Holding
the Fort

Books by Regina Jennings

LADIES OF CALDWELL COUNTY

Sixty Acres and a Bride
Love in the Balance
Caught in the Middle

OZARK MOUNTAIN ROMANCE SERIES

A Most Inconvenient Marriage
At Love's Bidding
For the Record

THE FORT RENO SERIES

Holding the Fort

An Unforeseen Match
featured in the novella collection *A Match Made in Texas*

Her Dearly Unintended
featured in the novella collection *With This Ring?*

Holding the Fort

REGINA JENNINGS

BETHANYHOUSE

a division of Baker Publishing Group
Minneapolis, Minnesota

© 2017 by Regina Jennings

Published by Bethany House Publishers
11400 Hampshire Avenue South
Bloomington, Minnesota 55438
www.bethanyhouse.com

Bethany House Publishers is a division of
Baker Publishing Group, Grand Rapids, Michigan

Printed in the United States of America

ISBN 978-0-7642-1893-4 (trade paper)
ISBN 978-0-7642-3119-3 (cloth)

Library of Congress Control Number: 2017945717

This is a work of historical reconstruction; the appearances of certain historical figures are therefore inevitable. All other characters, however, are products of the author's imagination, and any resemblance to actual persons, living or dead, is coincidental.

Cover design by Dan Thornberg, Design Source Creative Services

17 18 19 20 21 22 23   7 6 5 4 3 2 1

Chapter One

JUNE 1885
WICHITA, KANSAS

The fumes of the gaslights at the foot of the stage protected Louisa Bell from the more noxious odors of her audience. On hot nights like tonight, the scent of unwashed bodies in the Cat-Eye Saloon could be overwhelming. Braving a deep breath, Louisa delicately placed her hand against her beribboned polonaise and crescendoed her way into the next stanza. She lifted her head and sang to the rafters so she didn't have to meet the eyes of her overly interested, overly intoxicated, overly male audience. Their approval meant she had a place to live and food to eat. And while she knew that performing on stage carried certain undesirable associations, it was the only path open to her.

She held the final note while Charlie resolved the chord on the piano. The applause exploded immediately. Whistles and hoots filled the air.

"That was dandy, Lovely Lola." Slappy flopped his loose hands together in appreciation.

"Lovely Lola, will you marry me?" She didn't know his name,

but the cowboy was there every summer when the cattle made it up the trail.

"You're an angel!" Rawbone cried.

Louisa might not be the youngest, most coquettish performer at the saloon, but the purity and emotion of her voice couldn't be denied. She curtsied elegantly, holding her flounced skirt to the side. Cimarron Ted held up a glass to toast her. She returned his smile as she prepared for her last song of the night. Charlie started the intro on the piano, and Louisa mentally recited her pre-song mantra.

I am Lovely Lola Bell. They will be enchanted by my performance and will love my show.

She caught movement out of the corner of her eye. It was Tim-Bob, the owner of the Cat-Eye Saloon. With his hand wrapped firmly around Persephone's white, shapely arm, he was marching through the stage curtains and onto the stage, right in the middle of Louisa's nightly performance.

"Hey, Charlie," Tim-Bob called, "cut off that music. I have an announcement to make."

The pianist wasted no time in stopping and taking a swig from his bottle. The crowd wasn't as quick to simmer down.

"Let Lovely Lola sing!" a man hollered.

"It's Saturday night! Can't have Saturday night without Lovely Lola."

Whatever was going on, Louisa wished it didn't have to happen in front of a rowdy mob. Persephone showed promise as a performer on Tuesday nights—that was Louisa's night off—but she showed more promise as Tim-Bob's next ladylove. So why was she here now?

Persephone's blond hair—Tim-Bob always preferred blondes—had been arranged to swoop dramatically over one eye. That same eye was kept carefully trained on the scarred stage floor, but there was a self-satisfied twist on her tinted lips. Louisa's stomach twisted, too, and it had nothing to do with stage fright.

Tim-Bob held up the hand that wasn't busy touching Persephone. "If y'all would settle down and listen. It's not often that an establishment is graced with two such talents as Lola Bell and Persephone, but when it is, then it owes its customers the opportunity to appreciate both."

"It's Saturday. I came to town to hear Lovely Lola!"

Through the smoke-filled room, Louisa could make out Cimarron Ted shaking a fist. Tim-Bob shaded his eyes, then dropped his hand as he recognized the complainer.

"I understand we have some old admirers of Miss Lola's, and that's just dandy, but they'll soon grow to appreciate the charms of a new face . . . a younger face. I'm thinking of you, my friends, knowing how you'll thank me after you hear Persephone perform the finale tonight."

Persephone fluttered her eyelashes and smiled up at Tim-Bob. He gazed deeply into her eyes as Charlie jumped into action and played the opening notes to the song.

Louisa's song.

The audience, those traitors, barely noticed as Louisa backed away into the shadows. No one interrupted Persephone's slightly flat opening to call for Louisa's return. No one tried to stop Louisa from disappearing into the poorly lit hallway. No one except Tim-Bob.

"Lola, we need to talk." He stood next to a wall sconce. The gaslight flicked distorted shadows over his face. "Persephone's talent deserves a bigger audience, and she's young. With more experience, there's no limit to how she could develop."

Louisa pulled her cascading hair over her shoulder. Tim-Bob had said that about her at one time, but then she'd refused his advances. She'd thought her voice was enough to keep her job. Had he been looking for her replacement all this time?

"Is she taking every Saturday performance, then?" Louisa relied on her stage skills to keep her voice level—cheerful, even. "I suppose I could use the break from the daily—"

"Lola, just stop. It's best just to say this and get it over with. The Cat-Eye doesn't need two singers. Now, that doesn't mean I'm just going to dump you out on the street. You can keep your room while you find another job, or at least for a few weeks. I was a friend of your mother's, after all."

Her mother hadn't had any friends. Not in the end.

"Thank you," Louisa mumbled, and her feet moved toward her room at the end of the dark hallway. She ignored his weak excuses as they faded behind her.

This couldn't be happening. What would she do? Where could she go? She fumbled blindly with her door, and when her eyes focused again, she was sitting at her vanity stand. Reaching for a cool rag, she began wiping the rouge off her cheeks.

"Come in," she answered to the knock at her door. Not because she wanted company, but because she was too stunned to refuse it.

Cimarron Ted entered, scratching at a spot of mud dried to his white beard. The metal on his gun belt jangled as he shifted his wiry frame to avoid bumping up against a satin dress hanging from the clothing rack. "I had some news for ya, but I don't figure you want to hear it right now."

Louisa's lips settled into a rare frown. "Tim-Bob is kicking me out. I don't know where I'm going to go."

Through the thin walls, she could hear the applause as Persephone sang the last of her number. The men were fickle. As long as they had some pretty entertainment to go along with their drink, it wouldn't matter much who it was. The important thing was that Louisa find another place to work. Something to keep her head above water so she didn't sink to desperate measures.

The lace on her wide neckline chaffed against her collarbone.

Snapping out of her daze, she hopped up. "Here, help me out of this gown. I need to make plans." She turned her back toward the old mule driver as she considered her options.

Where else could she sing? She knew every house of entertainment in Wichita, and none were looking to hire. Finding a job outside of the smoky rooms on Douglas Avenue seemed unlikely, too. Even if her singing career hadn't tainted her, her mother's reputation had forever doomed her.

"My old fingers aren't as nimble as they used to be," Ted said. And he wasn't lying. The gown loosened slowly.

Louisa held the ribbons of the decorative front lacing in her hands, her feet tapping through her options. She'd always thought about giving voice lessons, but no respectable family in Wichita would welcome Lovely Lola into their home. If she had enough money for train fare, could she find work in another city?

"There you go," Cimarron Ted said. "If it weren't for you being like a daughter to me . . ."

Louisa stepped out of her gown. From the red tint spreading up Ted's neck, she should've asked him to wait outside before stripping down to her corset cover and petticoats, but for the company Louisa kept, she was dressed as modestly as a bride.

She reached for her silk dressing gown. "I met my father, and he wasn't you." Although she'd much rather have a crusty mule skinner as a father than the wastrel that sired her. Bradley's pa wasn't any better, either. Best that they just relied on each other, as they always had.

Thinking of her brother brought a terrible suspicion to her mind.

"Ted, you said you had news for me?" Her hands shook as she hid them in her fur-lined pockets.

"Well, I thought you should know that Bradley is in trouble again. From what I've heard, he's been thrown in the guardhouse."

Louisa clutched her hands into fists. There couldn't be a worse time for him to mess up. "What's he in trouble for?"

"Nothing for you to worry about. Just a little drinking, from what I hear. I doubt it amounts to much. Major Adams is known for having a stiff collar, and Bradley's known for tomfoolery. You got troubles of your own."

This was no time for Bradley's hijinks. As bad as her situation was, at least she'd been assured that her younger brother was out of the rain. How could she fix him when she didn't know what to do herself?

"I'll go see him." The decision was made even as she spoke. "I need a job, and maybe they're hiring at the fort. Besides, he needs to know that he'd best walk the straight and narrow, because I can't help him right now."

"Pardon me for saying it, ma'am, but you ain't going to Fort Reno. There's nothing there but a passel of ornery cavalrymen and some irate Indians. There's no way you can help Bradley while he's under Major Adams. You've done all you can for the boy."

But even as he was talking, a plan was forming.

As long as she'd been in Wichita, Kansas, Louisa had never known the Cat-Eye Saloon to send performers on a tour, but with that many men in one place, there had to be a need for diversions. She didn't know if the officers at Fort Reno would allow it, but it was worth a try. If only she could convince the U.S. Cavalry that their troopers would benefit from some wholesome entertainment. Or halfway wholesome entertainment, at least.

Even if she wasn't a respectable lady, Louisa had her standards. No drinking, no carousing, and no fraternizing with the customers—even if all the women in town assumed she did. Even if such behavior would make her as popular as Persephone.

"Where is Fort Reno, exactly?" Hangers skidded across the clothing rack as she examined her wardrobe. She might have to fight Tim-Bob for them, but she'd sewn most of these costumes herself. They were the only gowns she owned.

"It's in the Cheyenne and Arapaho Reservation, due south of here, but maybe you should write your brother and have a look-see over what to do next. I'd be sorrowed if you went all that way only to have to come back."

But she had to go somewhere. There was nothing in Wichita for her. She'd collect her last pay from Tim-Bob, pack her bags, and go see her only blood kin in the world.

It sounded like he might be in as much trouble as she was.

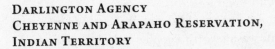

DARLINGTON AGENCY
CHEYENNE AND ARAPAHO RESERVATION,
INDIAN TERRITORY

A line of sweat ran down Major Daniel Adams's back as the gate opened and a cow stumbled out of the chute. His horse's ears twitched, and the animal shifted beneath him as war whoops rose around the corral. Daniel stroked the neck of his horse to calm it. With no buffalo left to hunt, the Cheyenne men looked forward to some fun before the women came in to butcher the animals. Better the livestock catch their arrows than his troopers. The cow blinked at the wide-open prairie before it and then, to the delight of the braves, took off with hooves flying.

Mondays were distribution day at the agency. The women left their tepees at the river's edge to come to the agency for their weekly rations, and the men looked forward to finding sport with the poor cattle each family received—a rowdy practice that Daniel would rather not allow, but with the growing tension, it was best to let them have their fun. Another perceived attack on their way of life, and the Cheyenne might want to revive some of their other traditions—traditions that were better off forgotten. Daniel looked over his young troopers with a protective eye. Right now, he didn't have the numbers to defend the fort and agency both. He needed every man. Even men like Bradley Willis.

Daniel himself had written the report, and he had to admit it contained an impressive list of accomplishments for an intoxicated man—improper discharge of a firearm, insubordination to his superiors, and endangering the troopers and property of the U.S. Cavalry. Not that Private Willis wasn't capable of jumping his horse over the cannons, but he'd been standing in the saddle and shooting at the lanterns when he'd done it. And when Daniel had ordered an end to his merriment, it took four men to subdue him.

Or one bullet. Act like a fool in front of the wrong man, and Private Willis's life wasn't worth a gopher hole. In fact, he might have a better future in a gopher hole if he didn't straighten up.

But since being released from the guardhouse, Private Willis had been on his best behavior. Currently he was manning the door of the agency's brick commissary store. Using rudimentary sign language, he motioned an Arapaho woman back to her place in the line, even though her Cheyenne sisters were bunching together, refusing her entry.

Daniel urged his horse away from the stock pen and toward the dispute. Private Willis paused in his communication with the women at Daniel's approach and saluted.

"Sir, I want to thank you for returning me to duty. That guardhouse is no place to rot on a day like this." The young man's eyes were level and quick. While others seemed to be wilting in the heat, he looked as cool as the springhouse.

The U.S. Army needed men like Bradley Willis. Men who were brave, fearless, and—to be honest—just a little reckless. Sometimes Daniel envied his boldness. A widower with two daughters couldn't take the risks that Willis took, but that didn't mean Daniel wasn't brave. And just because, years ago, he'd had to learn how to braid hair and play dolls didn't make him less of a man, either.

"You'd still be there, were we not shorthanded," Daniel said.

"I appreciate you giving me another chance, sir."

"Don't mess up again. Your antics put your fellow troopers in danger."

Willis's eyebrow rose a fraction of an inch. That movement was a challenge, and Daniel didn't walk away from those.

Speaking with a patience he didn't really possess, Daniel said, "Those lanterns exploded when you shot them. Someone could've been hit by flying glass."

"I reckon," Willis allowed.

"Or a stray bullet could've killed someone, had you missed."

Willis squirmed. "No, sir. That's not likely."

Daniel's hand tightened on the reins. "Are you contradicting me, Private?"

Willis seemed to realize his mistake. "No, sir. Upon reflection, I allow it is possible that under the influence of strong drink, because of the extreme angle I had from standing in the saddle, and on account of the amazing speed my horse was traveling, that I could have missed my shot."

Evidently the guardhouse hadn't taught him enough. "You have sentry duty for the second watch every night this week as further punishment," Daniel said. "I'll notify whoever is on watch with you that you are not to leave their sight."

That took some of the sass out of him. "Yes, sir," he replied.

"And you are not allowed in a saddle on the campgrounds. When you reach the boundaries of the post, you will dismount and walk your horse to the stable unless drilling with your company."

Judging from Willis's grimace, that was the punishment that

hurt. At least it was the one that would have bothered Daniel the most.

"Yes, sir," Willis finally said.

"You have many talents, Private. Keep your nose clean, and you might—"

"Major Adams!" Sergeant O'Hare appeared from nowhere, holding out his field glasses in shaking hands. "Over there, past the corral."

Daniel didn't need O'Hare's panic to understand the urgency. Leaving Willis behind, he took the glasses, spurred his horse, and galloped to the edge of the settlement, narrowly missing the latest bovine victim.

The calls reaching him were not the war cries of the braves or hurrahs of his troopers. These voices were higher, feminine.

"Pa! Pa!" The strong voice of Daniel's eldest daughter carried across the prairie. "Tell Daisy to give it to me!"

He jerked the field glasses to his face with enough force to blacken his eyes. The two girls streaked toward him, their horses leaping over piles of cattle bones and avoiding the mangy dogs that scattered as they approached town. In front was the youngest, Daisy, who'd been playing Indian again. Her long braids whipped in the wind, the hawk feathers she'd woven in barely hanging on. Her feet were covered in high-lacing moccasins.

Caroline chased hot on Daisy's heels. Even though the sixteen-year-old girl resembled a full-grown woman, she was far from emulating one in maturity. Arms pumping on the reins, heels digging into her horse, skirts flying, and hair a mess, Caroline was easily the most interesting thing the troopers had seen in months. And it wasn't just the troopers who were stunned. Even the hunters had paused in their pursuit to watch.

This was just the sort of incident that had his mother-in-law insisting the girls come to Galveston to live with her.

Daniel recognized the familiar tension that often preceded a battle. He tossed the field glasses to Sergeant O'Hare, who was trying to disappear and leave him to handle his family alone.

He reached Daisy first. Gasping for breath, she looked over her shoulder. "Caroline is trying to take it away, but it's for me, too."

He would not raise his voice at his own daughters in public, but a raised voice was imminent. "We will discuss this in the agency office. Go."

But then Caroline darted between them. "Give me the letter," she commanded. Daisy attempted an escape, and Caroline caught her by a braid, nearly pulling her from the saddle.

"Ow, ow, ow!" Daisy cried. But her outstretched hand did not relinquish the prize.

It took a pointed glare from Daniel to snap his men's attention back to their distribution.

"Inside Agent Dyer's office! Now!" he ordered his daughters.

Still swinging at each other and bickering, the girls rode down the dusty street of Darlington and dismounted at the office. Finding the building empty, Daniel shut the door with a mighty crash.

"Do you have any idea what a spectacle you've created?"

But far from cowering, the girls continued to argue. "She took the letter Grandmother sent," Caroline said. "She won't let me read it."

Daisy's eyes darted from her father to the stove. Daniel's life often depended on predicting his opponent's next move. He had Daisy's arm in a tight grip before she got two steps closer to her goal.

"You will not burn that letter," he commanded.

"It's made out to me, too," Caroline said. "She has no right to destroy it."

"It's a stupid letter," Daisy hollered. Her face was streaked with sweat and tears. "You don't need to read it."

How could Daniel expect to keep his troopers under control when his own daughters were insubordinate? Without further comment, he snatched the letter from Daisy's hand.

"Sit." He pointed at the nicely trimmed sofa. Thank goodness Agent Dyer was busy and not around to witness this. Daisy stomped over and threw herself down. "You too, Caroline," he said.

Caroline rolled her eyes and crossed her arms over her chest. He would never allow a trooper to have such a poor attitude or posture in his presence. So why couldn't he figure out how to teach his daughters?

For starters, he couldn't use the same rules he used on cavalrymen. He couldn't throw them in the guardhouse if they misbehaved or assign them to a lonely task. Ever since their mother died, he'd been too lenient with them. Sure, he'd taught them how to ride and shoot like nobody's business, but now they were growing up, and there were new problems to face. Problems that even a courageous man couldn't handle. They needed a woman to direct them, but ladies weren't readily available in Indian Territory.

The girls needed their mother. He needed her, too.

Instead, he got to deal with his mother-in-law. He unfolded the letter. Daisy was telling the truth. It had been addressed to her and Caroline. Not to him.

For all the faith that the U.S. Army put in him, his former mother-in-law had none. Then again, the death of her daughter, although not his fault, could have colored her opinion.

"I don't want to live with her." Daisy beat the soft heels of her moccasins against the wood floor. "It would be so boring."

"No, it wouldn't," Caroline said. "Living here is boring. There's no one to talk to. No girls our age at the fort. The only people are a few old washwomen and the troopers. And Father acts like the troopers carry an infectious plague. I can't speak to any of them."

Darn right, she couldn't. He quickly scanned the letter and found more of what he'd come to expect from Edna Crawford. She presented the girls with the option of a rose-colored future in Galveston with her and their grandfather, the banker. Beautiful gowns, a musical society, life in a genteel city with all the advantages a young lady needed to be a woman of substance. They'd have everything they desired.

Everything except their father.

Of course, Edna didn't think he was doing an adequate job raising her granddaughters. His eyes flicked over Daisy's unconventional mishmash of calico and Arapaho. He took stock of Caroline's dress, which had grown too short and too snug to be worn in a camp full of lonely men. Edna was right. He wasn't adequate, but that didn't mean he didn't love his daughters. They were his chief delight out here on the prairie. They were all that kept his house—and his heart—from being empty. She couldn't have them.

"Why did you take this from your sister?" he asked Daisy.

Her green eyes flashed. "It belongs in the fire." She jumped from the sofa and threw her arms around his waist. "I don't want to leave you, Pa."

Daniel laid a hand on her head. Sweet, impulsive Daisy. So like her mother. Then there was stubborn, hardheaded Caroline with her blazing red hair, who was just like him.

With a sigh, he handed the letter to Caroline. She had a right to read it, even though it broke his heart that she wanted to move away.

"No more fighting," he said. "And you cannot leave the fort without me ever again. I know I'm not able to teach you everything, but I have taught you that, haven't I?"

Caroline only glared at her little sister. He was about to reprimand her when he happened to look down and saw that Daisy had her tongue out.

He was fighting a losing battle, but he would never tire of looking for ways to win. As always, he fell back on his training. When in trouble, call in reinforcements. He'd considered bringing in a teacher for months now but didn't want to ask Edna for a recommendation. If only he knew whom to call.

Agent Dyer came through the door with a bounce in his step. He removed his bowler hat and brushed at his thinning hair. "Major Adams, I hope everything is alright." He caught sight of the girls and seemed to breathe a sigh of relief. "Ladies, from the way you were riding, I was afraid someone had been hurt."

"Not yet." Daniel narrowed his eyes at Caroline. She looked away. Well, too late. She and Daisy had brought their quarrel to a place of inspiration. Right in the shadow of the Arapaho school, where the Bureau of Indian Affairs and the Mennonite missionaries were doing their best to assimilate the native people.

"Mr. Dyer, I need your help," Daniel said. "I see what a fine job your missionary teachers are doing with the Arapaho children, and I think my own household would benefit from something similar."

"Noooo." Daisy fell back onto the sofa. "Not school."

Caroline remained ramrod straight but turned her head away.

"Our teachers wouldn't be able to travel to the fort regularly, and I doubt your girls would learn much in class, since many of the students speak Arapaho, but I could ask the Mennonite Society for a recommendation for a governess."

Which was exactly what Daniel had in mind. "Not just any lady," he said. "We require a mature older lady, one not given to frivolity or idleness. A strict disciplinarian is what I'm looking for, and as you know my daughters, you understand the need. She must be capable of keeping them under control while I'm out performing my duties. Charm and personality are unnecessary."

And frankly, undesired. Daniel was used to military interaction. You gave an order, and it was obeyed. Better to hire a woman who'd earned her place through discipline than one who beguiled her employers with feminine manipulations.

Dyer looked at the girls sympathetically. He'd always had a soft spot for them. "I think I understand you, sir. I will pass on your request."

"This is the worst day of my life," Daisy wailed into the sofa cushions.

"It's your fault," Caroline said. "If you'd just agree to go to Grandmother's, then this wouldn't happen."

"At attention," Daniel ordered. Daisy rolled off the sofa and stood with slumped shoulders. Caroline's pride wouldn't allow her to slack, but her eyes focused somewhere far over his shoulder. He'd seen troopers on heaven's threshold jump to attention faster.

"I'll be outside." Mr. Dyer took his hat and left.

Daniel clasped his hands behind his back and paced before them. When had his darling children grown so unruly? Were these the same girls who used to wait for him to return with their noses pressed against the glass of his office window? The girls who, when older, insisted that they'd rather be with him than the nursery maid who had diapered them? He'd tried to be both mother and father to them and had failed. But it wasn't too late. His resolve grew.

"Leaving the fort today was the last straw. You two know better than anyone the dangers of riding across Indian Territory alone."

"It was only across the river," Daisy said. "We knew you—" At his look, she went quiet.

"This misbehavior will be addressed. The older you've grown, the less propriety you've observed, and it's up to me to reverse that tendency. You want more attention, and you'll get it. Both from me and from a matron experienced in training young ladies. Just remember, you've brought this on yourselves."

There was more he could say, but actions spoke louder. They would know he was serious on their first day of lessons with their new instructor. He didn't like relying on others, but the unity of his family depended on the success of the missionary board's referral.

It was a lot to leave in the hands of a total stranger, but Daniel was desperate.

Chapter Two

A week ago, Louisa had been sitting in the Cat-Eye Saloon with her feet kicked up on a chair, humming along as Charlie tinkered on the piano and Rawbone tried to best her at chess. Today she was bouncing along the endless, lonesome grasslands of some Indian nation, wondering if she'd ever see civilization again.

Not that the Cat-Eye represented all that was right and good about Western civilization. When someone with a voice as limited as Persephone's could be considered a star attraction, you had to question the values of your society. But Louisa didn't lay any claim to being society. Her days weren't spent doing whatever it was that society ladies did.

Usually of an afternoon, during her chess matches, the only paying customers were perpetually tipsy Slappy, who relied heavily on the bar to resist gravity, and teams of Indian freighters grabbing their last hot meal before delivering their goods. Anyone new meant an unsuspecting victim to her skills, which made Louisa sorry she hadn't bargained with Tim-Bob for a chessboard to claim for her own. She dared a glance at the plainsmen riding in the stagecoach with her, covered in dust and sweat. They'd be easy pickings.

So far they'd ignored her, and she'd ignored them. Would it be any different if she were a real lady? Her mother had always told her to stay away from the uptight women of Wichita. The snobby cows liked to trample anyone who wasn't their own, she said. Louisa believed her, and yet . . .

She rested her forehead against the faded curtain hanging inside the coach. What lives they must live in their secure houses and their fenced gardens. To have a kitchen of your own, rooms that were private, relationships that lasted a lifetime? It was her dream, but it wouldn't come true in a town that already knew Lovely Lola and who she was.

Louisa and Bradley had barely survived their mother's abuse. When alcohol had brought an end to her mother's miserable life, Louisa continued to make money the best way she knew how— with her voice. As long as she could perform, she'd be fine. Louisa loved music. She loved the rich costumes, the dramatic characters, and the stirring performances, but she'd always feared her time was limited. The clients of the Cat-Eye Saloon didn't appreciate music enough to patron a mature singer, no matter how beautiful her voice. And when Persephone began sharing the limelight—not to mention a bed with Tim-Bob— Louisa felt the steady approach of destitution at her back. She just hadn't expected it to catch her so quickly.

The man next to her bent to tighten up the laces on his boots. Louisa leaned his direction to look out his window and saw a large log building surrounded by some small soddies. Whatever this place was, they were going to stop.

She pulled her adorable chocolate lace-up boots off the seat across from her and did her best to brush off the trail dust that covered her. When the coach stopped rocking, she was more than ready.

"Welcome to Red Fork Ranch," the driver announced. "Get on out of that hot box and stretch your limbs."

The cheerful banter between the driver and their host could be heard over the creaking of the springs and the lowing of cattle in the pen to the west. Louisa allowed her two traveling companions to exit before her. Remembering his manners, the one with the leather braid around his hat turned to help her down from the coach.

As she emerged, all speaking ceased. Their host, a stout-bodied and weathered-faced man in his prime, rubbed his mouth as he stared. A young boy at his side didn't hide his interest in her brightly colored gown or dramatically plumed hat. Dressed like a miniature version of the other ranch hands, the lad looked as amused by her clothes as she was by his.

If the men at the Red Fork Ranch were shocked by her arrival, what was the fearsome Major Adams going to say when she showed up uninvited, unannounced, and looking for a job at his fort? Well, she was who she was. Dressed in her gaudy outfit that clearly proclaimed her association with the fancy set, there was no use trying to hide it. She just hoped he'd accept a one-woman operatic troupe on the fort grounds.

"Welcome to Red Fork, ma'am. I'm Ralph Collins. You are traveling straight through?" Officially it was a question, but it was delivered in such a way that it would be hard to contradict.

She understood his concern. If she could have spared the time and the money, she would've bought herself some suitable clothing. As it was, she'd had to fight Tim-Bob tooth and nail to get the wardrobe pieces that she had, and she wasn't about to leave this beautiful blue silk for Persephone to wear.

She'd picked the most conservative pieces she could find, but that didn't keep her from looking like a soiled dove. She wished there were some way to let them understand the difference, but in most minds, if a woman performed on the stage, she was no different than one who performed in the bedchamber.

"I'm going straight through," she said. "Going on to Fort Reno."

Mr. Collins shifted his weight on steady legs. "Are you sure about that? The only hotel out there is the Cheyenne House. It's run by the Darlington Agency, and they're Mennonite folk. All the other land thereabouts belongs to the Indian nations. Unless you have an invitation by the Major . . ."

All nice ways of saying her kind wasn't welcome here. Louisa's stomach tightened into a familiar knot. "I bought a ticket for the stagecoach, just like everyone else. I'll leave when it does."

She didn't like the pity she saw in his eyes, but he didn't seem to be one who worried himself over other people's foolishness. "Then grab yourself a bite to eat, and the stage will pull out in an hour."

"Hey, Ralph." The driver popped his head out from beneath the stage. "We got a problem here. Take a look at this axle."

"In a minute."

Louisa left the coach to find the meal that had been offered. How could she explain her plan when she didn't really have one? Had she been foolish to think that she could just waltz up to Fort Reno and ask for work? After two days of riding across the flat plains of the Indian lands, she'd realized that a woman appearing in this forsaken territory would incite concern. It wasn't as if she could just blend in with the other ladies in town. There was no town. Only wives of government men or soldiers.

But then something caught her eye. In the shade of the porch stood a lady's travel valise.

She looked at the young boy. His mother's, perhaps?

"Come on inside," Mr. Collins offered. "We always look forward to the stagecoach. It's our source for news about the States."

The States? Did they forget that they lived in the United States? Then Louisa remembered what the driver had said when they crossed the border south of Wichita. The Indian nations. They truly were in a foreign country, then.

Inside, the thick log building smelled like animal hides and unwashed bodies. In vain Louisa looked for any sign of a woman. Like as not, if there was one here, she'd want nothing to do with Louisa, but still, to have some feminine advice about what lay ahead would be handy.

They were offered the use of the washroom and some simple refreshments while the stable hand tended to the horses. Louisa had just about given up hope when the lad approached.

"You don't dress like the other passengers I've seen. Especially Mrs. Townsend." He bit his lip as his eyes ran greedily over her velvet-trimmed hat.

Slowly and gracefully, Louisa unpinned it and set it between them. "Do you want to touch the material?" she asked. "It really is soft."

He grinned as he ran his hand lightly over it. "Feels like rabbits," he said.

She waited while he practiced rubbing it backward, then smoothing it again. "Who is Mrs. Townsend?" she asked.

His eyes never left the velvet. "She came yesterday, but she's feeling poorly. She ain't going to make it to Fort Reno, so she's waiting for the next coach north."

A woman going to Fort Reno? That must be who the valise outside belonged to. "Where is Mrs. Townsend?" Louisa asked. "I'd like to make her acquaintance."

"Boy, don't you talk fancy?"

The word *fancy* had been applied to her more than she'd like to admit.

"Mrs. Townsend is holed up in the cookhouse," he said. "I'll take you to her."

Louisa followed, enjoying the exercise after two days of jostling in the coach. She also enjoyed the absence of the jangling reins and creaking wheels. She could actually hear some birds here. Without even thinking about it, she began to hum. She hadn't heard any music for three days. Hadn't sung. For her it was like going without butter on your bread.

All too soon, they stepped across the threshold of a small soddie. An Indian woman turned toward them. If she was surprised to see a woman in silk, she didn't show it, but the woman seated at the table did.

"My, oh my, Hubert," she said, "who did you bring me?" Her thick gray hair was twisted into a neat bun and covered by a black doily. Louisa's throat caught. She'd learned to expect nothing but scorn from women like her.

The boy, Hubert, stole a piece of jerky off a drying line and answered, "She wanted to talk to you."

"My name is Miss Louisa Bell." Louisa trained her face to mimic the sternness of the Indian and not break out into the welcoming smile that was so popular on the stage. "I understand you are traveling to Fort Reno."

The woman's dress pegged her as one in mourning, although from the age of the fabric, Louisa guessed that she hadn't been recently bereaved. Then she looked again at her bloodshot eyes and dripping nose. As Hubert had said, this woman was ill.

"I'm Mrs. Townsend, dear," she said, "and I *was* going to Fort Reno, but my plans have changed." She wiped at her nose. "I've suffered from hay fever ever since I started this journey. My eyes itch. My nose runs. I spend the night coughing endlessly. If I don't find a remedy, I'll catch pneumonia, surely."

Young Hubert nodded. "Ralph says it affects a lot of people who come through. Especially in the spring."

Louisa filled her lungs, relieved to feel them expand unencumbered. Catching a cold would ruin any performances she might arrange.

"I'm sorry for your suffering," she said carefully. She didn't want to offend this woman who'd managed to hide her revulsion so far. And revolted she must be, for Louisa had met plenty of her kind before.

When she was young, a few good-hearted women had befriended her, giving her their children's cast-off clothes to wear, bringing her to church. She'd felt like she someday might be like them, until that Sunday afternoon when the children were invited to sing at the picnic. Even then Louisa's voice had been remarkable, so she hadn't thought twice about volunteering. But when it was her turn, the ladies had been outraged. Proof that her mother was right in this one respect.

"Believe me, young lady, I'm terribly discouraged that I won't be going." Mrs. Townsend dressed prudishly, but so far she hadn't snubbed Louisa as expected. "I felt like this trip was my mission, that God had called me to go on this adventure. I don't understand why He closed the door. Now I've wasted some of my late husband's funds on the trip, and I won't ever be able to put these books to use." She gestured to a crate near the door. "I thought I was acting in obedience, but all I've accomplished was catching a cold and inconveniencing Barbara Spotted Fawn by being underfoot."

The cook glanced up at the mention of her name but continued slicing potatoes.

Louisa looked at the box, and a plan began to form.

"Can I deliver those for you?" she asked.

"Oh, my dear, that would be won . . . won . . ." Mrs. Townsend broke out into a series of tight sneezes. "Wonderful. I've already been reimbursed for them and must not fail to have them delivered."

Without a word, Barbara Spotted Fawn set a cup of water before Louisa. She thanked her while eyeballing the crate.

That Sunday years ago, the song she'd sung as a child was

deemed inappropriate. Within minutes, the truth of her parentage had been revealed, and she stood shamed as her peers were whisked away from her by their shocked mothers. She'd been told she could visit church, but her singing was not welcome. Well, if she had to choose between God and her singing, it was her singing that had kept her fed over the years, not God.

"What kinds of books would I be delivering?" she asked. "Religious?"

Mrs. Townsend smiled. "You are astute. I am Mennonite, but these books are not for religious instruction. They are for general education. Major Adams ordered them."

Major Adams? Louisa hiccupped suddenly. Grabbing her cup, she took a big gulp of water to hide her surprise. Dare she travel with his property? On the other hand, what better way to guarantee an audience with the stern major?

Louisa smiled. She didn't think God cared enough to worry about where she was going, but maybe He cared about Mrs. Townsend. Maybe helping Mrs. Townsend was Louisa's ticket to success.

Chapter Three

Their stay at the Red Fork Ranch would last longer than anyone had planned.

Mr. Collins had come into the cookhouse to inform Louisa that the axle on the stagecoach needed to be replaced. They were working on it even now, but it would probably be late afternoon before they were rolling again.

Mrs. Townsend was leaving for Kansas on the northbound stage immediately. Still pronouncing blessings on Louisa with every sneeze, she gave her arm a firm squeeze.

"Meeting you has filled me with peace. I know this was ordained."

Louisa bit the inside of her mouth. Did Mrs. Townsend have to make it sound like she was dying? "I'm not after your eternal gratitude, ma'am," she said. "I'm only delivering a crate on my route. Nothing heroic."

"Well, you should be there by nightfall. And hopefully I'll be away from this insufferable dust."

Nightfall? Louisa surveyed the rolling grasslands stretched before her. What was there to do until then? She wasn't sure Barbara Spotted Fawn spoke English. The men had no interest in shooting the breeze with her. In fact, they acted as if they'd been warned not to speak to her at all. Right now, she missed all the busyness and conversation of the Cat-Eye Saloon. Not that she'd tell Miss Missionary that.

"I left you something in the kitchen," Mrs. Townsend said. "A more serviceable blouse and skirt. You don't want to ruin your fine things traveling in a coach."

Louisa looked down at her tightly fitted bodice. Her gown was sky blue and likely to pick up a stain or two. And she'd already noticed how the elaborate ruffles along the hem collected grass and burrs. Perhaps Mrs. Townsend didn't approve of the outlandish costume, but she was offering a solution. It was an unexpected, kind gesture.

"May God make your trip good and no sinning and everything good," Louisa said. She imagined that was what one said under the circumstances. She hadn't had much opportunity to talk to church women.

Mrs. Townsend's eyes twinkled. "That, my dear, is the most original benediction I've ever received." She gave her valise to the coachman. "I only wish I could be there on your arrival." Then she was handed up to her seat.

Louisa covered her face as the four-horse team pulled the coach away from the ranch. It was a wonder she wasn't as afflicted as Mrs. Townsend. Well, she'd deliver the crate of books, see about employment, and then figure out how to catch Bradley by the ear and straighten him up. At least one of them needed a future they could rely on.

Mr. Collins turned to her. "We should get this stage under way in a few hours, but I'm afraid we don't offer much amusement around here."

"I could take her fishing." Hubert had been hauling water and firewood to the kitchen all morning. It seemed that everyone at the Red Fork Ranch put in their fair share.

"The lady doesn't want to walk that far," Mr. Collins said.

"It's not so far." Hubert's eyes shone. "She can handle it."

Mr. Collins weighed his decision. "It's up to Miss Bell," he said finally.

"I have nothing else to do," she said. After hours in the stagecoach, she would enjoy a chance to get some fresh air.

"Then it's settled. Hubert, you can go down by Turkey Creek, but stay clear of the Cheyenne lands. They're feeling their oats. You should be back within . . ."

He continued to give instructions while Louisa went inside to get her hat. True to her word, Mrs. Townsend had left a bundle of clothes on the table. Barbara Spotted Fawn followed Louisa with her eyes, and seeing that she was headed toward the bundle, turned again to her stove, uninterested.

Multiple washings had faded the cotton fabric from black to a midnight shade. The material was soft and obviously of a more generous cut. Louisa could loosen her stays, which would be more comfortable in the coach. And the material would breathe well for relief from the heat. So far, the shade trees were few and far between.

Hubert appeared in the open window. "Miss Bell, are you ready?"

No time to change now. Besides, she'd rather keep the new clothes fresh for the coach ride.

Mr. Collins carried two canteens along with a fishing rod and a small rifle out of the main house. "Hubert, you bring Miss Bell back when she says. If you hear three shots, that means the stage is ready and you get your tail home."

"Yes, sir."

"Teddy and his crew are out past the creek. If they see any Cheyenne about, they'll sound the alarm. If you need anything, shoot twice and they'll come to you."

Hubert handed Louisa a canteen and an empty basket. "And we'll try to bring home some perch for supper."

"That's the idea. Good day, ma'am." Mr. Collins lifted his hat, pulled it on more firmly, and then headed to the corral.

"It's this way." Hubert shouldered the rifle and the fishing pole, then forged through the tall, dry grass with a skip in his step. Wishing she'd had time to change after all, Louisa lifted her hem and followed.

It wasn't long before they found a trail and she could stop worrying about the burrs and thistles. The wide sky was as vibrant and blue as her gown. The tall grass on either side of the road was as golden as the brass chandelier at the Cat-Eye Saloon. In fact, she'd love a canvas painted with this expansive scene to use for an aria she'd learned, if she ever got a chance to get on stage again.

Soon her humming had broken out into a full-throated rendition of the aria from *Don Carlos*. Louisa wasn't sure the lyrics were appropriate for young Hubert, but she felt it safe to assume he didn't speak Italian.

There was satisfaction in knowing that your voice could travel so far. She'd never had such a large stage. She performed some of her favorites as they trotted briskly along. No appreciative audience followed her every gesture, but she still felt like someone important was listening.

Even Hubert agreed. "That's mighty fine singing. I never heard the like."

Louisa patted him on the shoulder. "Thank you, Hubert. I guess you don't get much entertainment at the ranch."

"Oh, we put together some music of an evening, but it's just us old cowhands." He stood a little straighter at including himself with the men. "I can pick at a piano—I learned it at home—but there ain't no piano here."

At home? Louisa had noticed that Hubert called Mr. Collins by his given name instead of Father. Was he an orphan?

"How did you come to be at the ranch?" She kept her eyes

peeled for signs of a town but only saw grassland in every direction.

"Ralph is my brother. He wrote my parents in the States and told them that the city was no place for me. I needed to come to the nation and learn to be a man. And I can do so much more than my friends back home. I bet they're all sitting in school today. Ain't none of them carrying a gun, a fishing pole, and"—he ducked his head—"accompanying a pretty lady."

Louisa laughed aloud. "You are a smooth talker, Hubert Collins. I'd heard to watch out for you cowboys." Actually, she'd met scores of cowboys at the saloon. Most fell into one of two parties—either they favored being alone to sit and drink, or they were smooth talkers who'd had a month on the cattle trail to think up charming things to say to young ladies. Louisa could tell which Hubert would grow up to be.

Soon a cool line of trees appeared in a shallow valley. The creek wasn't far. "You only brought one fishing line," Louisa said.

Hubert waved a bee away. "I didn't figure on you wanting to fish."

Louisa smiled. "That's fine. I wouldn't mind exploring a bit, as long as you promise not to leave me."

He grinned, his too-big front teeth fully exposed. "You bet, but don't forget about the coach. We gotta get back when they signal, no questions."

Louisa nodded. She hadn't traveled much in her life, but she supposed such delays were typical.

More singing, that was what she'd do. She'd see this creek of Hubert's and then take a stroll from there.

Fort Reno more resembled a deserted village than a military outpost. From inside his home, called the General's House, Major

Adams had a perfect, centered view of the parade grounds, the barracks and mess halls arranged symmetrically on either side. And right now, most of those barracks were empty.

Daniel watched as the troopers went through their afternoon drills. Some of the troops were aligned on the southeast side, with the colored troops of the Tenth on the northwest. They looked to be in good form, but they needed reinforcements.

Picking up his letters, he stepped outside to his porch, where an always-ready assistant was waiting. "Post these letters," he said. "And saddle my horse."

"Should I get an escort ready?"

"That's not necessary."

The trooper saluted and turned to his tasks. The letters would go to the base post office and from there to Fort Supply to remind the powers that his fort was understaffed for the volatile location. Nothing had happened yet. He just prayed that he was prepared before something did.

The main purpose of Fort Reno was to keep peace among the Indian nations and tribes that surrounded it, and although always ready for battle, more likely than not you'd find Major Adams stuck behind his desk, away from the action.

But today he needed to get out. He needed room away from his men, away from his family. Daniel was a bloodhound when he scented a mystery, and lately he had a question that he couldn't puzzle out on the parade grounds. Because of his rank, the sentry wouldn't question him as he left the gate, but there'd be questions aplenty if they saw what he was up to.

Once astride his horse, Daniel pushed it into a canter. He didn't get enough time in the saddle. Paperwork and managing the troops kept him tied to the fort. Having his daughters there alone meant that he rarely accompanied troops out on patrol. Even if he asked his cook, Private Gundy, to keep an eye on the house, he hated leaving them. But today he needed to get away from questioning eyes. Something was eating at him, and he wouldn't rest until he found an answer.

He headed north and then turned east once he'd skirted the agency. He didn't need an audience. He needed some time and a lot of space, something Indian Territory had in abundance. But it was imperative that he was absolutely alone.

Was ten miles far enough? He kept going. Fifteen? His horse was in good shape, and he was traveling light. Besides, time on a horse was never wasted. It cleared his head and gave order to his thoughts.

Agent Dyer had come through with a recommendation for a governess. The widowed missionary lady sounded perfect for Caroline and Daisy. She would impose some sanity on the girls' dramatic turns, and her age and status would guarantee that the troopers afforded her respect. The last thing he wanted was to introduce a flighty female into the company of his men. He had enough trouble keeping the troopers in line.

He passed Turkey Creek, which meant he was nearing the boundary of the Red Fork Ranch. Daniel reined in his horse. He couldn't afford to run into any cowboys at the Cherokee-owned ranch. He found a mild depression in the land—a place where he wouldn't be as exposed.

Nights of turmoil had already framed his plan. As usual, he'd considered every variable until he came up with the most favorable option. He dismounted and began unbuttoning his coat. Off went all his accoutrements—his gauntlets, his saber, his sidearm, and his eagle-and-wreath belt plate. He had more gear than a peddler. He stacked it carefully, then covered it with his blue dress coat. The horse surveyed his white shirt with droll amusement. Daniel had determined that the cavalry coat was unnecessary to his experiment, but no use explaining it to the horse.

With a grunt, he tugged off his boot and immediately followed with his sock. He looked beneath him to make sure there weren't any goat's head stickers before he lowered his foot, and then the other boot followed.

Perhaps it was immature competitiveness, but knowing that someone had accomplished something made him eager to achieve it as well. Which was how he'd climbed to the position of major. And that same energy and planning would help him climb again.

He ran his hand over the McClellan saddle. Surely with his bare feet he could balance on it. Bradley Willis had done it in his boots, but he'd been full of liquid courage. Daniel wasn't looking to break his neck. He just had to see if he was equal to the challenge.

He moved the boots next to his coat and then hopped up in the saddle. He got the horse going at a smooth lope over flat ground before he pulled his feet up. Getting his feet under him was a trick. He'd expected it to be tough, but his feet held fast to the rawhide saddle. Maybe this wouldn't be as hard as he'd feared.

How could it be, when Private Willis made it look so easy?

Feet in place, he rocked with the movement of the horse, getting the rhythm. Slowly he rose, straightening his legs. A few bumps had him stopping at a crouch, but soon he was standing at full height. The reins stretched their full length. As he leaned back to steady himself, the reins pulled tight. His horse, well trained and sensitive to his movements, slowed. That was a problem. The change in pace unsettled him. Swaying, Daniel leaned forward to put slack in the reins.

"Giddyup!" he encouraged. The horse's ears pricked. It reached a gallop again. Daniel's bare toes curled around the edges of the saddle. Riding while standing up wasn't as tricky as he'd thought. He wished he could perform the feat for his troopers, because all they'd talked about for days was how amazing Private Willis was. If only they could see their commander. He knew more about horses—

The horse had nearly reached Turkey Creek. The last thing Daniel needed was to run beneath a tree. Could he turn the horse from here, or would he need to sit first? Ever so gently, he tightened the left rein. The horse responded, and he felt the satisfaction of exceeding his own expectations about his performance.

But then he heard something strange. A woman's voice. Singing. He didn't know where it was coming from until he was barreling toward her. A gorgeous apparition in blue standing directly in his path.

He hadn't reckoned on this complication.

Daniel always held that a well-trained horse could read its rider's mind. This horse was well trained, and whether it knew instinctively that Daniel wanted to stop, or if Daniel unconsciously pulled on the reins, the horse did what it had been trained to do. It stopped.

But Daniel did not.

Instead, he went flying over the head of the horse. His last thought was that he hoped he didn't die barefoot, but if he did, he prayed that someone would put his boots on his feet before they carried him back to the fort in front of his men.

Chapter Four

Hubert was happily situated at a bubbling brook, and he didn't appreciate Louisa's singing. He said it scared the fish away. She had to laugh at that. Tim-Bob had always said her singing drew men into the saloon like stink bait. She guessed men and fish hankered after different lures.

Before she'd set out down the creek bank, Louisa had promised Hubert that she'd keep her eye on the sun and not let it get too late. The wind was strong, hot, and rarely let up, but in the shady protection of the trees, it didn't overly provoke her. Once she'd walked far enough that she wouldn't offend Hubert's fish, she started singing again. First she ran her scales to strengthen her range. After she did a full warm-up—something she'd missed in the three days since she'd left home—she began a maudlin song of unrequited love that never failed to bring tears to the eyes of her intoxicated customers.

> *O don fatale, o don crudel*
> *che in suo furor mi fece il cielo!*
> *Tu che ci fai sì vane, altere,*
> *ti maledico, ti maledico, o mia beltà!*

She was approaching the apex, the stanza where she allowed her voice to soar to its zenith. Rawbone always grabbed his handkerchief during this portion. In dramatic fashion, she stepped into the sunlight and extended her arms to either side. Eyes closed, she was awash with music, with the warmth of the sun on her face, her neck, her arms. The emotion of Princess Eboli had never been as strong, and neither had her voice. Louisa had found a piece of heaven.

But it was the earth that was vibrating beneath her feet. Despite the distraction, she wasn't ready to let go of the moment. Dropping her voice, she repeated the final couplet, weaker now, more tenderly, so those poor sots would buy another round to drown their sorrows in. Eyes still closed, she clasped her hands at her breast.

The vibration increased, jarring her out of the song. What was that noise? More than a little irritated to be interrupted, Louisa opened her eyes.

A man was standing—standing!—on a horse that was running toward her. She was too stunned by the spectacle to be scared. With his white shirt open at the neck and his bare feet—bare!—he wasn't dressed as a cowboy. Who was he, and what in tarnation was he doing?

Uh-oh. He'd seen her. His face filled with alarm, even more alarm than a man standing on a saddle should show. He wobbled, swayed. The horse tossed its head. He pulled on the reins to steady himself, but that was the wrong thing to do. The horse stopped. Louisa covered her mouth as he pitched headlong over the horse and landed in a pile on the ground.

"Great Saturn's rings!" she breathed, then took off in a run for the crumpled figure in the grass. His blue pants were easily spotted. A stripe of yellow ran along the seam. A cavalry uniform. Probably a ruffian like her brother.

Forgetting about her elaborate gown, Louisa fell to her knees next to the lifeless figure. Was he dead? His face was buried in the dirt. Frantically she dug the soil away from his nose. He was breathing. At least that was something. But while dusting more dirt away, she hit solid rock. The soil was thin here. With a few swipes of her hand, she laid bare a slab of sandstone. He'd knocked himself out. But what did he expect, standing in a saddle? What kind of immature, reckless—

He groaned, and she left off listing his failures. He pushed against the ground to raise his head, then wavered dizzily.

"Shhh," she said. "Lie down for a spell. You're not ready to get up."

He didn't seem to understand. He stared stupidly at the ground beneath him. A thin, steady stream of blood was soaking into the soil. He squinted at the pool of blood. His arm shook as if his own weight was too much for him. He was in imminent danger of dropping to the ground and hitting his head again. She had no choice but to act.

She took him by the shoulders and slowly rotated him so that if he passed out again, his face wouldn't land in the dirt. He'd land on her. She barely had time to get her legs arranged beneath her before he crashed onto her lap.

Louisa didn't know quite what to do. She was no prude— being raised in a bawdy house had numbed her sensibilities—but she wasn't accustomed to having a man use her as a pillow. And he was a good-enough-looking man. His face looked wholesome and innocent, and she'd known enough guilty men to tell the difference.

Blood seeped through his light brown hair, sticking it to his forehead. Gingerly she pushed his hair back from the wound. The knot expanded right at his hairline. She dug a hankie out of her reticule. It was extravagant, lacy, and nearly useless, but she used it to mop up the blood and get a better look at the cut. She'd seen a lot worse inflicted when someone interrupted her performance, but how long could she sit here with a cavalry trooper in her lap?

The trooper's horse had returned. It bent over him, blowing its hot breath on his face and hers. Louisa brushed it away. Where were the man's boots? His coat? If her brother got in trouble for a little drinking, what would Major Adams do to this man, caught away from the fort out of uniform and behaving recklessly? Well, she'd just do what she could to make sure Major Adams didn't find out. She didn't want this fun-loving young trooper to get the guardhouse.

Fun-loving and fine looking. But maybe not as young as she'd first thought. She smoothed his hair again. His mouth twitched, bringing the merest hint of a dimple. What if he never woke up? What should she do? She couldn't let him derail her plans. Or maybe, when he came to, he could help her. Did he have any influence at the fort?

She looked for any sign of Hubert, but it was useless. He was too far away to summon with a call, as being out of earshot had been her goal when she'd left him and his discriminating perch. "My fate rests in the hands of an eight-year-old," she murmured.

Then she grew very still, as she had the distinct impression that she was being watched. Slowly she shifted her gaze downward to meet a pair of honey-colored eyes studying her.

He was confused, poor thing. She laid her hand against his cheek to calm him. "It's alright," she said. "You took a spill." She brushed back his hair again, enjoying the thick texture of it.

His horse nudged him. He lifted his hand to the horse's muzzle and closed his eyes but didn't get up.

"Now that you're feeling better, I can go get help."

But that seemed to startle him. He shook his head weakly. Again, he tried to push himself up and managed to reach a sitting position. He pulled his knees up and rested his head against them.

"Your head is bleeding," she said. "You have a knot."

If only he'd show some sign of understanding her, but all he was showing was stubbornness. Holding onto the reins, then the horse's head, he pulled himself upright.

Louisa scrambled to her feet. "What are you doing? You need to sit down. You're not ready."

But by the strength of his will, he made it into the saddle with her handkerchief still stuck to his face.

She did not like this. Not one bit. "Where do you think you're going? You're in no condition to ride."

He stared at her dumbly, as if he couldn't believe she was real. Slowly his eyes traveled from her plumed hat to her festooned gown, then back to her face, but he was either unable or unwilling to make any kind of response. By its own volition, the horse began to move forward. His bare feet in the stirrups were all that kept him from toppling over again.

Stubborn man, she fumed as he rode away. Not willing to admit he needed help. But who knew what the price would be if he were caught in that condition? Obviously Major Adams had put the fear into him. She only hoped his dread of his commander didn't endanger his life.

Daniel couldn't get the vision of the woman out of his head. This wasn't the first time his life had been in danger, but never had he been sent such an apparition to comfort him. With difficulty, he found his coat. His head pounded as he bent over to pull on his boots. He yanked the handkerchief off his face, stuffed it in his coat pocket, and gathered his gear. That done, he turned his horse toward the fort and did his best to stay in the saddle.

His thinking was befuddled. He knew he'd lost his faculties the minute he opened his eyes to see a beautiful woman holding him. Being widowed for the past decade, he wasn't surprised that his dream would take that bent. What was mildly embarrassing was the inappropriate dress of his guardian angel. He would've thought his imagination would produce someone more saintly to come to his aid. Not someone arrayed like a fancy woman for hire. He rubbed his forehead. He didn't even like thinking such thoughts.

And the singing. Her voice was still in his ears. He knew the song—had heard it performed at the opera house in Galveston when he was courting his wife. But why that song? If he was truly that close to meeting his Maker, he didn't want Princess Eboli's plight on his lips. It was obviously the product of his confusion. No one sang that beautifully. Or looked that fetching. Or dressed that sumptuously.

Oh, Lord, please make it stop. His head was about to explode.

Come to think of it, was he riding in the right direction? Was he even riding at all? For all Daniel knew, he might still be lying on his back, looking at her sweet face, wondering why he'd ever want to get up.

But he had gotten up, right? He was going back to the fort because of something important. Yes, his daughters. He would check on them. And there were troopers there, of course—troopers who were his responsibility. They would know if he stayed on the ground and never came back. So he'd go back. And he'd tell them . . . what would he tell them?

What had been an easy ride out turned into an arduous ride back. Slowly the horse carried him to the fort, but no matter how hard he tried, he couldn't remember what he'd been doing out here in the first place. Something important. Something concerning Private Willis. Something that he had to figure out.

The sun had started to set when he saw a handful of troopers riding toward him. They looked like they were floating across the prairie, hooves barely touching the ground. Were they real? They wore blue, but not blue silk. He tried to focus on faces, but everything looked blurry.

"Major Adams, sir. Do you need assistance?" The cavalryman was a good trooper. Daniel remembered that about him, but little else.

"No. I'm just headed to Fort Supply. General Custer is going west. He wants to consult with me before he goes." That made sense. That must be why he was out here. General Custer wanted him.

But the trooper was acting strangely. Was everyone going to be strange today? "General Custer wants to see you?" Daniel didn't miss the concern on his face. "Where have you been?"

Daniel knew where he'd been. He wasn't crazy. He just couldn't get the words in his head. Something about Willis and Custer. He waved the question away, but the movement made him dizzy. Next thing he knew, there were horses on either side of his. He heard words like *head wound*, *blood*, and *possible attack*.

"No," he said. "It's not the Indians. It's Private Willis."

"Willis did this to you?" The nice trooper's brow lowered. "Byrd, go to the fort and alert Lieutenant Hennessey. Tell him to have Dr. Bowen meet us. We're right behind you."

Daniel knew he'd said the wrong thing, but he didn't know what the right thing was. They weren't listening to him, and his head hurt with every step of his horse.

He should've stayed on her lap and never left.

Chapter Five

Bradley Willis loved the cavalry. Growing up in a tiny room shared by his drunk ma and his bossy sister was like being hog-tied and stuck in a barrel. Out here in Indian Territory, he had space. Space to run. Space to breathe. Space to holler if he had a mind to. Space to get himself in a heap of trouble, which was exactly what he did, and that was why he was out here painting the never-ending fence.

He slapped a dripping paintbrush of whitewash against the boards and blinked the sweat out of his eyes. At least he hadn't spent too much time locked up. Watching life go by from behind bars—there wasn't nothing fun about that. Even if Louisa thought he didn't have any sense, he had sense enough to know that the cavalry was good for him and that if he didn't toe the line, he'd be discharged with no pay, no honor, and no future.

Major Adams wasn't all that bad. Had Bradley not dulled his wits with rotgut, he wouldn't have carried on like that. Too late to do anything about it now. He'd enjoyed himself, and the fellas were still talking about his daring jumps and spot-on shooting, so a few nights in the guardhouse had been worth it, after all.

Bradley squinted toward the fort's center. Was that Captain Chandler heading his way? Two grunts from the Eighteenth

Artillery were walking out with him. Bradley splashed a final swipe on the fence before dropping the brush into the pail of whitewash. He wiped his hands on a rag and waited to see what they were coming out after.

"Private Willis?" Chandler kept his head high, showing his roughly shaved neck.

Bradley saluted. "Yes, sir!"

"You are under arrest."

Bradley almost laughed. "Arrested for what? I've been out here painting all day."

But no one else was laughing. The soldiers took him by the arms.

"You are accused of attacking Major Adams," Chandler said.

Attacking the post commander? Now Bradley wasn't laughing. Even slopped, he wouldn't dare lift a hand against the major. He loved the cavalry, and nothing would get you kicked out quicker.

Louisa was going to kill him.

───※)(※───

Buildings appeared on the horizon ahead. It was Fort Reno, according to the call of the stagecoach driver above her. Louisa tugged at the tight collar of the faded cotton blouse. She wasn't used to material against her throat. Maybe that was why all the proper ladies were so dour. They'd feel more relaxed with more of their neckline exposed.

The ride to the fort hadn't taken as long as the wait for the stagecoach repairs, but her time at the ranch had been more exciting than she'd anticipated. Despite Hubert's insistence that cavalrymen could take care of themselves, she'd made him walk along the creek for a while in the direction in which the trooper had disappeared before they'd returned to the ranch.

The only sign that the soldier had existed was the scar of red earth he'd disturbed and a dried patch of blood.

"That's nothing," Hubert had said. "They tell that a cavalryman can get scalped and still need a haircut the next day."

Mr. Collins at the ranch didn't listen to her concerns, either. Troopers were expected to take care of themselves. The ranchers wouldn't worry about them.

Those cowboys might not be bothered by his plight, but Louisa was determined to check on him once she got to the fort. She couldn't shake the image of him riding away, hunched over, barely able to stay in the saddle. What if he'd fallen off somewhere and was even now being carried down a hole by a colony of well-coordinated prairie dogs? She couldn't risk it.

As they drew nearer the fort, it became clear that she'd had the wrong idea when she'd pictured it. There was no high fence guarding it. Instead, the fort presented itself like a goose on a platter, open for everyone to view. Even though it wasn't quite dark yet, the wide avenue down the center was lit on both sides by lanterns, although a few were shattered. The stagecoach turned right and drove past rows of long white buildings.

Louisa reviewed her plan. She had come to deliver the crate of books to Major Adams. That excuse would get her in the door. And once she had his attention, perhaps she could suggest a small concert. Who knew? If worse came to worst, she might could get work as a washerwoman.

The stagecoach pulled up at an office where a trooper came out to meet them. The stage rocked as the driver hopped down and swung the door open. He offered her his gloved hand, and she stepped down on a white gravel walkway. Two young cavalrymen were passing by. One darted a glance at her, then his head whipped around, and he started walking backward. His companion frowned until he, too, laid eyes on her. She wasn't on stage, but she'd never had such an attentive audience.

"Troopers!" The man who had come out to greet them had some golden stripes on his upper arm. The soldiers spun around, and their backs went straight. Under the officer's watchful eye, they marched away, never looking back.

Could they tell by looking that she didn't belong in the clothes she wore? Did the scent of the Cat-Eye Saloon linger? She couldn't imagine they'd carry on that way with Mrs. Townsend.

I am Lovely Lola Bell. She mentally went through her performance warm-up. *They will be enchanted with my performance and will love my show.*

"Ma'am." The officer tipped his hat. "Lieutenant Hennessey at your service. I apologize for your reception. We rarely host unaccompanied ladies here at the fort."

It wasn't every day she was treated so politely. She choked back her stage smile to appear more demure. "No offense taken."

"May I ask what brings you to Indian Territory?"

He was young for a lieutenant but seemed affable enough. Hopefully he'd be agreeable to her suggestion.

"I'm looking for employment. I thought you had work available."

"Here at the fort? I don't know of anything in particular. We can ask . . . Pardon me, ma'am." Lieutenant Hennessey had spotted something behind her. "I'll be right back."

He rushed past her. Louisa turned to see what the hubbub was. Someone was being escorted across the green. Dragged across, more specifically. The lieutenant met them. The conversation was short but intense. With a nervous glance at her, he dismissed them to go on their way. Louisa wondered what the man in custody had done. Was he a dangerous man, or just high-spirited like her brother?

Just like her brother! Louisa narrowed her focus. She hadn't seen Bradley in months. The boy she remembered was thinner, paler, and his hair was not quite so bleached by the sun . . . but that was him. It was her brother being arrested. Again. This time right in front of her eyes. But what could she do about it? No job for her. No help for him.

"Forgive me." Lieutenant Hennessey had returned. "I didn't mean to leave you waiting. As I was saying . . ." He stared at the crate at her feet. "Are these your packages?"

How could she talk about a delivery when they were arresting her brother? She dragged her eyes away from Bradley. Her performance must continue. No distractions.

"Yes, sir. I'm to deliver these educational materials that Major Adams requested."

Her response must have been correct, for his countenance changed. "Why didn't you say so? Of course, we have a position for you, and I apologize for the confusion. When Major Adams told me that he'd sent for a teacher for his girls, well, I didn't expect those missionaries to send . . ." He looked away. "My apologies again, ma'am. Normally Major Adams would be here to greet you, but he's indisposed at the moment. I'll have your things delivered to your quarters."

His hand rose into the air. Instantly a soldier appeared. The lieutenant barked some orders, and her things were carted away. But Louisa didn't quite understand.

"Excuse me," she said, pushing away her worries about her brother, "did you say *teacher*?"

With an extended arm, he motioned in the direction that her bag had been taken. "Do you prefer *governess*? I beg your pardon, Miss . . ."

"Miss Bell," she said.

"Miss Bell. You will be a great asset to the Adams household, I'm sure."

A governess? Louisa bit her lip. It was the old clothes—they were throwing him off. Otherwise he'd never consider a woman like her to teach book learning. Not if he knew.

She should correct him. She should tell him that she wasn't the governess. But with no other jobs available and Bradley in trouble . . .

The gravel path they traveled encircled the middle grounds of the fort. Long buildings lined two sides of the main square—barracks, perhaps—but the orderly setting did not calm her emotions. She had to do something for Bradley, but what? The only way to stay at the fort was to go along with the lieutenant's mistake. It wouldn't be for long.

Ahead was what looked to be very comfortable houses—at least houses finer than any in her part of town. They'd be more fitting in a nice neighborhood or on a prosperous farm. And she was to live here? Louisa had never lived in anything this fine or conversed with anyone who did. She was beginning to wonder if she and Bradley had any business with these people at all.

They stopped before the center house, the one lined up perfectly across from the flagpole in the middle of the parade ground. It was so big, she wasn't even sure which door was the entrance—the center one, or the French doors that flanked it on each side?

"Private Gundy assists with the house," Lieutenant Hennessey said. "He can show you to your room. Major Adams has surely been in contact with you about your students."

Louisa twisted a blond curl around her finger. She'd always been half afraid of those respectable ladies who scorned the likes of her mother, but she'd hoped someday to be able to pass as one of them. She just hadn't counted on doing it so soon. And a governess had different expectations than a music teacher. Governesses were staid, respectable, severe, while music teachers . . . well, everyone expected a music teacher to be flighty.

Then again, all she had to do was spend a day watching over some children and maybe teach them the alphabet and their numbers. It was work and a roof over her head. And it would give her a chance to see what kind of trouble Bradley was in now.

A governess? Just another role to play. Only she wished it wasn't in Major Adams's household. Hopefully his wife would be understanding. That was usually how it was with these imperative men. The more insufferable the man, the more saintly the wife. She hoped it held true for the Adams household.

"Major Adams?" she asked. "Where did you say he was?"

The young officer's face showed a trace of concern. "He is unavailable. I'll post a sentry at the house. Should you need anything, they will alert me immediately."

Nice Lieutenant Hennessey was in command now? Then he might be in a position to show some mercy to Bradley. She'd do well to earn his trust while she had the opportunity.

She stopped in front of the porch, where a trooper stood guarding her bag and the crate of books. "Lieutenant Hennessey, may I have a word with you in private?"

Her request surprised him, but she had his full attention. "Of course, ma'am." He offered her his arm and escorted her off the gravel path onto the green, away from any eavesdroppers behind open windows. "Is this private enough, or would you like to visit my office?"

Louisa looked both ways. "It'll do. I didn't want to say anything in front of the others, but I'm concerned about one of your troopers."

The good humor vanished. His young face settled into determined lines. "Go on."

Actually, she was concerned about a couple of his troopers,

but she couldn't ask about Bradley. Not yet. "Earlier today, while waiting for the stagecoach, I came across a cavalryman. I couldn't tell you his rank because he'd removed his coat, but he was riding near the Red Fork Ranch."

"He was alone?"

"Yes, completely alone. He rode by me at a great speed but lost control of his horse and went flying to the ground. I ran to help him, but he'd suffered an injury to his head and didn't respond to any of my questions."

The lieutenant crackled with energy. "You saw his accident? And you say he was alone? No one attacked him?"

"There was no one else there. When he recovered enough to get up, he rode off without a word. I fear for his well-being, if he isn't recovered."

"Let me get this straight." The lieutenant spoke slowly. "He fell off his horse? Just like that. No one was pursuing him or harassing him?"

This was the part Louisa didn't want to admit. She didn't want to stir up trouble, but telling the truth might help them identify the injured trooper.

"I don't want to get him in trouble."

His eyebrow rose. "There are no secrets here on base, Miss Bell."

She sighed. "He was trick riding. Standing in the saddle."

Lieutenant Hennessey must not have heard her. His face went completely blank. His mouth opened, but it took him a few tries to come up with something to say. "I'm afraid I'm going to need more information. He was standing in the saddle, out of uniform?"

"Well, he had his shirt and his trousers on. I would imagine the boots were too slick to balance in."

"He was riding in his sock feet?"

"No socks. Barefoot."

At this, he turned his back to her and commenced with the most frightful fit of coughing. She couldn't tell if he was moved by concern for his fellow officer or merely shocked. When he turned to face her again, he was mopping his eyes with his handkerchief. "Excuse me," he said. "This cavalryman that you saw was standing in the saddle when he lost control of his horse and was thrown onto his head. Is that the account you wish to report?"

"Oh, no! I do *not* wish to report it. I only want to make sure he's safe."

"Did he see you?"

"Certainly. I tried to give him aid, but he wouldn't accept it. He left without a word."

"Could he hear you?"

"I'd say so. He was lying in my lap."

Was Lieutenant Hennessey having some kind of an attack? He'd marched away to wheeze with his hands on his knees, leaving Louisa convinced that the last part probably should've gone unsaid.

"Lieutenant Hennessey?" she called. He raised a hand, asking for time while he caught his breath.

"I beg your pardon." Again he wiped his eyes. "Your account has been most, most helpful."

"Aren't you concerned about the rider?"

"He made it to the fort. He's being cared for now."

"But I don't want him to get into trouble. I thought by telling you instead of Major Adams that you might be lenient with him."

An unabashed smile spread across the lieutenant's face. "You came to the right man, no doubt about it. But there's no reason for you to mention this to anyone else."

Which was what she wanted, but . . . "I thought you said there were no secrets at this fort."

"We need to know what our troopers are up to, but when officers have secrets, we call that information confidential." He gestured toward the crate of books. "Shall we go?"

Louisa hiccupped and then smiled to cover her sudden nerves. "Lead on."

Chapter Six

Louisa's stomach let her know that supper time had passed. This world of saluting and marching was foreign to her, just as foreign as the quiet, tidy row of houses.

Just a few hours, she told herself as she waited on the porch. *Fill in as the governess until you have time to find Bradley.* If something went wrong, then she'd claim, like the missionary lady, that the environment didn't agree with her, and she'd hop back on a stagecoach to Wichita. No one would ever know that Bradley Willis's sister had visited him. The last thing he needed was to get in even more trouble because of her.

At Lieutenant Hennessey's knock, the door was opened by a thin man with a shock of brown hair. He wore a stained apron over his cavalry uniform, and his feet splayed wide, like the floor was rocking and he had to keep his balance.

"Private Gundy, this is Miss Bell. She's the new governess."

Private Gundy vigorously scrubbed his hands on the apron, which probably only made them dirtier. "Here, let me help you with that case." He hooked the handle and swung it away from the trooper. "The girls have been waiting for you."

His welcome felt as warm as the three-o'clock sun.

"Nice to meet you, Private Gundy."

"Those your books?" he asked. "Just leave them by the door, and I'll fetch them later."

"Gundy, do you know what room Miss Bell is staying in?" Lieutenant Hennessey asked.

The private grinned. "I have to say, she don't look like a Darlington woman."

"She is here at the request of Major Adams. Her room?"

Louisa was on the verge of asking who the Darlington women were when she remembered hearing that name before. Something to do with Mrs. Townsend. Perhaps she should keep her questions to herself.

Gundy turned and headed toward the staircase, but his steps were uneven. Just below his knee, a strange crease appeared in his trousers with each step. A brace?

Seeing her confusion, Lieutenant Hennessey said, "Private Gundy has a wooden leg, but he didn't want to leave the cavalry. He'll rustle you up something to eat when you're ready. Have a good evening."

"Wait." Louisa kept one eye on her host and the other on the man stomping up the stairs. "I'm staying here?" There had to be a mistake. This house was finer than any she'd ever been in before. The candelabra sparkled with crystals dripping from its curved arms, and a white tablecloth adorned a long dining table in the room to her right.

"What arrangements did you make with Major Adams?"

Louisa chewed her lip. Of course, she had no idea what arrangements had been made. Could it be worse than a room behind the kitchen at the Cat-Eye? Better not to rock the boat. "I'm sure everything is satisfactory." She smiled as if delighted. "Thank you for your help."

"Yes, ma'am. And if you need anything, I'm right next door."

The floor creaked as Gundy climbed the stairs. "This blamed leg. I don't make it up here often, but when I do, I take my time."

"I appreciate it," Louisa said. She didn't want to irritate him, not if her next meal depended on him.

The stairs ran up the right side of the entryway. The beautiful wood paneling had been well cared for, and she imagined that the white painted balusters had to be washed frequently with small children in the home. The stairs opened at the top to a small landing surrounded by closed doors.

Private Gundy pointed to the door in the far corner. "That one's yours."

He turned to face Louisa and watched her closely as she made her way down the spotless hall. She turned the brass knob and peeked into the room. By the light of the lamp on a little table, she saw a virginal metal-framed bed with a white coverlet. A wardrobe painted robin's-egg blue stood next to the window. A dressing screen was set aside to show the washstand and the ceramic pitcher and basin. Louisa stepped into the room, picked up the lamp, and worked her way to the mirror. Its gilt frame glowed warmly in the lamplight. Louisa was almost surprised to see her reflection looking back at her. She didn't feel like herself in this drab clothing, but at least the same face greeted her from the mirror.

Her lodging secured, the next step was to find Bradley. She set the lamp on the end table next to her bed and turned to Private Gundy. "So how long have you been at the fort?"

"Since the beginning. 1874. But I'm not in the cavalry proper anymore." He swung his leg forward. "But I don't mind. No more marching. I get kitchen duty now."

Louisa tried for some information. "I've never been to a fort before. I wondered what all those buildings out there are, especially the brick one over that way."

"The guardhouse? Why would you be asking about that?"

Realizing she had no good answer, she went to the window and opened the sash. "It's stuffy in here," she said. "I'll come down for a bite to eat as soon as I wash up. Thank you."

Gundy nodded and whistled as he left.

Back at the Cat-Eye Saloon, Louisa's room held racks of clothing—odds and ends of expensive fabrics that she'd eventually rework into new costumes. Stacks of music littered every corner, and cosmetics spilled out of every open drawer. And before she moved to the saloon, she'd shared a small space with her energetic younger brother and her tipsy mother. Keeping Bradley out of her mother's angry reach had been a challenge. She couldn't imagine having a room this size to herself.

There was no need to unpack, or maybe there was. If she'd come as a governess, then she needed to at least give the appearance that she was planning to stay. She gripped the handle of her traveling case and braced herself for the heavy load. The bed frame squawked as she deposited the case on the mattress.

Louisa closed the door and turned the lock. A governess. Who would've thought? She might have made a good teacher had the wheel of luck granted her a better opening act. Had she gone to school, had a father who paid for her books and a mother who had the time to help her with homework, she might have found a respectable position like this, after all.

Facing the mirror, she wondered if she could look respectable. Her china-doll complexion was prized by her admirers, but would children take her seriously? She could perform, she could keep an audience's attention, but could she impart any kind of wisdom? Her brows lowered. If she had the kind of wisdom people prized, she'd do a fine job imparting it left and right. But most parents didn't want their young ladies to learn how to keep a chair between themselves and a besotted admirer. They didn't want to discuss the application of cosmetics or which foods you should avoid to keep from belching during a performance.

She couldn't teach anything that proper children needed to know.

The locks on Louisa's old traveling case had a bad habit of sticking. She jostled the case to loosen the latch, then when that failed, she pounded it with the heel of her hand. One at a time, they sprang open. The lifted lid released the warm, fruity smell of her perfume. Louisa shook out a red taffeta skirt trimmed in black velvet. Taking a hanger, she placed it in the wardrobe. Even if she left tomorrow, it wouldn't hurt to air out the clothes after the harsh ride they'd had.

Next, she lifted her yellow silk, which had never been her favorite. The only thing she could find to admire about the outfit was the matching fringe-covered shawl and gloves, but they would look out of place on the prairie. She set the gloves on the washstand and tried to hang the shawl on the hanger with the gown, but it fell to the floor next to the bed. Louisa deposited the gown in the wardrobe, then came back for the shawl. But it was gone.

She stopped in the middle of the room. Her eyes traced the floorboards from one corner of the room to the other. They'd dealt with rats at the Cat-Eye Saloon, but they weren't known to snatch accessories right out from under your feet. Something was wrong.

Trying to be as quiet as a church mouse, Louisa stepped next to the bed and knelt to lift the coverlet that draped to the floor. Pinching the fabric between her finger and thumb, she lifted it gingerly. Instead of a fringed shawl, she saw an Indian's face, painted for war.

Louisa's holler echoed off the wallpapered walls. She sprang away from the bed and would have jumped out the window had it not been on the second story.

Her door rattled. The knob shook. A girl's voice yelled, "Daisy, is that you? Open the door."

Keeping an eye on the bed and her back to the wall, Louisa slammed the door to her wardrobe closed, then slid her way around the room. Passing the washstand, she grabbed the pitcher to smash over a head if necessary. With shaking hands, she unlocked the door, jumped across the threshold, then slammed it closed behind her.

Which brought her face-to-face with a young woman with blazing red hair. The girl's eyes widened, and her mouth dropped open. "Who are you?" She stepped backward to scan Louisa from head to toe, paying particular attention to the pitcher Louisa held above her head.

"There's an Indian in there." Louisa tightened her grip on the doorknob. "We have to get Lieutenant Hennessey."

The girl's mouth twitched. "If you're going to scream every time you see an Indian, it's going to be an irksome association."

The redhead grabbed the doorknob as the door began to shake and held it firm, but the voice coming through from the bedroom sounded nothing like a member of the Cheyenne or Arapaho tribes.

"Let me out, Caroline, you ugly lizard."

Louisa startled. What was going on?

"We shouldn't open the door," the girl said. "She's quite dangerous. You should heed your inclination to fear her, that's for certain."

But Louisa had lived by her wits for years. She knew when someone was mocking her. With a warning glare at the redhead, Louisa motioned for her to let go of the doorknob. Louisa kept the pitcher raised and ready as the door flew open. A younger girl with paint streaking her face and feathers woven into her braids stomped out. She seemed confused to find Louisa standing there, but her focus soon fell on the redhead.

"You told her to lock me in!" The younger one dove at the older girl.

"You'll wish you'd listened to me and kept her trapped inside," the older girl said to Louisa as she tried to fend off her opponent, who was swinging at her like a windmill.

Sisters? Their oval faces and doe-like eyes evidenced family blood. Their squabbling guaranteed it. Well, Louisa hadn't expected to find girls this age at the base, but they were none of her business. Still shaking, she darted into the room to set the pitcher down, returned to the hall, then closed the door behind her and walked past the warring siblings.

"Hey," the little one said, "aren't you going to make us behave?"

Louisa had dodged hundreds of fights at the saloon. Why would she get involved in such a paltry—?

Her fists tightened. Could these girls be Major Adams's children? With a deep sigh, she turned. The oldest wasn't a child at all, and the younger fought like an alley cat. But Louisa was the governess. Even if it was only for the evening, she had a duty to perform. Both girls held each other at arm's length and waited for her to intervene.

"Are you Major Adams's children?" she asked.

The older one tossed her red mane. "You might as well catch the next stagecoach before you embarrass yourself."

Louisa had faced some tough audiences before. She'd been jeered at and heckled, and she wasn't about to let this young lady prevail.

Louisa's posture was always excellent, so she didn't need to set her shoulders or stiffen her spine, but she did remind herself to use her proper diction. "I beg your pardon, Miss Adams, but you will not address me in that manner."

"Or you'll tell my father?" Her little sister—Daisy, hadn't she called her?—had stepped away. Whatever qualms Daisy lacked about getting under beds and scaring people, she didn't want any part of this rebellion. Her eyes darted to the staircase nervously, but while she feared her father, her sister did not.

"Tell your father . . ." Talking to Major Adams was something Louisa would rather avoid just yet. Not until she knew why Bradley was in trouble this time. What other punishments did parents inflict on their progeny? Whippings? Somehow, she didn't think governesses could do that to girls nearly grown, but she wasn't sure. She'd have to be creative. "You will speak to me with respect"—she used her stage elocution—"or I will punish you in a dozen different ways. I'll give you extra schoolwork. I'll give you extra chores. I'll make you stay in your room on lovely days." The older girl just scoffed. Louisa hadn't hit on the right target yet, so she continued. "I'll make you wear hideous old dresses like the one I'm wearing. I'll feed your desserts to Daisy."

"Hooray!" Daisy cheered. "Caroline loves her sweets. She never shares."

Caroline of the red hair shoved her sister away. "Don't tell her anything. Whose side are you on?"

"I'm on the side that lets me stay at the fort and doesn't make me go live in Grandmother's boring house," Daisy replied.

Grandmother? There was something missing.

"Where's your mother?" Louisa asked.

"We haven't got one," Daisy said. "She died after I was born."

"Who's been taking care of you?"

Caroline's chin jutted. "We don't need anyone to take care of us."

"When I was a baby, I had a nurse," said Daisy. "But she didn't stay with us when we moved here. Colonel Keyes's wife watched us when we were little, but he got reassigned, and Pa is the post commander now. We're too big to need a nanny."

Louisa didn't like this one bit. She'd hoped that Major Adams's wife would be reasonable, but from the sound of it, Louisa would be answering directly to the man himself. Not as a musician who would spend her days practicing and evenings performing. Not even as a lowly washerwoman. She would answer to him, live in his house, and care for his children. She hadn't planned on this type of work, and if she failed, he would surely send her packing. But what choice did she have? It looked like her best option. And she had nowhere else to go.

"I can promise you," Louisa said, "I have never been mistaken for a nanny. Now, I haven't ate supper yet—"

"Eaten," Caroline interrupted. "You haven't *eaten* supper yet."

Daisy squinted up at her. "You don't look very old. Are you sure you're a governess?"

This was going to be harder than she'd imagined. These weren't babies to be rocked to sleep. These were intelligent, even if uncouth, young ladies who could riddle her story full of holes in minutes. She had to give a convincing performance.

"I'm a hungry governess," she said. Then with a smile as warm as she could muster for a child who'd endangered her life just minutes before, she added, "Would you mind showing me to the kitchen?"

The painted stripes on Daisy's cheeks crinkled as she smiled. "Yes, ma'am." She skipped to the staircase.

Louisa rattled her doorknob and looked Caroline in the eye. The fiery redhead hadn't backed down an inch. "Please respect my privacy, and I'll respect yours."

"You've already invaded my home," Caroline said. "And throwing out intruders is the family business." She turned and marched away.

Major Adams might be the least of Louisa's concerns.

Chapter Seven

Was that a trumpet? Louisa lifted her head off her pillow. It was still dark outside, and some amateur musician had decided to play a concert. Wasn't this an army base? What kind of discipline did they have if they were up at all hours tooting away on a horn? Groaning, she dropped her head back on the feather pillow and pulled the blanket over her head.

She must have dozed off, because the next thing she heard was knocking at her door. Throwing the covers away, she saw light streaming in through the window. It had to be early yet. Probably not even ten o'clock.

"Miss Bell, are you in there?" It was a child's voice.

Where was she? Louisa reached for her silk dressing gown and got a better look at the room. The fort. Now she remembered. And obviously they got around earlier than the performers at the Cat-Eye Saloon.

"Keep your drawers on," Louisa called.

"What did you say?"

Louisa rolled her eyes. She was supposed to be a governess. Her memory was coming back to her. "Daisy? Sorry. Give me a minute."

She plumped her mass of messy curls and tied the ribbon closed on the rose-colored gown. After checking her face in the mirror, she went to the door.

"Private Gundy said that our lessons start today." Daisy's face was clear of paint, and her hair was unbound from its braids and flowing over her shoulders.

"What time is it?" Louisa peeked carefully around the hall, making sure she wasn't in front of an audience before she'd gotten into her role.

"It's already after seven," Daisy said. "Drill is over, and the troopers have started their fatigue duties. But if you're not ready for lessons, Caroline and I don't mind."

Lessons today? What kinds of lessons? Louisa's education had as many holes in it as the lace on her old pantaloons. She hadn't considered that lessons would be required of her so soon.

"I think I'll spend the day becoming acquainted with the grounds. This fort is rather large. Can you take me around?"

Daisy laughed. "Pa doesn't like us to be around the troopers. He'd whup us for sure. Sometimes Caroline makes us walk slow so the men will catch up with us—"

"Daisy." Caroline popped her head around the corner of the stairwell. "What are you telling her?" She took a long look at Louisa's robe. Her eyebrow rose.

A missionary lady probably didn't have a robe like this. Was everything about her totally unsuitable?

Louisa tugged the neck of the robe closed all the way to her chin. "I'll come down as soon as I'm dressed. We can eat breakfast together and then decide what to do next."

"Breakfast is already over. You missed it."

"At seven o'clock?" No one Louisa knew got up so early.

"She can eat if she wants, Daisy." Caroline shook her head in disapproval. "Let her take all the time she needs. That means less schoolwork for us."

So education wasn't Caroline's forte? Finally something was going Louisa's way. The last thing she needed was a scholar to teach.

She shooed Daisy out of her room, closed the door, went to her wardrobe, and reached for one of her more flattering gowns. But as her fingers touched the rich fabric, she stopped. A governess wouldn't wear anything interesting. No feathers, no velvet, no lace. Nothing that would draw attention to herself. With a last lingering touch, Louisa turned again to the faded blouse and black skirt thrown over the chair. The longer she kept up the ruse, the more time she had to plan her next step.

The girls had gone downstairs already, so the sure tread of boots in the hallway outside her door made her stomach heavy with dread. Major Adams was in the house. Feeling like she was trapped in a mouse hole with a cat prowling just outside, Louisa went through her morning routine, minus the cosmetics, and tried not to make a peep.

～❦～

Daniel's head throbbed with every step down the stairs from his room to his office. He'd slept through reveille, slept through drill, but that was what he got for listening to Dr. Bowen. Had his thinking not been so muddled last night, he would have insisted that Doc send him home sooner. As it was, he'd whiled away half the night answering imbecilic questions while sitting on an uncomfortable cot in the same room as a consumptive trooper. When Daniel finally recovered his wits enough to command the doctor to release him, they declared him well enough to go home, because frankly, what else were they going to do? He was still commander here. He did remember that much.

He remembered other things, too. Things that didn't make sense. Like the fact that he was standing in the saddle when he fell. And how he'd hit his head hard enough to see a fancy woman out at Turkey Creek. Not just see her, but feel her hand on his face, hear her voice singing from the trees, and then later the sweet sound of her calling after him to come back.

A siren, tempting him to linger in the underworld and forget his duties in life. Such thoughts weren't consistent with what he knew about eternity, but that didn't mean much when you got hit hard enough. She was the product of hammering his imagination against a hard rock.

He reached the bottom of the stairs with teeth gritted. He touched the bandage on his forehead and decided that he'd wear a hat today, even inside. He didn't want to be bothered with more questions, although he couldn't hide forever. Going to the front door, he stuck his head out. A trooper stood guard on his porch.

"Are you waiting for something?" Didn't they think Daniel was capable of protecting his own house?

"I'm supposed to report to Lieutenant Hennessey as soon as you're about."

Blast it, Jack. Why did he have to be such a nursemaid?

"Tell Lieutenant Hennessey that I'm just fine. I won't need his assistance." Daniel tried to turn in the doorway, but the open door bounced against something. A wooden crate. "And what in tarnation is this? Has my entryway become the commissary?"

"I'll ask Lieutenant Hennessey what to do."

"I don't need Lieutenant . . ." But the trooper hurried off.

Turning his back on his commander? Daniel should have him thrown in the guardhouse. And he should make a note of that, because he wasn't confident he'd be able to remember past the next ten minutes.

He eased himself into his office and sat behind his desk. His brain felt too big for his skull. Daniel picked up the nearest newspaper—the *Cheyenne Transporter*—and read a headline about the ongoing dispute over grazing land that the Texas cattlemen had leased from the Cheyenne and Arapaho. The cowboys claimed that their cattle were still being stolen, despite them paying rent. The tribes claimed it was justice done for their shortened rations, and that much worse could happen if they weren't fed better.

Daniel tossed down the paper and covered his eyes. The throbbing had to get better soon. If he could just keep his eyes closed for the rest of the day . . .

Why did Jack have to pound on the door so loudly? Daniel yelled at him to come in, then prepared himself for the worst.

Jack appeared with a cup of steaming coffee in his hand. "How are you feeling?"

The concern of his post adjutant embarrassed Daniel. A commander shouldn't show any weakness to his men.

Gathering his wits—which had been scattered considerably by yesterday's events—Daniel took the coffee. "Thanks for seeing to everything last night. It's best that we don't allow a minor injury to distract the troops from their tasks." Because he was distracted enough. He took a swig of coffee. He'd need a strong dosage of it if he was going to make it through the day.

"They haven't been disrupted in the least. Only the few you sent to arrest Private Willis." Jack leaned forward. "Do you remember what happened yet?"

Daniel leaned back. "What has Willis done now?"

"You mentioned his name when we found . . . when you rode into camp last night. You said he was responsible for your injury, but we don't know how that's possible, since he was here all day."

Daniel didn't need the concern on Jack's face to tell him he'd made a mistake. "Let him go. He didn't do anything." What had he said about Private Willis? His memory was full of holes.

"And I apologize about that crate. The governess got here last night, and Gundy said he'd move it. I'll remind him before I leave."

The new teacher had arrived while he was indisposed? Daniel got to his feet so quickly that his head spun. A strict disciplinarian—that was what he'd requested, and a woman like that wouldn't appreciate him keeping her waiting. Daniel had wanted her welcome to be appropriate and civilized—two traits he heartily wished his daughters possessed, as well. He didn't want to start out on the wrong foot. Women with book learning could hold a grudge longer than Queen Victoria could hold a throne.

"Where is she now?"

"Here, I suppose. Haven't you seen the girls?"

"I'm sure you've got better things to do than keep track of my daughters and a matronly widow."

"I'm going to check the kitchen. Stay right here." Jack dipped his head.

"They should've been done with breakfast an hour ago." But it was too late. Jack was gone, his boots clomping right through Daniel's home—against his orders.

Daniel took his seat, had another drink of coffee, and flipped open his ledger. Show no weakness. Just pretend to be doing the job until he could do it. His eyes blurred over the page. More purchase orders from the quartermaster needed to be logged. Also on his desk were reports from the various Indian agencies and wanted posters from Fort Smith. By tomorrow, he might not remember anything he read with this headache, but he should appear busy, at least.

Footsteps. Daniel needed to snap out of his foul mood. He didn't want his knuckles rapped by the governess's ruler.

The door opened, and Jack motioned a woman into his office. Daniel lifted his cup to his mouth and took stock of the black skirt. A widow, Mr. Dyer had told him. Still in mourning, as was proper. But then he saw a face that was anything but proper.

It was a face he'd thought he'd never see again.

The coffee scalded Daniel's lungs as he inhaled it. Determined not to erupt, he locked his jaw despite the burning. His chest heaved, his eyes watered. Seeing his distress, Jack turned the governess away, but not before Daniel got a clear look at her face.

Her beautiful, unforgettable face.

Daniel spun to the window to gain his composure. She was real, but how was it possible that she was in his house? Had he regained his senses, or not?

From his window, the parade grounds looked the same as they did every other day. The flag flew in the middle. The turf wrinkled where Private Willis had performed his riding feats earlier that month. Ben Clark, their guide and interpreter, and Sergeant O'Hare walked from the adjutant's office to the post office, chewing over some new bit of information, while a crew of troopers unloaded the wagons of the latest mule train at the commissary.

Everything outside his office was routine. Inside his office, his world had just been turned upside down.

"Major Adams?" Stinking Jack and his impatience. "Major Adams, may I present Miss Bell?"

Daniel rubbed his eyes and prayed that she wouldn't look the same when he turned around. Couldn't he ask for that one favor?

Jack cleared his throat. It was time for Daniel to face the music. While the events of his mishap weren't clear, he remembered enough to know that whatever she had witnessed put him at a disadvantage. He touched his hat, making sure it covered his bandage, before he turned to address her.

He had to look her in the eyes. A commander couldn't go skulking around. Steeling his nerves, he raised his gaze. It was her, alright.

Her blue eyes widened. Was that a spark of recognition? And why was Jack smiling?

⊶⧓⧓⧓⊷

She had expected Major Adams to be intimidating. Standing in the small office, framed by the morning sun at his back, he radiated authority, but she got an even stronger sense of restless energy. Restless energy and a sensitivity to hot coffee.

It was up to her to keep in his good graces, but now that she'd been introduced as the governess, how did she ask for another position? That was a question for another day, so she studied the chessboard to her left and pretended nothing was amiss until he'd recovered.

"Pleased to make your acquaintance, Mrs. Bell," he said.

Finally, she could look him in the face, but between the sunlight at his back and the hat he was wearing, she couldn't clearly make out his features. His words were short and clipped, as if he were in a hurry to get through his script.

"It's Miss Bell," she said. "I'm unmarried."

Lieutenant Hennessey rocked from toes to heels, heels to toes. "Unmarried?" he asked. "How interesting."

"I was told that you were a widow." The major's voice was stern.

"I'm not."

"I was also told that you were . . . old."

Louisa blinked. Of all the qualities he could disapprove of, he chose her age? Well, she'd already taken to this role. Now it was time to see how well she could perform it.

"Mrs. Townsend became ill. I am here in her place, but I am old enough to handle your daughters. That's all that's required." She kept her chin level. Hadn't she handled rowdy cowboys, drunkards, and cardsharps? How much trouble could two well-off girls be?

"You are not what was promised." He had an orator's voice, but his words were less than inspiring. And once he made a decision, she could tell it would be impossible to change his mind. She only had this one shot, and she might as well shoot for the moon.

"Give me a week," she said, surprising herself. "You don't have anyone else for the job, and I've come all this way."

His hand dropped from his collar as he pondered his decision. Her eyes were adjusting to the light in the room, bringing his features into focus. His blue uniform coat stretched over broad shoulders. The belt defined a trim waist. Now that she'd met his daughters, she knew he wasn't young, but his face had a youthful innocence that his years in the military hadn't been able to erase. Still, even without all the decorations on his coat, she would recognize him as the major.

Or would she?

She narrowed her eyes. Was there light brown hair beneath that hat? Hair with a touch of red in it, just like Daisy's?

"One week," he said, "but I'll be monitoring your progress. Now, if you'll excuse me."

He tapped the brim of his hat as a dismissal, but Louisa was fixed in place, unable to look away. It couldn't be. Couldn't be! The man she'd helped out at Turkey Creek couldn't be Major Adams. It was too terrible to contemplate. In vain she searched for his wound, but the hat's placement made it impossible to see.

Lieutenant Hennessey stepped to the side of the doorway. "This way, please, Miss Bell."

It was time to leave. Both men were watching her as if they expected something to happen. Did he not recognize her? He had suffered a hard fall, so maybe he didn't remember. It was on the tip of her tongue to ask, but to ask what? *Do you recollect a gaudily dressed woman who held you on her lap?* For her and Bradley's sake, she had to hope that he didn't. She'd just been introduced as a governess. If he remembered her dressed in her performance clothes, he'd kick her out immediately. No father wanted a chorus girl around his daughters.

She hoped she could count on Lieutenant Hennessey to keep a secret, because if Major Adams ever remembered their encounter, she'd be the last woman he'd want under his roof.

Chapter Eight

On stage, Louisa had been caught unprepared before. Once she'd forgotten the words and stood there with her mouth hanging open like a broken gate as the music played. She'd almost lost her job. This time the stakes were even higher.

Without thought, her feet carried her away from the office and to the parlor. That was Major Adams? That man? Had she known, she would have never stepped out of the trees. Now it wasn't just this job at stake, but Bradley's also. If Bradley's commanding officer found out who she was, and that she'd lied to him in order to stay beneath his roof, Bradley might be in even more trouble. But why hadn't the major said anything? Maybe Mrs. Townsend's God was taking care of her after all.

Morning light streamed across the room, painting a golden square against the lavender wallpaper. She'd only traded the major for another audience, his children. She had to get her bearings and continue with the show.

"Aww, now you're going to make us study?"

Louisa startled to see Daisy lying on the ground beneath the sofa. Her legs stretched out behind her, and her foot pushed against the fireplace hearth.

A governess. That was what Louisa had to be for the next week, or until she could find Bradley. If only she had a clue what a governess actually did.

Daisy's freckled face was scrunched up, watching her. Louisa had only gone to school here and there, but she did know that studying didn't happen beneath a sofa.

"Where's your schoolroom?" she asked.

"We don't have a schoolroom."

"Then where do you do your lessons?"

Daisy slapped the flowered rug beneath her. "Right here, if I'm of a mind. Or in the tree behind the house. Or in the kitchen. Lieutenant Hennessey helped me learn how to carry-over on my ciphering using pinto beans."

"And your last governess allowed that?"

"We've never had a governess. There's an old schoolhouse here on base, but the teachers don't stay very long. Which is fine with me. I don't fare so well with teachers. I'd rather be outside."

They had that in common, but Louisa thought it best not to admit it. She'd been hoping she could take her cues from the girls on how to behave, but it turned out that they didn't have the slightest idea either. She smiled. Finally, a lucky break.

"Bring out your books." Louisa stepped around the child on the rug and moved the sofa cushions to make room for the two of them. If Miss Caroline didn't want to participate, Louisa would leave her be for now.

"You were supposed to bring books, remember?"

The crate. It still sat by the front door, right next to Major Adams's office. Louisa drew in a deep breath. No use in losing her nerve now. She'd already gotten her fancy boot in the door. She had to pretend to belong.

With every ounce of courage she could muster, she sashayed past the open office door. From the corner of her eye, she saw him look up, but she didn't stop. Lieutenant Hennessey was gone, and she could think of nothing she had to say to the major alone.

The wooden crate barely budged when she grasped it. Should she try to hoist it up? Would a real lady do that? Feeling the major's eyes on her, she tested the lid of the crate and puffed a blond lock out of her face in satisfaction. The top had already been loosened for her.

Quickly she set it aside and pulled out the books, dismay filling her as she looked at the titles.

Ray's New Higher Arithmetic
A Primary Spelling Book of the English Language
Heath's Common School Music Readers
Gray's Botanical Textbook: Structural Botany
The Practical Linguist . . . The French Language, Volume 1
A Practical Reader with Exercises in Vocal Culture

Higher arithmetic? Besides counting measures in a song, Louisa hadn't had much call for ciphering. And she wasn't one-hundred-percent certain what structural botany was, either. Houses made of plants? This was going to be harder than she'd thought. She lifted a last book, *Sermons for Boys and Girls by Eminent American Preachers*, and groaned. Hadn't Mrs. Townsend pledged that this box wasn't full of religion books?

Those would be the last subjects she taught—sermons and math. Louisa gathered the books in her arms.

Daisy called from the parlor. "We need a slate and chalk. Father keeps them in his office."

A sudden bump sounded from the office, as if the legs of a chair were lowered too quickly. Major Adams had heard Daisy's request. Louisa chewed her lip. There was no avoiding the encounter. With an armful of books, she stepped into his doorway.

Major Adams held a sheet of correspondence high before his face. His pen had stilled. He had to know that she was standing there. With a sigh, he lowered the paper and met her eyes.

"How may I help you?"

Louisa's heart rocked inside her chest. He no longer wore his hat, so the bandage on his head was easily visible. So were the lazy waves of his hair and his soft brown eyes. She dragged her gaze away from him and studied the chessboard instead.

"Daisy informs me that her slate and chalk are in here." The board showed a game in progress. The pieces held each other in check. Whoever was playing the major was his equal. One more hard look at the board, and Louisa knew she'd be able to re-create it in her memory later that night. Just like the notes on a scale, she could summon their arrangement at will.

He stood. "Let me help you with the books."

"No thanks," she said too quickly. "I'm only carrying them to the parlor."

His head drew back just a whisker. Obviously, Major Adams wasn't used to being refused, even if it was an offer of help.

"I could use help getting the slate." She smiled to soften her refusal. "And the chalk."

"I will do that," he said. "And carry the books."

Without giving her time to prepare, he reached for the stack of books in her arms. Louisa felt a bit breathless at his sudden proximity. She shoved them toward him so there was no risk of him coming closer—although by the creek he'd gotten really close to her. In her lap.

Great Saturn's rings! She had to stop thinking like that!

He tucked the books beneath his arm and marched to his bureau as sharply as if he were in a parade. When he pulled the drawer open, pieces of chalk clinked against each other.

The wooden frame of the slate caught on the drawer top as he removed it, and he lowered it and tried again, with less fluster this time.

But why should he be flustered? He was the mighty commander of this fort. He had nothing to prove to her.

He balanced the slate and chalk on top of the stack of books. When he spun to face her, the chalk rolled, hopped over the slate's frame, and fell. He grabbed handfuls of air as he tried to catch it, but the chalk bounced off his fingertips and rolled under his desk. Had Louisa not been so terrified of him, she might have laughed at his fumbling.

Instead, she held her skirt aside and dropped to her knees. With her head under the desk and stretching forward, she was finally able to retrieve the chalk. She could feel the warmth in her cheeks as she stood. Major Adams looked flushed as well, and he did not strike her as a man who was easily unsettled. Perhaps that head injury still had him addled.

"You've hurt your head." With the piece of chalk, she motioned to his bandage. "Are you sure you've recovered?"

His eyes lit at the challenge, but instead of answering her, he made an inquiry of his own. "As you know, I requested a strict, experienced governess from the missionary society. I understand you are a replacement, but are you sure you're up to the task?"

Louisa was walking a high wire without a net. No stopping now. "Has the missionary society ever misled you before?"

He took a moment to savor her reply. The intensity of his gaze had her on her guard. "From this stack of books, it appears you are very ambitious."

"I'm sure your daughters will do just fine."

"I'm not worried about my daughters," he replied. He tilted the books to get a look at the spines. "French? You speak French?"

Louisa had never had a French lesson in her life, but she'd learned several songs in the language. Classical, fancy music at that. But instead of singing, she demurely quoted one of her favorites, carefully removing any musical inflection that might expose her as a performer.

> Belle nuit, ô nuit d'amour
> Souris à nos ivresses
> Nuit plus douce que le jour
> Ô, belle nuit d'amour!

Major Adams's jaw went taut as he blinked. Hadn't she pronounced every word correctly? Mimicking was one of her strengths, and she'd heard this song performed several times, although it was usually a duet.

"Will that be . . . will those be the phrases you teach my daughters?"

Poor man was probably concerned they couldn't keep up. Louisa smiled. "Nothing like that to start with. They'll have to learn the basics first."

"Let's hold off on the French lessons." He nodded once, then waited for her concession.

"Whatever you say." She'd delay teaching them anything, if possible.

Evidently Major Adams had no more time to visit with her, because he spun on his heel and strode to the parlor. By the time Louisa caught up, he'd deposited the books with the girls—Caroline having deigned to appear—and was making his departure.

"And now I need to go out to supervise work detail," he said. "I mean, Sergeant O'Hare can do it, but he might be . . . it'd be better if I wasn't here."

He was flustered again. Louisa stepped out of the doorway

to allow him to pass. The front door shut decisively behind him, leaving them alone in the house.

"Father is supposed to stay at home." This from Caroline as she carved her initials with a needle in the base of a candlestick. "He's injured and not supposed to work. And then there's you, who should be working but aren't. A real governess would've started class immediately after breakfast instead of wasting time organizing her materials."

"Caroline's a grouch." Daisy was hopscotching the brick hearth in front of the fireplace. "She doesn't know anything. She's never had a governess."

"But I've read plenty of stories about them, and they are more professional than Miss Bell."

What stories were those? Louisa's job would be easier if someone would tell her what to do. This was almost like taking on a role with no script.

Actually, it was precisely like that.

"Let's get started," Louisa said.

Caroline stabbed her needle into the candle as she looked at the stack of books her father had left. "I'm too old for a slate," she said.

For crying aloud. Even considering all her customers at the Cat-Eye, Louisa had never worked for such particular people before. "Then you can use a pencil. Where are they?"

Caroline tilted her head toward the major's office. "There's a pencil holder on Father's desk. Help yourself."

Now that the major had left the house, the office didn't intimidate her nearly as much, even if the stately bookcases and the impressive desk looked more like a fortress than the rest of the fort did. Louisa took a pencil off his desk and tested its point. Then she took another, because she supposed she'd need one, too. But when she considered what she might actually write with it, she returned it to the pencil case. Better not to have a pencil at all than to have one and not know what to write.

She was about to join the girls in the parlor when the chessboard caught her eye. A quick look over her shoulder told her that no one was about. Her hand tightened on the pencil. She held her drab skirt tight against her legs so she wouldn't bump the little table and scatter the pieces as she moved closer. Without effort, the battle sprang to life before her eyes. She saw strategy and defense. She saw mistakes made—although not gross mistakes—and she saw a plan unfolding. Whoever had left the pieces there was a good match for the major, for who else would be playing the game in his office? One of the girls, perhaps? She didn't think so. The skill was too advanced. Probably Jack Hennessey.

Like always, the way illuminated before her. Jack, if he was the black army, seemed unaware of the opening the major had left him. In a few short moves . . .

Louisa slid a pawn forward one space to open a path for a rook. She gave the board one last look, but it was unnecessary. Like anticipating the next bar of music, patterns and predictions leapt out at her. Lieutenant Hennessey would appreciate the help.

If only arithmetic were as easy.

When she returned to the parlor, Daisy bounced on the sofa cushions. "What are we going to do first?"

Caroline haunted the corner by the fireplace, unwilling to admit her curiosity. Her gingham dress, although well made and of quality fabric, looked uncomfortably tight in the shoulders. How many years had she had it? Louisa gave Daisy's dress another evaluation. It fit similar to how Mrs. Townsend's dress fit Louisa. The waistband sagged against her flat stomach. The sleeves flopped past her wrists. Daisy's gown wasn't new. A hand-me-down from Caroline, no doubt. Poor things. How they must yearn for something beautiful to wear. Instead of trying to teach them botany, she should be teaching them how to sew.

But her first crusade was finding out what Bradley was accused of and informing him of her break with Tim-Bob and the Cat-Eye. Then maybe she could help prettify the Misses Adams.

"Let's see where you are in your studies," Louisa said. She picked up the spelling primer and ran her finger down the page. The words in the front of the book seemed simple. She looked again at Daisy, perched on the edge of the sofa, eager for the test to begin. What could a ten-year-old spell? She'd know soon enough.

"Spell *tooth*."

Daisy turned to grin at Caroline, who rolled her eyes.

"T-o-o-t-h."

That was too easy. Louisa flipped through another year's worth of lessons. "Spell *copper*."

Daisy's answer matched the book, so Louisa had to admit she'd been bested.

The clock chimed. She lowered the book. "Time for lunch."

"It's only ten o'clock," Caroline replied.

Ten o'clock? She should just now be getting out of bed. She'd go crazy if she had to sit in this parlor all day when her brother was so close. While trying to ease the furrows on her brow, she flipped the pages of the primer until the words looked more difficult.

"Let's try *trifling*."

Finally, Daisy was stumped. Feeling much relieved, Louisa handed her the book. "Copy these words on your slate, and we'll test you tomorrow."

Daisy promptly arranged her slate on her lap. Probably a real governess would insist on her sitting at a table, but why did proper people think the only way you could learn was if you were uncomfortable?

Daisy's head popped up. "Do I have to copy the saying at the end?"

"What's it say?"

"'Never shirk the truth to tell; What is false is far from well.'"

Louisa ran her hands over the pile of blond curls that cascaded over her shoulder. She pulled her hair over her heart and twisted a curl around her finger. "Why would you want to copy that?"

"Isn't it part of the exercise?"

Louisa took a deep breath. Daisy was just a child. She didn't know that Louisa was a sinner pretending to be a saint. Besides, who was Louisa hurting by being there? She might accidentally teach a ten-year-old a few spelling words if she wasn't careful. What would be the harm in that?

Tired of being ignored, Caroline reached for the *Practical Reader*. The spine creaked as she forced the pages to part for the first time. Instead of starting at the beginning, she opened it near the back. With a shake of her head, she snapped the book closed.

"This is for children. There's not a passage in there that I can't read. Simplistic."

Truthfully, Louisa wanted nothing more than to drag Mrs. Townsend into the room and ask her why she'd chosen these books for the girls, for there didn't seem to be anything appropriate or interesting to them.

"I thought you hated school," Louisa said.

"Only because it's too easy. The teachers that come to the fort never challenge me."

Louisa's teeth ground against each other. "Then read this." She shoved the botany book at Caroline and let go before the girl could push it back at her. "Unless you've studied botany already . . ."

Please don't let her know botany. Please don't let her know botany.

Louisa nearly cheered when Caroline flounced away and flopped into the armchair by the fireplace. The girl took no pains to spare the pages from her juvenile frustration, but Louisa could not care less. She'd bought herself some time. It had to get easier from here.

≈≈)(≈≈

The line of horses seemed to flicker in the sun. The sharp uniforms of the drilling troopers faded into a foggy blue haze. Daniel knew he could fool everyone into thinking that he was critiquing their drill—until he collapsed on the ground, at least. Trying to lead while lying facedown in the red dirt of Fort Reno wouldn't be his finest moment. He had to look like he was in control, even when he couldn't control his own spinning head.

Actually, everything seemed to be spinning out of control, not just his head. Ben Clark reported that the reduced rations from the agency had the Cheyenne riled up. With the fort holding only a fifth of the troopers it was meant to house, Daniel couldn't afford any kind of trouble. Not until Washington got around to resupplying his men. He hated this pointless waiting. If it were up to him, he'd solve the problem immediately. Answer the request. Dispatch the troops. Why let a problem fester when you knew the solution?

But Daniel didn't know the solution to the mystery under his own roof. Who was this Miss Bell? Why hadn't she said anything about meeting him before? Unless his memory was faulty, which it very well could be, she'd been the soul of concern. Perhaps even more concerned than was seemly for a woman of her position. Then again, his actions had hardly been appropriate. If she never mentioned the incident, so much the better. His nose twitched. Something about her didn't add up, and he wouldn't rest easy until he figured out what was wrong. The situation called for extra vigilance, and he was more than willing to watch her like a hawk.

He owed her hospitality, as she'd come at his request. And he owed her the respect he'd give any lady, especially a Christian sister sent by the missionaries he admired. Beyond that, he prayed that God wouldn't allow his judgment to be clouded. A pretty face was no substitute for character.

Daniel forced the scene before him into focus. Command Sergeant Major O'Hare stood under a tree with his field glasses. The parade grounds weren't big enough for him to need field glasses, but the stout Irishman preferred looking official. Going to him gave Daniel an excuse to wait in the shade.

"These are all the men we have?" Daniel asked as he motioned for a trooper to bring him a canteen of water.

Sergeant O'Hare pulled on his brown goatee. "I hope the Cheyenne aren't keeping count."

Daniel was of the firm opinion that when Washington proposed any new Indian regulations, they should go ahead and send extra troops with them. Especially for edicts as unpopular as the short rations. If conditions worsened, Agent Dyer would let him know. He'd ring Daniel through the telephone line that ran directly between the agency and the fort.

But more was ringing in his head than the telephone. Daniel took the canteen from the trooper and tossed back a quick drink, but the sudden movement made his head swim.

"Are you feeling alright?" O'Hare asked. "Beg my pardon for asking, but . . ."

Daniel glared at his officer. At least he hoped he was glaring at him. From the way the light reflected around everything, he couldn't be sure exactly where his eyes were pointed.

"I'm going to get Doc—"

"No," Daniel said. "I'm fine."

But even in his confused state, he could see Sergeant O'Hare discreetly waving for help. Daniel fumed. He didn't want to cause a scene. Didn't want to give these tightly wound troops any reason to question his fitness. Maybe it was better to retreat while still showing strength.

"I have correspondence to attend to," he heard himself say. As he walked out from under the tree, the bright light stung his eyes. He knew he'd recover, but he hated being weak, even if it was just for a day. How could he take care of his duties, of his girls, if he wasn't one-hundred-percent fit?

He kept his eyes down on the neat lawn of the green as he made his way back to the house. He'd always prided himself on his ability to take care of things, of people. Anything less was a failure.

But he had failed. He was on a campaign when Daisy was born. Margaret had been taken by a fever suddenly, and a week and two days later, she was buried while Daniel held the infant in the crook of one arm and six-year-old Caroline by the hand. The sobs of his mother-in-law had battered him like artillery.

No wonder Edna didn't trust him. He'd failed her daughter. Daniel didn't know what he could have done to save her, but he had never forgiven himself for not being there. He wouldn't fail his girls this time, which meant making sure that this governess lived up to her promises.

The white house reflected the hot sun at him. Inside it would be cool. He had to take care of himself, but he couldn't let the new governess see him ailing. He'd get a cool rag for his forehead, then slip into his office and pull the shades.

He walked past the front porch, breathing in the scent of the roses that meant home to him this time of year. No use in alerting everyone that he was back. He didn't want Miss Bell to think that convalescing was a frequent practice of his. Walking around the side of the house, he took stock of his firewood and the progress of his kitchen garden. He might be understaffed, but he still ran a tight ship. He stepped through the back door into the kitchen. Every muscle in his body ached, from his neck down. How he wished he could blame Bradley Willis, but this was solely on him. No one made him act the fool.

Daniel took a cheesecloth towel from a hook and doused it in cool water from the pump. If only he could get to his office without drawing the attention of the new governess. He didn't want to see her again until he was feeling his best.

"So how many soldiers are stationed here?" His hearing sharpened at the sound of Miss Bell's voice, especially as the topic concerned his men.

"I don't know," Daisy said. "The companies come and go a lot. Even those stationed here spend a lot of time patrolling the reservation. We don't see much of them unless they're here to restock their supplies."

"Don't forget the new recruits," Caroline added. "They stay until they get the drills down and are ready for service. And some of them take longer than others."

Ah, Caroline. What was he going to do with her? She was always comparing, always evaluating—and not much met her standards. Another trait that he and his eldest shared.

"But if there was a particular soldier you wanted to see, how would you meet him?"

Daniel's jaw tightened at the inappropriate question. Meet one of the troopers? What exactly did she have in mind? Miss Bell's beauty made him wary. This conversation only deepened his mistrust.

"You could ask Pa," Daisy said. "He could order them to his office."

"No, I wouldn't do that," Miss Bell said, a bit too hastily. "I wouldn't want to trouble your father over anything so inconsequential. Now, open your books."

His fist tightened on the towel in his hand, causing the

water to drip on his boot. She knew better than to broach the subject with him but had no qualms about questioning his daughters?

Such behavior would not do.

Daniel knew some of the officers' wives advertised for homely maids and governesses, because odds were they wouldn't be able to keep a single woman single at an isolated outpost full of lonely soldiers. Now he understood the practice. But he'd always supposed the maids were struck by a case of regiment fever upon seeing the men in uniform. From the sound of it, Miss Bell had taken this post for that specific reason.

A week-long trial period? With her fetching attributes, she wouldn't need half that time to get a proposal, and then he'd be left without help once again. Although his request for a referral had been answered immediately, the appointment had gone awry somewhere. What had happened to his strict missionary widow? Perhaps he should consult Agent Dyer before allowing Miss Bell to get too comfortable in his home.

"You told me to read the first chapter," Caroline said, "but what are phaenogamous plants?"

Daniel grunted. Caroline and Daisy needed someone with Miss Bell's academic training. That much couldn't be denied. He'd just have to watch her closely to make sure she conducted herself in a manner befitting her station. Extremely closely.

"Daddy, what are you doing home?" Peering around the door-frame, Daisy smiled up at him. "I didn't hear you come in."

He crossed his arms over his chest, hiding the rag. "Aren't you supposed to be at your studies?"

Her eyes sparkled. "I am doing my studies. Remember how I learn my spelling words better if I walk around while I practice them? I'm practicing."

His estimation of Miss Bell went up a begrudging notch. With his own governess, Daniel had never been allowed to get out of his seat, and like his daughter, he did his best thinking on the move. At least he'd found a teacher who understood Daisy.

Now that he was out of the sun, he felt revitalized. His head was slowly but surely clearing up.

"You work hard for Miss Bell," he said, trying not to wince with each step. "If you get a proper education here, then there's no reason for you to move to Galveston."

Daisy held her spelling book in one hand with her thumb stuck between the pages. "If Caroline knows that, then she'll mess up on purpose."

Daniel pinched her cheek and whispered, "Caroline can't stand to fail. I don't think she could do it even if she wanted to. Now get back to work."

Daisy scratched at her ribs, then turned and ran back to the parlor.

Daniel made a beeline for his office and purposefully refused to look in the parlor as he passed. Closing the window shades was a trick. It took him a few tries to find the precise angle to tug the lines, but he finally got them down. At least he could use this convalescence time to get something done. And he could also call Mr. Dyer about his unorthodox governess.

As he crossed to his desk, Daniel passed his chessboard. Sometimes he'd study it for hours, trying to think of the best move. That would take more effort than he was prepared for today, but something caught his eye.

His white queen was in jeopardy. The black rook was ready to pounce on her. How had he missed that? He squatted next to the board, his focus sharpening. If the rook had that opening available during his last play, he wouldn't have left his queen there. And according to the arrowhead he kept on the bookcase, it was black's play. Had black already moved? He fished through his memory. The pawn. It was in the wrong place. He was certain of it. So if black had moved, then it was white's turn again, but who had moved it? Daisy? Caroline? Jack?

Or had he? Daniel touched the knot on his head. Had he moved it and forgotten? Anything was possible. He moved a bishop into the path of the rook to stop the assault, then double-checked that the arrowhead still pointed to the black side of the board.

That fall might have hurt his memory, but evidently it had improved his chess game.

He left the board and walked to the telephone box hanging on the wall. Lifting the receiver, he settled into his chair to wait for someone on the other end to answer. Outside, the line draped over the telephone poles and across the river like patriotic bunting until it dipped down toward the riverbank and disappeared from sight. Finally, he heard Dyer's voice, scratchy over the miles of wire.

"This is Agent Dyer."

"Major Adams, here. How are you prepared for Monday?"

Dyer hesitated. "We have the goods. We have more than enough goods, but no permission to distribute them all."

Because the tribes wouldn't learn to farm until the easy food stopped coming. Daniel understood the theory, but these tribes had faced starvation before. The children would be lost first. How far was the government willing to go in their reeducation plans? How could they expect the tribes to embrace their ways when they'd been bitter enemies?

"We'll be there to keep a tight rein on things, as usual," Daniel said.

"I kinda planned that you would be." Dyer sounded confused. Why was Daniel calling on the rarely used telephone to tell him what he already knew?

Daniel took a deep breath. "There's another issue I wanted to discuss. The governess arrived yesterday."

"Excellent. I hope Mrs. Townsend is settling in."

"Mrs. Townsend didn't make it. Her replacement is named Miss Bell."

There was another pause. "Hmm. That name doesn't sound familiar."

"You don't know her?" Daniel leaned into the receiver. "I suspected as much. She isn't what I asked for. Doesn't dress like a Mennonite, doesn't—"

"Major Adams, if I may." Daniel could just imagine Dyer running his hand through his thinning hair. "I don't think anything is amiss. If Mrs. Townsend is unavailable, I'm sure they sent a suitable replacement."

"If you could only see her."

"Why? What's wrong with her?" Then, aside, "There's no trouble, Ida. Don't bother me now."

"Well, she's . . . she's . . ." Daniel didn't know what to say. A godly woman was beautiful in her own right, but somehow Miss Bell didn't fit. And it was something he couldn't quite identify. Something that made her different from other women he knew. Her clothes, her manners, the very fact that she'd accept a lowly position out in Indian Territory when she obviously had other opportunities, made him question her motives.

But how to describe it? "She's a thoroughbred," he finally said, "trying to pass herself off as a mule."

❧❧❧

Louisa's heart pounded against her ribs as she listened in at the office doorway. She hadn't fooled Major Adams. Not for a second. She waited for the click that would signal the end of the phone call and the end of her ruse, but instead the conversation continued.

"Yes, she did bring the books," Major Adams said into the

receiver. "She must have some training, although from her French vocabulary, I don't think it was at a seminary."

Louisa clenched her fists against her waist and closed her eyes, as if through concentration she could hear the voice on the other end of the line.

"I guess it couldn't be a coincidence. Someone had to send her. But if you'd do me a favor, Dyer, next time you talk to those committee men, ask them exactly what experience she's had. I'd like to know where she's taught before. Yes, a letter with her references. That would be preferred, because some of the stuff she's said has me curious."

Louisa tiptoed back to the parlor, thankful that her worn cotton skirt didn't rustle. Major Adams had his doubts about her? Well, she had some questions for him. Like, why was her brother put in the guardhouse, and was he still there? When would it be safe to admit the family relationship? And what was a dignified, ambitious cavalry officer doing trick riding away from his fort?

Lieutenant Hennessey had been wrong. Fort Reno was full of secrets.

Chapter Nine

After three days, the knot on his head had finally disappeared, but his problems with the new governess had not.

Daniel sat in his leather chair by the fireplace in the parlor. After supper, Private Gundy had cleaned the kitchen and then quietly made his way to the barracks, leaving Daniel alone with his girls. But they weren't alone anymore. Miss Bell had taken up residence, and the change was not all positive.

Daniel had wanted a matron, someone old and respectable to work with his girls and put his mind at ease. Miss Bell was by very definition uneasy on his mind. True, dressed in her dull and dreary clothes, she was attempting to minimize her beauty, but the gorgeous traveling gown he remembered was another mystery. How did a governess acquire such a dress? And there was a bearing about her that one did not acquire in the schoolroom, a sparking vitality that didn't seem forged by hours of study.

He was having improper thoughts about the woman he'd hired to teach his daughters propriety. Improper only in that he shouldn't be thinking of her at all, besides to winnow out her secrets and assure himself that he'd been mistaken in his first assessment.

The girls must have completed their lessons, because they'd been left to their own devices after dinner. Caroline stitched a white pillowcase for her hope chest while Daisy doodled pictures of Indian mothers and their children on a notepad. The ever-confusing Miss Bell sat opposite him with an arithmetic book held to the light of a lamp. Her pretty mouth scrunched into a bow, and her brow furrowed as she slowly traced over the ciphers with her finger.

Was there something amiss with the book? He squinted to make out something on the page, but from his vantage point, it was useless. Besides, studying her was more interesting than trying to read her book.

Had an observer no insight on the scene, they might very well suppose them to be a loving father and mother spending an evening around the fire with their two growing daughters. The observer might comment on the youthfulness of the parents—he didn't look old enough to have a daughter nearly grown, either—and the tastefulness of the parlor. What they wouldn't know was that the parlor had been furnished nine years ago when the General's House was built. The furnishings didn't belong to him, and he'd never even considered them until this moment, when he suddenly wondered what sort of impression his household had made on Miss Bell.

His wife, Margaret, had never lived at Fort Reno. He'd already been widowed when he received the assignment and moved his girls from their grandmother's house in Galveston. He never worried about impressing his superiors when they traveled through Indian Territory. Fort Reno was an oasis after sleeping in a tent. Thanks to the quartermaster, no one in the army would find his home lacking.

But did she?

Eavesdropping was a time-honored method of information gathering, and so far, he had heard nothing further from Miss Bell that raised concerns. Instead he'd been confused by her pealing laughter, her lighthearted encouragements to the girls, and how she kept her good spirits even in the face of Caroline's ill temper.

High-spirited during the day, but a bookworm in her spare time. As soon as her duties with the girls were completed, she buried her nose in books that were obviously far below her abilities. Was she that conscientious about being prepared? Did she memorize the upcoming exercises? Why did she appear to be studying so intently?

And how was he to learn anything if she never spoke to him? He couldn't call her in for an interrogation. Actually, he could, but what if her story was true? Word would get back to all the missionary folks at Darlington of how he'd doubted them, and then he'd have some explaining to do. He'd have to think it through, but he was thinking of her too much already. Thinking of what a study in contrasts she made, with her ethereal, angelic features wasted in the faded mourning gown she wore every day. Thinking how her beautifully cultured voice and graceful movements contrasted with her lack of table manners and decorum. No answer seemed to satisfy.

She looked up, then looked away, embarrassed at meeting his eye. Daniel smacked the arm of his chair, ready to break the silence.

"Father, must you fidget?" Caroline whisked her needle through the fabric. "I was enjoying the peace."

"How have their lessons gone?" he asked. The woman was a teacher, after all. Wasn't that a topic they could converse upon?

Miss Bell raised an eyebrow. "I'm still evaluating them, to see where we should begin. I don't want to frustrate my pupils by starting them below or above their abilities."

Daisy giggled. "She thought I would still be working on my sums. And me, ten years old."

Caroline rolled her eyes. Daniel felt the uncomfortable prod of dissatisfaction. He'd done his best with the girls—enlisting the help of the fort's transient teachers and any learned man who came through to examine their progress—but had it been enough?

"And you passed the test. Next we'll study . . ." She flipped ahead a few pages. "Multiplication."

"I already know that, too." Daisy held her notepad at arm's length to better appreciate her sketching. "You're going to have to find something more challenging."

"Daisy, mind your tone with Miss Bell. She knows what she's doing. There might be gaps in your education that we are unaware of." It was his job to question the governess, not his girls'.

Miss Bell looked surprised. "Yes," she said at last. "That's what I'm doing. I'm starting at the beginning and finding gaps."

Caroline flipped her embroidery over and picked up her little scissors. "Grandmother would have me taking real lessons by now." She snipped a thread. "Instead I'm stuck proving that I know the most rudimentary parts of speech."

"Caroline Adams, you apologize to Miss Bell." Daniel would brook no insubordination. "It is not your place to criticize. You forget the chain of command here."

Caroline appeared shaken by his reaction, but she stood her ground. As he'd come to expect. With lowered eyes but a defiantly raised chin, she replied, "May I be excused, sir?"

"You will prepare an apology and present it tomorrow morning. Go to your room."

The room was uncomfortably silent as she gathered her stitching and glided out of the room.

Daisy pulled her skirt up to scratch at her knee. "I guess I'll go up, too." She came to him and planted a kiss on his cheek.

"Good night, Pa. Good night, Miss Bell," she added with a shy smile, then skipped to the stairs.

And now it was up to him to smooth over Caroline's rudeness. Or would a teacher prefer to deal with Caroline herself? Either way, Miss Bell would be uncomfortable until she was assured that she would be treated with respect—

What was she doing? Instead of being flustered by Caroline's criticism, Miss Bell had calmly unlaced her boots, slipped them off, then turned on the sofa and stretched her legs out in front of her.

Her white stockings were clean enough to be on the upholstery, but Daniel had never seen a woman sit like that in a parlor. It was almost like she was sitting in bed.

Thoughts like that were not helpful.

Perhaps, with her back against the arm of the sofa, she caught more light from the lamp. That was probably the benefit she sought. A benefit for him was that it allowed him to better study her profile. Her eyebrows were thin and light. Her large blue eyes looked able to produce tears at a moment's notice, although she'd kept them dry so far. Her lips moved silently as she pored over the page before her. But as innocent as she appeared, her position was scandalous.

"You are obviously the adviser in this matter," he said, "but is it proper for ladies to . . . um . . . elevate their feet in society?"

She lowered her book and stared at her charming toes as if they, like a naughty pup, had surprised her by jumping up on the sofa without permission.

"I'm sorry." She sat up. "I'm not used to being in company after my work is done." She shifted to sit properly, with her feet hidden beneath the hem of her skirt. "I'll try not to distract you any further." She lifted her book, effectively hiding her face from him.

He was distracted, but her turning the conversation back on

him was a ploy he wasn't falling for. And a mere book would not hide a subject of interest from his observation. She had to know he wasn't put off so easily. And was this the first time he'd been alone with a woman since Margaret had died?

What did that have to do with anything?

Maybe he'd stir the pot. See how she responded if he too adopted informal manners. "We had a unit come in from the field tonight," he said. "By the time we got everyone settled, my uniform had taken a good amount of punishment. And it's so muggy tonight. I hope you won't be offended if I remove my coat."

Her blue eyes caught his over the edge of her book. Was she shocked by his lack of propriety? He felt a little reckless as he unfastened the brass buttons and tossed his coat aside. Maybe he should let her put her feet up. If they were living together, it only made sense that they be allowed some level of comfort at the end of the day.

"You had a unit come in?" She closed her book. "How interesting life at the fort is. Are the troops allowed to socialize during the evening?"

"Yes, once they've completed their duties for the day."

"And what about the troopers in the guardhouse? Are they allowed out?"

Daniel paused. What a strange question. How did she know anything about the guardhouse?

"If they are being punished, then they aren't allowed to socialize, but at the moment the guardhouse is empty—"

But she'd stopped listening. Instead she was lacing up her boots and heading for the door.

~≈)(≈~

Bradley was out of the guardhouse and possibly strolling on the green. He'd be so surprised to see her. Louisa found herself striding to the front door before she considered the consequences.

She turned in the hall to see Major Adams right behind her. He hadn't said a word, but obviously he wasn't letting her out of his sight. She stumbled for an acceptable excuse for her behavior. One wrong word, and he'd telephone Agent Dyer to tattle on her again.

"I've been inside all day," she said, "with my nose in a book. A stroll would do me good."

He might have removed his coat, but he was still intimidating. So was the questioning look he gave her. "But it's evening. It's dark. Surely tomorrow would be better."

Since when was darkness a reason to stay inside? No one expected Lovely Lola Bell to worry about such things. She hated to argue with him, but she had to see Bradley. What excuse would a lady give?

"The sun," she said. "The sun is so hot during the day, and tomorrow the girls will have their lessons. Don't worry about me. I won't stray off the fort. I just want to—" she held her hand against her rib cage and inhaled like any good singer knew how to do—"to stretch my lungs."

Major Adams looked so very interested that Louisa nearly lost her nerve.

"Miss Bell, you've probably lived such a sheltered life that you don't understand the temptations these men face. They are good troopers, and if any of them treat you as anything less than a lady, they would be most severely punished, but all the same, there's no call for you to be out after dark alone. I would not submit you to their company at night, when they are the most lively and reckless."

And maybe it was when she was feeling the most lively and reckless, too? She laced her hands together, fearful of his reaction if he had any inkling of her thoughts. Had she finally convinced him that she was proper enough to teach his daughters, only to have it backfire on her? No one besides Tim-Bob and Cimarron Ted really cared for her well-being, and Tim-Bob had thrown her over at the first chance. But protecting her was part of the major's duties, and he was probably one of those men who never failed to do his duty. Unfortunately, he'd determined that she was too genteel to rub elbows with the ruffians outside.

If only one of those ruffians weren't her brother.

"You want to take a stroll?" The lamplight picked up traces of auburn in the waves of his hair.

With him? It might be the only way she could escape from the house. It was a dangerous prospect, but she'd learned to face fear on the stage.

I am Lovely Lola Bell. He will be enchanted with my performance and will love my show.

"Yes, sir. I would like that very much."

"Do you need a shawl or something?"

She started to turn and then remembered that the only shawls she had were made of fabric that Mrs. Townsend probably considered worthy of hellfire. "It's warm enough."

"I'll tell the girls. Excuse me." His tall boots flashed as he strode up the stairs. Louisa nearly collapsed against the wall. What was she doing, going on a stroll with the major? How long before he discovered who she really was? *What* she really was?

She heard voices as he bade the girls good night. Would he tell them that they were going on a walk together? Alone? Louisa was lost at sea without a map. If only she'd had someone to teach her what was acceptable in society. As it was, she had to trust the major's sense of propriety and hope this wasn't a test of her character.

Down the stairs he came. He slid on his coat, racing through the buttons but forgoing his hat and gloves. He held the door open for her, standing as tall and brave as she'd expect an important military man like him to stand. She passed through the doorway, trying to keep her shoulder from brushing against his chest. Already she was jittery.

This was just a performance, and a performance for only one man, at that. One very powerful, very observant, very intelligent man.

He escorted her down the porch steps, but instead of heading toward the green, they walked to the officer's quarters next door. Major Adams hammered on the door with his fist.

"Lieutenant," he yelled. "Lieutenant, come down at once."

The house was dark save a faint light in an upstairs window. Louisa followed the light's progress down the stairs until the glow appeared at the front of the house. The door flew open, and Lieutenant Hennessey appeared with shirt untucked and sock feet.

"Yes, sir! What is it?" He caught sight of Louisa and began hastily tucking in his shirt.

"Miss Bell wants to stroll around the base."

Lieutenant Hennessey's eyebrow rose. "Oh? Right now?"

"Yes, right now. She's spent after working with the girls, and she needs some relief."

Great Saturn's rings, what was he doing? Was he going to wake the whole camp to announce her walk? "There's no need to wake Lieutenant Hennessey," she said. "I don't have to—"

"Yes, sir." The lieutenant didn't require an explanation. All he heard was a command. "Five minutes, and I'll be ready. Do you want to wait inside?"

"That's unnecessary," the major said.

The lieutenant saluted and disappeared inside the house.

This was ridiculous. "I fully intended to go by myself," Louisa said. "If you don't want to go, there's no reason to wake Lieutenant Hennessey instead."

"Who said I don't want to go?" Major Adams stepped back

as if she'd offended him. "I'm going to accompany you on your stroll."

"Then why summon the lieutenant? Does he have to guard the house while you're gone?"

"Not at all. He's to act as our chaperone. Even out here in the nations, I'm committed to providing you with the protections you're accustomed to."

Louisa ran a shaking hand over her eyes. They were from such different worlds. If only he knew the kinds of protection she was accustomed to.

She looked across the dark parade grounds to the long barracks, where light came through the windows and voices could be heard laughing. A cluster of men stood outside the guardhouse, red dots of light attesting to the fact that they were enjoying cigars before turning in for the night. Metal rang out from east of the commissary as some troopers played horseshoes. Shouts came from the west as some men tested their skills at arm wrestling. Was Bradley one of those men? Was this her best chance?

The door opened, and the lieutenant appeared. "Reporting for duty." He tightened his gloves and smoothed his blue tunic—dressed perfectly, when he should be in bed.

Her impulsive request to take a stroll had led to this? Louisa wanted to hide, but Major Adams saw nothing unusual in the procedure.

"Then we're off. Fall back behind us, Lieutenant. Maintain a position twenty feet to the rear."

Oh, dear heavens. They set off on the gravel path that lined the parade grounds. The uncomfortable man from the parlor was obviously in his element as he strode ahead of her, not a jot worried over whom their outing would inconvenience. Thankfully he had nothing to say, because she was so embarrassed she could hardly breathe. Instead she searched the darkness for a familiar form or gesture, glad that the major had forgone escorting her. It had been hard to concentrate with her arm tucked into his.

Would she recognize Bradley? She'd spotted him easily enough the day she arrived, but it was darker now. They approached a cluster of men. Their voices carried across the green as they laughed and shoved each other playfully. But their fun halted abruptly when Louisa and the major appeared out of the darkness. Immediately the men snapped to attention, frozen like opossums caught by surprise—minus the tongue sticking out.

They didn't move a hair, even as she approached, giving her a good chance to search each of their faces. No brother.

"Good evening," Major Adams said. "Carry on."

Their shoulders lowered, but they didn't carry on. No more laughter, no more horsing around. They just stood in awe until Louisa had passed.

"Hey, Teddy, did you get your horse shod?" the lieutenant called to one of the men. Evidently Lieutenant Hennessey wasn't nearly as scary as the major, something Louisa had sensed from their first meeting. The men chatted with him amicably as she and the major continued around the walk. Major Adams looked over his shoulder, and his steps slowed. Finally, he stopped walking and turned.

"We're going to outmaneuver our coverage," he said. "Might as well wait on Jack. He's my eyes and ears. These fellows will tell him things that they'd never want me to know."

And so had she. She studied the major as he watched his assistant. He stood straight and tall with his chest expanded as he surveyed his domain. What would it be like to be as respected as he was? Louisa couldn't imagine.

With a playful slap on the back, the lieutenant left the men, who acted as if they'd forgotten the commander. One fellow started dancing a jig while his friends clapped their hands. They would never act that way if they'd remembered that Major Adams was nearby.

In the last three days, she had managed to avoid him almost entirely. Evening meals were the most dangerous, but she watched Major Adams closely and mimicked his manners so she wouldn't be caught messing up. She should have noticed that he never put his feet on the furniture.

And yet he'd stood on his saddle.

Louisa darted a glance at him, hoping to see the daring man who'd undertaken trick riding once out of sight of his responsibilities. She knew that playful man lived somewhere beneath his stern uniform and guarded expressions. No wonder he'd ridden so far from camp before trying the stunt.

A group of men sauntered toward them, lost in their own conversation, until they saw who was waiting on the walkway. They snapped to attention, too, and Louisa was surprised to see that they were all black men. Major Adams greeted them as he had the last group and let them pass.

"Now Jack will have to talk to them, too. I apologize for bringing him. I forgot how he likes to chat."

"That's alright," she said. "I didn't realize you had black troops stationed here."

"The Indians call them buffalo soldiers, because they say their hair is curly like the buffaloes'. They are fine troopers. They feel like they have a lot to prove."

Like Bradley did. If she ever got her hands on him . . .

"Let's go," Major Adams said. "Jack can catch up."

They started forward again, into the path of half a dozen men. Louisa was beginning to understand why the major preferred to sit in his house of an evening instead of walking around. His presence disrupted everyone. Like when the sheriff showed up at the poker games after the music.

How lonely he must be. That respect came at the price of

companionship. He let Lieutenant Hennessey take the role of confidant while he remained aloof—ready to reprimand, ready to punish, ready to send these young men to their deaths if required. Who could he talk to? Who lent him an ear for his struggles?

Daisy had mentioned her mother's death, but it had been so long ago. Why hadn't he remarried? Then, as if to answer her own question, Louisa looked around. Rolling prairie in every direction. The missionary woman back at Red Fork Ranch had been the only unmarried white woman she'd seen since getting on the stagecoach.

The next group of troopers saluted, but with a casual wave, the major urged her past them, intent on getting her the fresh air he'd promised.

"There's no need to walk so—" Suddenly her voice failed her and her heart began to race. That was Bradley, passing her now. She had to stop him.

With little time to act, she deliberately stumbled. Twisting her ankle was easy in the heeled boots she wore. She grabbed Bradley's arm to keep herself from falling to the ground. Major Adams immediately took her other arm and suspended her between them.

"I'm sorry," she said. "I turned my ankle. If you could help me to the bench over there."

She looked Bradley full in the face, but he was looking at his commander.

"I can assist her, Willis." Major Adams had pulled her closer to him. "Go your way."

If only Bradley would look at her. She dug her fingers into his arm. She felt him tense, and he stole a glance in her direction. He was already pulling away when his eyes widened. His mouth fell open as recognition dropped on him like a cask of whiskey.

"What . . . what are you doing here?" he gasped.

Before she could come up with an excuse, the major stepped between them.

"What did you say, trooper?" Major Adams's voice was cold and steady.

Stunned, Bradley stumbled backward and stuttered a pathetic, "Nothing, sir."

"You will not address this lady unless she addresses you first. Do you understand?"

Poor Bradley! He stood at attention, blinking rapidly as if he'd just been doused in water. Louisa felt tears in her eyes, but the last thing she wanted was for him to get into more trouble. She had to act. She had to distract the major.

"Do you understand?" Major Adams repeated.

"My ankle," she cried. "I need help." The major already had her arm, so she had to do something more drastic. "Please stop. I feel faint."

The major couldn't threaten Bradley and tend to her at the same time. She waved Bradley away, frantic that he leave while he had the chance. His retreating back was the last thing she saw before she closed her eyes and let her body go slack.

To his credit, the major didn't allow her to hit the ground. He gathered her in his arms and walked away from the troopers.

"Should I get Doc?"

Louisa opened one eye to peek. Lieutenant Hennessey jogged along beside them.

"Let's get her to the house first. It was that impudent Willis who upset her."

Louisa's throat tightened. Bradley had nothing to do with it. Why did the major assume the worst of him?

Major Adams carried her like she weighed nothing, but her heart was heavy. Hiding her frustration was a challenge, especially while being carried in his arms. Really she wanted nothing more than to be able to pinch him hard at that moment. Or leave another egg-sized knot on his noggin.

They went up the steps of the major's house, and Lieutenant Hennessey threw open the front door. Next thing she knew, she was lying on the sofa. How did one credibly recover from a faint? Probably by acting weak and groggy, not angry and ready for a fight. Thinking through her response, she began by fluttering her eyes and moaning.

"Here's some water," Lieutenant Hennessey said.

"You can go now." Major Adams's hand brushed her hair from her face with unaccountable tenderness. Where had that come from? She began to calm. Now wasn't the time to confront him. She needed his favor. She needed to stay longer if she was going to turn his opinion of Bradley. She needed to stop enjoying the attention the major was paying her at that moment. Maybe she felt weak and groggy, after all.

"Don't you think that Doc—"

"Jack, I can handle this."

"I'm not so sure about that, Daniel."

Louisa opened her eyes and caught Jack's knowing grin, but Daniel—Major Adams—was watching her.

"Feeling better?" he asked.

She nodded. Jack's eyes darted between the two of them. Without another word from his commander, he left, humming a ditty in three-quarter time.

Seated on the sofa next to her, Major Adams lifted a glass of water to her lips. She sat up and took it out of his hand. She was thirsty and eager to end the charade. Maybe too eager.

"How's your ankle?"

She'd almost forgotten her injury. "It's fine, really. The sharp pain made my head spin, but now it's gone."

His face betrayed no emotion, only intense interest as he took in her words. She felt there was more to be said.

"I wasn't offended by the trooper's question," she added. "There was no call for you to talk to him like that."

The major leaned away. He took the glass from her hand and set it on the hearth, out of her reach.

"I apologize for not practicing better judgment," he said at last.

"Some people just let their temper get the better of them."

"I'm not talking about my temper," he said. "My mistake was taking you out after dark. It won't happen again."

Louisa pressed her fist against her chest to stifle a sharp hiccup. So far he'd treated her respectfully and expected his daughters to do the same. This was the first time he'd openly opposed her. She understood the warning, loud and clear.

He stood, and although he didn't speak, an order had been given just the same. Their night was over. She'd disappointed him, but she didn't know how to avoid it. Despite her regret, Bradley's career came first.

Worried that she'd ruined everything, Louisa headed to the stairs, so distracted that she forgot to limp.

Chapter Ten

The morning sky had just begun to lighten in the east. A yellow cast on the horizon chased the stars to the west, where they'd stay cool and out of the blistering sun that could wreak havoc on any summer day.

Daniel had dealt with sun sickness in his men before. He'd revived men who had fallen from exhaustion. He'd tended to injured troopers who had passed out from pain. He'd carried unconscious victims of Indian raids to safety. He'd recently been knocked out himself and was still suffering from a painful knot on his head.

But Miss Bell had not been unconscious last night.

Instead of heading toward the green, he turned just outside the gate. His footprints marred the wet grass until he left the lawn and hit the longer grasses of the field. He nodded to the dairyman driving the milk cans in from the barn, but he didn't stop to talk. He had some thinking to do.

For starters, one did not heartily declare their intention to faint, then direct someone else to leave before proceeding to drop. For whatever reason, Miss Bell had arranged for Private Willis to escape in the midst of her distress. Secondly, unconscious people did not hold their heads upright while being carried. They did not keep their hands clasped neatly together while being handled. He'd known the instant she was in his arms that she had no need for the service, but he'd carried her anyway.

And he'd do it again.

The post commander didn't need to get his hands dirty. He could have ordered anyone, including a verified doctor from the fort's hospital, to attend to Miss Bell, but he'd rejected the idea immediately. Instead, he'd played along with her ruse. But why? Maybe because she'd been so kind about his injury. Maybe because she hadn't told anyone about finding him crumpled up on the prairie. Maybe because he enjoyed cradling her against his body . . .

Daniel stopped and watched the sun rise over the horizon. What was happening to him? Not once since Margaret had died had he felt his loneliness so keenly. The cavalry had kept them separated for much of their marriage, and after her death, he used to pretend that she was still at her parents' home in Galveston, waiting with the children for him to return. Over time, that fantasy could not be maintained, but by then his grief had been replaced by determination to plow ahead with his family and succeed in his career. When he was moved to officers' quarters, the girls had joined him, and he applied himself to caring for them and the hundreds of troops who relied on him.

He'd thought he could raise the girls on his own, and if Edna hadn't meddled, he would still think that. But his former mother-in-law was right. Caroline and Daisy needed a woman in their life. And perhaps Daniel did, too.

Miss Bell. Educated, poised, nurturing, and kind—she was a beautiful, fascinating woman. But something was amiss. Yes, she was comely, but attraction did not siphon away his intellect. It would take more than beauty to draw him off the scent, and something smelled rotten. What had she gained from her performance? And why did she want to keep Private Willis away from him? That might be at the root of the mystery. She'd asked the girls how she could meet a trooper. Was Private Willis her intended target?

He started back toward the house, the center abode on Officers' Row. It was Sunday and quiet on the fort. He was surprised Miss Bell hadn't asked about their Sabbath observance at the fort chapel. He'd expect a governess sent by Mennonite missionaries would think ahead to worship. Perhaps she'd forgotten what day it was.

Or perhaps Miss Bell had more on her mind than he had accounted for.

He slipped inside the house. The girls should be coming downstairs soon. Breakfast would be sparse, as it was Private Gundy's day off, so he might need to lend a hand to help Caroline get food on the table this morning.

He walked past his office and caught sight of the chessboard. Where was his white bishop? He'd moved it to stop the rook's attack on the queen, but he hadn't expected the knight to take it out. Why hadn't he seen that?

And the even bigger question . . . had he moved it himself and forgotten? No one else had been in here.

As far as Daniel could tell, his head was fine. The headache had faded, but would he know if he'd knocked himself cattywampus in the fall? And how could an accident improve his chess skills?

He stuck his head out the office door and bellowed, "Come on down and get breakfast ready."

The sound of feet in the rooms above signaled progress, so he returned to the chessboard. His first inclination was to take out the knight, but was he walking into a trap? Or could he move his queen somewhere safer? This time he wouldn't make a hasty decision. They might be late for church, but he wasn't leaving the board without knowing that he'd played his best move.

By the time the girls were in the kitchen, Daniel was confident of his play. It was subtle, it was sophisticated, and it was the correct response. Now if he could only station a guard in his office so he'd know if he himself was playing the opposing team. Actually, he could station a guard—one of the benefits of being the post commander—but he'd have a hard time explaining why he wanted his office guarded from himself.

One last look at the board, then he reached up to move the arrowhead, but again it was already pointing to the black side. Head-injury Daniel might be a better chess player, but he kept forgetting to move the stone. Daniel smiled at the ridiculousness of the situation. It was Sunday, the sky was clear, and his household was running efficiently. He deserved a laugh—especially if it was at his own expense.

Still musing, he walked around the corner and collided with Miss Bell.

He caught her by her arms to keep her from falling backward. Her hands flew to his chest. He froze at the sight of her, his fingers registering the softest fabric. Her blue eyes opened wide, her lips parted, and her lively blond hair draped over her shoulder. He couldn't bring himself to release her. Then he became aware of their surroundings, of her surroundings, of her clothing in particular. The prudish schoolmarm dress had been replaced by a rose gown of satin. He felt her beauty all the way to his gut. And she was probably wondering why he still had a hold of her.

"I'm doomed," he breathed.

"What?" she asked.

What was he talking about? He released her like she was

wrapped in barbed wire. Was he having another vision? He rubbed his eyes, but she hadn't disappeared. And the gown she wore, narrow and clinging, didn't magically change into an ugly mourning dress, either.

"What are you wearing?" he finally managed. Maybe it wasn't a polite question, but he desperately needed to know.

"It's a dressing gown." Her forehead wrinkled in uncertainty. She shoved her hands into its fur-lined pockets. "Is something wrong?"

"You can't wear that to church."

At the word church, she lowered her eyes. "I've worn the same dress all week, so I thought I'd better wash it today. I didn't think you had a church out here. As far as this old thing—" she lifted the pockets up, her hands still inside, then flopped them against her—"this is just an old dressing gown, but I have to wear something around the house, don't I?"

"Yes, you most certainly do," he barked. What was he doing? He ran his hand through his hair as he tried to collect his thoughts. Something holy. That was what he needed to focus on. "I assumed you would be looking forward to Sunday services. The chaplain is quite good."

A black sash at her waist held the robe closed, and now she was twisting it around her wrist. "Maybe next week, then. But I don't want to make you and your family late. I was just headed to the kitchen for some breakfast."

Which was where he had been headed, but not anymore. He took another look at the silky wrapper and wondered. Could she be so innocent that she didn't understand the effect she had on him?

"I was just going upstairs," he said, "to get my Bible."

Not waiting for her to leave, he stepped around her and stomped up the stairs. He hadn't told her what to expect on Sunday, but still, he was disappointed. He wanted her to set a good example for his daughters instead of lounging the day away in a silk robe. In his house. While he was away.

If anyone needed church at that moment, it was him.

～❦）❋（❦～

Louisa used to enjoy Sundays, but yesterday had been the longest day of her life. With the family gone, the house had been as quiet as a tomb. Too afraid to look for Bradley in broad daylight, Louisa had wandered around the house in her dressing gown, feeling unaccepted, unclothed, and unwelcome.

She couldn't go where everyone else went. She couldn't be who they were. And now, as she looked over Caroline's botany essay, she wondered what it would have been like to grow up without the shame and dread that followed her every step. Maybe her dreams for the future were impossible. Would living in a respectable neighborhood really make her a lady, or would she feel as inadequate as she did here? Her mother had always claimed that Louisa was no better than she was. That Louisa shouldn't judge her because sooner or later, she'd be earning a living selling her favors as well.

Louisa never knew how to tell her mother that the gentlemen callers weren't what Louisa detested. It was her mother's abuse, the harshness, the stolen childhood that she rued. But maybe those things rode along as stowaways on the track her mother had chosen. So far, Louisa had proven her mother wrong, but since she had her singing, she'd never been tested by hunger and desperation. Without it, what came next for her?

The governess story had fallen in her lap. For now, it was like a gift from heaven, but it was only a matter of time until she was found out. Until that day, she had meals on the table and a roof over her head—a very nice roof over her head. And she had a reprieve from the sordid world that she belonged in. As long as she could keep up the act.

If only Major Adams wasn't so suspicious. It seemed that she couldn't do anything without attracting his attention. Of course, his activities didn't escape her notice, either.

Major Adams had been called away early that morning. Mondays were distribution day at the agency, he'd said, and with so few men, the major wanted to be vigilant. Louisa felt odd knowing a man's schedule so intimately. From her room, she heard his boots in the hall when he went to bed and recognized his tread when he rose in the morning. Three meals a day together, unless he decided to eat in the officers' mess. She saw his laundry carried out by the camp's washerwoman and his correspondence delivered to his desk. She knew so much about him, and he knew nothing about her.

Nor could he.

Louisa wrote an *A* on the top of the paper. Caroline took it from her without drawing her gaze from the window. The troopers were at roll call, which was immensely more interesting to Caroline than the grade on her theme. Not that the grade meant anything. How was Louisa to know if her thesis was sound? Even the younger Adams girl had already surpassed her own book learning. Thankfully, Louisa's attention to voice and presentation had helped her mimic finer ladies, so her vocabulary and manner carried her farce, but they couldn't help on paper. She spent hours each night trying to catch up with the girls' level. The arithmetic procedures came easily enough. The movement of the numbers—carrying over, borrowing, keeping remainders—were like the movements of chess pieces. Everything had a place and moved in prescribed manners. But memorizing the tables was more of a challenge. She'd set the seven multiplication table to music but still couldn't come up with the correct number without humming through the song.

But hiding behind her books in the evening served more than one purpose. It also prevented excessive conversation with

Major Adams. The more Louisa talked, the more he learned about her, and that was dangerous.

With Caroline at the window, Louisa looked over Daisy's shoulder at her penmanship. Thankfully the impatient youngster had never perfected her script. That was one area Louisa could judge accurately.

"Very good work, Daisy," she said. "Your capital letters are improving."

"I'll be extra careful on my next letter to Grandmother. Maybe she'll think my penmanship has improved enough to let me stay here."

Another mention of the grandmother. Louisa took a seat next to Daisy. "Your grandmother doesn't approve of you being here?"

"Nope. She says we'll grow up as wild as the jackrabbits if we don't live in town. She blames Pa for not giving us a proper education."

Caroline dropped the curtain and turned toward the table. "She promised me comportment classes, elocution, painting, music, French—all the things I need to be an accomplished young lady. Father doesn't understand why that's important."

At this, Louisa's ears perked up. Here she'd been trying to learn sums, memorizing spelling lists, and deciphering the parts of speech, but if Caroline wanted lessons on presentation, why, that was one thing Louisa was qualified to teach.

"I think your grandmother is correct. Those are all skills you should develop. They will be important to your career."

"Career?" Caroline's mouth twisted, and an eyebrow rose.

"I mean they'll be important if you . . ." Louisa couldn't think of anything besides performing. She had to come up with something. "If you want to be a governess."

"Oh yes." Caroline fluttered her hand before her face like a fan. "Being a governess is my highest ambition."

"Don't be mean," Daisy said. "We should feel sorry for Miss Bell. She isn't having any fun being a governess."

"But I should be, shouldn't I?" Louisa was tired of moping around with her nose in a book. Her bed was soft and clean, and she hadn't gone hungry. She didn't have to endure the catcalls of an inebriated audience or the bickering of the ladies backstage. Why shouldn't she enjoy her time here? Her future couldn't occupy her thoughts from sunrise to sunset. She had to appreciate the day.

Guilt had nagged at her, reminding her that she wasn't giving the girls the education they needed. But here was something that she was qualified to help with. How could someone like Mrs. Townsend teach Caroline how to get a man's attention? How could a gently raised governess handle Daisy and her wild ways? For this, Louisa was the perfect teacher.

And that was what she'd try to convince Major Adams of, as soon as she could work up the courage.

⁂

Thursday evening, after Private Gundy set the meal on the table before them, Major Adams took the hands of his daughters. Daisy reached for Louisa's, but Louisa had to catch Caroline's to complete the circle. They bowed their heads, a custom that made Louisa nervous. One night Major Adams called on Daisy to pray, another night it was Caroline. What would she say if he called on her? She didn't know, but it wouldn't be the right thing, of that she was sure.

As soon as Major Adams began his prayer, Louisa's spirit calmed. She'd dodged the bullet again. But the gratitude coming from the major annoyed her. Of course he was thankful. God had given him everything he needed, where she had to make it on her own. But before he said *Amen*, she silently added her own requests, just in case someone was listening.

"We have to eat pheasant again?" Daisy pushed her plate away. "I don't like the way it tastes." She flopped back against her seat.

Major Adams pinned his pheasant with his fork and elegantly sawed it with his knife. "Your tastes are not the only consideration for this household. Captain Chandler's unit went hunting yesterday and brought this back for us to enjoy. I will be expected to tell them how delicious it was when I thank them for the gift."

"Well, tell Captain Chandler that I didn't like it." She pulled her feet up in her chair and hugged her knees.

Louisa cast an anxious glance at the major. What would a governess do in this situation? Was it her role to correct Daisy, or would the major prefer to deal with her? His eyes darted to her. She nodded.

"Daisy, you shouldn't put your knees up at the table. All the boys will see your knickers and whistle at you."

Major Adams stopped chewing. He pinned Louisa with that lazy stare that completely masked his thoughts. Daisy's face turned scarlet as she slowly lowered her feet. Caroline's eyes were as big as chicken eggs. After a silent, painful moment that stretched as long as the Wichita train, Major Adams resumed chewing. He took a swallow of his tea, then turned his honey-brown eyes on Louisa.

"Miss Bell brings up a good point. You girls are outgrowing your dresses."

Caroline rolled her eyes. "Father—"

"You are both growing up, and I can't have my daughters in rags. Besides, don't you want something new?"

"From Darlington?" Caroline snorted. "The gowns they sell at the agency are all boring colors that the Mennonites pick out for the Indians. There's nothing suitable there."

"I'm a decent hand at alterations," Louisa said. "You wouldn't believe how many times I've made over my wardrobe."

The room grew silent again as each of the three Adamses looked apologetically at the old mourning gown she wore.

"No, not this. I mean the gowns I wore at my last job."

"Miss Bell," Major Adams said, keeping his face absolutely even, "you've worn that same gown every day since you arrived. Do you own any other clothes?"

He knew good and well that she had something else, or had he forgotten?

"Yes, she does," Daisy chirped. "She had a wardrobe full of clothes when she arrived. I saw them in her room."

She hadn't opened that wardrobe since the night she'd found Daisy hiding under her bed. She'd done her best to forget about those clothes.

"Most of those don't fit me anymore. I shouldn't have brought them."

Caroline smirked. "You said that you're a talented seamstress. Can't you alter them?"

"I . . ." Louisa was flummoxed. "I . . . can't alter them that much. My waist has thickened so, you wouldn't even believe it."

Major Adams's eyes focused as if he could see right through the table to her waist. She half expected it to start smoking under his burning gaze. Louisa smoothed her gown, which hung loose on her. This was ridiculous.

"Tomorrow I'll escort you ladies to Darlington," Major Adams said. "I think all of you could use something new."

Her, too? Louisa traced the cavalry emblem embossed on the silverware with her finger. "That's very kind of you, Major, but I can't afford anything new."

"Your payment is due."

"It is? Already?" How was she going to pay him? She looked nervously at the pheasant on her plate. How many of his meals had she eaten? How much was the rent on the room?

"I'll pay you biweekly," he said. "Tomorrow is Friday."

Louisa's mouth dropped open. "You're going to pay me?"

His eyes narrowed and his mouth quirked. "Don't your employers usually pay you?"

Louisa gulped. "I get tongue-tied. I don't even know what I'm saying. Don't pay any attention to me."

But with her luck, he would remember every word.

❧❀❧

Don't pay any attention to her? Oh, but that was impossible. Miss Bell made a fascinating study. She carried herself like a woman of substance, used to accepting the fawning admiration of her acquaintances, but right beneath the surface was an insecure lady who wasn't quite confident of her abilities. What had happened to her to make her doubt herself so? Or was she trying to be someone she was not?

"Major Adams?" Her blue eyes reflected the light of the silver candelabra on the table between them. "With your permission, I've decided to undertake the girls' studies in a new area."

With all Caroline's dramatics about the academics, he didn't blame her. But . . . "I hope you aren't surrendering to their onslaught of complaints. That would be rewarding them for their bad behavior."

"Not at all, but they also need instruction in music, painting, dance, and deportment. They could practice these lessons after their books. More as a reward."

"That's a logical suggestion. They can practice their manners in Darlington tomorrow." The situation at the agency was tense. Maybe a family appearance would ease some of the hostility. Daisy especially was a favorite among the Arapaho girls at the school. Plus, he'd be interested to see what Agent Dyer thought of his governess in person. Dyer had only shown amusement at Daniel's desire to ferret out her secrets. Once the agent met her, he'd better understand.

Caroline groaned. "As if Darlington's anywhere special."

"Stay behind, then." Although he knew she'd never do that. "We'll leave in the morning. I'll have the horses prepared." He looked at Miss Bell. "Do you ride?"

She shook her head, bouncing her curls against her neck. Had he mentioned how interesting he found her unbound hair? Or at least it was only barely controlled by a ribbon at her neck. No Mennonite that he'd ever known wore her hair like that.

"I've only ridden in trains or buggies. And this trip was the first time for either of those."

No wonder she was at a loss so often. She hadn't seen much of the world. A wave of protectiveness surged through him, momentarily melting his suspicions. How well he could imagine her as the youngest child of a busy family. As the sheltered daughter of a doting father. It seemed strange to have her at his table, with his family, and not know anything about her own.

"Have you written your parents?" he asked.

The tines of her fork scraped against the china. "My parents? Why would you ask that?"

"Because you're away from home. They must care where you are. If Caroline were to go on a journey, I'd be waiting to hear from her."

Her usual gentle expression seemed tacked in place. Why didn't she just answer him? Had he overstepped his bounds?

"They . . ." Her eyes lowered as she studied the fowl on her plate. "I'd rather not discuss my family."

"I didn't mean any offense."

She didn't say a word. Merely picked up her fork and took another bite.

As unpredictable as the spring weather. Daniel went back

to his meal, but he studied her with the same intensity that he studied his chessboard.

He'd invited Miss Bell here because he had girl trouble. Now his female complications were only multiplying. How many secrets did Miss Bell have?

Chapter Eleven

July mornings on the Cheyenne prairie were like a disappointing treasure chest. From the outside, they looked full of the promise of brilliant sunshine and gentle breezes, but once you lifted the lid, all you found was the blistering sun and a hot, dry wind that peeled the skin off your bones. Which was why it was better to leave for Darlington early.

Taking a wagon would be the correct way to transport three females, but Daniel wasn't altogether comfortable with the ponderous transportation. Tempers between the tribes and the troops could flare like dry prairie hay. Although the fort and agency were only a few miles' distance apart, he needed to be able to flee if necessary.

Daniel had insisted that his daughters learn how to ride. He couldn't consider himself a proper cavalry officer if he didn't train his own flesh and blood how to handle a horse. And somehow, as part of his household, that obligation now covered Miss Bell, too.

From his office window, he watched as his four mounts were delivered. Their reins were left looped on the banister of his porch. A whole day with Miss Bell. What surprises would she reveal today? He already had a test planned.

"Girls!" His voice echoed up the stairwell. "Let's get going."

Their chattering rose with their hurrying. How long did it take two girls to get ready for a trip to town? But the first person down the stairs was Miss Bell. She wore the same sad everyday dress, but she wore it like it was the finest satin—neat and tidy, except for her cascading mass of blond curls.

"Miss Bell, I have your wages." He motioned her into his office and went to his desk. Reaching into the drawer, he produced an envelope. "Is this amount still satisfactory?"

What would she say? He'd added a dollar to the weekly allotment they'd agreed on through Dyer's correspondence. Did she have the character to mention it? Did she even know the details in the offer he'd made?

She slid her finger under the flap and pulled out the money. Her thumb moved and fanned the bills. He waited, barely breathing, for her to make a mistake.

But instead she whistled. "Are you sure this is right? It seems like too much."

Daniel relaxed, surprised to find that she'd answered just as he'd hoped she would. She was honest. At least they'd established that.

"After all," she continued, "you're putting up my room and board, and—"

"There's nowhere else on base for you to stay, and even if there was, we can't have you wandering around at night, looking for your lodging."

Her face turned crimson. Him and his rough manners. He had to remember that a missionary lady like Miss Bell wasn't used to soldier talk.

"I beg your pardon," he said. "I wasn't implying anything. I did overpay you this first time, but I assumed you might require some supplies as you get comfortable here on the fort."

"Pa, let's go." Daisy ran into the office, then skidded to a stop, missing Miss Bell by inches.

A reprimand was on his lips, but Miss Bell wrapped an arm around his impetuous daughter and hugged her. "Is Darlington this exciting?"

Daisy smiled up at him with shining eyes. "No, but going riding with Pa is."

She was such a sweet girl. He wished he could spend more time with her. But then again, he never knew what to do with the girls. He feared that Daisy was already too wild. Any activity he could provide—hunting, fishing, riding, shooting—would only exacerbate the problem. And Caroline was so busy trying to prove that she'd be better off in Galveston that she made a point of not enjoying anything they did together. As she came down the stairs, she primly tied on her bonnet and tucked her red hair beneath the brim. She used to love riding as much as Daisy, but now she felt she had to eschew anything fun if she wanted to be a lady like her grandmother. Daniel was at a loss.

Daisy swung open the front door and raced outside. "It's Gunpowder! He's my favorite." She clapped her hands. The horse nickered in greeting, probably relieved he wasn't carrying Daniel today.

Daniel dropped his hat on his head and pulled on his gloves.

Miss Bell twisted her hands. "Which one is mine?"

"There's nothing to be nervous about. We brought you the gentlest horse in the stables. Her name is Mary Todd."

"As in Lincoln?" she asked.

"Yeah. Maybe not the best name for a calm horse, but she doesn't live up to the reference."

Daisy had already scrambled onto her horse, sitting astride

and patting its neck. Caroline gracefully pulled herself into the sidesaddle of her mount. She arranged her skirt, which rode up to cover only a little past her knee. He'd be fixing that too-short dress problem today. And then there was Miss Bell.

"I don't know how to get started." She stood a short distance away, afraid to approach her horse. She hiccupped.

"I'll admit, you ladies do have it a bit harder. Step up here with your left foot." He bent to hold the stirrup in his hand, but when she lifted her foot, he drew back to give her sensibilities some room. The horse shifted, and she hopped, trying to keep her balance.

Her forehead creased as she removed her foot from the stirrup. "I'm not doing it right. Maybe I shouldn't go."

"And leave me to take the girls shopping for dresses on my own? I don't think so." He had to smile at her laughter.

"Point taken," she said. "I won't abandon you, Major."

He ignored the jolt of pleasure her words produced. It was just a phrase. "Getting up in the saddle is the trickiest part," he said. "Let me help you."

He stepped forward and placed his hands around her waist. His chest grew tight, but he had a job to do. Before he lifted her, she braced herself by resting her hands on his shoulders. He knew he shouldn't look, knew he should just focus on his task, but sometimes a soldier had to plunge headfirst into the fray regardless of the danger. His eyes sought hers. Their gazes locked, and he knew the truth. She felt the same breathless curiosity and, like him, would never admit it.

He lifted her into the saddle and was finally able to breathe again. A nervous glance at his daughters told him that Caroline wasn't paying a lick of attention, and Daisy was beaming happily at everyone, although probably unaware of how vulnerable her father felt. He was surprised by the revelation himself.

"I feel off-balance," Miss Bell said.

So did he. "Hook your leg over the horn. Yes, like that. You might have to scoot over a little."

She made a tiny bounce and scrunched her nose. "I don't feel very secure."

"Which is why my cavalry don't ride sidesaddle. But you'll get used to it."

"Can we go now?" Daisy asked.

Glad for the excuse to get away, Daniel mounted his own horse. "Yes, but not too fast. Miss Bell won't be able to keep up." What had passed between them just now? Had Miss Bell noticed? Daniel arranged his hat against the morning sun. There was no room for infatuation. He had to stay objective.

"Look, Father," Caroline said. "Is that unit going out with us?"

They were leaving now? Why now? He motioned for the ladies to wait until the two parallel columns of horses passed them. They looked sharp, his men in blue. Everyone rode by except for the trooper in the rear, who was on foot, leading his horse.

"What's he walking for?" Caroline asked. "Private Willis is an excellent horseman."

When had she noticed that? And how did she know his name? "He's forbidden from riding on the grounds," Daniel said. "He pulled some fool stunt and could've gotten someone killed." Willis had almost reached them, so he lowered his voice. "Not the sort of man you want to rely on."

"I'm slipping!" Miss Bell's backside had slid to the left of the saddle. She dropped the reins and held onto the saddle horn with both hands. "Help me!"

The girls' horses were between Daniel and Miss Bell. He maneuvered his mount around, but Private Willis reached her first. Leaving his horse behind, the young man raced to her side and caught her by the ankles.

"Hold on to the horn," Willis said.

Pulling a saber on a man was never more tempting. "Unhand her, Trooper."

"Please," Miss Bell said. "He's helping me."

And he was, much to Daniel's dismay. Using the trooper's grip on her feet—would Daniel ever be able to erase the sight of her shapely ankles in Willis's ungentlemanly hands?—Miss Bell was able to steady herself.

She stretched her hand down to Willis. "I am Miss Louisa Bell, the governess for the children of Major Adams. I come from Wichita, and I am educated and proper. But I do declare, I have never met such a helpful and gentlemanly young man."

What? Daniel narrowed his eyes. What was she doing? Why did she have to tell him her life story? Last time they'd crossed Willis's path, she'd manufactured a dizzy spell. Something was amiss. He didn't like the influence the trooper had over her.

Willis stared at Miss Louisa Bell as if thunderstruck. As if he couldn't comprehend the words she was saying. The temper Miss Bell had chided Daniel for was about to make a reappearance.

"That will be all, Private Willis." Daniel had to get Willis away before he got hurt, and it wasn't an Indian attack Willis should fear right now.

"Yes, sir." Willis caught the reins of his horse and ambled past them. As he got to Caroline, something fluttered to the ground.

A lady's glove. Caroline's glove.

Willis stopped. He stared at the glove as if it were a poisonous snake. To Daniel, it was even more deadly for the jackanapes.

Don't pick it up, Daniel warned in his head. *Don't be a fool.* But Willis was every shade of a fool. With a tip of his hat at Caroline, he retrieved the glove, dusted it off, and placed it in her hand.

"Thank you," she cooed in a voice Daniel had never heard before.

First his governess and then his daughter. Did this man have no sense of decency?

"Get on your horse and go," Daniel ordered without stopping to consider which encounter bothered him the most.

"But, sir, I'm not supposed to get on a horse until I leave—"

"Go."

The young man listened, and wisely so, because Daniel wouldn't let down his guard until he got his womenfolk out of the range of Private Willis.

~><)(<~

Thinking while bouncing in a saddle was nearly impossible. Louisa tried to listen as Daisy excitedly described the charms of the agency and town ahead, but Louisa was too distracted by what had happened at the fort.

All in all, she thought she'd done the right thing in bringing Bradley to the major's attention. By pretending to fall out of her saddle, she'd given Bradley a chance to prove himself, but she hadn't wanted him to expose her disguise. Thankfully, Bradley seemed to understand the situation immediately and didn't ask any questions about her story. After such a gallant rescue, how could Major Adams think poorly of Bradley? And Caroline, bless her heart, had turned inexplicably clumsy at just the right time. Could Caroline have designs of her own?

Louisa smiled through her wincing. Her brother had done her proud. Progress had been made. Hopefully the major wouldn't forget what a gentleman Bradley was.

They rode over a gentle ridge, and morning sun reflected off the red water of the Canadian River. The sharp tops of a hundred tepees stabbed their poles into the cloudless Arapaho sky.

Daisy, who'd been wearing her pony out by galloping around

them, asked, "Have you ever been inside a tepee? I wish I lived in one."

"And give up your beautiful home?" Why was no one satisfied with what they had?

"It'd be so fun. A fire right in the middle, furs on the ground. And in the summer, they're cooler than the house. They just throw a flap open, and the breeze comes right in."

And being next to the river was probably cooler, too, but the sight of tepees still took some time getting used to.

Riding into town made Louisa nervous. Up and down the sidewalks stood groups of Indians. Most of the men wore white sheets wrapped around them. Here and there was a flash of bronze skin, feathers in dark braids, or leather moccasins, but many of the Indian men preferred to stay hidden and peek out from the gap in their blankets. Others, however, had even less modesty than Louisa's friends at the Cat-Eye. She gawked at one man walking down the street in nothing but a loincloth and a whole palette of paint decorating his shining skin. Major Adams caught her eye, and she turned away in embarrassment.

The women wore leather dresses that covered them from neck to ankles. These dresses were adorned with every bauble imaginable—beaded jewelry, bones, ribbons, and rows of oddly shaped white buttons hung from their chest. Louisa appreciated the dramatic mix as only a stage performer could. Wasn't there a song about a desperate Indian maiden and her lost love? If she ever found herself on a stage again, she'd love to fashion a costume like these.

A small population of Indians called Wichita home. They weren't unknown to Louisa, but she'd never been in the minority like this. And these Indians were different, still speaking their native tongues and retaining their customs. She was truly in a foreign nation. She understood why little Hubert Collins at the ranch had talked about going back to the States.

Her arms and hands ached from holding so tightly to the reins. The last thing she wanted was for her horse to dart away and embarrass her in front of all the curious onlookers. Of course, none of the Adams family seemed the least concerned. Daisy looked back at the people with equal curiosity, even waving at a tall boy roughly her age, while Caroline stared straight ahead, just as she had since they'd left the fort. Major Adams continually scanned the crowd. Occasionally he'd nod to someone and a sort of greeting would be exchanged, but beyond that, he seemed to be at ease.

The last few yards to the store were the worst, as she anticipated getting off the horse. Her legs had cramped from their unusual position, but eventually the pain had faded, and now she was just plain numb—as dead as the columns on either side of the stage at the Cat-Eye Saloon. This would not be pretty.

The girls hopped off their horses like the experts they were. Major Adams looped the reins over the hitching post, making sure to give the horses their space, and then came for her as the girls disappeared into the store.

"Do you need help?"

He looked so honest, so helpful, so . . . good. Louisa felt a twinge of conscience. She'd never intended for her performance to mean anything personally. Maybe the major was a good man, but there was nothing she could do to change her course at this point. It was just a pity she had to continue deceiving him.

"I don't think I can get down," she said.

"That's why I'm here." He reached up and took her by the waist. Louisa tried to turn in the saddle, but she couldn't. "You . . . ah . . ." He lowered his voice. "You've got to lift your leg over the horn. It's holding you in place."

Louisa winced as she tried to push life into her useless limb. She gripped the major's forearms for balance and wrenched her leg free. He lifted her and set her easily on the ground.

Except her legs just didn't want to work.

No sooner had Major Adams released his hold on her than her knees buckled and she started downward.

"Whoa," he ordered. The horses at the post flicked their ears at the command, but Louisa was helpless. All she could do was hold on to the man who held her. "I shouldn't have left you in the saddle that long," he said. His arms were wrapped around her, holding her up. Her face was pressed against his wool coat, her arms clutching his coat. "You never complained."

"It stopped hurting after a while." She tried again to put weight on her legs, but needles of fire shot up from her feet. She gasped and tightened her hold.

"You're in pain," he said. With a quick movement, he swung her up into his arms.

Giving in to her appreciation for the dramatic, Louisa laid her cheek against his shoulder. Yes, she should have remained rigid and kept as much room between them as possible, but the romance of the moment swept her away . . . just like the handsome trooper.

He still smelled good from his morning shave. She fit well in his arms. That was about all she could observe before he lowered her to sit on the edge of the general store's porch.

"There you go." He stepped back, arms akimbo with his fists against his belt, and looked down at her. "And this time you didn't have to manufacture a faint."

"What?" Her warm fog of contentment vanished. Louisa sat up straight. "I don't know what you're talking about."

"Don't you?" A dimple was threatening to appear, but his eyes were sharp, waiting for her reaction.

Forcing herself to look calm, Louisa held her feet out before her and drew circles in the air with her toes. "Perhaps you thought I was feigning an illness, but it didn't stop you from carrying me, did it?"

He quirked an eyebrow. His expression registered a new respect. "I suppose we both had a part to play. I just have to wonder what audience you were performing for."

Louisa lowered her feet and pressed them firmly against the ground, unsure of where the conversation was leading.

Seeing her hesitation, he took her by the hand and pulled her upright. When he didn't release her, she was forced to meet his gaze. He was bending close. So close that her throat bounced with the sudden need to swallow. So close that she saw both curiosity and a hint of fear in his brown eyes. But the dimple had returned.

"You are a mystery, Miss Bell. And I make it my business to know everything about everything in my territory."

❦

What a surprise. Normally just the suspicion of wrongdoing was enough to send his staff into lengthy explanations and apologies. Miss Bell not only defended herself, but she'd turned the tables and accused him of just as serious a deception. It was true. He hadn't thought twice about sweeping her into his arms that night, and he'd done it again right there at the store. Had Miss Bell exaggerated her inability to stand just then? Had she tried to fool him twice?

He couldn't help but smile. What woman would go to such ridiculous lengths? Was he that desirable?

Daniel had to hide his grin as White Horse spotted him. His long black braids were threaded with leather thongs and beads, and he wore his sheet like a Roman senator, draped gracefully around his body. Daniel felt Miss Bell shrink back at his approach. There was nothing to fear from White Horse. He was a fair man and an honest dealer. Daniel greeted him in the sign language that the tribes used between each other.

According to White Horse, he was in town to talk to the

chiefs. Daniel nodded. The more the Indians self-governed, the more content they were, which he figured was true for just about any group of people.

It's the cowboys, White Horse signed. *Going up the trail. They have paid for passage through the Cheyenne and Arapaho lands. They say that our people are stealing from them, even though they paid. Arapaho say it is Cheyenne stealing cattle. Cheyenne say the cowboys are lying. They are lazy, and the cows are running away.*

Lives had been lost over less. Monitoring Indian Territory was like watching over a lit match in a hut made of straw while standing in kerosene up to your knees. Disheartened Indians, displaced from their homes and made to live here, didn't feel the need to play by the U.S. government's rules. Cowboys only saw open prairie—good grassland for their herds being driven to Kansas. How could someone own something so vast? Why should they pay to merely walk their cattle across it? Outlaws saw an uninhabited kingdom that would hide them from lawmen, and trigger-happy cavalrymen saw a threat in every uninvited rider in the territory.

All the elements needed for a disaster. And here Daniel was, trying to raise his daughters in the midst of it.

Do the braves want to fight? he signed.

White Horse didn't blink. *I'll talk to the chiefs. The chiefs will fix it.*

That answer didn't satisfy Daniel. Had his requests for more troops been received? It might be time to send a courier directly. He'd see to it after their shopping. Since he was in Darlington, he could assess the situation for himself.

He turned to find Miss Bell watching him. The admiration in her eyes was unmistakable. Daniel dropped his gaze. She was a young lady. Younger than him by many years. Several, at least. Well, maybe just a couple, now that he thought about it.

Either way, she didn't need to look at him like that. Not when he was moving heaven and earth to catch her in a lie.

"Come." He took her by the arm and escorted her into the shop, where Caroline and Daisy were causing a commotion.

Caroline had already instructed Mr. Evans to set aside three canisters of candy for her to choose from. Daisy was cradling a baby chick in her hands, holding it up to her face and rubbing its downy yellowness against her cheek. "Can I buy this?" she asked when she spotted Daniel.

Miss Bell bent over the little creature and exclaimed as she stroked its head. "It's so precious."

Daniel's side felt cold and empty with her gone. Maybe this game of proving her a fraud was going too far. She had her peculiarities, but she'd done them no harm. Daisy loved her, and even Caroline had begun to soften. Should solid evidence appear of some deception, then he'd show no mercy, but for now . . . He watched her caress the chick with a gentle touch.

He cleared his throat. "We came for material," he said. "Material and whatever else Miss Bell decides young ladies need. A chick is not on the list."

Miss Bell smiled up at him with sparkling eyes. "Don't be so sure, Major Adams."

At that moment, he would've bought her a whole henhouse if she'd asked.

"Maybe next time," he said finally. "Now, what about their clothing?"

Miss Bell glided over to the dry goods counter. The way she held her arms, elbows out slightly, hands clasped gently before her, made it a pity there wasn't an audience to appreciate her every move. What was she doing, hiding away in his house in Indian Territory? She deserved to be admired by the masses, not spend her days sewing dresses for children.

Miss Bell frowned as she reached the bolts of fabric. Caroline had separated out two. One had flowers all over it, and the other was some sort of plaid. That was as far as his descriptions could go in regard to material.

"Either one of these would do," Caroline said, but to his surprise, he realized that she was asking Miss Bell, not telling her. Had she decided Miss Bell might be helpful after all?

"No, no, no." Miss Bell rummaged through the bolts. "You are a beautiful young lady with striking coloring. There is no call to hide your light under a basket." She looked through the limited offerings once, then twice. Then she motioned Mr. Evans over with a wave of her arm. "Excuse me, but where do you keep your finer material?"

Mr. Evans looked to him. Daniel shrugged.

"I don't know what you're talking about," the storekeeper said. "That is fine material."

"No, I mean silks, velvets, some brocade or taffeta. Don't you have any of that?"

He pushed a thinning lock of hair off his forehead and back into place. "No, ma'am. The white folk who work at this agency generally prefer simplicity."

"What about the Indians?"

Before Daniel could interject, Daisy gave a war whoop. "I'll wear Indian clothes! That would be splendid."

"Not Indian clothes, exactly," Miss Bell said. "But maybe there's some colorful trim, lacework, or something to dress up what you already have."

"No, ma'am."

"How about handkerchiefs? I lost my nicest handkerchief on the stagecoach, and I dearly want it replaced."

"No, ma'am." The storekeeper's finger tapped against the countertop. "We have boots, if you need new boots."

Daniel leaned forward. "You do have a tendency to twist your ankle. Maybe something sturdier . . . ?"

He loved how she turned pink.

She shook her head. "We're shopping for the girls, not me."

Her heart was in the right place, but even he was getting tired of seeing the same dress day after day. Margaret had always enjoyed getting new fabric to sew a skirt. If Miss Bell needed persuasion, he'd do his best.

Marching forward with new orders, Daniel pushed all the fabric to the side and cleared a spot. Then he reached for the top bolt and thunked it down in the center of the counter. He unrolled a span of the light brown fabric, then looked at Daisy, at Caroline, and at Miss Bell. "Nope," he said. He pushed it aside and took the next bolt. This one was a rust color, almost the color of his hair when he was a boy. Before he'd even found the end of the bolt, Miss Bell stopped him.

"That one is a definite no." She'd come to stand beside him. Shoulder to shoulder. "I've already turned down most of these, but we might have to reconsider."

"How about we pick the least offensive?" he said.

The next bolt held a pale yellow. He studied it, then looked up to meet Miss Bell's blue eyes. The yellow was cheery, much better suited to her disposition than the ugly gown she wore every day, but she shook her head.

Taking a handful of her own curls, she held them up. "Blond hair. It just doesn't suit."

"What about the girls?"

"Too light. They'll stain it immediately."

That made sense. He'd always thought women's clothing was a matter of folly and whim, but he was learning that there was some strategy after all. And Daniel was all about strategy.

"How about this?" He held up a dark flowery print. The roses were so tiny, he could barely make out what they were.

Miss Bell ran her hand over the material. "It's not as fine as I prefer, but I could dress it up for Caroline."

As fine as she preferred? He bit back a smile. Better to leave her pride intact and not mention the hideous thing she'd been wearing.

Caroline flipped her hair over her shoulder. "I wouldn't hate it." Which was as good as he was going to get.

"Then this will be for Caroline. What would suit my Daisy?"

"Buckskin," Daisy cheered.

"Daisy," said Miss Bell, "look at this gingham. Don't you love the blue checks? They're almost violet."

Daisy picked up a string of colorful Indian beads. "As long as I can wear this with it."

Miss Bell looked to Daniel. "It really wouldn't hurt anything," she said. "She's only a child."

"Fine."

Daisy squealed and skipped to the register. In time, they picked another fabric for each girl.

"Now how about something for you?" Judging by her continual donning of the ugly dress, he assumed that getting her to wear the pretty blue dress he remembered from his accident was out of the question.

"No, really. I hate to waste my wages on this fabric. It doesn't seem suitable."

"It's exactly suitable. This is what the women at the agency wear."

"But by the time I get the girls' dresses sewn . . ." She looked at the material, then again at her reticule, which held her money. "I suppose I can't keep wearing this dress, can I? But you go on. I can do my own shopping."

He supposed she was right. Buying clothing for a lady wasn't appropriate, and if she was paying for the fabric herself, she didn't have to answer to him.

Before long, she'd instructed Mr. Evans on the yardage they required, and as he was wrapping the packages, she joined Daisy at the counter of trading goods. Here one could find jewelry and beadwork made by the Arapaho and Cheyenne women. Naturally, the Indians didn't buy their jewelry from the store, but the mission traded it out for other goods on their behalf, and until it was traded, it was on display.

And Miss Bell was drawn to it like Daisy was to the candy jars. Her delicate, tapered fingers danced over the beads and shells as if she could only be acquainted with them through touch. She laid hold of a disk the size of a half-dollar, then fished its mate from the grass-woven basket. Grinning, she turned to him and dangled the earrings from either side of her face.

Daniel had never been torn like this before. Usually his gut led him to the truth, but now his gut had him reaching out and nicking an earring. It swung like a pendulum, bouncing against her cheek, which was still rosy.

"If I had these," she said, "they'd be the first real earrings I'd ever owned."

"Your other earrings aren't real?"

"Imitation." She set them back in the basket. "Imitation ruby. Imitation emerald. At least the shells aren't counterfeits." She stretched out a couple strings of beads and set them with the fabric. "And what are these white beads? I saw them sewed in rows on the Indian women's dresses."

Daniel took one from her hand. His fingers brushed against her open palm. He held the oblong piece before him, enjoying her suspense.

"These are elk teeth."

"Ew!" She dropped the remaining teeth out of her hand into the basket. "We don't need any of those."

He laughed. "I favor the shells."

"What about scissors?" she asked. "Needles? Thread? Buttons?"

Daniel tapped his foot as he tried to recall the whereabouts of Margaret's sewing kit. "I couldn't swear to it. You'd better get what you need here."

There was a bounce in her step as she left the counter to find a sewing kit and notions. And a smile on his lips as he added the earrings to their growing stack of goodies.

Chapter Twelve

If there was one thing Louisa was not looking forward to, it was getting back on that horse. Major Adams buckled their packages onto the back of the saddles while Daisy and Caroline climbed aboard their mounts. Louisa watched carefully to see how Caroline managed her flawless balance while ascending to her seat. And how exactly did she position her legs so that they didn't go numb? Louisa had felt like an utter and complete ninny when her knees refused to work. If it hadn't been for Major Adams . . .

She inhaled deeply, and the dusty road transformed into the cedar scent that came off his coat when he'd carried her. But the fun would end if Major Adams saw through her ruse, and he already had suspicions. Every time they were together, she felt like he was studying her. A casual observer might wonder if he was besotted, but she knew better. To a person with a guilty conscience, it was a heavy burden to work under.

"Ready to try again?" His honey-colored eyes crinkled with concern. "Let's make sure you don't wear yourself out this time." He fitted his hands around her waist. Louisa grasped his arms and couldn't fail to notice the play of muscle beneath the coat as he lifted her into place. Many of the characters that

Lovely Lola played would have batted their eyes and smiled shyly, as if embarrassed to discover how strong he was. Instead, Louisa took up the reins without even a sigh over how much she enjoyed his help.

Another thing to dream about when her adventure was over.

They set off beneath the strong afternoon sun, full from a good meal at the Darlington restaurant and a hundred unique sights she hadn't imagined before. The colorful streamers of ribbons and beads in the hair of the women. The little girls with their black braids and gingham dresses flying as they played at recess at the reservation school. The solemn baby with giant eyes, strapped on the back of its mother as she came to town to do her shopping. No wonder Daisy felt such a kinship with the tribes. From her limited experiences on the fort, they represented most of the families she knew.

Even now Daisy was racing ahead, racing behind, her knees clutched to the sides of her horse so that she was controlling it almost entirely by feel.

Major Adams reined in beside her. "You probably think I should stop her."

"She's a joy to behold." Louisa pushed the brim of her bonnet back to watch as Daisy streaked past them again.

"It might not be proper for a lady to ride like that, but there could come a day when she will need to. Caroline puts on fine airs, but should the fort ever come under attack, I know she wouldn't slow the troops down if we had to evacuate."

Louisa scanned the plains around her for hostile forces. "Is that likely?"

He looked at the tepees at the river's edge. "Did you notice the broken ones?"

Louisa shook her head, but with a second look, she could pick out a few crumpled piles with broken poles. "What does it mean?"

"It means the Cheyenne Dog Soldiers are punishing those

who are cooperating with the government. White Horse knows that if they come into his part of the village, he's to have Agent Dyer call me immediately."

"Call you?" Louisa asked. "I'd forgotten the phone." It was difficult to wrap her head around the contrast of such a modern invention among the tepees, more than one hundred miles from the nearest railroad or town. What kind of world were they living in?

She shifted in the saddle. The ache had returned.

Major Adams noticed immediately. "We aren't that far out. Would you like to walk for a bit?"

"I'm afraid I'd better, or I might not be able to walk at all later." She somehow managed to pull on the reins and stop the horse. And when the major lifted her down, she managed not to take too much notice.

"You're walking?" Caroline rolled her eyes. "This is going to take forever."

"Go on home, then," the major said. "Tell Gundy we'll be there for supper."

Without changing her stoic expression, Caroline shook her reins, and her horse bolted forward. Just as the major had said, she glided effortlessly on the galloping horse, even while sitting sidesaddle. Daisy's head popped up as her sister blazed by, and she dug her heels into her pony and took off after her.

"I'm jealous," Louisa said. "They make it look so easy."

"Practice. Isn't that what you tell your students?"

Of course. The myriad students she'd taught over the years.

A bumblebee zoomed between them. It came back, hovering to inspect her. Louisa shrank away, swatting at it.

The major laughed. "You don't want to hit it. It probably wouldn't hurt you anyway."

Louisa shuddered. "My brother has a sensitivity to bees. Seeing what happens to him is enough to give me a deadly fear."

"You shouldn't be afraid," he said. "Not here. Not with me."

Her eyes darted to him. He didn't understand. For the time being, he was all that stood between her and an uncertain future. If there were anyone she would be afraid of . . .

"Your probation period is over." His head was down as if he were embarrassed. "If you enjoy your position here at the fort, I'd like for you to stay."

The high grass brushed against the back of her hand as they walked. Louisa had only counted on being a governess for a week, maybe a couple, but why not? She'd come here looking for employment. Did it matter so much that they needed a teacher more than a performer?

And despite her lack of schooling, the girls did need her, as the day had proved. So did Bradley. He could hardly act irresponsibly when she was at the fort with him. Maybe she could be of help on a more permanent basis. What wouldn't she do for a home, a family, somewhere safe?

But the risk. Did she have the courage to remain at her station?

"I accept your offer," she said. "I'm honored that you're putting your trust in me."

She was Lovely Lola. She could enchant with her performance and make them love her show. Could she make them love her, though? Because she was already falling in love with this family.

"I expect you to report in to me regularly with their progress, especially on their basic subjects."

"Of course."

"Then that's settled." He sauntered along, looking more like the cocky horseman she'd seen that first day.

And she was settled. Not a music teacher, but a real teacher of reading, writing, and arithmetic. Louisa could do this. She could learn and study and keep up with the girls. It was the best offer she had.

It was the only offer she had.

They strolled over ground that was strangely absent of rocks or stones. The biggest stumbling blocks were the thick tufts of prairie hay or an occasional rodent hole, but for the most part, she was free to study the wide blue sky above her head. To watch the hawks spiraling above them lazily, until a quick movement caught their attention and they dove with deadly precision.

"I didn't mean to upset you the other night when I asked about your family."

Louisa hiccupped. She covered her mouth with her hand, but out here on the prairie, there was nowhere to hide from this conversation.

He continued. "There was a time when it would've been painful for me to talk about my family, so I understand." His gaze settled somewhere beyond the horizon. "My uncle was the only family I ever knew after my parents died."

Louisa's eyes widened. "You didn't have parents?" She almost cheered before realizing how completely inappropriate that would be. But this meant that he did understand. If he knew about their upbringing, he'd probably be more sympathetic with Bradley. "I never would've guessed that we have that in common. I lost my parents, too." The words poured out with her relief that Major Adams wasn't so different after all. "Most days, I try not to think about it, but after being here and seeing you with your sweet family, it's shown me what I missed growing up. But I assumed you came from one of those perfect families that had everything."

"Far from it."

The brim of Louisa's sunbonnet swayed as she shook her head. "But you must tell me. It would help me to know . . ." To know she wasn't the only one from shameful beginnings? To know that he wouldn't be prejudiced against someone rising up from their past? ". . . to know you better."

Was that too forward? Evidently not, because Major Adams's only response was to start his story.

"My father died of whiskey poisoning when I was six years old, and my mother of consumption not too long after. I moved to town with my uncle. Luckily for him, he could afford to hire people to take care of me so he didn't have to dirty his hands." He kept his voice even, yet Louisa could hear the hurt of an abandoned little boy. At least she'd had Bradley. Major Adams had been alone.

"When I thought I was old enough to make it on my own, I ran away. I tried life on the streets. I lived with the drifters, hoping to find work for the day to feed myself."

Louisa's heart pounded. She'd been so wrong about him. If anyone understood her journey, Major Adams did.

"For a while I didn't care if I lived or died, really," he said. "I felt like no one cared what happened to me, so why should I? But then one day I met someone who showed me unconditional love."

"Your wife?" Louisa asked.

"No. My God." He studied the horizon. "I met a God who made me, loved me, gave His Son so that I could know Him. That changed my life. I realized that I had a purpose, and if staying with my uncle prepared me for my future, then that was what I had to do. My lot might have been hard with my uncle, but at least it saved me from compromising my convictions on the streets."

"Oh." That wasn't what she'd been expecting. Unease began to grow in her heart. He was so earnest, so full of belief. This didn't bode well for her.

"You see, we have more in common than you think. We were both orphaned, but we both looked to Christ to redeem our circumstances."

Maybe one of them had, but Louisa would have had to get

past the church people to meet God, and they weren't moving out of her way.

"I'm grateful for how you care for my girls," he said. "I guess you know how they feel, missing their own dear mother, as you do."

Her own dear mother? Not exactly how Louisa would have ever described her. The only impression her mother had left after all these years was a dull, callous spot that protected Louisa from hurtful memories. Besides a missing mother, Louisa's childhood had nothing in common with the major's girls.

But he was waiting for her to make a response. "Your daughters are lucky they have you," she said.

"They have me for now, but every time I ride on a campaign, I'm faced with the knowledge that I could be leaving them as orphans. What would become of them? That's why hearing about your childhood reassures me that you're the right person for the job."

"Why am I the right person?" she asked.

"Because of all that you've accomplished. You were orphaned, but you didn't turn to sin for easy money. With your beauty and charm, it would've been natural for you to rely on your looks, but you took the high road. You eschewed low connections, stayed away from unladylike professions." He'd turned and faced her full on. "Despite your humble circumstances, you managed to procure an education, refined habits, and make something of yourself. Look at you, Miss Bell. You are a genteel, educated woman. That's something to be proud of."

The sharp wind stung her skin, just as tears stung her eyes. This was worse than she'd thought possible. Nothing he admired about her was authentic. What excuse could she ever offer to the man who'd come from the same situation without stain?

She suddenly felt tired and ready to climb back in the saddle.

Anything to end this conversation. She'd rather have numb legs than an aching heart.

⁂

Daniel was growing increasingly frustrated, but he didn't know who bore the blame—Miss Bell or himself. The more he tried to get to know her, the more confused he became. He'd decided to go with his gut and give her the benefit of the doubt, but his intellect opposed him at every turn. What was at the bottom of her many inconsistencies?

Daniel handed their horses' reins to the private who rushed from the stables to collect them as Miss Bell limped into the house. What should have been a compliment had ruffled her feathers, and for the life of him, he couldn't figure out why. Perhaps he'd insulted her family with the comparison to his. If so, she could have corrected him or at least discouraged him from blabbing on. He'd never told anyone else on the fort anything so personal. And what did she do when he bared his soul? Clammed up and moped her way home.

Well, it wasn't over. Here was just another question she'd have to answer. Another reason he wished Agent Dyer had been in his office when they visited Darlington.

From the adjutant's office, Lieutenant Hennessey appeared. He beelined straight for Daniel with a folded paper in his hand. Official business.

"You've got a guest."

Daniel's stomach tightened. People didn't come this far without a strong inclination to stir up trouble, and he was out of patience. He opened the paper and frowned.

"Not a guest, a prisoner." He handed the paper back to Jack. "I should leave him in the guardhouse to rot."

"Oh no. He's already sent in his meal request to Private Gundy. He even asked me for a razor so he could get spiffed up for dinner."

"I thought after David Payne died that this nonsense would end, but no, Frisco has got to keep their empty hopes alive." Daniel looked at the house. "Tell him I'll send for him when dinner is ready."

"Yes, sir."

"And, Jack, you might as well come, too. I'm sure there'll be enough for everyone."

Jack's eyes darted to the side. His voice lost its military tone at the subject change. "Thank you, Daniel. I appreciate what you're trying to do, but I'd rather have some time to myself tonight."

"Did you get another letter?"

He nodded. "My ma says Hattie's parents are determined that she's going to marry that man." He shrugged. "Maybe I never had a shot, but I wish I had made my case before I left home and enlisted."

"I could give you a leave of absence. Find her. Propose. You won't know unless you try."

"She'd laugh me out of the county. No, it's been too long. All that's left is for me to feel like a dolt and wonder what could've been."

"Then you can do better," Daniel said. "If she doesn't appreciate you, you'll find someone who does." He had worked with Jack for three years now and feared that no woman Jack would ever meet would measure up to his youthful infatuation with Miss Hattie Walker. Jack had held out hope that someday he'd return and win her hand, but the letter from home made it appear unlikely. Hopefully he'd get over her soon. Then again, getting over a woman wasn't the easiest thing to do.

Daniel repeated his invitation, then bid Jack good-bye and headed to the house. Had he gotten over Margaret yet? It wasn't like that with her. He'd loved her deeply, truly, and without reserve. He'd mourned her death hard, sorrow triggered by a thousand different things a day. But that sorrow had mellowed. Now the memories brought more joy than pain, his deepest regret being that his daughters couldn't remember the fine woman she'd been.

Was he over her death? Yes. The strongest feelings remaining were the memories of love shared and burdens divided. Good memories that made him yearn for a companion again. It would never be the same, but life continued. He would make the best of the situation and carry on.

Only his situation wasn't the best right now.

Getting a governess for the girls—someone they could learn from and emulate—had been his goal. He knew that without their mother, they were missing out on an important part of life. Never had he expected Miss Bell to reveal what he'd been missing, too.

He entered the house, stopped at his office long enough to toss his hat on the desk, and looked at the chessboard. Another piece had been moved, but supper was waiting. He headed to the dining room, where instead of their nice china and silver, brown paper packages littered the table. Caroline snipped a string. It had barely popped apart before Daisy ripped through the paper.

"It's the gingham. This one is mine!"

"Two more to go." Caroline's eyes sparkled. Finally, something she was excited about. Daniel leaned against the doorway to soak up the moment. It had been the right thing to do, taking them out today. They would do it more often. Hopefully Miss Bell wouldn't oppose the idea, even if the day had ended on a sour note.

He straightened and looked around. "Where is Miss Bell?"

Caroline held some material beneath her chin and gave him a dazzling smile. "Doesn't this color look good? I wouldn't have thought about it with my red hair, but Miss Bell . . ." She lowered the material. "I didn't see her come in, but maybe she went upstairs. I wonder whose dress she's going to sew first. It should be mine. I'm about to pop the buttons on my—"

Daniel held up his hand. This was not a conversation he wanted to hear. "You girls get this table cleaned off and then put the place settings out. Mr. Smith is a guest of the base again tonight, so set an extra place."

"He got arrested again?" Daisy looked at Caroline, then dissolved into giggles.

"Really, Daisy," Caroline huffed. "You're the one who can't control herself, yet you claim that I set my cap for everyone."

"At least I didn't drop my glove for that handsome private today," Daisy answered.

Another conversation Daniel would rather skip. "Get the table cleared, and then get yourselves cleaned up. Miss Bell won't appreciate sharing a dinner table with dusty young ladies," he said on his way out of the room.

When he got to the top of the staircase, he moved to stand in front of Miss Bell's door. Maybe having a widowed woman twice his age would have made the living arrangements less awkward, but what was he supposed to do with Miss Bell? Stand at the foot of the stairs and yell her name when he needed to talk to her? He might treat his troopers like that, but never a lady.

Making up his mind, he knocked on the bedroom door. "Miss Bell, may I have a word with you?"

He heard a door close inside. Her wardrobe, no doubt. Then the knob turned, and she appeared, the door only open wide enough for her face to be pressed into the crack. She didn't say a word. Only looked at him with eyebrows high.

"I came to tell you that a Mr. Smith will be joining us for dinner. He's the orneriest scalawag you'll ever meet, but he knows what's going on in the Unassigned Lands. I find him useful. If he offends you, I will hold him accountable. Of that you can be sure."

"A scalawag?" Her blue eyes caught his. "He probably associates with all tiers of the lower class."

What was she getting at? "He most certainly does associate with scoundrels, ma'am. So be on your guard."

Her face still looked sorrowful, but resigned. "Yes, sir. By suppertime, my guard will be back in place, and we'll have an enjoyable evening. Until then . . ."

She eased the door closed, leaving Daniel staring at the white painted panels.

Chapter Thirteen

What are you going to wear?" Daisy's voice could be heard through the open window in Louisa's room. "Frisco Smith always says something about the way we're dressed."

"I wish we'd had time to sew our new dresses," Caroline grumbled. "Father should've taken us shopping months ago."

For once, Louisa was apt to grumble along with Caroline. She'd worn the same dress every day for nearly two weeks. Her only respite had been on Sunday, when she kept to the house in a dressing gown. Like Caroline, the thought of the new material made her old clothes insufferable. Maybe a guest, even a scalawag, presented a special occasion? Didn't ladies dress up for special occasions? Couldn't she find some combination in her wardrobe that would be suitable?

The most demure skirt she owned was the red taffeta. Yes, it caught the light and rustled, but it had no bustle. Only very simple lines that dignified the color. But the white blouse she usually paired with it would not serve. The collar hung right at the edge of her shoulders and the neck scooped low enough that someone could tell exactly how long she could hold a fermata

153

just by looking. The shawl she'd purchased at Darlington that morning might be her salvation. If she could fashion it with a brooch, then she'd only be showing an acceptable amount of flesh for the major's unpolluted table.

With the fichu pinned tightly beneath her neck and the ends arranged over her bosom, she was ready. Part of her wanted to throw caution to the wind. Show her true colors and see if the major thought her as fine of a lady after that. But there was still her brother to consider. Until she was sure that he was back in the major's good graces, she mustn't give up her post.

The front door creaked. Lieutenant Jack's voice could be heard. Louisa left her room and rapped on the girls' door. This was her chance to instruct the girls in something she knew more about—making a gentleman feel welcome.

"Our guest has arrived," she said. "Time to come down."

Judging from the pitch of the girls' voices, they were frantically trying to get ready. No sense in standing at the door waiting. Louisa double-checked to make sure her fichu was in place and then descended the staircase.

Major Adams stood with his arms crossed, looking as welcoming as Tim-Bob when the temperance ladies tried to get inside the Cat-Eye Saloon. Their guest had stopped inside the door, his hat set at a rakish angle and dark curls spilling down his neck as he held out his manacled wrists.

"Honestly, Daniel, I don't see why you make Jack lock me up like this. We both know I'm no danger."

The rattle of the iron cuffs might have been unfamiliar to the nice parlor, but it wasn't to Louisa. More than one member of her audience had been escorted out under duress.

"On the fort, you are a prisoner, and I don't want any of my men to forget it," Major Adams said. "Only in my house are you a guest."

Major Adams turned suddenly, as if he hadn't heard her coming down. At seeing her dress, he couldn't blink away his shock. His reaction embarrassed Louisa, but their guest seemed to enjoy the major's surprise.

"My, my, my, Daniel." Mr. Smith whistled, and his blue eyes sparkled with mischievousness. "Who do we have here?"

"Miss Bell, may I introduce Mr. Frisco Smith. A career criminal who has spent his young life being strongly influenced by people of poor character."

Lieutenant Hennessey succeeded in removing the manacles just in time for Frisco Smith to sweep off his hat and bow deeply. "And now I'm the one with poor character doing the influencing. So beware."

Jack rolled his eyes. "I'll set these here by the door. Let me know when you're done with him. Oh, and the laundress found this in your coat pocket." Jack waved a small, lumpy envelope. "I'll leave it on your desk."

"Are you sure you don't want to stay? See what Frisco has to say for himself?" the major asked.

"No, thank you. My time would be better spent reading a book." With a tip of his hat, Jack fled.

Major Adams looked Louisa over as if he'd expected her to have changed while he wasn't paying attention. "Miss Bell is the governess for my daughters," he informed Frisco. "Keep in mind that you're in the presence of a lady."

Frisco tossed his hat into the major's office, letting it land with a gentle plop on his desk. "What do your daughters need a governess for? Isn't Miss Caroline grown? It seems like the last time I saw her, she was marrying age."

Louisa had to choke down a giggle. No wonder Major Adams had warned her about this man. He seemed determined to do everything in his power to upset the poor major.

"Miss Adams is *not* of marrying age, as every man on this

base is made aware before they set foot on Fort Reno soil. She is a child, and I am her father. Do you understand?"

Frisco's youthful face showed not a hint of fear. "I do hope when I have daughters, they are homely."

"Undoubtedly they will be," Major Adams said.

"Otherwise, what would I do when they run into fellows like me?" He winked at Louisa. Then he stilled. "Wait a minute. Don't I know you?"

Louisa's fingers went cold. She stepped closer to the banister and gripped it to steady herself. "We've never met."

"We've never been introduced," Frisco said, "but I'm sure we've met. I don't forget a face. Have you spent time in Kansas, by any chance?"

Major Adams shot her a warning glance. She was more than happy to let him do the talking, because there was little she could say at the moment. "Miss Bell is from Wichita, but it is unlikely that she's associated with your kind."

"Wichita? Maybe that's where I've seen you, but I can't place you. Give me time," he said. "It'll come to me."

Why hadn't she worn the ugly dress just once more? Even covered with a shawl, her clothes were too fine for this job. Too close to what she really was. Louisa glanced up the stairs, but running away would only cause more questions. With her stomach churning, she forced herself to remain. Maybe Mr. Smith wouldn't say anything else.

Caroline and Daisy raced down the stairs. Daisy threw herself into Frisco's arms and asked if he'd brought her a present. Caroline hung back, waiting to be acknowledged, although impatient that he should do so.

"You look very nice tonight." Major Adams had come to stand at Louisa's side. "Such fine clothes. Why have you hidden them until now?"

Louisa smoothed her skirt. The red taffeta rustled beneath

her palms. "I didn't think they were appropriate for a governess."

He had to recognize the brooch as the one she'd just purchased. Then he followed her collarbone to where the fichu ended and her bare shoulder peeked out. He looked at her face again, as if she should be aware that something was happening. But what? Did he see something of beauty in her, or was he merely judging her suitability in training his daughters? If only she knew what he was thinking.

Without saying a word, he tugged the edge of her shawl over her shoulder. His fingers brushed against her bare skin as he arranged the covering. With the girls happily chatting with Frisco, no one else noticed the exchange, but Louisa felt it to her bones.

"Perfectly suitable for an evening dance, but perhaps too fine for dinner."

"The red skirt?" she asked.

"The shoulder," he answered. His eyes twinkled as if they'd shared a private joke, but then they settled again. "Have you recovered from your injury of this afternoon?"

His expression made it clear he wasn't referring to her saddle soreness.

"I apologize," she said. "I'm usually quite adept at controlling my emotions."

"If I knew how I offended you . . ."

"No offense. Let's leave the past in the past."

"But such recent past?" There was that look again. As if he was trying to read her mind. "And if we are going to abide each other in the future . . ."

"Pa, let's eat." Taking him by the cuff, Daisy tried to pull him away.

"Patience, child," he said. "Patience rewards those who wait." With a last meaningful look, he turned to direct everyone to dinner.

Louisa sat in her usual place opposite the major, but Daisy had to scoot down so that Frisco could sit at her father's right hand with Caroline across from him. Once everyone took their seats, Louisa got another good look at their guest. The name Frisco Smith didn't ring any bells. Despite his confidence, he was very young. He wouldn't have been to the Cat-Eye Saloon in years past. He had to have seen her recently. Recently enough that the memory would return soon. What would she do? She couldn't call him a liar. Major Adams might not care for him, but Louisa couldn't slander him. She took the tureen of soup, set it down, and ladled out a bowl for herself. She'd just have to hope he didn't come back to the issue.

"If your soldiers had given us just a few more hours, we'd have had some good wells dug over on the Canadian River south of Mustang Creek. That looks like some good farmland. Good for orchards, too."

"Sorry to inconvenience you," Major Adams said. "How many did you bring with you this time?"

"Three dozen. Most of them are repeaters, but a handful are first-timers. And there's more coming. This is going to happen."

The hot soup loosened Louisa's throat, and her curiosity wouldn't be held back any longer. The whole situation was so strange. "What exactly did you get arrested for?" she asked.

Frisco's smile lit up the room. "For being an industrious individual and a community leader."

"For squatting on government property," Major Adams said. "He leads settlers into the Unassigned Lands to stake homesteads, which is purely illegal."

"Those lands are unassigned, and it's about time someone made use of them."

"I thought all the land in the territory belonged to the Indian tribes," Louisa said.

"No, ma'am." Frisco leaned forward, obviously needing little inducement to speak on the subject. "To our north and west is the Cheyenne and Arapaho Reservation. That's their land now, but there's still land available. And there are other people who've been run off their homes, too. Not just the Indians."

"Who else is being kicked out of their homes?" Louisa asked. With the war a score of years behind them, she hadn't heard of people losing their property in a long time.

"Our shores are teeming with families, people who know how to turn the soil and produce crops, streets crowded with farmers from Ireland, Germany, Russia, who were run off their land, whether by famine or war. They're already here, living in crowded tenement apartments. In the meantime, all this land, millions of acres, is sitting fallow. All I'm asking is that the government do the same thing for them that they did for the Indians. Give them a chance at a homestead, too. Assign that land for settlement—white, Indian . . . shoot, I've even got freedmen wanting a chance at it. Opening up the Unassigned Lands would be good for the country."

"You're not asking the government," Major Adams said. "You're trying to force their hand."

"Yes, sir, I'm a bona fide boomer."

Caroline lowered her spoon. "'Carnival barker' is more appropriate."

Frisco leaned toward Louisa. "Miss Caroline has trouble expressing her admiration for my skills. I go from town to town giving speeches, letting people know what fine land is available. Until he died, David Payne was our leader, but the movement lives on. We're making an impact. More and more senators are seeing the sense of opening the Unassigned Lands for settlement."

The change that came over Caroline was remarkable. Gone

was the indifferent air she adopted around her family. Absent was the simpering flirtation designed to attract the soldiers' attention. She seemed to be honestly moved by what moved him. Genuinely thinking about someone other than herself.

But just that fast, Frisco swung his attention to Louisa. "I know where I saw you. You were on the stage, weren't you?"

The room spun. The stage? Louisa hiccupped violently. She fisted her hand against her chest, trying to suppress the next one. This was it. Her final curtain call. But they'd have to drag her away. "I've been here"—she hiccupped again—"for some time."

"It was two weeks ago," he said. "That's when I saw you. C'mon. It had to be you."

Major Adams looked puzzled, which was better than him leaping to his feet and throwing her out. "Two weeks ago? That'd be about right, wouldn't it?"

Why wasn't he shocked? Did he already suspect she was a performer? She couldn't take the chance. Louisa prayed there would be no more painful hiccups and lowered her hand. "I don't think you saw me on the stage," she said.

Frisco threw back his head and laughed. "You look so worried. Major Adams here is a tough man, but I don't think he'll throw you into the guardhouse for riding on a stagecoach."

"A stagecoach?" Louisa gasped. Her knees felt watery. Her head was spinning. All eyes were on her, and she wanted to be under the table. "The stagecoach," she repeated.

"What did you think I meant?" Frisco asked.

Slowly she gathered her wits. "I don't remember you," she said. "How could you have been on the stage and me not know?"

"I didn't say I was on the stage. I said I saw you. At the Red Fork Ranch. Y'all were pulling in as I was loading up supplies for my settlers."

Louisa bit her lip. At the ranch. That was all. One simple

misunderstanding, and she'd almost been exposed. What was she thinking? Wichita wasn't that far away. Her deception could be uncovered just that easily.

~⚬⚬⚬~

What was wrong with Miss Bell? Had something happened on the stagecoach? Had Frisco embarrassed her? Daniel didn't think Frisco would have been inappropriate to the governess. He was her junior by several years and not likely to have his head turned by a missionary woman. On the other hand—

Daniel took another look at the vision she made over the candelabra in the middle of the table. Her perfect white shoulder peeked out from her scarf again. With her beauty and her dazzling smile, she'd turn any man's head no matter how she was dressed. But put her in a sky-blue gown . . .

Frisco had continued painting his idealistic picture of a future territory here among the nations, and it seemed that Caroline and Daisy were only too eager to listen.

"I didn't invite you to dinner to have you proselytize my family," Daniel said to Frisco. "I want to know what news you bring."

Frisco served himself some game fowl off the platter. "Besides the fact that hundreds of people in the surrounding states are insisting that the U.S. government loosen the stranglehold on this territory? Well, there's talk at the end of the trail that the Cheyenne aren't honoring their contract with the cattle drivers. They're losing several head of cattle a day."

Daniel took a drink of his tea, the cool brew washing down the dust of the day. "What are the cowboys saying?"

"Some of the bosses say they aren't going to pay for passage anymore. They'll cross the reservation without it. Instead of paying for protection that they'll never see, they'll hire their own armed men to accompany their herds."

Daniel stabbed at the fowl on his plate with his knife. "They can't cross the reservation without paying the tribes. The chiefs don't want trouble, but the question is whether they can rein in their braves who would love to see another war."

"That wouldn't be good for anyone," Frisco said.

Which was why Daniel tolerated his lawbreaking guest. Frisco wasn't a gunslinger. His war was against the government, and his weapon was popular opinion. The more settlers he could bring down to show the promise of the land, the more pressure would be applied to their representatives. He played guide for the curious. He brought them across the nations, dug some wells, surveyed homesteads, then when the troopers finally found them, he and his followers good-naturedly accompanied them back to the fort. Usually the followers would be escorted back to the States while Frisco awaited a court date and a trip to Arkansas for his appointment with the judge.

"Come across any known men?" Daniel asked. The U.S. Marshals from Fort Smith had jurisdiction over Indian Territory, but the vast uninhabited areas of land meant that you could never have too many eyes watching over it.

"Came across Marshal Bass Reeves hot on the trail of a bad character named Jim Webb, but we hadn't seen hide nor hair of him, so we weren't any help. Naturally, we're not looking for company on these treks. We avoid being seen as much as possible."

"But Marshal Reeves saw you and didn't bring you in?" Daniel tried to act shocked. "Doesn't he know you're a wanted man?"

Frisco's eyes darted to Caroline, as if she might help him out of a pickle. "Reeves was going to bring us in, I reckon. It just seemed that . . . well, he said . . ."

"I assume Jim Webb is a dangerous criminal," Caroline said. She assumed the proud look she got whenever she'd managed to correct someone. "Since Frisco wasn't going to harm anyone, it would've been foolhardy for the marshal to waste his time arresting Frisco when someone's life could be in danger."

"Yes, I suppose only the cavalry has the time to chase harmless people around." Daniel glared at his daughter. "And it's *Mr. Smith* to you, young lady. Not *Frisco*."

"I don't mind." Frisco held up his glass of tea as if he were toasting Caroline with champagne. The nerve.

"Well, I do mind." Daniel shot his daughter a warning, as the boomer was beginning to look more and more dangerous all the time.

Throughout the rest of the meal, Daisy and Caroline peppered their guest with questions. Daisy sought to bring Louisa into the conversation, but she remained uncharacteristically aloof. Her elbow rested on the table—which even Daniel knew was bad manners—and her hand was touching her face almost constantly. Covering her mouth, shading her eyes, pulling her hair across her cheek—almost like she was trying not to be seen.

"I heard about the last resident of the guardhouse." Frisco grinned as he wiped his mouth on his napkin and pushed his plate away. "Sergeant O'Hare told me that one of your own men got locked up not too long ago."

Daniel nodded. "Usually I'm not forced to detain my own men like that, but Private Willis has got to learn some discipline. We need every man. Until reinforcements arrive, we can barely hold the fort. This isn't the time for a trooper to be imbibing illegal alcohol and shooting out the lanterns."

Louisa fumbled her goblet. Tea splashed on the table. She quickly righted her glass and covered the dark wet spot with her napkin. "He . . . he did that?" she asked.

Daniel's interest keened. Twice she'd crossed paths with Bradley Willis, and both times she'd managed to arrest his attention. How well did she know him? Whatever the case, it was best for her—and Caroline—to know what Willis was capable of.

"He most certainly did. Just the fact that he was in possession of alcohol was bad enough, but he furthered his offense by becoming intoxicated, which led to dangerous behavior."

Frisco leaned forward, anxious to impart another tidbit. "And according to O'Hare, he did all that shooting while standing in the saddle."

Daniel would have preferred that part to have gone unmentioned. When he'd done the same thing, Louisa had aided him. Then again, it wasn't the same thing. Not at all. Daniel hadn't endangered anyone but himself, and while Louisa probably would have offered Private Willis the same compassion, that didn't mean the young man deserved it.

"I'm sure he didn't mean any harm," she said.

"What would you know about his intentions, ma'am?" Daniel replied. "The way he was shooting at every light, and from such a precarious position, he could've easily killed someone. Then I would've lost two troopers, and despite what you might think of me, I do not wish to have one of my men executed for recklessly taking another's life." Voicing this fear set his teeth on edge. "The important thing is that Private Willis earned his stay in the guardhouse." The room had gone silent. No one at the table moved. "I'd rather deal with a hundred misguided boomers than one reckless trooper."

Too easily people from the civilian world thought that being in the cavalry was like a camping expedition. They forgot that it wasn't just about braving the primitive conditions and the elements. The troopers were often in life-and-death situations. They had to trust each other. Their lives depended on their buddies. Stunts like Willis's hurt morale and disrupted the discipline that they relied on.

From the look on Miss Bell's face, he'd upset her again, but he'd spoken the truth, and she needed to hear it, no matter how it made her eyes water.

As much as he respected her ability with his girls, he was worried that the governess was in desperate need of some instruction, too.

Chapter Fourteen

She was trapped. Louisa pulled her eyes from the major's. There was nothing she could say to soften his opinion of her brother. Her defense of Bradley seemed only to hurt his case.

Frisco Smith bravely plowed on to another subject, but Louisa couldn't follow the conversation. It took all of her concentration to keep Major Adams's words from settling in her heart. She had to contain her sorrow until she could be alone.

Finally, after the last course had been served, she made her excuse. Although she tried not to depart abruptly, Major Adams's unwavering gaze showed that he recognized her distress, but this time he was unwilling to apologize.

And that hurt even more.

Once upstairs, Louisa locked her bedroom door behind her. She might not be in the guardhouse, but she was the major's prisoner just the same. Her utter lack of freedom was suffocating. She couldn't wear her own clothes, couldn't talk about her life, and she was expected to sit at a fancy dinner and hear her brother insulted without saying a word in his defense.

And the worst part was that it was all true.

How could Bradley be so stupid? Shooting out the fort's

lanterns while standing in the saddle? Louisa twisted a curl around her finger. It was a wonder he was still in the army after that stunt. As much as she wanted to pretend that Bradley was harmless, she understood the major's concern.

Bradley had made mistakes that could hurt people, but he was still her brother, and she still loved him. She always wanted the best for him—hoped that she'd done well by him—and to hear someone's unsympathetic evaluation cut her to the quick, but she couldn't deny the truth. Major Adams had been where Bradley was, but he had made something of himself. If there was a man she wanted her brother to emulate, it was her strong, honest, relentless employer.

She tossed her hair back off her shoulders. All was not lost, but it would be if she didn't maintain her composure. Someday, if everything went as planned, she wanted to live around respectable citizens like Major Adams. Hearing his opinion was painful but instructional. Could she and Bradley ever measure up? Not unless they worked very hard, and that was what she intended to do. Once Bradley straightened up, he could earn a place in Major Adams's regard, but as for her—she could never tell him about her previous life. Women weren't given the same forgiveness as men. While Louisa hadn't come to Fort Reno with the intent to deceive anyone, continuing the deception had become necessary.

Having nothing to do, nowhere to go—even a walk around the base was forbidden—Louisa pulled out the arithmetic book and studied for the rest of the night.

At dusk, Frisco Smith was escorted back to his cell, and the family retired. After taps had been played, the only sound outdoors was the unrelenting wind that rattled the windowpane. But then the windowpane rattled a little too hard. Louisa lowered her book. Had a bird flown into the glass? There it was again. As quietly as she could, she rose, blew out her candle, and pushed aside the curtain.

Bradley! He was crouched beneath the window, watching the green carefully. He looked up again and saw her, then pointed to the back of the house. Louisa hurried to unfasten the window and warn him of the danger, but he'd disappeared to meet her by the kitchen.

Great Saturn's rings! Didn't he realize the danger of what he was suggesting? Forgetting her shoes and shawl, she eased down the stairs and to the kitchen. The door lock clicked when she turned it, but the door was well oiled, and she slipped out noiselessly. Looking both ways, she darted out onto the lawn, but there were no trees behind the house, probably to assure no one could sneak up on it—or away from it. The only place to hide out of sight of the house was a woodpile stacked between rain barrels. And that was where she found her brother.

"Bradley!" She'd lecture him soon enough. Right now she wanted a hearty hug from the only blood kin she had in the world. He was so much bigger and stronger than she remembered.

"What in tarnation are you doing here?" he whispered as he held her at arm's length to get a better look. "You are out of your mind."

Her spine stiffened. "I'm the one out of my mind? What's this about you getting drunk and riding through camp using the lanterns as targets?"

He dropped her arms. "I didn't miss a single shot, so I wasn't that drunk, was I? Besides, I served my time. Everything is fine now. Or was, until you showed up. What are you doing in his house? Do you want to get us arrested?"

"I'm a governess—"

"Have mercy." He slapped his forehead. "You? A governess? You've spent less time in school than a cat spends in water. And I can't believe Major Adams would hire my sister—"

"He doesn't know. What kind of idiot do you take me for?"

"The kind of idiot who lies to my commander. Major Adams will find out, you know. Nothing gets past him. And when he does—"

"He's not going to find out. Besides, even if he sends me away, he won't know I'm your sister. It won't hurt you any."

But Bradley's jaw had set in stubborn lines. "Why are you here, anyway? To convince me to behave myself and walk the straight and narrow? That's rich, considering you're calling yourself a governess."

"I came here to get a job. Tim-Bob sent me packing."

Bradley shrugged. "Perform somewhere else."

"That's why I came here. That and because my brother can't stay out of the guardhouse."

"I'm out, aren't I?"

He wasn't taking her seriously. "Bradley, without my job, I don't have anything to fall back on," she said. "And I can't be a performer forever. It's only a matter of time before I'm out in the street." Or upstairs. But she couldn't voice that fear. Not even to her brother. "That's why I'm here. You need to be reminded that I can't bail you out this time. You need this enlistment."

"Don't you think I'm trying?" He held his hands out in supplication. "It's hard work here. Always being bossed around. Always have to say 'yes, sir,' and 'no, sir.' I hadn't tasted whiskey for months. Thought I'd just have one glass. Thought I'd just blow off a little steam. Next thing I knew, I was having the time of my life . . . and then I was in the guardhouse. It won't happen again, but it's not nearly as serious as what you're doing. Really, Lola? What do you think the major will do when he finds out that a dance hall singer has been living under his roof, spending time with his girls?" His nose wrinkled as if disgusted by the very thought of her. But just as quickly, he softened. "Look, I didn't mean it that way. I'm not embarrassed by who you are, but

I am embarrassed that you're here. Can you imagine if the fellas found out that my big sister came here to make me behave? I'd never live that down. You have to leave. This was a bad idea."

It was. She could see that now. The best way to fix it was to leave before Major Adams learned of her and Bradley's relationship, but she didn't have anywhere to go. She needed this job. Without it, she was looking at a dead end.

~※)※~

The first rock to hit the window had Daniel out of bed. The second one had him throwing a robe over his nightshirt and reaching for his saber. He'd seen the looks Frisco Smith and Caroline had exchanged during dinner. So help him, if the boomer thought to lure his innocent daughter outside for a tryst, Daniel would run him through without a twinge of regret. But the man beneath the window wasn't Frisco. It was a trooper, and he didn't have to take a second look before pinpointing exactly who.

Bradley Willis.

Perhaps Edna was right. Why did Daniel think he could raise two daughters amid so many men of questionable character? But they were his responsibility, and tonight, asserting that responsibility might be something he relished. This was the last straw for the private.

But before Daniel could step into the hall, he heard a door open. Easing his door open as well, he peeked through the crack and saw Miss Bell in the hallway, her white blouse gleaming in the moonlight.

His heart dropped as she descended the stairs. Going back into his room, he tossed his saber on his rumpled sheets and watched at the window. As he feared, she emerged from the back of the house. Willis had disappeared into the shadows, where she ran to meet him.

How had the boy won her trust so quickly? They'd only seen each other once, no twice, at the fort, but here she was, sneaking out, risking her reputation, risking her safety. His concern grew. He pulled on his britches and a shirt, still getting dressed as he hurried down the stairs, while jealousy warred for his soul. His first concern was that she was safe. If Willis laid a hand on her, he'd rue the day. But beyond that . . .

Daniel peered out the kitchen window. They huddled on the other side of the woodpile, trying to use it as a shield. She was so naïve. She probably felt sorry for Willis after Daniel criticized him at the dinner table. He had to be careful. With her tender heart, he'd probably only increased her infatuation.

While every bit of manly impulse in Daniel urged him to rush outside, grab the villain by the collar, and haul him to a court martial, he fought for control. A public spectacle would hurt Miss Bell. He couldn't expose her to the scandal. He ran his fingers through his hair. He had to protect her, even if it meant allowing Willis to go unpunished.

He tasted the sharp flavor of jealousy, but he had to master it. She was at the fort under his protection. Besides, a woman as beautiful and vivacious as she wanted nothing to do with a widower and father. He couldn't even stand in a saddle without nearly breaking his neck.

They were parting. To his relief, he saw no hug, no token pass between them. Willis sulked away, hands in his pockets, while Miss Bell watched him go with wistful regret. She turned to the house. Daniel stepped away from the door but stopped in the dark kitchen. He wished he could ignore the exchange. He wished he could let it go unmentioned and repair the tenuous relationship between them, but he had a responsibility to her and to his government. The meeting had happened on his watch. He couldn't turn a blind eye.

The hem of her red skirt was dark as she entered the kitchen, probably damp from the grass. Her white blouse hung off both shoulders, showing what the shawl had hidden during dinner.

She was exquisite, but she hadn't dressed that way for him.

Bending over the lock, she slid it into place and then turned. He knew the moment her eyes adjusted and she saw him standing in the darkness.

❧❦❧

There was no mistaking the silhouette of the man in the doorway.

"Major Adams!" Her pulse sped up, and she covered her heart with her hand. "You startled me."

A match struck. A flame flared as he lit a lamp and adjusted it. He'd dressed in a hurry, his white shirt unbuttoned, his suspenders crooked.

"Just imagine," he said, "how startled I was to hear someone entering my house at this time of night."

Her throat tightened. He deserved the truth, but for Bradley's sake, she couldn't tell him. Instead she'd accept the blame and his contempt.

She threw her shoulders back. Was this the final straw? Would he send her packing? She lifted her chin and tried to speak with confidence. "I apologize, Major Adams. I should've notified you that I was going for a stroll. My room felt confining tonight."

There was no escape from the intensity of his gaze. He didn't mock her. He didn't call her a liar. But neither did he look away and give her the dignity of pretending to believe her.

"You may be on a fort, but there are still dangers for a woman alone after dark. And even more danger for a woman who is not alone."

Louisa bit her lip. He'd seen her. Did he know who she'd been with, or was he hoping she'd reveal it? She had to maintain her bluff.

"I feel much better now that I've had some fresh air. If you'll excuse me . . ."

"That's it?" he asked. His hair was ruffled, his eyes tender. She shifted her weight, wondering what to do. One minute he looked like he was about to rain down judgment on her, but now he looked as if she'd hurt his feelings. "That's all you have to say?"

"I don't feel like talking."

"But I do." His voice was low, but the calm was deceiving. He had the authority to eject her from the house that very moment. He could summon a troop of men to carry her away, throw her in the guardhouse, or put her in stocks on the village green if they still had such a thing. He was calm, but he was not happy.

"I apologize again if I've displeased you," she said. "In the future—"

"Why?"

"What?"

"Why?" He looked genuinely confused. "Are you lonely? It must be difficult for you, here with the girls every day, but that is the task you've taken. We could go to Darlington more often, if you'd like to socialize with the ladies there. Whatever it takes, because I want you to be content. You are doing a good job with my daughters, and they . . . and I don't want you to leave."

She was trying to find her footing. He'd gone from commander to employer to now, something else. His plea was more of a personal request than an order.

"I don't want to leave," she said. "This is where I need to be."

He held her gaze, conveying how much her statement meant to him. But then he blinked, and the spell broke. With a sigh, he picked up the lantern. "But you will leave. If you are caught alone with a trooper at night, you will leave, and that trooper will be dishonorably discharged. This is a military base, and I cannot bend the rules. Do you understand?"

Her head was spinning. He'd always been the major. Standing in his rumpled clothes, shirt unbuttoned and hair disheveled, he knew who he was. The boyish looks didn't change the man.

Just like her. No matter how acceptable she dressed, she had to remember who she was, and that she was in no way his equal.

Chapter Fifteen

Despite knowing full well that Private Willis had been sent out on patrol and wouldn't be back for at least a week, Daniel found himself watching for him all day. He wanted someone to take the brunt of his frustration, but he couldn't bring Willis up on charges without endangering Miss Bell's reputation. The only thing to do was to send him on an assignment and hope he realized what a mercy was being given him.

After extended meetings with the officers and scouts today, Daniel should have been longing for home, but uncertainty kept him away. He'd even stayed at the mess hall to eat supper with the troopers—something Jack encouraged him to do more often for morale purposes—but now dinner was over. Was he ready to face Miss Bell? Or more accurately, was she ready to face him?

He slowed as he approached the house. If only God would lead him to the correct decision. If only God would show him where mercy was warranted and where correction was needed. But wasn't godly correction a mercy in itself? Daniel shook his head. He'd better leave such thorny questions to the reverends. Miss Bell was probably innocent of any true offense. Maybe she only longed for adult companionship. If so, she would hardly turn to him, not with the way he corrected her at every pass. He wanted to reassure her that this indiscretion alone didn't ruin his opinion of her. That her actions weren't irredeemable. As the sun went down, he knew he could delay no longer. He had to return home and deal with the trouble they'd stumbled into the night before.

But instead of festering resentment, the front door of his house opened to a flurry of fabric, measuring tapes, scraps of ribbon and lace, and laughter. Daniel stood in the doorway as a heavy burden eased off his shoulders. Miss Bell had taken his advice in stride and was proving her maturity, even as she laughed like a girl with Caroline and Daisy.

The wife of the last post commander at Fort Reno had left behind an old broken sewing machine in the attic of Jack's quarters. A few hours with the fort's smith, and it was spinning in his parlor, much to the delight of the ladies. Daniel had imagined sewing to be a quiet pastime. He'd never heard a word from the girls when they were at their embroidery hoops. Then again, he couldn't be sure that they'd ever finished a single embroidery project, either. He'd never thought to ask.

The machine creaked as Caroline pedaled it. While the material was feeding through smoothly, they chattered excitedly, but then it snagged, and howls and protests filled the air.

This ruckus was at least productive. And they were having fun. Thanks to Miss Bell.

She stood behind Caroline, her white blouse demurely covered with the shawl again. No perfect shoulder visible, just her fetching eyes. Her skirt was another extravagant piece of work he'd never seen before. Canary yellow with rich, chocolate fringe edging it and gathered in the back to make a—he caught himself, wondering at his attention to her outfit. Well, if he wasn't currently living in a tailor shop, he wouldn't be as observant of the details.

"Yes, just keep it feeding through. Slow down a little when you come to the curve." Miss Bell's thick blond curls were gathered over one shoulder, leaving her neck bare on the opposite side.

"Pa, look what we're doing!"

Daisy's announcement startled the governess. Her eyes rose to meet his, shy, uncertain, and oh so blue. He wanted to help her, and the only remedy was to see that she didn't find herself lonely again. If necessary, he was willing to sacrifice his own time to entertain her. In fact, he had a pastime she might find diverting enough to keep her out of trouble once the girls were asleep.

He entered the room and crouched next to Daisy, his boots squeaking as he knelt. "Is that for your dress?"

She beamed and held up a wicked-looking pair of scissors. "It is. Miss Bell measured it for me. She said that she's going to add a touch of—"

"Shhh." Miss Bell's finely arched eyebrow rose. "I thought we were keeping it a secret."

Daisy covered her mouth, her eyes dancing.

For that moment with his daughter, he'd forgive Miss Bell just about anything.

Caroline had yet to look up from the sewing machine, so intent was she. It'd been years since he'd seen her take such an interest in anything—besides uniformed soldiers and rebellious boomers. He'd gone a whole day without worrying about where his daughters were or what they were doing. Proof that he had to find a way for Miss Bell to succeed here.

"You worked late today," Miss Bell said. Her eyes flicked to the window. "And I just realized how poor the light is in here now. Girls, we should gather our things up for the night. You mustn't strain your eyes."

The sewing machine continued to whirl until Caroline reached the end of her piece. She snipped the threads, then held it up for inspection. "My shoulders are tired," she said, "but we got a lot done."

Not knowing where the odd scraps of material belonged, Daniel stood aside as they tidied their work, then gave each of his daughters a kiss on the cheek as they went up the stairs for the night.

"Do you need help?" he asked Miss Bell.

"No, thank you. I thought I'd work on my own dress, now that the girls have gone up."

He wanted to mention that it was just like her to put their needs before her own, but it felt like too personal of a compliment. Having no excuse to stay, he headed for his office. All the new dispatches had already been delivered to him in person. So why did he spy an envelope beneath his ledger? As Daniel slid it out, he could feel something inside it. Something besides paper. Taking his letter opener, he cut a slit in the envelope and grasped a dainty square of lace. What in the world?

He held it before him. It was a lady's handkerchief. Delicate and showy. Not the least bit useful. He picked up the envelope again, but there was no name on it. Then he remembered Jack's message. He'd said the washerwoman had found it, didn't he? In Daniel's jacket pocket? There had to be some mistake.

"Major Adams, do you want me to put out the lamp in the parlor?"

He dropped the handkerchief on his desk and came to meet Miss Bell at the door of his office. Now that the house was quiet, she seemed embarrassed to face him. He wanted her to shake off their last encounter and act as his peer. An equal was hard to come by when isolated with only the men under his command.

But what would give her the courage to face him? Daniel had an idea.

"I have a favor to ask, if you have a minute." At her startled expression, he added, "It's nothing important, just a diversion."

Her eyelashes fluttered as she thought through her next move. Seeming to sense no danger inherent in the offer, she accepted. "What did you have in mind?"

"I know so little about you, but there's one thing I'm becoming more and more sure of."

Louisa's throat jogged. Did she not know what he was talking about?

To end her misery, Daniel stepped back and gestured grandly to his chessboard, where their game was already in progress. "Someone has been challenging me on the board."

She hiccupped. He smiled at the now-familiar response, a sure sign she was nervous.

"You aren't upset?"

He pulled the chair out for her. "You have no idea how thrilled I am. I haven't had a true opponent in ages."

His chest loosened as she accepted his invitation. She arranged her yellow skirt between the arms of the chair, but her focus was already on the board. Her blond curls swung forward as she leaned closer, tucking her hands beneath her as if to prevent herself from making a premature move. Daniel stroked his jaw in pure enjoyment at the prospect of such a beautiful challenger. How was he ever going to concentrate on the game?

"Take your time," he said. "There's no hurry."

The flash of confidence in her smile took his breath away. "I'm ready when you are," she said and moved her rook.

Who was this woman? One minute she was all fragile beauty, the next extreme confidence. Judging from her demeanor, she felt safe at the chessboard. She felt secure. She obviously felt she couldn't fail.

But she could, and it only took a few moves.

"Check," he said. His black rook moved into line with her king. And no sooner did he make the move than he wished someone would sock him right in the nose. Why hadn't he played a little more gently with her? If he won too easily, she wouldn't want to play him again.

But if he expected her to crumple, he was surprised. Instead, with lightning precision, she swung her knight around to wipe out his rook. Daniel let some tension out of his shoulders. He should have seen that coming, but surely she'd make another mistake. Players without patience often did.

While he studied the board, she studied the room. As he worked out the tactics he'd need to corner her king, he occasionally looked up to see her reading the spines on his bookshelf. Once, just before he was ready to commit to a move, he caught her watching him—which was fair, he supposed, since he'd spent hours studying her. With a bold move, he slid his bishop across the board to pick off her knight. Then he kicked his foot over his knee and leaned back, ready to accept her congratulations.

Her hand shot out. A piece tapped against the board. "Checkmate," she said. But before he could recover, she made an even more shocking pronouncement. "And what's my handkerchief doing on your desk?"

~∞)(∞~

She was probably seeing things, but Louisa bounded to his desk and picked up the lacy cloth. Where had she lost it? Here? She knew she'd had it at the Red Fork Ranch, but after that, she hadn't seen it. Holding it in her hand, she smoothed it with her thumb. It had been freshly laundered, but in a fold of the lace was a stain the laundress had missed.

"That's your handkerchief?" Major Adams sounded as shocked as she felt. The pieces on the board could only move in prescribed ways, but Major Adams surprised her at every turn. Who was he now? The commander of the fort who'd chastised her about leaving at night, who had the power to send her packing, or the gentleman who seemed to enjoy her company?

"Did someone bring it from the Red Fork Ranch?" But as soon as the words left her mouth, she wished them back. She had an uneasy feeling she might know where she'd left it after all.

Major Adams began to clear the board.

"You win," he said, then, "Do you mind if I close the door?"

"I don't mind." But she barely suppressed a hiccup as she settled into her chair and tried to hide between the arms. What could he want to say that warranted a closed door? She was already in trouble for meeting with Bradley. Was he now going to criticize her behavior at the ranch?

He returned to the table, his hand trailing over the back of her chair on his way to his own seat. How little the table looked as he leaned forward, his forearms resting on his knees.

"I'm sorry to make you uncomfortable, Miss Bell, but there's something we've never talked about—an event that we share." His handsome face looked apologetic. "It only exposes myself as an immature—"

"Then why—"

"Because I believe in knowing the truth, even when the truth is uncomfortable. Are you comfortable with the truth, Miss Bell?"

Louisa folded her hands in her lap. The truth could destroy her. "I don't know what you mean."

"The truth will set you free, right? That's what you and your missionary friends teach us, anyway. Well, I'm ready to be set free. You see, I have a question I've wanted to ask." He took a deep breath. His shiny boots shifted on the floor. "That day when you found me by the creek, why did you do what you did?"

Louisa wet her lips as she saw him again, injured, helpless. How much more she knew of him now. How unbelievable that she'd cradled him in her lap and brushed the dirt off his face.

"You needed help. You were hurt."

"But you could've called for help. I assume you weren't out there alone."

Because in Major Adams's world, a lady never went around unchaperoned. Louisa pushed the handkerchief's lace aside and looked at the stain again. "Where did you find this?"

"The washerwoman found it in my coat pocket, covered with my blood, no doubt." He picked up a chess piece and rolled it between his fingers. "Going out by myself and risking my neck was foolish of me. I deserved your scorn, but you responded with kindness."

"And now I know why you did it," she said.

"A challenge. After seeing Private Willis's skill, I had to know if I could do it. And then I was caught by my governess."

Louisa raised her head. "I am your children's governess, not yours."

"True. You are not *my* governess." His eyes traveled over her face. She felt her skin grow warm. "Yet my embarrassment is the same. Thank you for not telling anyone."

He wanted the truth, right? Louisa ducked her head. "I told Lieutenant Hennessey."

"Jack knows? What did you tell him?" Major Adams looked like nothing more than a little boy trying to get his story straight.

"That you were standing in the saddle, and you fell and hit your head."

He groaned. He rested his elbows on his knees again and covered his eyes. "He's known all along?"

"He promised he wouldn't say anything," Louisa said. "Especially about me holding you on my lap."

The major pulled his hands down and peered at her over his fingers. He'd gone very still. "That's the part I remember best."

With the major awake and possessing his wits, discussing the incident was more intimate than the actual event. Their gazes remained locked as both relived the moment. Louisa's memory had to be superior, since she wasn't hurt, but from the way Major Adams looked, it had moved him, too. The girls could be heard murmuring quietly upstairs as they settled into their beds. Horses at the stables whinnied. What did he think of her, behaving like that?

Louisa started to rise.

He was on his feet immediately. "You can't go. Not until I thank you for caring for me while I was incapacitated. That was very brave of you," he continued.

"No need to mention it again." She was finding it easier to breathe.

"What is your given name, Miss Bell?"

Her breathing got tight again. "Louisa."

"May I call you Louisa, please? Not in front of the children, of course, but when it's only us talking together as adults?"

She couldn't deny that the memory of him in her arms was coming back with a strength that confounded her. And now it was bolstered by the knowledge of him, of his character and all that he'd accomplished. This handsome man had been only handsome before. Now he had her respect.

"You may." She gulped and, forgetting all about the role she was playing, said what was honestly on her mind. "And your name is Daniel?"

His gaze deepened. "Be my guest."

He watched her lips, as if waiting for her to repeat it, so she did.

"Daniel."

Strange to call him that. She knew him as the commander, and she knew him as the girls' father, but now, in possession of his name . . . he was a man to her. Just a simple man. It was better, she decided, that they'd had this conversation. Better for it to finally be out in the open.

"I'm glad we met that way," he said. "It tells me something about your character. It tells me that you are tenderhearted toward people who should know better. It tells me that you have a lovely singing voice, although you hide it, and it makes me wonder what else you keep hidden." He halted. "The blue dress," he said. "You brought a satchel full of clothes. There was a crate of books, but there was also a bag of clothing. And yet you wore the same outfit all this time."

"I've worn a few nicer skirts," she said, "and the dressing gown. Don't forget the dressing gown."

His eyes warmed. "I could never forget the dressing gown, but where are the rest of your clothes?"

Louisa caught her reflection in the dark windowpane. How calm she looked. How ashamed she felt. "They're not really appropriate for teaching children," she said.

But then again, neither was she.

Chapter Sixteen

Indiscriminate grace. Was that the term for it? Obviously, Miss Bell suffered from some sort of fondness for miscreants, or else she never would have come to his aid. Daniel chewed on the end of his pen as he gazed out his office window the next week. He'd wondered what a beautiful, graceful, educated woman like Louisa was doing, taking a lowly governess position in Indian Territory. The truth appeared to be that she was too kindhearted for her own good. It would be un-Christian to consider that a flaw, but it was a characteristic that merited monitoring.

Unscrupulous men preyed on such women, eliciting their sympathy and taking advantage of them. Daniel's job was to protect all the Cheyenne and Arapaho Reservation, the Darlington Agency, and Fort Reno. It was no stretch to include Miss Bell in that assignment.

"Major Adams, mail call."

"Come in," he called. Sergeant Byrd was a capable soldier who, although healthy, somehow evoked the sense of one who had survived a life-threatening injury. Another man Louisa would be inclined to save.

Daniel took the letters, dismissed the trooper, and started

thinking how there were generous souls like Louisa who needed protecting, and then there were women like Edna Crawford.

The top envelope bore the familiar handwriting of his mother-in-law. He'd written Edna to assure her that he'd found a suitable governess, but evidently his report didn't suffice. According to her letter, if she didn't receive more specific information about Miss Bell's qualifications, she would travel to Fort Reno and interview her herself. Daniel dropped the letter on his desk. He'd asked Agent Dyer to check into Louisa's records, but he hadn't heard anything yet. What was Daniel supposed to do? He didn't have time to investigate a governess. He had a fort to run.

But the next letter wiped away his excuses. The agency stationery was still crisp and firm, having traveled just a few miles and never going into the leather mail pouch. Daniel eyed it warily. His letter opener sliced through the envelope, and a smaller, sealed envelope fell onto his desk as he pulled out Agent Dyer's letter.

Major Adams,

As you requested, I wrote the Mennonite Missionary Society concerning Miss Bell. I am forwarding their response to you unopened. I hope the answer is satisfactory.

Your servant,
Agent Dyer

Daniel lowered himself into his chair. A letter with Miss Bell's qualifications and references? That was just what Edna wanted. He could open that envelope and in a few moments have an answer that would put her in her place. He picked up the envelope from the missionary society and reached for his letter opener. The razor edge scratched against the paper, and he paused. What if the answer didn't please Edna? What if, for instance, Louisa's schooling wasn't vigorous enough to suit his mother-in-law? What if Edna expected, like Daniel had, an older widow to teach her granddaughters?

The neat print on the envelope took on a sinister cast. What did he need to know about Louisa beyond what he already knew? Yes, she was unconventional, but hadn't she proved herself already? There was the issue of her behavior with Private Willis, but now that Daniel had identified Louisa's generosity as the problem, he didn't doubt her character.

He dropped the letter opener and picked up his pen. He would write Agent Dyer, thanking him for getting the information. As for Edna, he didn't need to answer to her. They were his daughters, and Miss Bell worked for him. She was his responsibility, so why was everyone acting like Louisa was any of their business?

His pen moved on the paper.

My Dearest . . .

The words startled him. He hadn't meant to write them—not to his mother-in-law and certainly not to Agent Dyer. So who was he addressing? The answer was only too obvious.

He sat with eyes closed and pen readied, but instead of reliving the moment he'd awakened to feel her cool hand on his brow, he had even better memories to cherish. Her sparkling eyes as she bested him at chess. The way she curled up on the sofa with Daisy pulled tight to her side as they read a book together. Showing Caroline how to arrange her hair. These memories meant more to him now.

His pen moved on the page again, and what he wrote had nothing to do with employment.

Every time I see you, I'm filled with the desire to know you more, but something is holding you back. Is it fear?

Whatever you're afraid of, I wish you'd trust me to take care of it, but with all the eyes watching our every move, I must be careful.

He paused. He wasn't going to give her this letter. It was too personal. Almost a journal entry. He shouldn't even put it on paper, but writing his thoughts clarified them.

I must be careful, not just because I want to protect your reputation, but because I need to protect my judgment. At times, I feel like I'm being unwise where you are concerned. And at times, I desperately want my heart to win at any cost.

How empty his house would feel without her. How off-balance the dinner table would be. How long his nights without her company in the parlor.

Boots on gravel. He glanced out the window and saw the top of Sergeant Nothem's head. He was coming this way. Daniel slid his lonely musings into his portfolio as if the correspondence were top secret. A guilty conscience caused him to grasp the unopened envelope as well. He'd asked for this. He'd wanted answers. Did he still want answers? What if it didn't contain the answers he was looking for?

That was ridiculous. Daniel took out a match and struck it against his desk. Hadn't he discussed with Louisa how the truth could set one free? He held the flame to the envelope, then shook out the match. He knew the truth in his heart. Louisa was a good woman. He didn't need a piece of paper from a stranger to tell him that. The flame warmed his fingers as it licked the paper brown, then black. He would trust her. That was his decision.

Sergeant Nothem knocked as the ashes started to crumble.

Daniel tossed the burning letter into his cold fireplace, picked up his portfolio, and hurried to answer the door.

～◦)(◦～

Louisa dipped her paintbrush into the canning jar and gave it a swirl. Caroline had continually grieved over the finer arts she was supposed to learn at her grandmother's, supposing that Louisa was dead-set on book learning, but nothing could be further from the truth.

On the back porch of the house, the ladies could practice their painting uninterrupted. While the view of endless prairie didn't offer much by way of inspiration, the porch did keep them out of the troopers' curious view. And after last week's visit with Daniel, Louisa could use a bit of breathing room.

"What are you painting?" Daisy sat on the porch step with a canvas propped against a washtub.

"It's a surprise," Caroline said. "We aren't supposed to show it until we're finished."

That had been Louisa's idea. While she had painted many a backdrop for the stage, she'd never taught painting and didn't have a clue how to help improve theirs. Better to let them go their own way and compliment the painting when it was done.

Two thoughts warred in Louisa's breast as she dabbed her brush into the blue and began to splash a vast sky on her canvas. First, her time in the Adams household was forming her dreams into solid, concrete possibilities. Before, she'd had vague ideas about the kind of work she could do once her performing days were over. Now she knew exactly what she wanted. Being responsible for the girls, being a mentor, exploring the world with them—she never thought the connection would mean so much to her.

Second, the more she grew to appreciate the respectable life, the more important it was that she continue doing something disreputable—mainly misleading Daniel about who she was and why she had come to the fort. She was in a quandary. Only through her dishonesty could she someday be a proper lady. She wasn't hurting anyone, she told herself. And what other option was available?

"Do you want to see mine?" Daisy scrambled to her feet, carrying her picture, and Louisa saw a field of daisies spread over a gentle hill.

"Daisy, that's beautiful," Louisa said. She caught the canvas by the corner and held it up. The colors of the field faded, giving the painting a sense of depth that was impressive, considering the age of the artist. "You surprise me. This is really good."

"Thank you. I just painted what I saw in my head." Daisy's eyes sparkled, and she bounced on her toes.

"There!" Caroline made a last jot and then stepped away from her canvas. "I'm done, too." She picked up her canvas and proudly turned around to display it.

"Oh . . ." Louisa covered her mouth. Caroline had painted a similar landscape, but without the skill of her younger sister. On top of that, she'd ambitiously added a few cows to the pasture. Or were they horses? Louisa cocked her head and stepped back. Had she not known better, she would have thought the girls had traded canvases.

"Goodness, Caroline. I can't believe you did that all by yourself," Louisa finally said.

Caroline beamed. "It's been years since I used these watercolors, but I guess you never forget how." She smiled at Daisy. "And if you keep practicing, soon you'll be as good as I am."

Louisa drew in a quick breath. Could Caroline really not see what a mess her painting was? If not, Daisy would soon set her straight.

But Daisy responded with surprising grace. "I'll keep practicing. But show us yours, Miss Bell."

Louisa didn't claim any special talents in painting. Usually her work was only viewed from a distance by moderately intoxicated men, but at least one could tell that the painting was of a party. A room full of gaily dressed gentlemen and ladies who, although simply drawn, had very colorful costumes.

"What is that woman wearing?" Caroline stuck her nose just inches from the surface. "And that one? Is that how they dress in the city?"

"It's formal attire," Louisa said, "for fancy parties."

Daisy joined in. "I don't think so. When we visited Grandmother in Galveston, no one wore anything that bright. And look how much skin is showing on top."

"End of painting lesson," Louisa said. "Let's bring these inside so the wind doesn't blow them over."

"Or stick dirt and grass to the wet paint," Daisy said as she held her masterpiece at arm's length.

As soon as the girls went inside, Louisa grabbed her paintbrush and swirled it against the black paint. Then, biting her tongue, she covered each of her ladies with a cheerless, dark shawl. There! She stood back to look at the figures. Honestly, their dresses hadn't been scandalous for evening wear, but out here she'd only seen simple cotton gowns that buttoned up to the neck. Didn't these ladies have any imagination?

Louisa's imagination, on the other hand, had been working overtime. Lately, she'd been imagining a future where her position as governess lasted for years. Where she belonged with a family like the Adamses.

The girls had run their paintings upstairs to their room. They were supposed to return with their books. On the excuse of looking for their slates, Louisa headed toward Daniel's office and heard the crinkle of paper beneath her foot just outside the door. Pivoting the toe of her boot, she saw a sheet of stationery on the floor. The only crease in it was the one she'd just added. The girls in their hurry had run right past it.

Had someone left this for the major? She picked it up and carried it into his office. It didn't feel as strange going in the room as it used to. The wood varnish of the desk smelled masculine. Ink, wool, leather—she closed her eyes and took a deep whiff of the now-familiar mixture. She'd know what room she was in without even looking. A noise from the open window reminded her that she didn't want to be caught lingering. She just needed to put the letter on the desk, and . . .

My Dearest,

Louisa's jaw dropped. Her eyes jumped to the end, but there was no signature. She started at the beginning again.

Every time I see you, I'm filled with the desire to know you more . . .

She tried to digest what she was reading. Who would have the nerve to slide this beneath the door of their commander's house and risk his fury? The naked yearning on the page made her blush. What would it be like to have a man think those things about her? She pressed the letter to her chest, trying to imagine a man declaring his love to her, and that man bore a shocking resemblance to Major Adams.

She chided herself. She should be content with him allowing her in his house. She didn't dare ask for more.

But who was the letter for? There was only one explanation— Caroline. Louisa folded the letter and, after looking around to make sure no one was watching, hid it in her corset. It wasn't like she was taking something from the major's office. The letter had been at the door, probably slid beneath it in hopes of Caroline finding it. Louisa shuddered at the horribly reckless move. If this man knew what was good for him, he'd listen to his head. His heart was fixing to lead him into a world of trouble.

Her step faltered. Bradley wouldn't dare, would he? But the handwriting wasn't his. Whose, then? Lieutenant Jack's? Surely not. Perhaps that soulful Sergeant Byrd? He'd caught Caroline's eye when they walked across the green the day before. Perhaps he was going to tell her to look for the letter, but Louisa had interrupted him.

All her chess matches at the saloon had not taught her the strategy for supervising a young woman of courting age.

Chapter Seventeen

The punishing noon sun found Private Bradley Willis on the prairie, watching as Lieutenant Hennessey and the interpreter Ben Clark approached the band of Arapaho men. Bradley kept his pistol hand free from the reins. Tempers had been running high. Not too long ago, a prominent Cheyenne Dog Soldier by the name of Running Buffalo had been accused of trying to steal ponies from a Texas herd passing through the reservation. When the cowboys had tried to recover the ponies, guns were drawn, and Running Buffalo was shot down. Running Buffalo's family had then cornered the Texans in a stone bakery, where they were surrounded until the cavalry could rescue them.

Frustrated that the troopers hadn't allowed them to enact their own justice, the Dog Soldiers refused to allow their people to participate in the yearly census of the tribe. They stood outside the agency office to scare away anyone who thought to cooperate with Agent Dyer's mandate.

Now there was more trouble, but this time with the cattle, not ponies. And Bradley had been chosen for the small band that would protect the fort's interpreter as he tried to get an accurate report on the goings-on.

Were these the ones who'd stolen the cattle from the trail drivers? Lieutenant Hennessey chatted amiably with them through Ben Clark. If they didn't speak English, then they hadn't attended the Arapaho school at Darlington, which could mean they were troublemakers. Or it could mean that they didn't see much sense in sitting at a desk when they could be riding the prairie.

Bradley understood that only too well.

He hadn't missed going to school growing up, but Louisa had. Once she'd found a schoolbook buried in mud behind the saloon after a big rain. She'd saved every page she could and pored over them night after night, trying to learn anything she could from the smeared words. Bradley had felt sorry for her even then. She was made for something better, whereas he didn't figure he'd ever amount to much. Luckily for him, the cavalry was looking for poor boys with no education to ship off to the dangerous frontier.

He'd thought he was brave, riding out with other soldiers, armed to the teeth, but his sister was playing a much more dangerous game. What made Louisa think she could fool a man like Major Adams into thinking she was one of his set? Didn't she know how likely she was to get hurt? Louisa had always longed for a respectable life for both of them. No wonder she'd jumped at the chance to play like she was a lady, if only for a few weeks. As long as she didn't ruin his chances at a career in the cavalry.

His grip loosened as Clark and Hennessey finished their questioning, and his fellow men-at-arms began to breathe easier. These Arapaho men weren't interested in taking up the Cheyenne's grievances. They were worried about the decreasing rations and wanted more protection from the Cheyenne Dog Soldiers, but they posed no threat to Darlington or the fort. While Bradley could feel a twinge of disappointment that there'd be no excitement today, he could also appreciate the fact that he would go to bed tonight with no new holes poked through his hide.

They fell into their lines, riding across the vast Cheyenne and Arapaho Reservation. Bradley had never regretted anything before. His stunts had consequences, but what was life, if you didn't drink it to the lees? But seeing Louisa with those girls, seeing her walking on his major's arm, he realized what his sister had missed out on. Who would marry Lovely Lola from the Cat-Eye Saloon? Not a decent man like the major. Who would treat her like the fine lady she secretly hoped to be someday?

Bradley slumped in the saddle. Big sisters could rile you up like the dickens, but Louisa had been there for him when he needed her. All those years that she preached at him to straighten up and make something of himself, she hadn't done it just to ruin his fun. She'd done it because she was trapped and didn't want the same life for him.

And he hadn't listened to her.

Bradley studied the horizon, feeling a sudden urge to spur his horse and flee the thoughts that were settling on him like a biting cloud of mosquitoes. Thoughts like how he should be responsible. Thoughts like how he should be trying to settle down and make something of himself. Thoughts like how he owed his sister that much at least. No matter how fast he ran, Bradley feared that when he slowed down, he'd remember that he could've been a better man.

He'd try for her. He'd be the best soldier at the fort if it meant Louisa got a shot at being a respectable lady and all. Maybe she'd read enough schoolbooks to keep her job as a governess. Wouldn't that be something? What if the major decided that he needed her at the house permanently? What if he decided . . .

A grin spread over Bradley's face. The major was a widower. No wife. Louisa was uncommonly beautiful. He'd seen the way the major had glared at him when he ran into them on the way to Darlington. That was jealousy, or he was a parson.

Adventures didn't always mean risking your neck by getting liquored up and standing in the saddle. Sometimes you could take on a challenge closer to home.

But a challenge was already coming at him.

Two riders thundered toward them from the west, their bodies curved and sticking to their horses as close as a sandbur.

Clark cast a nervous glance at Hennessey. Even with a bandanna in the way, Bradley saw his Adam's apple jog.

"There are only two of them," Lieutenant Hennessey said. But he didn't look like their armed group of five reassured him one bit.

Clark lifted his hand. "It's Coyote and White Horse. They're looking for us."

Sure enough, the riders' horses pulled up, stiffening their front legs and nearly sitting back on their haunches as their cloud of dust caught up and coated them.

The conversation was short and tense. Then the horses were spurred again, and the two men raced toward the settlement of Darlington.

"We gotta get out of here." Clark looked at Hennessey. "You're in command, but if you want us to stay, I'm turning in my resignation."

Hennessey studied the western horizon. Bradley did too, but the only thing that met his eyes was the grass snapping beneath the constant wind and a stack of white clouds towering to the heavens.

"What is it?" the lieutenant asked.

"Six or seven hundred Cheyenne warriors are headed this way, led by Old Crow. Coyote and White Horse are going to Darlington to warn Agent Dyer and the others." Clark's horse shook a fly out of its ear.

"Old Crow is on the warpath?"

"And us at an empty fort," Clark answered.

No more words were needed. The men turned their horses toward the unguarded, unprepared fort and prayed for the employees at the agency as they rode to raise the alarm.

With the girls busy working on their school assignments, Louisa had returned to her sewing. Taking a last stitch, she flipped Caroline's dress over, tied off the thread, and then bit it off short. She rustled through the cloth, turning it right-side out, then held it up at arm's length to appreciate her handiwork.

The apple-green dress was cut modestly enough for the daughter of a major in the U.S. Cavalry, but she'd added enough trim and ribbon from her own retired wardrobe that no one would mistake Caroline for a governess herself. Louisa ran her finger over the collar. She hoped it wasn't too showy, but she'd been limited as to what she could salvage from her clothing, and goodness knew the shop at Darlington didn't offer any frivolities.

"Caroline, come try it on."

Above her head, someone squealed. Boot heels pounded down the hallway and then the stairs. Perhaps Louisa shouldn't encourage Caroline to look more fetching. She was already attracting too much attention. Still uncertain what to do with the swain's letter, Louisa had stuffed it into her sheet music until she had a chance to ask Bradley about it.

Without breaking stride, Caroline swept through the parlor, snatched the dress from Louisa's hands, and hurried back upstairs, nearly plowing down her sister, who was on her heels.

"How about mine?" Daisy's eyes were shining. "I'm almost done with my arithmetic."

Louisa scratched at her wrist. If she never saw another column of sums, she'd die a happy woman. Daisy was proving to be a quick study, which meant Louisa had to stay up late each night to keep ahead of her.

"Good, then it's time for your spelling exam. But first you may try this on." She pulled Daisy's gown out from behind her. She'd been working on it between lessons and finally had the Indian beadwork added.

Daisy spotted it immediately. Her mouth made a perfect O, and she ran her fingers over the beaded design that adorned the cuffs. "It's beautiful. And it looks like a proper dress, so even Grandmother couldn't complain."

From what Louisa had heard, Grandmother was capable of complaining about anything, but far be it from her to say that.

"Go try it on, and then we'll see if you can spell anything while wearing it."

Daisy was a sweetheart. Although Louisa wasn't quite old enough to have a daughter that age, Daisy brought out every nurturing instinct she possessed. Louisa always found excuses to smooth her hair, clean her face, or share with her some intricate flower or bright butterfly to make her beam. And she smiled so easily. Joy—that was Daisy.

Joy didn't come as easily for Caroline. Old enough to remember her mother and feel the loss, Caroline struggled to find her place in the world. She strained at the ties that kept her bound to the family, but had no idea what to do when free. And the frustration she felt, she attributed to her father.

Then there was Major Adams. Daniel. Initially Louisa had viewed him only through his relationship with his daughters. She judged him either as the antagonist to her brother or as the stern disciplinarian to the girls. Now she saw him as a man who doubted his ability to raise the girls alone. He'd been too proud to ask for help until his mother-in-law forced his hand. But if Louisa wasn't mistaken, he felt that hiring her had been the perfect solution to his problem.

It pleased her that she pleased him.

The front door opened. Louisa smiled at the sound of his familiar step. The girls heard him, too.

"Pa, look!" Daisy cried. "Look at my new dress!"

Louisa rose to meet them at the foot of the stairs. Daniel whistled. "Don't you look beautiful!" His eyes shone warmly and held their warmth as he smiled at Louisa in appreciation. "Is that Indian beadwork?" He bent forward to look at the sleeve Daisy offered him. "That is perfect for you, honey."

His eyes caught Louisa's. *You are amazing*, he mouthed over Daisy's head. Louisa felt like dancing, just like Daisy was.

"Ahem!"

All eyes rose to look at Caroline, who descended the staircase like a debutante at a ball . . . or like Louisa when singing the part of Venus. Oh, the power of a simple dress to turn a girl into a refined young lady. Louisa's heart swelled with pride.

Daniel must have felt the same way. "You look stunning, Caroline. So much like your mother." Had his eyes grown misty? Louisa yearned to reach out to him, but this moment was between him, his daughter, and a memory she had no part in.

Caroline glowed. She turned slowly to show off the dress. Even Louisa was impressed with her handiwork.

She supposed they'd just stand there and admire Caroline forever, but Daniel was looking at her. "What about your masterpiece? Didn't you finish one for yourself?"

"The girls needed theirs more than I do. Until I get it finished, I'll keep wearing what I have."

"When her new dress is finished, we can have a dance!" Daisy cheered. "Miss Bell painted a picture of a dance—"

"Forget about the picture," Louisa interrupted. "If your father could arrange for a ball with the troopers—"

But the stern commander was back. "Absolutely not. I will

not offer my girls up as dancing partners to a hundred lonely men."

"Then maybe there's another venue to show off your dresses. Are there any social events around here? At Darlington, perhaps?"

"There are powwows," Daisy said.

Powwows weren't exactly the kind of dance Louisa was looking for. "What about here on the fort?" she asked.

Caroline's face lit with hopeful joy while her father's brow lowered.

"If there were enough officers' families here, we might could have a dance, but the fort is nearly empty. The boys put on shows to entertain themselves all the time. Nearly every company has a band of some kind. For the most part, I've done my best to keep the girls away from those events."

"But we can hear them when the windows are open," Caroline said. "The band is really good, and someone can play the piano."

"There's a piano?" Louisa's eyebrows shot up. "I didn't know there was a piano here."

"In the upstairs of the commissary," Daisy said. "Do you play?"

"Well enough to accompany my students." Louisa hugged Daisy to her side. "Wouldn't you like to practice your French with music?"

"You taught them the French?" Daniel cocked his head and fixed her with a stern gaze.

"Italian," Louisa corrected. "I taught them a few songs in Italian." She scratched her brow. "Do you speak Italian?"

"No," he admitted.

"Perfect!" she said.

The girls' enthusiasm was contagious, but they held it in check as they waited for their father's response.

"If I could arrange for you to have the room to yourselves daily, would you want to practice with the girls in there?" he asked.

The girls erupted in squeals. Daisy jumped into Caroline's arms, and Caroline swung her around.

"That would be marvelous," Louisa said over their cheers.

"Would you sing?" he asked quietly.

His posture was casual as he leaned against the banister, his uniform straining across his shoulders, but something in his eyes showed that there was more at stake.

"Me, sing?" Louisa had performed under trying circumstances before. She'd sung a lighthearted song about a riverboat on the Mississippi while her mother was dying in her back room. She'd cried over a fictional lost lover on stage while she was secretly seething over a drunk's treatment of her and swearing that she'd never speak to a man again. She'd had practice making her face convey emotions that her heart knew were false. That was what she relied on now. "You want me to sing? I would be embarrassed to sing for you, Major Adams."

Beg me. Beg me to sing, she silently pleaded. He'd seen her at her worst. He'd seen her mistakes. He saw her poor attempts to teach math and writing. And then the horse . . . she could barely walk after that. If only she could sing for him—the one talent she had, besides beating him at chess.

Daisy was fidgeting, wanting her father's attention for herself, but he was still watching Louisa. Did he see the truth? Did he see how badly she wanted to perform for him?

"It would embarrass you?" A fine wrinkle appeared on his forehead as he gazed at her. "Are you afraid I'd find your performance unladylike?"

She ran her fingers over the banister. Why didn't she just give in and do it? He was asking. How could he disapprove if she accepted?

Because in her experience, men often asked women to do things that they knew were wrong. She had to be above reproach. She conjured a vision of Mrs. Townsend in all her Mennonite modesty. Would she sing a popular tune for her widower employer? Absolutely not!

"You'll do very well without me performing."

"But you're teaching my daughters to sing. Why is that different?"

Louisa shot a glance at the girls. Worry clouded their eyes at the thought that their new gowns might go unappreciated.

"In general, for a woman to sing on stage—"

Daniel held up a hand to stop her. "Whoa, whoa, whoa. I meant only to practice in private. We're talking family entertainment. No one said anything about singing on a stage." He shook his head in amusement. "It's not as if I'm going to dress my innocent daughters up in velvets and parade them on a stage in front of a crowd of rowdy men."

Louisa's mouth went dry. "Of course not," she stammered. "That would be . . ." Disgraceful? Indecent? All of those words referred to her.

"Father, that's not fair," Caroline said. "Grandmother said there are events where society meets and the young ladies perform their skills. They're called *sorties*, and they are a legitimate method of gaining a young man's attention."

"Sorties are attacks made by a small group of soldiers." He rolled his eyes. "Is there any hope for my daughters raised on a fort? What I think you meant to say is a *soiree*, unless you were planning an ambush in the midst of your performance."

Daisy let loose one of her blood-curdling war whoops.

"Great Saturn's rings!" Louisa blurted and grabbed Daniel's sleeve.

Daniel covered Louisa's hand with his own while choking on shocked laughter. She guessed a lady didn't utter oaths aimed at the heavens. She made to pull her hand out of his grip before the girls noticed, but he held her fast.

"Daisy, you startled Miss Bell. Tell her you're sorry, and no more screeching in the house."

Daisy flicked at the beaded fringe on the end of her belt. "Sorry, Miss Bell. I just got excited thinking how fun it'd be to attack all the soldiers while they were busy watching Caroline sing. I can sneak around as silent as a brave. I bet I could get to half a dozen before anyone noticed."

"Daisy must learn how to sing," Caroline said. "She should be good at something besides frightening the starch out of people. And I need an audience to practice on before I meet grandmother's friends. I wouldn't want them to think me amateurish."

"I wouldn't want them to think you professional," Daniel shot back. He smiled at Louisa as if he expected her to share his joke. If that was the response he was looking for, he was disappointed.

Louisa was still trying to think of an answer when she heard raised voices.

"What are they cheering?" she asked.

But Daniel didn't answer. He rushed to the door, flung it open, and settled his hat on his head as he marched outside.

When he slammed the door behind him, the whole house shook. What had happened?

Only later did Louisa realize that it was the boom of the cannon that had rattled the windowpanes.

Chapter Eighteen

The pulse-raising scent of gunpowder reached Daniel as he strode toward the adjutant's office. The door to the office burst open, and Captain Chandler raced toward the stables. The enlisted men not running to their horses were hitching wagons and pulling the cannons out of the middle of the green to the edges of the fort. The lookout's bugle sounded again. It was from the west. Daniel seethed in frustration. By now Jack would have found him some field glasses. Where was Jack?

Sergeant O'Hare saluted and produced the necessary piece of equipment.

"What am I supposed to be looking at?" Daniel marched to the western portion of the grounds so he could see around the post office.

"The riders are headed in, and they're running hard."

"Anyone chasing them?"

"Not that we can see."

"Who is it?"

"From the size of the unit, we think it's Jack and Ben. They left yesterday with a small party."

Daniel lifted the glasses to look at the approaching horsemen. Yes, it was Jack, taking on the toughest assignments for himself.

"Distribute arms. Cavalry in the saddle, infantry on the perimeter, with the bulk of them protecting our west. And get me my horse."

"Yes, sir." A quick salute, and O'Hare went to do what he already knew to do.

The troops hustled, no steps wasted—everyone to their station. But there were so few of them. Officially, Fort Reno covered nearly ten thousand acres. There was no possible way for them to hold all that land, but it was absolutely essential for them to protect the sprawling campus that huddled on a spot as naked and vulnerable as any that existed in the natural world. Essential, because everything Daniel held dear resided in the center house on Officers' Row.

"Here they come," the sentry bellowed.

As Jack and his men sped past the mule teams pulling the cannon to the perimeter, they spotted Daniel. Foam from the horses' mouths flecked out with each blow, their sides slick and wet. Jack and Private Willis were abreast of each other, with Ben and two others on their heels.

"It's the Cheyenne," Jack began as soon as he was close enough to be heard. "Six or seven hundred men heading to Darlington. Old Crow is leading them. White Horse and Coyote went to Darlington to warn them."

Daniel's gut clenched. Seven hundred men. They were hopelessly outnumbered. Decisions had to be made immediately. By now the adjutant's office had emptied. Several officers waited tensely for orders.

"Send half the troops to evacuate Darlington. Bring the civilians here. The rest of the troops will hold the fort but will be organized to intervene if the rescue squad runs into trouble."

"Yes, sir," sounded around him as the officers scattered.

"Private Willis," Daniel said, "tend to these horses. Rub them down, care for them personally."

"But, sir, I'm ready to go. All I need is a fresh horse. Those people in Darlington—"

Daniel raised a hand. "Never question my orders, Private. Especially now."

Willis clamped his mouth shut in what looked like genuine shame. "I apologize, sir. I let my desire to fight get the best of me. Excuse me." He gathered the reins from the other men and pulled the spent horses toward the stable.

Daniel would never admit it to anyone, but he wasn't about to send Private Willis on that mission. If something happened to the boy, Daniel would always question whether he'd done like King David and sent his rival to his death. Willis was safe for now. Or as safe as any of them could be.

He marched to the green-roofed house he called home. What if White Horse never reached Darlington? Daniel had to call Agent Dyer. Seconds could make the difference. Seeing his approach, Louisa opened the door. Her eyes looked stark against her blanched skin.

"I sent the girls to the cellar," she said. "Was that the right thing?"

If there was one thing Daniel couldn't dwell on, it was what the Cheyenne did to their female captives. Probably this uprising was just a warning, probably they weren't going to attempt a direct attack on the fort, but the fear was always there in the back of his mind. And if the Dog Soldiers prevailed, a cellar wouldn't save them.

"I want to help," Louisa said. "Let me help you."

He took her hand and dragged her behind him to the telephone box on the wall. Calling Dyer came first, but he couldn't bear to send Louisa away. Not yet. Releasing her hand, he picked up the earpiece and heard Dyer on the other line immediately. He was yelling at someone in the room.

"Just one bag. That's all you have time for. Get on a horse and ride."

"Agent Dyer!" Daniel called. "Can you hear me?"

There was a crashing noise. Daniel closed his eyes to block out everything but the sounds. He had to know what he was hearing.

"I'm here, Major. I know why you're calling."

"We got our news from the same messengers you did. Any chance this is a false report?"

"No." Dyer didn't even pause before answering. "I know Coyote. He's telling the truth. We're evacuating the agency and the school staff. The missionaries—everyone is headed your way."

"And we have troops running toward you as an escort for safe passage, but that's all we can do. We can't hold the Cheyenne out of Darlington. Not until reinforcements arrive."

"I understand. Let's pray it's enough. And if the rebels think Ida and I are at the fort, that would be helpful. We want them to think the station is deserted."

Daniel's stomach dropped. Dyer couldn't mean he was staying in Darlington. "We can't protect you there. Weren't you listening? I order you and your wife to come to the fort."

"I'm not in the military, Major. I don't answer to you. We've spent our time here building trust with the Cheyenne and Arapaho. How would it look if I ran and hid behind the might of the army when they have a grievance? I have a post, and I won't abandon it."

"Don't be a fool, Dyer. This is more than airing grievances."

"We'll hide from those who want to harm us, but if the Cheyenne decimate the Arapaho village, I need to be ready to open the storehouse for them. Wait—" Raised voices sounded in the room. Dyer called out an answer, then he was back. "I'm needed in the street. Your troopers are on the horizon, and everyone is in a hurry to quit the place. I'll contact you when it's safe to do so. Pray for us."

Daniel had yet to open his eyes. "God be with you," he said, then replaced the earpiece on its receiver. They all had their duties to perform. Unfortunately, until reinforcements arrived, he was hampered from completing his. But the people were the most important. They could rebuild Darlington if needed. It was the lives that couldn't be replaced.

He opened his eyes to find Louisa watching him.

"The agency people are coming?" She wrung her hands. "They will be so scared. We need to be ready to receive them so they'll be out of the troopers' way. I can clean rooms, move furniture around. We can even get supplies from the fort commissary and stock some of the kitchens so if they don't feel like eating in the mess hall, they can feed themselves and their families."

The urgent activity outside the window demanded his attention, but Louisa was speaking sense. They had civilians headed toward them. The last thing they needed was women and children crying on the parade grounds, getting underfoot if they came under attack.

"Excellent idea. Get Caroline and Daisy and prepare the officers' houses that are vacant. They won't have much when they get here, so whatever you can lay out will be helpful."

"Yes, sir." She drew her skirt to the side to slip past him, but Daniel caught her arm.

"Louisa, at the first war cry or gunshot, you get yourself and the girls locked into the nearest cellar. I don't care if everyone else is left standing on the green, you can't let the Cheyenne get ahold of you."

Her smile was weak but true. "I will take care of your girls,

Daniel. They come first. But they don't want to lose their father. Be careful."

He paused, listening for words she didn't speak—how she wanted him safe for her sake, how she couldn't stand to lose him. Of course, she didn't think that, but he was surprised at how badly he wanted to hear it.

❧✦☙

Louisa flipped a mattress, glad for something to do. She'd go mad sitting in the parlor when all the fort buzzed with activity.

"Caroline, sheets." Louisa didn't have breath to spare as she wrestled the mattress into place.

Caroline unfurled the sheet, and when it had settled onto the mattress, she pointed to the window. "They're here," she said, and then she raced out of the room.

Louisa was right behind her. Together they ran down the stairs, through the nearly empty house, and out onto the porch. A shiny black buggy was turning off the avenue from the agency. A man in his shirtsleeves held the reins, a tight-mouthed woman at his side. Next came a wagon with two men on the bench in front and the back teeming with bonnets, trunks, and skirts.

Louisa wrapped her arms around her stomach. The teachers. That wagon was full of real teachers from the Arapaho Indian School. Teachers who would know she was a phony. Suddenly all the work she'd done to prepare for their arrival seemed pointless. Maybe she should have saddled a horse, dodged the Cheyenne, and bounced painfully away.

"C'mon, let's help them unload." Caroline walked across the porch in a stately manner, just like the daughter of the commander should. "Daisy, let's go!" she hollered, ruining the illusion some. Daisy scurried out the front door with a duster still in her hands. Caroline stopped and watched Louisa over her shoulder.

Louisa's feet felt anchored to the floor. There'd only been a few women at the fort since Louisa arrived. Ben Clark's wife was Cheyenne and kept busy with their large family. Besides her, few of the officers at the fort were married, and the washer-women certainly didn't visit the post commander's home. But there'd be no way to avoid these women, and once they finished crying over their banishment, they'd judge her with dry eyes and hard hearts.

Growing up, there had been a few women who had shown Louisa mercy. A few women who felt sorry for the dirty little girl with the cruel mother, but when Louisa began to mature, even they shunned her. At first only the songs she'd sung had been wrong, but soon her very appearance became unsuitable. And there wasn't much she could do to change that. By the time she had money to buy herself something besides her mother's cast-offs, she was performing at the Cat-Eye.

"Miss Bell? Aren't you coming?"

"There's work to do here," Louisa said. "You go along."

Caroline's gaze softened, making Louisa feel like a child who had to be humored. "Don't be afraid, Miss Bell. You are every bit as good of a teacher as they are," she said. Caroline, like her father, seemed to read Louisa's fears as easily as reading Daisy's primer.

The unexpected kindness made Louisa's guilt even heavier. She was a horrible teacher and an even more horrible person. Being around church people only made her feel worse.

"Your father will be looking for you," Louisa said. "Don't wait on me."

Turning her back, she returned to the house, then watched out the window as Caroline left. The buggy had reached Officers' Row. Lieutenant Hennessey was the first to greet them.

Daniel appeared next, doffed his hat to the ladies, and asked Caroline a question as she approached. Caroline gestured to the house, and Louisa jumped away from the window, her heart pounding. The shame and fear had caught her off guard. Turning from the window, she tiptoed back upstairs and began straightening another room.

"Louisa?" It was Daniel. He was inside the house. The floor in the empty parlor creaked. "Are you in here?"

She backed away from the half-made bed. "I'm up here." Her voice sounded weak even to her own ears. When he stepped around the corner, she frantically grabbed the sheet and began tucking it into place.

"Everyone is going to the chapel for prayer," he said. "You're free to join them."

"No, thanks." Her hands shook. "That'll give me more time to prepare their lodgings. I haven't checked the room Daisy was in, but there's no telling what she's left undone."

The corner of the mattress kept slipping from her hands. Instead of helping, Daniel stood silently and watched her.

"Stubborn mattress." Louisa let out a sharp laugh. "Don't wait on me. You must have a thousand things to do. I'll take care of this."

"I guess I assumed you'd want to go to the chapel with the ladies. They are unfamiliar with the fort. It would be a comfort to them to have you along."

Had he forgotten that she'd never been to the chapel, either? Each week she had managed to come up with one excuse or another. Louisa picked up a lightly quilted coverlet. A bead of sweat ran down her neck and past her shoulder blades at what she was about to say. The fort was in danger. He had an uprising on his hands, and she was refusing to cooperate.

"Caroline and Daisy can guide them. It'll be good for them to take this role—"

"Miss Bell, we are in a crisis. I am ordering you to escort our guests and my daughters to the chapel immediately." She'd disappointed him, but he wasn't appealing to her friendship. He was giving an order. He stepped out of the doorway, clearing her path, waiting for her to obey.

It wasn't fair. Louisa wanted to help. She'd work hard for him, do nearly anything, but he was asking the one thing that might end their association. The one thing that had the power to expose her.

But he wasn't giving her a choice. She made her way outside, where the women huddled in the shade of the porch. Tear-streaked faces, red from sorrow and the heat, looked her way. Louisa worried about the taffeta skirt she wore. The color wasn't the same muted hue of theirs. She adjusted her fichu to cover all the skin it could. Hopefully the ladies would be accepting in their distress.

Daniel cleared his throat and waited for their desperate whispers to die down. "Everyone who wanted to evacuate Darlington is here safely. Our soldiers are at their stations, and the fort is secure. If the men will organize themselves, we will put you to use."

"Excuse me, Major." A bespectacled man raised his hand. "We Mennonites are peace-loving people. Our consciences won't allow us to fight, but we can help with any defenses you want built, tending to the horses, or any other task—"

"I understand," Daniel said. "Thank you for your offer. In the meanwhile, your women might be best occupied entreating the Lord on our behalf. It's understandable that they would want to pray for peace so you can return to your homes. Miss Bell is the governess of my daughters." At this, Daniel motioned to her. Louisa had never felt butterflies like these before on the stage. "Some of you might know her through her connections with your Mennonite Society. She'll lead you to the chapel."

Ignoring the questioning looks shot her way, Louisa took Daisy's hand. She wasn't about to let the girl get away from her. Summoning her skills as a performer, Louisa spoke in calm, rounded tones.

"If you would please follow me, I will show you where the chapel is." Holding on to Daisy with a death grip, she made their way through the women and started across the lawn. Louisa had seen what direction the Adams family went on Sundays, but once they turned past the barracks, she wasn't sure. She hurried Daisy along to get her out of earshot.

"Daisy, you have to show me where we're going. Can you do that without anyone knowing?"

"The chapel? Sure. Do you want me to show you the secret way?"

"No. Don't do that. And no jumping out and scaring anyone for a while, especially in war paint."

Daisy pouted. Louisa wanted to pout with her, but she was too frightened. Why had Daniel mentioned her connections? Did any of these women know Mrs. Townsend?

It turned out the old schoolhouse doubled as the chapel. It was set on the corner of the main avenue entering the fort. Louisa's steps faltered.

Caroline put an arm around her waist. The friendly gesture was as unfamiliar as the chapel, but much more welcome. "Don't be scared," Caroline said. "I haven't seen any smoke from Darlington or the tepees. Looks like the Cheyenne just wanted to stir the pot."

Louisa leapt at the excuse. "Yes, I'm so concerned I'm beside myself. Do you mind taking the lead? I'm not sure exactly what your father's orders were for this prayer service."

"Orders?" Caroline asked. "He didn't have to order them to pray. It's what you do at times like this."

Louisa held Daisy's hand tighter as Caroline pulled away.

Why were they eager to talk to a God who demanded the impossible—perfection—from them? But then again, they were perfect. These women hadn't lived in the gutter like Louisa had. No wonder they didn't mind gathering to parade their holiness before each other. They had some. Louisa didn't.

Louisa waited at the door as the women filed in. Many of them held hands. Some hugged each other as if being reunited after a long journey. For the most part, they were occupied with comforting one another and paid Louisa no mind. Eventually they arranged themselves on the benches in the church. One matronly woman who still wore an apron splashed with her dinner preparations had gathered Caroline beneath her wing, obviously having some relationship with her from the past. Daisy finally pulled away from Louisa to join them. Not wanting to be the only one standing, Louisa perched on an empty pew behind everyone else. A few eyes drifted her way, but most people watched the older woman sitting with Caroline and Daisy.

"Well, sisters," the matron said, "we didn't expect to be here today, fearful for our lives and anxious for our homes, but God is not surprised. He's known this day was coming, and now He's watching to see if we'll fret and stew or if we'll turn to Him. Frankly, I don't know what the fretting and stewing will accomplish, so why don't we just go ahead and tell our Father about our trouble?"

Louisa nearly jumped out of her seat at the *amens*. If she wasn't careful, the terrible day from her childhood would be re-created here. Expecting to be identified and called out at any moment, Louisa trembled on the bench. This time, instead of merely getting expelled from church, she had so much more to lose.

The ladies sat in silence with bowed heads and closed eyes, but on the inside, Louisa was rioting. Her palms grew damp with sweat. Her legs ached with tension. What did God think of her sitting in this chapel, pretending to be holy? He knew the truth. He knew she was no friend of His.

She couldn't suppress her panic any longer. Giving freedom to her anxious nerves, she stood and quietly slipped out the door.

Chapter Nineteen

The situation was tense, but there were no attacks yet. Daniel had sent out the necessary telegraphs notifying Washington of their predicament and again requesting more troops. The perimeter of the fort was heavily guarded, and he had their positions marked on the map spread over his desk. There was no word from Agent Dyer at Darlington. While Daniel appreciated his sense of duty, he dearly hoped his troopers wouldn't be called on to make a frantic rescue if the Cheyenne carried out their threats. He'd lose men, and there was no guarantee Dyer and his wife could be saved.

According to Captain Chandler, Dyer had some trusted Indian guards among Old Crow's men. They would try to dissuade the band from doing any damage to the property and, as a last resort, would break away to ferry the Dyers across the Canadian River to the fort.

Either way, Daniel preferred to be by the phone in his office. Everyone knew where to find him, and find him they did.

"Major Adams, telegrams."

"Come in," he called, little expecting to see Private Willis step inside his office. "You're finished with the horses?" he asked.

"Yes, sir. I was coming this way to tell you when the fellas at

217

the post hall suggested I bring you these telegrams along with some mail that came in before we went under siege."

"We aren't under siege, Private. There might be hostile Indians in Darlington right now, but we could leave if we wanted." Which of course they didn't want.

He ripped open the first telegram, then read it once, twice, three times with dry eyes. "President Cleveland has ordered General Sheridan to come here immediately."

Daniel had asked for more troops, not for the Commanding General of the entire U.S. Army to come. General Sheridan's aide thought they'd be there within the week. Daniel's jaw set. One week? It was a long time to hold off invaders, but not long enough to prepare for a visit from General Sheridan. He read through the rest of the letter carefully, making notes for his staff of particular requests. A hunting outing, the general's favorite meals, the number of staff they'd need to find lodging for. Details Daniel hadn't been expecting in the midst of a siege. Wait, not a siege. But now not only did he have to hold the Indians at bay, but he also had to plan a holiday for the army brass.

Daniel turned in his chair to look over the green fields that stretched to the horizon. He hoped that the Cheyenne could be placated before any loss of life occurred, but would General Sheridan be satisfied with a peaceful solution? General Sheridan of the scorched-earth technique, first against the Confederacy and then against the Kiowa and Comanche tribes? And weren't the Cheyenne attacked by him that winter, too? Daniel grimly crumpled the telegram in his hand.

"That bad, huh?"

Daniel spun around. He had forgotten he wasn't alone. With everything going on, Private Willis didn't realize the danger he was in. An accident could happen, like getting stabbed with a letter opener.

"Report to your sergeant. Your delivery is complete."

With a "yes, sir," he was gone, but Daniel's worries stayed. The second telegram alerted him that three companies of the Fifth Cavalry were on their way, along with three companies of the Eighteenth Infantry. They definitely needed the help. The Cheyenne had shown a reluctance to challenge the fort directly, but one never knew when they might find the courage.

Everyone was prepared. Every trooper was in place. Daniel had learned not to expend valuable energy anticipating an attack that might not come. Once the defenses were up, it was his job to look to the contingencies. *What if . . . ?* And while the attack wasn't a certainty, General Sheridan's visit was, and they'd better be ready to receive him.

Returning to his list, Daniel began to assign the tasks. With so many of his men required to walk the picket line, he'd ask the Mennonite men for help with the carpentry and painting work needed to spruce up the fort. What if the Cheyenne didn't let the mule trains pass? They might be running low on food by the time reinforcements arrived. Daniel would consult with the quartermaster on the situation and see how much could be shared with the agency families that had sought shelter here. They might need to bring in the gardens early. And then there was the entertainment that high-ranking officers required. The upstairs of the commissary needed to be spiffed up and decorated.

His pen scratched against the thin pad, writing task after task that had to be done. First priorities were starred, then those that were less important added later. So much depended on the Cheyenne and what they had in mind. No use decorating the commissary if it was aflame the next day.

After the tasks were identified, it was time to assign them. Easily, Daniel sped down the line, knowing exactly which of his staff and which units were the most capable for the various duties. He even remembered to include the Darlington men and women where applicable.

And Miss Bell.

Daniel lowered his pen. Why was she so shy around the other women? With her poise and confidence in the face of a motley unit of soldiers, he'd thought her beyond intimidation. But here came some simple, sacrificing women, and Louisa was reduced to a mess of nerves.

Maybe he was being too hard on her. More likely the Cheyenne threat had her rattled, not the Darlington ladies. He was proud of the way Louisa had responded at the first news of the attack. Give her a few moments, and that courage would come back.

He heard sharp orders and the familiar sound of boots marching across the green. They were changing the guard. He wanted to be there, to encourage his men and tell them of General Sheridan's approach. He opened the front door, and behind the straight lines of soldiers, he noticed a lonely figure huddled next to the chapel.

It was Louisa, hiding, while the rest of the ladies were inside.

The prayers had finished. Soft voices floated through the chapel window to where Louisa was hiding beneath a pecan tree. Somehow she needed to blend back into the group when they left the building without them realizing she'd been absent the entire time. Even better if she could disappear completely before some innocent question destroyed her story, but Daisy and Caroline would be looking for her.

And so was Lieutenant Hennessey, evidently.

He'd spotted her. Not knowing what to do, Louisa bowed her head and made the sign of the cross, or at least something close to what she'd seen some religious people make while praying. Surely, he'd know she was busy and not bother her.

Lieutenant Hennessey paused, but after a curious shake of his head, he marched up to her. "I thought you were Mennonite."

"Shhh." Louisa squinted with her head bowed as if not completely finished with her prayers. "God will hear you."

"God hears everything," he said.

From the twist of his mouth, Louisa could tell she'd answered wrong. He wasn't fooled. Before he could ask any more questions, she waved at the ladies leaving the chapel and called for Daisy and Caroline.

"Are we under attack?" Daisy asked a bit too loudly and much too excitedly as she ran to meet them.

"No, ma'am, but the telegraph wires are buzzing with news," Lieutenant Hennessey said. "General Sheridan is coming with four other generals and practically half the army. We don't have much time to prepare."

Louisa watched as the scared women passed in tight groups, comforting one another. "But that's good, right? All those soldiers will mean that the Darlington people can go back home and things will get back to normal."

"Yes and no. It's good as far as our Indian situation is concerned, but there'll be nothing normal about having General Sheridan at the fort. He's the supreme commander of the entire U.S. Army and could easily cause more problems than seven hundred Cheyenne. If the fort was burning down around us, he'd still expect to be entertained in style."

"Entertained? What does that mean?"

Caroline seemed to perk up at the question as well.

"There'll be some grand performance for the officers. The men will throw something together, of course, but Major Adams said that you and the girls were practicing a few musical pieces as well. If you have time to prepare, could they present their songs?"

Louisa threw her hands in the air. "Our lives are in danger, but we're supposed to practice some songs?"

"I'm sorry," Jack said. "When there's danger, the fort's response can be overwhelming, but everything is now in place, and we plan for the next mission. That doesn't mean we're going to be less diligent, just looking ahead. Besides, staying busy helps deal with the uncertainty."

Louisa chewed her lip as she looked about her. There was no more rushing around; the troopers had settled into their positions and were waiting. At least rehearsing with Caroline and Daisy would get her out of the way of the teachers from the Arapaho school. Caroline nudged her, hoping for a yes.

Louisa nodded. "We can be ready. We'll start practicing more."

"Perfect. And you shouldn't expect to see the major this evening. He'll be in the adjutant's office for the rest of the day. He didn't want the girls worried about him." Lieutenant Hennessey looked down at a list in his hand. "Now on to Major Adams's next command." With a salute and a wink at Daisy, he was gone.

They headed back to their house as some of the troopers were coming off their watch. Louisa knew Daniel would expect his daughters to be sheltered away from the high-strung troops, but then she saw Bradley. Taking Daisy by the hand, she stayed on the gravel walk, even though it led right into the path of the men.

That was a mistake. A young man with a dashing mustache and pomaded hair made a beeline for Caroline. Whatever he said had Caroline covering her mouth as she giggled. Was he the mysterious letter writer?

"Caroline!" Daisy yelled. "You're gonna get him thrown in

the guardhouse." She pulled out of Louisa's grasp and ran to them.

The trooper lifted his head. He stroked his mustache and, with a quick bow, hightailed it away. Bradley glared a warning at Louisa, but with the danger all around them, she had to talk to him.

"Be careful out there," she whispered as she slowed next to Bradley. "Take care of yourself."

"You shouldn't be here," he grumbled. "Do you have any idea how brutal the Cheyenne are?"

"I'm not worried about me. I'm worried about you." Bradley rolled his eyes, but that was all the time she had. "We'll talk later," she promised as she marched both errant girls to the house.

≈≫✦≪≈

A second day had passed with tense pickets and mourning refugees, but no attacks. The war drums pounded all night, and scouts saw riders blazing across the prairie in war paint, but no smoke from Darlington meant the Cheyenne were demonstrating their anger in less destructive ways.

No one was letting their guard down, but life inside the fort had found a tempo, and that tempo included preparations for General Sheridan and the oncoming units. Daniel made his way back to the house after a long day inspecting and evaluating what needed to be done. Again the ladies from Darlington had met at the chapel for prayer, but Daniel hadn't seen Louisa among them.

Now that he thought about it, she'd found an excuse each Sunday to avoid the church service. He'd wondered if her strict Mennonite upbringing prohibited her from attending the general Protestant meeting on the fort, but these women were mostly teachers and missionaries from the Mennonite mission. What could her objection be to praying with them? Besides, Louisa didn't observe Mennonite traditions as far as Daniel could tell. Bright colors, wearing her hair unbound, singing popular music—in many ways she wasn't what Daniel had expected. But was she what she claimed? How many inconsistencies could he ignore?

Light lingered on the faraway horizon. The day had lasted forever, but with the evening came a sense of normalcy. Daniel was stuck in his office, answering correspondence, until after dinner. By the time he'd finished, the sewing machine had stilled, and the girls had gone to bed. He set aside his pen and slid his papers into his Gladstone case. Was Louisa still awake? Would she grant him some time?

He rubbed the weariness from his face. He had a decision to make. Either he was in love with the kind, resilient woman living under his roof, or he didn't really know her and needed to reserve his regard until some questions were answered. He was impatient to have it settled. Just when he was determined to declare himself, some new startling behavior would have him questioning her again.

He went to the chessboard to place the pieces in anticipation of her visit. He even arranged her chair, pushing it a little to his side, though he suspected she'd move it back where it was directly behind her army.

Daniel had at various assignments been able to play chess against some challenging opponents, but as his skill grew along with his rank, he found true competition harder to come by. Even if a man in the barracks could best him, most would rather not, and that left him untested and every victory hollow.

But not anymore. In Louisa he had found someone who didn't care a dime about his feelings when it came to the game. She beat him joyfully. And the one time he'd bested her, her frustration showed that she'd fought her best against him. Satisfying—that was what it was.

When he'd finished arranging the table, he paused. What was he doing? She was under his protection, and under suspicion.

But he'd rather not worry about some vague uneasiness. He had enough real danger lurking out in the canyons and flatlands of the reservation. This would be the most pleasant reconnaissance he'd ever undertaken.

Louisa came to the door. No longer did she wear the old dress that disguised her beauty. Her red skirt warmed the lamplight and reflected it in rosy tones on her glowing face. Perhaps that was why she avoided the missionaries. Perhaps she was straying from their standards, but his standards were pleased.

"Finished already?" he asked.

"I thought I could cut some more pieces tonight—running the machine would be too loud once the girls are in bed—but I don't have the right measurements. It'll have to wait until they can help me."

His mouth went dry as thoughts of the chessboard faded. "Can I help?"

"I'm not sure."

"I might not be able to stitch a buttonhole, but I know how to measure." Then he saw the measuring tape and pad of paper in her hands. He smiled as he reached for them. "If you're half as excited as the girls about getting a new dress, I want to do everything I can to help."

She relinquished the measuring tape, her hand resting in his for a heartbeat. "There's nothing to it. I took my own measurements on my waist. I just need some help with my shoulders and back. It'll be simple."

He ran the measuring tape through his fingers as she turned her back to him and dropped her pad of paper on his desk.

"What do I do?" Standing behind her, he was free to appreciate the soft flowing fabric of the shawl pinned around her shoulders, their outline undisguised by their draped covering. He was glad both hands had to hold the tape. Otherwise, he'd have been tempted to span her waist and pull her against him.

Who was he fooling? He was tempted just the same.

"Take a measurement from one shoulder to the other," she said. "Right where the sleeve starts."

He put the tape against her back, then stopped. "The shawl . . ."

She tucked her chin as she fumbled with the brooch. Wordlessly she removed the shawl and folded it in her hands. It'd been so long since he had seen anything so beautiful.

He pressed the end of the tape to her shoulder, just low enough to avoid touching the bare skin exposed by the wide neckline, and stretched it to the other side. At the pressure, she braced herself and leaned back against him.

"Fourteen inches," he said. Why had he agreed to do this? It was pure torture. And yet he wouldn't miss it for the world.

She jotted down the number, then straightened again. "Only one more. It goes from the nape of my neck to the waist of my skirt."

Oh, heavens. He'd earned medals for easier assignments.

"This collar is lower than . . . other blouses. Where should I start measuring?"

She reached behind her and touched the spot where a red ribbon gathered the mass of curls that she kept draped over her shoulder.

"Your hair," he said. "I don't want to pull it."

She turned, her profile outlined by the lamp. "It's alright, Daniel. I trust you."

That made one of them.

Taking the measuring tape in one hand, he brushed away her curls with the other. He caught the scent of rose water as he pressed the end of the tape to the soft skin on her neck. Then, running his finger down the length of the tape, he passed the bump of her collar, down and down over every vertebrae between her shoulder blades. He encountered the firm edge of her corset, then traced the curve of her spine until he'd reached the band that marked the end of his journey.

Somehow, he couldn't bring the number on the tape into focus. It was too much. "Louisa?"

She turned her head to look at him, her jaw resting against her white shoulder. Her curls danced across his knuckles as he moved his hand away, dropping the measuring tape in the process.

"What's wrong?" she asked.

"Louisa, there's something I want to say."

She clasped her hands before her, as if startled, and that was the last thing he wanted. Taking her gently by the arms, he turned her to face him and gave her an encouraging smile. The words he'd written in his letter were perched on the tip of his tongue.

"I want you to know that you are—"

A tinny *pop* sounded from somewhere above his head. Was it the girls? No, it came from outside. Without hesitation, he pulled Louisa to his side. Were they under attack? Staying between her and the window, he turned his head, trying to isolate the sound. Another *pop*, and he knew it was coming from the back of the house. Where her room was.

Her body tensed. She'd heard it, too, and they both knew it wasn't the Cheyenne. Daniel looked out the dark window, but the only image that greeted him was the reflection of him holding Louisa. And her face was turned wistfully up and away, toward the staircase.

"It's getting late," she said. "It's time for me to retire." She pulled away to gather her notebook and pencil. Daniel stood, arms crossed, as she bent to retrieve the measuring tape.

A commander often had to squelch his emotions to lead fairly. The disappointment would come, and the anger, but not yet. Just because his vanity was hurt didn't mean that he could ignore the danger she was in.

"Miss Bell," he said. Louisa straightened slowly, keeping her eyes down as she folded the tape into her hand. He chose his words carefully. "I want to let you know how much I appreciate your help during this emergency, and how much I admire the progress you are making with Caroline and Daisy. You are perfectly suited to this station, or at least to my reckoning, you are. Do you feel otherwise?"

Pop! Another pebble thrown against her window. That idiot Willis. Who else would be so brazen when Daniel's lamplight was shining in his office? He would deal with Willis later. First, he had to prevent Louisa from making a mistake that he could not ignore.

"No, sir," she answered. "I'm very grateful for my position here. I have no wish to find another."

The words were right, but her body shook as if ignoring the signal anguished her. At her distress, Daniel checked himself again. Could he be acting out of jealousy? But what other option did he have? Allow females under his protection to frolic at night with his troopers? It wasn't an issue of vanity, but of decency. And as distasteful as it was to thwart a rival by pulling rank, Daniel had no choice.

"As long as we understand each other," he said.

"We do, Major Adams. I won't be downstairs again until breakfast. Good night." And just like that, she disappeared into the dark of the hallway and up the stairs.

Daniel made his way to the front door without stopping for a saber or a gun. He knew what lurked behind the woodpile, and he wouldn't need anything but a few barked orders to deal with it, although he'd prefer to use his fists. At the noise of the door opening, there was a scramble in the darkness and then footsteps receding around the back of the house, no doubt racing to the barracks. Daniel waited on his porch until he saw a shadowed figure between the buildings on the adjacent side of the square. When it darted into the barracks door—left open to catch the summer's night breeze—he knew that his household wouldn't be interrupted again that night. He'd prevented his governess from behaving poorly.

As an employer, he was satisfied. As a man, he was bitterly disappointed.

Chapter Twenty

Most of the trouble that Bradley had faced in his life, he'd brought on himself. Sure, he hadn't asked to be born to the mother he'd been born to, and he hadn't requested a pa who didn't even stick around to lay eyes on his son's sorry hide, but he could pretty much take credit for everything after that. He had a chip on his shoulder and a fire in his belly, and that didn't make for a peaceable life, no matter how hard his sister tried to keep him on the straight and narrow.

But this trouble wasn't his fault. Didn't he have enough to worry about, without his sister being at risk? In an honest-to-goodness attempt to protect her, he'd taken an extra pistol from the armory with plans to give it to her after everyone else had gone to sleep. No harm in her being prepared should they be overrun. But instead of finding her in her room where she ought to be, she was downstairs fraternizing with the major.

Bradley slapped more whitewash on the fence. He should've known not to throw those rocks while Major Adams's lamp was lit, but he'd thought the office was too far away for the major to hear some pebbles against her window. By the time Bradley realized his mistake, what had he seen? The major standing in front of the window with an arm around Louisa.

If that didn't beat all.

Bradley scratched at his army-issued shirt and appreciated that the messiness of his fatigue duty allowed him to wear the lighter cotton today. If he'd been caught red-handed last night, he wouldn't need to bother putting on that uniform again. As it was, the mere suspicion that he'd been out after curfew was enough to saddle him with the loathsome job of painting the eternal fence.

Let that be a lesson to her. His sister thought Major Adams could be reasoned with—that he'd make exceptions for Bradley if she only asked. She didn't understand military discipline. Neither did she understand that the major was completely besotted with her. His commanding officer had noticed the relationship between them, and just like a jealous lover, had been sending Bradley black looks ever since. Not that Bradley needed the attention. He'd already pushed his luck, and his sister and her meddling were going to be the death of him.

And here she came now. Had she gone plumb loco? The extravagant plume on her hat was sure to attract the major's attention. And if that wasn't bad enough, trudging along at her side were the major's older daughter, the one young enough and pretty enough to earn a firing squad over, and the little girl, swinging a basket with every step.

Bradley jammed his brush into the pail of whitewash and slapped it against the fence again. He kept his head down as they approached, praying Louisa wasn't up to what he thought she was up to.

"Why are we crossing here?" the older daughter asked. "The fence is wet."

Louisa answered in her stage voice. "This is the area that I saw the flowers in. If we want to truly comprehend your botany text, we must have real specimens to examine." Boy howdy. She was taking on this teacher role with a vengeance. "Besides, I don't think this kind trooper will mind us troubling him for a minute. Maybe he'll leave a dry patch for us to climb over."

It was a tad gratifying to see Caroline Adams fluster when she saw who he was. She would be trouble to someone, someday, but not as much trouble as his sister was.

"Good day, ladies." If he was walking the plank, he might as well be gallant about it. "I'm afraid I can't let you go across this fence. Not while the fort is on alert."

Miss Adams touched the fence gingerly, testing it for paint. "But our persistent governess insists there's something that can only be found on the other side."

Their governess? If Louisa wasn't irritating him so much, he'd find the idea funny. "Your governess isn't the boss here. It's your pa, and I'd rather make Miss Bell angry than him."

Louisa's brows had leveled into that warning look, but what could she say? For once in his life, he had the upper hand on his older sister.

"Then we'll have to find the flowers on this side of the fence," Louisa grudgingly said.

"Go look over yonder." He waved the dripping brush toward the stables. "Just don't go past the sentry. He's there for a reason."

The little one wasn't waiting. With her braids bouncing, she ran ahead through the high grass toward a patch of wildflowers.

"Oh, Daisy," Louisa said. "Caroline, run after her, please. Make sure she doesn't go too far."

Bradley didn't like the look he got from Caroline. It made him wonder if the whole household suspected him of ungentlemanly activities.

"I wanted to get a weapon to you last night," he hissed as

soon as the girls were out of earshot. "Something you could protect yourself with. I don't have it now, so move along."

"But I need your help," she said, "or else someone is going to get in trouble."

"You mean like me, when you get me discharged from the cavalry?"

She rolled her eyes. "I didn't mean to be in his office that late, but I didn't know you were coming. Sorry." She pulled a piece of paper from her sleeve. "This is more important. I found this on the floor by the front door. Someone has been writing inappropriate letters to Caroline."

"You don't think it's me, do you? Even I'm not that thick-skulled."

"Just look and tell me if you know who it is."

With a cautious look toward the adjutant's office, Bradley opened the letter. Louisa was going to be the death of him. But then his eyes focused, and at first sight, Bradley knew what his older and wiser sister had missed.

He couldn't keep the giant grin off his face as he dove into the writing. It was his major, no doubt, but he'd never heard the likes of these phrases coming out of his mouth. Just imagine, lovesick Major Adams penning this secret letter to his sister, Lovely Lola of the Cat-Eye Saloon. Bradley had never enjoyed reading in any form until now.

But he had to tread carefully. If Major Adams was this besotted, there was no telling how he might react if he knew Bradley had read the letter. And what would Louisa think? Time to do a little acting himself.

"What is it?" she asked. "You didn't write it, did you?"

"No. I most certainly did not."

"Then why do you look like that? You're up to something."

"I think I know the author."

"You do? Then you'd better tell him to leave off the wooing.

If I hadn't come home first, Major Adams could have found it. Can you imagine what a ruckus he would raise?"

"Or he might have done his best to keep it quiet."

She shook her head. "He's very protective of his girls. He would tear this fort apart to find the author."

Bradley couldn't play it safe. No matter what the stakes, he had to poke the cat to see how hard it could scratch. He folded the letter and handed it back to her. "Why don't you tell him you found it?"

"What? He'll be furious. You don't know the major like I do."

"Evidently not."

"I just feel like I need to tell someone. I wouldn't want this to reach Caroline and encourage her to do something ill-advised." She tucked the letter into her sleeve and picked up her basket.

"Show him, Lola. I promise, it's the right thing to do."

"Since when are you an expert on the right thing to do?" But she straightened her plain mourning dress and thanked him in her fanciest voice for the assistance. Then she went to join the girls.

Bradley had forgotten how fine Louisa could sound when playing a character. He wondered if this governess character would be a permanent one.

It sounded like if she played her cards right, a better role might be available.

Well, he wasn't much help. Louisa turned her attention to the two girls darting around behind the buildings. They didn't seem to be concerned about her talking to Bradley, but she knew their father would be.

What was she going to do about Daniel?

Louisa never should have mentioned the measurements. The girls at the Cat-Eye were always lounging around in various stages of undress and always had some project going to improve their wardrobe. Helping pin together a bodice or take measurements wasn't a particularly noteworthy event. And if Tim-Bob happened through, no one paid him any mind.

But last night hadn't been a friend helping a friend. What had made it different, she couldn't say. His hands were so warm, so gentle, and the difference had nothing to do with reporting some measurements. In this case, she wasn't just another chorus girl. She meant something. And what had he been on the verge of telling her?

Then Bradley had to ruin it. Of course, he was only looking after her, but what would have happened had he not picked that moment to throw rocks at her window? What had Daniel been going to say?

Louisa adjusted the brim of her velvet hat against the wind. She was growing comfortable in her role as a proper lady. She still made mistakes, and plenty of them, but so far she'd escaped detection. What if she put away her pots of rouge and her feathered costumes forever? Could this masquerade lead to a good reference for another teaching position? Being Miss Bell the educated governess had its perks.

And one of those perks was getting to spend time with the major.

"I found my flower," Caroline called. She held up a purple bloom with a yellow center. "It's *Anemone caroliniana*, or Carolina Anemone." Smiling, she dropped it into her basket.

"Excellent work," Louisa said. Making her way through the botany book ahead of Caroline had her eyes burning every evening, but it'd been worth it. No longer did Caroline accuse her of not being a real governess. Of course, arithmetic and composition weren't as easily mastered, but in the meantime, she could memorize the names of plants just like she'd memorized lines of foreign songs she didn't understand.

Yes, she could get used to this life, but a man like Daniel Adams wanted nothing to do with a woman like Lovely Lola. And the more she treasured his friendship, the more important it was that she be truthful. Being truthful would mean losing everything, and that wasn't what she wanted. For once Louisa understood her brother's need to take insanely dangerous risks.

Daisy bounded through the buffalo grass to Louisa. "I'm going to make a daisy chain out of Indian blankets." She held up a basket full of the flowers. Their petals fanned out flat like a red wagon wheel that had rolled through a puddle of golden paint.

"What's the proper name?" Louisa asked.

"*Gaillardia pulchella*," Caroline said. "How long of a chain are you going to make?"

"As long as I want," Daisy said. "It isn't any of your concern." She skipped off to another clump she saw near the fence.

Taking stock of the space afforded them, Louisa cleared her throat. "Since we have the whole outdoors as our amphitheater, let's practice our music for our upcoming performance. What do you say?"

"I'm singing alto this time." Caroline bent over and snapped a stalk of thick grass with a bushy head to it, then put it in her basket.

"Fine, I'll do the melody," Daisy called, although she was getting farther away and out of breath.

Louisa hummed the starting note to herself and then began the song. Both girls chimed in with charming voices, causing even Bradley over by the fence to lift his head in wonder. The song waxed and waned as they gathered their treasures—which was their primary objective, after all—and Louisa was happy to fill in when a voice lost its position.

She'd crescendoed to a lovely note when her ear picked up something unwelcome. A scream.

Daisy was dancing a frantic jig and whooping and hollering as she had a habit of doing. Louisa's lips pressed firm. Why would she interrupt now? She'd been doing so well with the melody line.

But there was something odd about her dance. The flailing of the arms, the stomping, the running. And then a phrase came out clearly.

"Help me!"

Daisy wasn't dancing. She was swatting at something. Louisa dropped her basket and sprinted to her. It was hornets. A ground nest, and Daisy was being stung over and over again. Louisa's legs strained against her skirts to cover the ground more quickly, but she felt like she was running through sand. She didn't seem to be getting any closer.

Then she saw Bradley racing toward Daisy.

"No, Bradley!" Louisa screamed as his boots flashed over the hard-baked ground. He had a sensitivity to stings. His body reacted violently to them. But he wasn't stopping. Holding out his arms, he snatched up Daisy. Her body whipped about from the suddenness of his approach, but he ducked his head and kept on running toward the center of the fort with the little girl held against his chest.

Louisa's stomach dropped. She angled toward them, but Bradley was already slowing down. Before he reached the first building of the fort, he fell to his knees and collapsed.

Louisa slid to the ground next to him and yanked on his shoulder to flip him over. Already his face, covered with red welts, was turning puffy and nearly purple.

"Is she all right?" he asked.

Daisy's sobs were muffled by the ground. Louisa crawled to her and flipped her on her back. "It burns," Daisy said. "My skin is burning everywhere." She, too, was covered in stings— more than Bradley—but absent the swelling.

"Get your father," Louisa ordered Caroline as she caught up. Caroline streaked toward the green, yelling to sound the alarm.

If Louisa had been torn between whom to treat, Bradley solved it for her. "Look after the little one," he said. "I'm fine."

He'd always been a poor liar, but Louisa obeyed. She swatted at a few lingering hornets, shook some out of Daisy's skirts, and checked over Bradley once again. Tears streamed down her cheeks as she placed a cool hand against Daisy's feverish cheek. "I should've brought us something to drink," she said.

"Doesn't matter," Bradley wheezed. "Ol' Major Adams doesn't allow that kind of drink in the territories."

"That's not what I meant," Louisa said. But her brother was teasing her through gritted teeth and tightening lungs. She took his hand. Tremors racked through it. He lay flat on his back, his mouth open wide as he gasped for air. "Why did you do that?" Louisa moaned. "Always being stupid, rushing in when you shouldn't."

"What my sister calls stupid, the army calls heroic." His voice had stretched out tighter and higher.

Louisa shushed him. "Rest," she said. "Don't wear yourself out." But even she knew that relaxing wouldn't help him any.

Thundering hooves approached. The sentry from the field was racing toward them while a handful of mounted men came from the fort with Daniel in the lead. He jumped out of the saddle, landing next to Daisy. He took his canteen, wrenched off the lid, and held it to her lips. Louisa moved closer to Bradley to give Daniel more room at his daughter's side. Bradley's trembling had turned into more violent shaking. Louisa brushed back his hair, but his eyes were swollen shut.

Suddenly there were troopers all around, and curiously, Major Adams was not in charge. Instead, a rotund young man with prematurely thinning hair was barking orders. With a gloved hand pointing at Daisy, he directed two troopers to lift her onto a stretcher and carry her back to the fort.

"She's my daughter," Daniel said as he waved the stretcher away. "I've got her."

The doctor nodded his assent, then knelt by Bradley to examine him.

"He's done this before," Louisa said, "when he was little."

The doctor spared her the merest glance as he placed a stethoscope to Bradley's chest. "They have the tendency to get worse every time," he said. "Breathe."

The whistling sound in Bradley's lungs scared Louisa. The doctor didn't like it, either. "All right, boys. Let's get him loaded up and taken to the hospital. And I need some chewing tobacco to apply to these stings. If you have any on you, get to chewin'. It'll draw out the poison."

Louisa continued to hold Bradley's hand until they got him loaded on the stretcher and hustled him to the hospital with the doctor at his side.

"Doc!" Daniel barked as he rode, carrying Daisy. "You haven't even looked at my daughter—"

But Doc faced him down, grimly determined. "Major, this trooper's life is in danger. Your daughter will recover."

Louisa covered her mouth. Was Bradley dying? Was this the last time she'd ever see him? Then she saw Daniel's face. It was drawn, white. His eyes flashed wild and scared. And it was her fault. She'd taken Daisy out under the guise of wildflower hunting when all she'd wanted was a chance to talk to Bradley. Look what her dishonesty had caused.

Two people's lives were in danger because of her poor judgment. Pretending to be something she wasn't had cost the people she loved most in the world.

Chapter Twenty-One

Daniel took the clay mixture from Private Gundy's hand, barely registering the gentle pat the trooper gave his shoulder as he exited Daisy's bedroom.

"Here, Father, let me do it." Caroline scraped the clay out of his palm and carefully began to reapply it to soothe the red welts that covered her sister. Daniel leaned back in the chair that had magically appeared next to her bed. Upon first hearing Caroline's voice raised across the green, he'd thought the girls were up to their usual antics. He'd wondered where Louisa was, how they'd gotten away from her. But then the tenor of her cries became more clear, and Daniel had mounted the nearest horse and raced to meet her.

Following Caroline's frantic gestures, he quickly reached them. With relief, he saw Louisa kneeling next to Daisy. He knew her first concern would be to get Daisy somewhere safe, just as his was. But somehow everyone from Louisa to Doctor Bowen seemed more worried about Private Willis. And where was Miss Bell now? Instead of looking after her charge, she stayed with that good-for-nothing man. Daniel stared through dull eyes at his baby girl. How could Louisa abandon her responsibility? Had she put his daughter in danger to arrange a secret meeting with the trooper?

Daisy stirred, but without the pained agitation she'd had before.

"How are you, honey?" he asked. Her face was covered with patches of Reno's red clay over her welts, but she had calmed.

"It hurts," she whimpered.

If it would help, he'd send his troops out to find every hornet nest in the territory, pour kerosene on them, and set them aflame.

"You are being so brave," he said. "The bravest soldier I've ever known. Dr. Bowen said it'll stop stinging by tomorrow morning. We've just got to be brave for a little while longer."

Her chin quivered. "Where's Miss Bell? I want her here."

So did he, but she'd abandoned her post. Again.

Before Daniel could answer, Caroline spoke. "Miss Bell is with Private Willis. He saved your life, Daisy, and he's doing poorly now. Worse than you."

"That's enough," Daniel said. "I won't have you making her feel guilty."

"But it's the truth." Caroline's jaw hardened, a sure sign that she believed what she said and wouldn't be hushed.

"Private Willis got caught in the same swarm as Daisy," Daniel said, "by the same dumb luck. He was supposed to be whitewashing the fence, not lollygagging in the wildflowers."

Caroline flung her hair over her shoulder, like she was getting clear for a fight. "He *was* whitewashing the fence. Only after Daisy started screaming did he run right into that cloud of wasps and carry her away. And now he might die for it."

Daisy's weak sobs only fueled Daniel's anger. "We'll talk about this later," he said. "We shouldn't upset your sister." But really he was the one who was getting agitated. What if it were true? What if he owed Private Willis everything? He held a glass to Daisy's mouth. "It's milk," he said. "Should help cool you down."

She only managed a sip before dozing off into another fitful trance.

Unfortunately, any kind of rest was out of Daniel's reach. Why would Private Willis give his life for Daisy? He didn't owe Daniel anything. Probably the boy thought he was impervious to the hornet attack. Maybe he was trying to prove himself. Either way, if it were true, some recognition was called for. As commander of the fort, it was Daniel's duty to check on Private Willis, no matter how badly he wished otherwise. He'd check on the trooper, and while he was at it, he'd remind Louisa of her duty. She wasn't on the fort to sit at the bedside of her secret paramour.

Private Gundy returned to the room with two plates of food. "You might as well eat something," he said. "It don't help no one for you to go hungry."

Caroline took the fork from his hand and started into her bowl of beans and flatbread. No reason to starve yourself if you had an appetite, but Daniel didn't.

After getting Gundy's assurance that he would stay with Daisy and Caroline, Daniel headed downstairs. Stopping to get his hat from his office, he wondered again at Louisa being gone so long. Didn't she feel any obligation to him and Daisy? He thought of Louisa as family, but obviously she didn't consider him that important. And to think he'd been composing sappy love letters to her.

Speaking of the letter—where was it? He scanned his desk, then riffled through the loose papers on the blotter. Had he put it in his pocket? Maybe he'd left it by his bed, although he didn't remember taking it upstairs. His whole world was out of control, and Daniel did not appreciate it.

Tamping down his frustration, he set out for the hospital.

A wagon of firewood was parked next to the kitchen. The troopers who'd been down to the riverbank to collect it were now unloading it and paused in their work to watch him walk by. No greetings, no salutes. They'd heard about Daisy and were uncertain how to respond. But one brave trooper stepped forward.

"Major Adams, we want to say how sorry we are about your daughter. It's good to hear she's going to recover."

"Thank you," he said.

"And we're really torn up about Private Willis. The Mennonites joined us in prayer for him, and some are still at the chapel, praying for him right now. He's too good a man to go that way."

Daniel's steps slowed. While the general sentiment shared by military men was that any death not earned in battle was doubly mourned, he was surprised by their concern. And irritated that he couldn't truthfully find the space in his heart to be worried about Willis, not while Daisy was hurting. But it was wrong of him. Had his love for Louisa prejudiced him against the private? Instead of seeing Bradley Willis as a trooper who needed to learn the discipline of the U.S. Cavalry, Daniel viewed him as a threat. As a rival.

A rival that had perhaps sacrificed his life for Daisy's.

Two sentries scanning the open fields for Cheyenne encroachers jumped to attention as Daniel approached the hospital. One reached around to swing the door open for Daniel as he passed inside, and the orderly on duty motioned him to a room down the hall. The light from the window behind him illuminated the doctor, who was bent over the bed with a stethoscope, listening to his patient's chest. What Daniel could see of the bloated figure between the linen wrappings looked nothing like Private Willis. Daniel only got a glimpse of the trooper's face before he had to look away. The disfigurement was equal to any he'd seen in battle. Eyes swollen shut, nose bulbous, lips cracked and bleeding. Had he done this to himself to save Daisy?

Daniel couldn't move. He'd thought Daisy's case was terrible until he saw this. Daisy could express her pain. Private Willis couldn't even communicate. Could barely breathe. If it turned just a tad worse . . .

Doc didn't acknowledge him, continuing to listen to Willis's labored breathing. Only then did Daniel see Louisa sitting in the corner. Red splotched her eyes. She held a yellow cavalry neckerchief to her face to mop her tears.

Had it been any other situation, he would have been moved by her distress. Daniel stood still, unsure of what to do. Manufacturing concern when he felt none was beneath him, and yet he realized he *should* care. Something was wrong with him if he didn't.

Daniel's chest stretched in a long, painful breath. When had he grown so cold to the sufferings of others? Had the duties that kept him from his family also kept him from feeling? Until Miss Bell had come, he'd gone about his day-to-day work, not allowing himself to feel anything beyond frustration at failure or satisfaction at achievement. His troopers were only pawns arranged for the best results.

With Miss Bell, the gentler side of his nature had awakened, but so had the ugly. He might be able to love again, but he could also hurt. And Miss Bell was testing him on both counts.

Shame on him. How many times had Daniel mourned the fact that a trooper had died alone? Louisa hadn't left Willis to his fate. She'd been sitting here with this hero, and no matter how Daniel's vanity protested, he owed her for that.

He sat on the bench next to her. Her shoulders shook as she wept. His anger seeped away, along with his hope. He'd been a fool to think he could stand between her and the man she so obviously loved. Putting away his own feelings, he took her hand. Louisa clung to it.

"I should've protected Daisy better," she sobbed. "I shouldn't have taken her outside."

His hand tightened around hers. "She's always run around here free as a bird. This could've happened at any time."

She took a long, shaky breath. "Logically, I know that's true. It's just my emotions getting the better of me."

"She's going to be fine, thanks to you." Leaning on his incredible military discipline, he added, "And thanks to Private Willis."

At that, Louisa dissolved into tears again. She fell against his arm and sobbed into his sleeve. Daniel lifted his arm to pull her against himself. Doc could think what he wanted. If Willis ever recovered, it would be clear enough that Daniel was only comforting the distraught sweetheart of the injured man. No one could accuse him of behaving improperly.

Slowly, as she began to regain her composure, he could feel his heart settling as well. She was in love with another. He'd thought it was only a passing fancy, but he had to face the truth. He could admire her, he could appreciate her, but he could never love her the way he wanted to. She wouldn't allow it.

She sniffled and looked up at him with those bottomless blue eyes. "Private Willis is a good man, as are you. It does me good to hear that you approve."

His arm felt disembodied, but he imagined that he'd squeezed her shoulder in affirmation. "I owe him a great deal for his sacrifice. Who could've known the price would be so high—"

"He did." She smiled fondly at the miserable mass of flesh on the bed. "He knew that a hornet sting could be deadly for him, but he did it anyway."

And how would she know that? But then Daniel remembered

her saying the same thing about her brother. Perhaps the two of them had discussed the similarity . . . while hiding outside his kitchen after dark. He forced away the unkind thought and tried to focus again on the situation at hand.

Seeing that Louisa had composed herself, he rose and moved to the cot where Willis lay. "Can he hear me?" he asked the doctor.

"I don't know how much he'll understand. His pulse is weak, but if you have something to say, now's the time."

Daniel had sent up many a prayer for Daisy already, but to his shame, he hadn't entreated God on Bradley Willis's behalf. And if anyone needed prayer right now, it was Bradley Willis.

Daniel dropped to his knees next to the cot. Taking Bradley's swollen, wrapped hand, he worked to put his heart in the correct place before speaking.

"Private—Bradley. This is Major Adams. You saved my daughter's life today. I don't know if you thought your actions through or if it was just an impulse, but she's going to be fine because of your sacrifice. No matter what else you do with your life—or whatever you've done in the past—saving a life is something holy, something that reflects the heart of God."

It was hard to reconcile this motionless body with the impulsive troublemaker who had so challenged him, but the longer Daniel thought about it, the more he realized that saving Daisy was just the reckless, impulsive thing that men like Private Willis specialized in. He should thank God that Bradley wasn't more careful.

"I don't know where you stand with God"—although Daniel in his more judgmental moments didn't give Bradley much hope—"and it feels wrong for me to sit here and talk to you about your sins when you just saved my daughter's life, but I'd be remiss if I didn't remind you that God is near. He waits to hear from you. He made you and loves you and offers you the most precious gift—Himself, in the form of His Son, Jesus."

There was no response, but what did Daniel expect? Maybe talking about the hereafter wasn't the best topic at a bedside, but it was often the last chance when more logical opportunities had been neglected.

"Foremost, I'm praying for your speedy recovery," he said. "And as soon as you get back on your feet, if it's alright, I want to bring Daisy over so she can say thank you. You saved the life of my little girl, and we're forever grateful."

Daniel's throat tightened as his eyes drifted toward Louisa. He'd have to be grateful for what Willis had given him, and not think of what he was taking away.

❧❦❧

What a bitter victory. Bradley finally had Major Adams's regard, but he might not live to benefit from it. Louisa believed there was a God, but she didn't want to believe He'd be so cruel.

Daniel and the doctor talked over the medical supplies that they had available and the possibility of ordering something more specific for the outpost once shipments resumed, but Louisa lost interest. Instead, Daniel's words still rang in her ears. God didn't care what you'd done, or who you'd been? It wasn't too late to become His child? That didn't fit with what she'd experienced. She couldn't understand how she still had tears left to cry, but they were trickling down her cheeks as Daniel turned toward the door.

Seeing her, he stopped. "Daisy is asking for you, but stay here as long as you feel you need to."

How could he be so generous when she'd gone against his wishes to visit Bradley? "Staying here must seem unladylike," she said. "I hope you'll forgive me."

He shot a glance at the doctor, who was busy measuring the contents from a green-tinted bottle. Leaning closer, Daniel whispered, "I myself have been hurt and received attentions that some might deem unladylike, but that were most appreciated. You have a tender heart. There's no shame in that."

Her heart almost burst. If he couldn't read the adoration in her eyes, he was blind. She thought she saw recognition there, but then he stiffened and, with a formal bow, made his departure.

But Louisa had questions.

"Wait." She followed him out to the empty hallway, feeling nearly suffocated by the afternoon heat and the weight of her questions. "What you said to Private Willis about God, did you say that just because he's hurt, or because he saved Daisy?"

Daniel paused, his eyes suddenly very focused. Had she said something wrong? Was what he said to Bradley not meant for her?

"What do you mean, Louisa? God has loved Private Willis from the beginning. He didn't earn God's love when he saved Daisy."

"I hope you're right," Louisa said. "But what if you're wrong? Maybe God isn't there for him. Maybe he has to find his way alone."

And the thought of her brother teetering on death's door alone, without any comfort, terrified her.

❧⁂❧

For the second time that day, Daniel felt like he'd had the wind knocked out of him.

Louisa didn't know Christ.

The revelation stunned him. He'd wondered about her reticence and thought it might be that as a Mennonite she kept her religion private. But that didn't explain her reluctance to attend the chapel services or her nervousness when he mentioned the missionaries at the agency. And now these questions. Something was missing.

"Louisa, God loves each of us, even though we're all flawed."

She twisted her hands in agitation. "But someone tainted—like Private Willis, for example—they can't come near God. God wouldn't allow it. He's too holy."

Daniel nodded, proud that she continued to ask, even when she was afraid of the answers.

"And that's where Jesus comes in. He lived here on Earth among us, but He lived without ever sinning. He did what we couldn't do, and then He paid our penalty so that we are forgiven. All we have to do is confess our sins to God and ask Him to accept Jesus's sacrifice on our behalf."

"I'm confused." Louisa twisted the yellow neckerchief. "I mean, I know all of this, of course, but I was just surprised you said it to Private Willis. That's all."

That couldn't be all. Her confusion was sincere, as were her questions. Just another inconsistency in her story, but this wasn't the time to call her out.

"We've been through a lot today, but having the peace, the assurance—"

"I have that." Her words were abrupt. "Thank you for answering my questions, but you've said enough." Her downcast eyes didn't meet his.

Daniel felt inadequate. Had he failed to say the right words? He prayed that she would give him another chance. If she'd allow it, they could talk about important matters, matters that reached to the heart of who they were and what God had in store for them.

"Let's go home," he said. "It's getting late—"

"You said I could stay. Daisy has you and Caroline, but Bradley doesn't have anyone."

Daniel felt his strength sapped. Talking about their future together was not going to happen. As far as Louisa was concerned, her future resided with the deathly ill young man in the room behind them. Not with Daniel.

Chapter Twenty-Two

She'd worn her new dress today, sewn from the material she'd purchased at Darlington. Bradley had felt good enough to notice it when she went to visit him, but Daniel hadn't mentioned it at all.

Now, in the cavernous second story of the commissary building, Louisa played the piano by rote as the girls practiced, and tried not to look as melancholy as she felt. Every day they ducked between buildings, heard scattered gunfire in the distance, saw mounted figures on the crest of the far-off horizon, but nothing came of it. The refugees prayed anxiously, the troopers were excitable, and the waiting put a strain on a person.

Daniel was right to give the girls this task. They needed a diversion. So did Louisa, because without a doubt, Daniel was avoiding her. Now that Daisy was tearing around the fort at full strength again, Louisa had hoped he would forgive her. And maybe he had, but the sight of her in the parlor was enough to send him darting up the stairs to his room for the whole of the evening. Certainly, he'd do more of that religious talk if she gave him the opportunity, but even the thought of the decision before her was terrifying.

Confess everything? She couldn't come to God and ask His forgiveness while still lying to Daniel. Even Louisa understood that. Confessing to Daniel, telling him the truth, would mean losing him, if she hadn't lost him already. How could she decide between a God she didn't know and a man she loved?

But she couldn't say no to God if He was as loving as Daniel said. Perhaps her one terrible experience at a church hadn't been because of God. Perhaps the people who claimed Him could be mean and hateful at times, just like everyone else. Perhaps they were loved by God, but frustrated Him at the same time—like Bradley and his wild ways embarrassed her.

From her intentionally limited contact with the agency women, Louisa hadn't experienced the censure she'd expected. Certainly, they didn't recognize her for what she was, but regardless, they accepted her. Comparing their conversation to that of the Cat-Eye Saloon girls was like comparing the purest spring water to swill. No petty bickering, no conniving manipulations. Whatever differences and conflicts did arise were usually brushed aside quickly and neatly.

If God could turn her into a woman like that, Louisa would volunteer immediately, but there was a complication. God had expectations, and Louisa couldn't take the first step. The thought filled her with dread. So did the thought of Daniel hearing the truth about her. But maybe it didn't matter. Daniel had kept her at a distance since Daisy's accident. He'd even discontinued the chess matches that she'd enjoyed so much. When he'd been out one day, she'd set up the pieces and made the first move, but in three nights he'd yet to respond.

Louisa was hurt. He had every right to censure her for taking Daisy into a dangerous area. He claimed it wasn't Louisa's fault, but perhaps he didn't recognize his resentment.

The song ended.

"You weren't even listening." Daisy's welt-covered arms were crossed in front of her chest, and her foot was tapping. "You aren't paying attention."

And the general should arrive in two days. They were running out of time. No matter what, Louisa couldn't embarrass Daniel in front of General Sheridan.

"Sorry, I was woolgathering. Let's do it again." She placed her fingers on the beginning chords. "On three . . ."

They practiced for around an hour. Louisa stopped the girls to improve certain phrases, to get the timing right, and most importantly to get the accent right on the Italian songs. She hoped it was right, anyway. All she knew was what she'd heard from Signora Giovanna when she sang, but then she'd found out that Ginny was from New Jersey and had faked her accent, so Louisa had no idea if her words were right or not.

"Wait." Caroline rushed to the piano and covered the keys. "We haven't heard your piece yet."

"No one needs to hear me. I'm only the governess. Now move your hands."

Caroline refused. "You said that it was proper for us to sing, so why wouldn't you? Do you think we're less ladylike than you are?"

If the poor innocent dears only knew. "You are performing to bring your father credit. There's no reason for me to perform. The general would have no interest in a governess's ability."

Boots sounded on the staircase. Someone was coming up. Louisa arranged her hair in expectation. At first glance, she was disappointed to see it was only Lieutenant Jack, but the major following him up the stairs made her heart skip a beat.

"Major Adams and I came to check on you ladies." Jack's grin showed that he was obviously unconcerned with his superior's unease.

When Louisa turned to Daniel, he spoke as if compelled by duty. "Do you need anything for the concert?"

After what had happened to Daisy, Louisa didn't deserve his regard, but the change in his attitude hurt. She kept her brave face in place, even if it was only a mask. If nothing else, she'd found work that she loved. If not here, then maybe she could leave the fort with a good recommendation. She'd have to learn to be content with that. "We have the music and the instruments," she said. "Are there decorations?"

"For the Commander of the U.S. Army? This room will be decorated, even in an uprising. Proper respect must be shown."

"And what news of Agent Dyer and his wife? Has their hiding place been discovered?"

Daniel shook his head. "No, they telephoned this morning. No one knows they are there. The Cheyenne have helped themselves to the storerooms, but the Dyers haven't been discovered."

Caroline and Daisy had taken to dancing with invisible partners in the spacious room. The opportunity to speak to Daniel and Jack together couldn't be ignored. Ever since his accident, Bradley had been after her to do the right thing and tell Daniel about her discovery. Hopefully Lieutenant Hennessey would temper Daniel's response.

"Major Adams, there is an issue I need to bring to your attention. With everything going on of late, I didn't want to bother you with it, so maybe you'd prefer Lieutenant Hennessey to assist—"

"I'm at your service," Daniel interrupted. Jack raised his eyebrows at Daniel's curt tone.

Louisa opened her portfolio of music and withdrew the missive. "Several days ago, I found this letter near your front door. Someone had slid it past the threshold. I can only surmise that it was intended for Caroline."

Daniel held the open letter before him. Louisa watched in wonder as his cheeks seemed to flame in sudden color.

Jack leaned over his shoulder. One glance at the letter, and his eyes widened. "That's your hand—"

Thud! The heel of the major's boot landed squarely on Jack's toes. "And that's your foot," Daniel said.

Jack's mouth went tight. "I'm not one for insubordination, but that was uncalled for."

"Did you read this?" Daniel asked her, ignoring Jack.

"It wasn't addressed to anyone, so I didn't know not to. Whoever left a love letter right outside your office was behaving extremely recklessly."

Jack, still fuming, took a wide step away from Daniel before saying, "A love letter? That is concerning. What exactly does it say?"

"Jack," Daniel growled.

But now at a safe distance, Jack couldn't be reined in. "Major Adams, Miss Bell wants us to identify the author of the letter. Of course I need to know what it says."

"It was a very well-written letter," said Louisa, "speaking of longing and affection, but not appropriate if the addressee is a young lady of Caroline's age."

"What if the addressee wasn't Caroline?" Jack's eyes twinkled.

"Who else could it possibly be?" Louisa asked. "I just thought diligence should be paid if someone is so besotted. While I sympathize with the desperate man, it's my duty to protect your daughters."

"A besotted, desperate letter?" Jack whistled. "Hand it over, Daniel. I really should investigate this."

Daniel shoved the letter into his pocket. "No need. I'll deal with it."

"I'm happy to start an inquiry. We'll make a list of all the suspects—"

"It's not Private Willis," Louisa said. Better to clear his name at once. "I showed him the letter, and he's the one who encouraged me to show it to you."

If Daniel looked embarrassed before, now he looked ill. "You showed this letter to Private Willis?"

Louisa squirmed. Even Jack's smile disappeared. She picked at a button on her new dress—the new dress he hadn't noticed yet. "I knew it wasn't him, but I wanted to make sure. He told me that I had nothing to worry about—Caroline was safe—but that you would be interested in knowing that I'd found it."

Daniel's face was blank. "Excuse me," he said. He spun on his heel toward the stairs, leaving Louisa confused.

Jack tipped his hat. "Nice dress," he said with a smile.

"Nice dress," Daniel called from the stairs. "Of course I noticed."

Jack winked at her, then ran to catch up with the befuddled major.

⁓ᴈ)(ᴈ⁓

Daniel halted in his march to the hospital to pull the letter out of his pocket and scan it. It was just as bad as he remembered. Louisa had read these words? And so had Private Willis. He groaned. He was doing his best, but he couldn't change how he felt for a woman just because she decided she loved someone else. Shoving the letter back in his pocket, he stomped on, ignoring Jack's attempt to catch up with him.

He'd told himself that he wouldn't be moved by her beauty. That from now on he was only concerned with her soul and her work with his girls. But seeing his true feelings written by his own hand only intensified his loss.

He missed Louisa's company. He missed her conversation, her compassion, her goodness. She might be impulsive and free-spirited, but she was faithful in the ways that mattered. Yes, she was faithful—just not to him.

That didn't diminish her good qualities, but Daniel was practical. He wouldn't allow himself to pine after a woman who had her sights set elsewhere. He'd only be getting in her way.

There had to be a reason she'd love a rogue like Bradley Willis. His rescue of Daisy showed that he too had qualities that Daniel had failed to recognize at first, and it was his duty to correct that oversight. He owed it to Willis to help him succeed. Perhaps the young man lacked fatherly guidance. Perhaps he needed a role model. Had Daniel already been too hard on him and missed that opportunity? He hoped not. And he mustn't be an obstacle to Louisa, either, as she learned more about God. She had to feel comfortable coming to him with her questions, no matter how hard it was for him to hide his regard.

"Is there anything you want to talk about?" Jack was a little out of breath but determined. "Usually when someone takes pen to paper with no intention of ever sending the letter, it means they want someone to listen."

"An immature and ridiculous thing for me to do."

"But honest. I'm sure whatever you wrote was honest."

Daniel wanted to walk away, but Jack had always been transparent about his own heartbreak with Miss Walker, and Daniel had never thought less of him for it.

"She doesn't love me and likely never will. I don't know when it happened, but she's in love with another." As hard as it was to say, he felt better for saying it.

"Here at the fort?" Jack rolled his eyes. "How would she have even met someone here?"

"I can't get involved. She works for me, and the man is under my command. I have no right to interfere."

"So you'll go moping around, pining for your lady? Let me know if you need help with that. I'm quite the expert."

"Thanks for the offer. Now go get a report from Ben Clark and see when we can expect the reinforcements."

"Yes, sir," Jack said. "But before I go, how is Private Willis faring?"

Daniel choked down his annoyance. Jack's shots always seemed to hit the mark. "I'm going to check on him now." Because he should. It was the right thing to do.

"I've been worried about him. We were so shorthanded that he hasn't had many visitors, but Miss Bell was good to look in on him."

Daniel was itching to whack Jack upside the head, but it was unnecessary. Jack slapped his own forehead. "Private Willis? Is he your rival? Why in the world would she prefer a private to an officer? I mean, he is a good horseman, I'll give him that. And you won't find a better shot, but—"

"I'm a better shot." Daniel might have had his heart broken, but his pride was still intact.

"Yes, sir, Major Adams. Absolutely, you're a better shot. Maybe you should challenge him to a contest to impress your lady, after the manner of Robin Hood. Unfortunately, poor underdog Willis has more in common with Robin Hood, and that'd make you the Sheriff of Nottingham, so a contest might not work out. And then there's the fact that he's in the hospital because he saved your daughter's life. Now, that kind of heroic act is nearly impossible to overcome. Ladies love a self-sacrificing hero on death's door." He shrugged. "Come to think of it, you might not have the strongest case, after all."

Sometimes, in his eagerness to come to a logical conclusion, Jack forgot to consider the delicate feelings of his superior.

Daniel filled his lungs with a long draw of the sultry summer air. "Forget about Miss Bell and Private Willis. Forget I said anything. And most of all, forget about that letter."

Jack saluted, one eyebrow cocked high and hidden beneath the band of his hat.

With nothing to do besides his duty, Daniel strode the short distance to the hospital.

He found Willis sitting on the edge of his bed in his undershirt and striped trousers. His pant legs stopped mid-calf, exposing bare feet. He flicked another playing card toward a clean spittoon—at least Daniel assumed it was clean—and grunted when the card missed and fell to join the other dozen cards on the floor.

At Daniel's arrival, Willis took a second glance before leaping to his feet in a sharp salute.

"At ease," Daniel said. While the young man hadn't quite regained his complexion, his movements were that of a healthy trooper. "Where's Doc?"

Willis swung his arm down and hitched up his britches. "He's rejoined his unit on patrol. He said I didn't need him anymore. I'm just waiting for permission to get back to work."

Doc hadn't released him? "Permission from whom?"

"From you, of course. Can I sit?" At Daniel's nod, Willis plopped on his bed and fished beneath the rumpled blanket until he located two socks, then began to pull them on. "I've been pacing this cell—room, but it feels like a cell—until I'm about to go mad. We're patrolling again, aren't we? I can hear the troopers ride past, and I'm flat-out itching to get into the saddle." He located his boots beneath the bed. "Another day in here and I'll go loco. So glad—"

He spoke just like he rode—fast and furious—but hitting all the marks. Maybe he wasn't intentionally a troublemaker. Maybe he was just high-strung. A lot of troopers on base would enjoy a few days' sick leave. It did Daniel's heart good to hear a trooper excited about getting back to his job.

Maybe Willis would be good for Louisa. Maybe he'd make something of himself, after all.

Daniel looked again at the young man. There was something

he needed to tell him. Something he owed him. But first he had a question.

"You knew, didn't you?" Daniel asked. "You knew that hornet stings could be deadly for you."

Bradley's head popped up. "I joined the cavalry to help my country. To make a difference. If saving a child's life doesn't fit that description, then I don't know what does."

Daniel felt some of the muscles in his neck unknotting. Maybe he could do this.

"I know your secret." Daniel pulled a chair over and sat across from Bradley, whose eyes had narrowed in suspicion. "I know you have been secretly meeting with Miss Bell, and that's what I want to talk to you about."

"Go on."

Daniel had never seen the private so wary. His fear did him credit.

"Such meetings will not be tolerated. Miss Bell is a lady, and were that activity brought to light, it would expose her to the harshest criticism. You are a young, reckless man. Many young reckless men sow their wild oats, then travel on to the next assignment, but Miss Bell will be held to a higher standard. Her reputation and her livelihood are in jeopardy."

"It was her idea," Bradley said.

And just like that, Daniel wanted to throttle him, but he mastered the urge and continued.

"I heartily advise you not to interrupt me again," he warned. "I will tell you when you can speak." He stood and paced the room. "What I came to say is that, while I disapprove of the manner in which you and Miss Bell are meeting, if you wish to court her properly, then, considering the grave danger you placed yourself in on behalf of my daughter—I can hardly disapprove."

Daniel found himself leaning against Bowen's medicine cabinet, the various jars and bottles blurring before his eyes. His chest was tight, but he forced out the final words.

"If you want to court Miss Bell, you have my blessing."

Instead of giving his thanks, as Daniel expected, Private Willis burst into laughter.

Chapter Twenty-Three

No one had ever accused Major Adams of lacking courage, and this proved it. Here he was, about to die of misery, and yet he was carrying through with his mission like a good soldier. Bradley was impressed, and it was in his power to end his commander's misery.

"Major," Bradley entreated, choking off his laughter. When there was no answer, he stood and went to his side. "Major Adams?"

The major stood before the folders of powders and curatives, bracing himself against the cabinet like the earth was shaking. "I've said what I came to say. From this point, if you want to see Miss Bell, apply to me first, and I'll arrange proper—"

"Major—"

"Are you interrupting me again, trooper?" Major Adams's chest puffed out as he turned to face Bradley.

"It's just that—"

"I'm trying to do you a good turn. If you had any sense at all—"

"That's what I'm trying to tell you. While I do want to see Miss Bell—"

"Keep talking, and that offer is in jeopardy."

Bradley paused. Major Adams had recovered from his agony. In fact, he was about to be raging mad if Bradley didn't tread carefully. He covered his mouth with his hand, showing his determination to wait until Adams was finished.

But the major had had enough.

"You have one chance to get this right. Don't make me regret my offer."

Expelling his news in one breath, Bradley blurted, "Louisa is my sister."

The effect was instantaneous. Major Adams sagged like his knees might give out and blinked like a fish tossed up on the riverbank. Now Bradley could smile unafraid.

"Louisa Bell is my sister. That's why she's been wanting to see me. I had no idea she was coming here. Nearly tripped over my own feet when I saw her."

Saw her dressed like a governess, he wanted to add, but he wouldn't tell the major all her secrets.

"So she—she already knew you?"

"As brothers and sisters are wont to do, yes."

"Then there was nothing untoward in her desire to speak privately with you?" Major Adams frowned. "But why didn't she tell me? Why hide it?"

Bradley bounced on his toes, never having had this much fun in his short, hectic life. "Would you brag about having a brother like me, sir?"

Major Adams cut him a sharp look, then with a shrug seemed to accept his excuse . . . which was fairly insulting, if Bradley thought about it, but he didn't spend much time dwelling on offenses. He'd rather be thinking of how to tweak the nose of his major. All in good fun, of course.

"You are her brother." Major Adams kept glancing out the window toward his house. "She mentioned she had a brother who was sensitive to bee stings."

"That would be me. And that's probably all she told you. But then again, I doubt you and her have had much time to converse, seeing as how she's only the governess and so busy teaching your daughters."

"Yes . . ." His voice trailed off.

"I mean, I doubt you've given her a second thought. Just another recruit at your command. No different than the rest of us poor grunts."

"No . . ."

Major Adams was mesmerized, still staring at his house. Bradley might as well take advantage of the situation.

"And then there's that fence that still needs painting. I think Private Stephenson would appreciate that duty. All you have to do is say the word—"

And just like that, Major Adams snapped to his senses. "As far as the fence goes, we don't want to expose you needlessly to the same hornet nest. You can trade duties with someone cleaning the dining hall. That floor needs scrubbing by someone who can do it with strength and vigor. I think you're just the person." He turned on his heel to leave.

"Excuse me, Major."

Major Adams hadn't been able to stand just a minute earlier. Now he could hardly keep from running out the door. "What is it, Private?"

"Please don't tell Louisa that I told you. She didn't want to hurt her standing in your eyes."

The major dropped his hat on his head and with a tap set it firm. "Who gives the orders around here?" he asked, then marched out the door.

If Bradley had had an advantage, he hadn't kept it long. That was how life went. Or his, anyway.

"And I enjoyed your letter," he said, laughing, but only when he was sure that Major Adams had left the building.

~≈)(≈~

The house was quiet, which to Louisa was not a good sign. Leaving the commissary, the girls had taken off without her. She'd chased them across the fort, but since they weren't opposed to lifting their skirts and running, she'd fallen behind. Now, standing in the doorway of the house, it felt as still as a tomb. Where were they hiding? A quick look in Daniel's office told her that he wasn't home, either.

Louisa was flummoxed. She'd come to Fort Reno to look for a job and to bring her brother into the major's good graces. Now he'd been restored, and she felt like she was banished. Common sense told her that she was free to make her excuses and leave. Free to go west and try her luck with the new skills she'd learned here, but despite the danger, she couldn't bear the thought of leaving. What would Caroline and Daisy do without her? Who would guide Caroline through the next years, when the most important decisions of a woman's life were made? Who would keep an eye on Daisy and not be critical of her high spirits?

And there was an even more important development. Louisa's prejudices against God were weakening. She had to give Him a chance, but she feared leaving this safe haven. Could she afford her new Christian virtues when she was on her own? Could she afford them here, if it meant unburdening herself of her lies?

Louisa tossed her portfolio of musical scores on the dining room table as she passed through to the kitchen. Where were the girls? So help her, if they got hurt again, she'd kill them. The lace curtains fluttered in the empty kitchen. A bowl of snapped green beans sat on the table. A crumpled dishrag had drawn a fly that she shooed away.

A board creaked. Louisa froze. Upstairs—in her room, if she wasn't mistaken. Her lips tightened. What mischief were they up to now? She crept up the stairs. Her smart chocolate lace-up boots weren't designed for stalking quietly, but the girls weren't listening for her. Instead they were oohing and ahhing like they were watching fireworks at the Independence Day celebration.

Standing outside her bedroom door, she could hear them clearly.

"Look at this, Caroline. Have you ever seen anything this lovely?"

"No. Not until I found . . . this."

Daisy squealed. "Why doesn't she wear these clothes? She always dressed so ugly."

"I don't know," Caroline replied, her voice nearly drowned by a swish of taffeta. "I would definitely have worn this."

Louisa hit the door so hard that it flew open and bounced against the wall. Both girls jumped. Caroline clutched Louisa's blue silk gown to her chest. Daisy stumbled backward and tripped over an errant crinoline. Her hind end thudded on the floor.

"You're as quiet as an Indian," she said.

"And you're as guilty as sin," Louisa replied. "Get out of my room."

She turned to Caroline, who wasn't moving. "Have these clothes been hiding in here all this time?" She held the blue silk beneath her chin. "How in the world could you forget them?"

Because Louisa had been trying to forget that part of her life existed for weeks. "Those are my private belongings." She caught the blue dress's skirt, but Caroline didn't let go, and they stood with it suspended between them. "You have no right."

"Louisa?" It was Daniel. He was in the house.

Carolina's eyebrow arched. *Louisa?* she mouthed.

"Put those gowns away," Louisa rasped angrily. Major Adams had distanced himself from her already. How cold of a reception would she get if he saw these highly suggestive gowns?

There was a mad flurry of fabric, lace, and feathers as the costumes were shoved into the wardrobe.

"Don't tell Pa we're in here," Daisy begged. At the sound of his footsteps in the hallway, she dove beneath the bed. Caroline followed as Louisa closed the door of the wardrobe and kicked the remaining pieces beneath the bed to join the girls.

"Louisa?" The doorway was filled with the blue of his cavalry uniform. The only pieces missing were his hat and his saber. He rested his forearm on the doorframe. "I'm glad I found you."

The July heat had dampened his hair, leaving it curly and sticking to his forehead. Louisa clasped her hands behind her back and moved away from the incriminating wardrobe. He'd just left her an hour ago. Had he thought of something else to say?

"Yes, sir. Did you need me?"

"I do."

His honeyed eyes were captivating. His voice low and rich. The two words sent chills up her back. What had happened? Something significant, for his manner had changed. He extended his hand. What was she to do but offer her own? He took it, slowly and deliberately raising it, and when he paused, holding it just beneath his lips, Louisa nearly came undone. She was on the brink of ordering him to kiss it and get it over with, when he did just that. His warm mouth caressed her knuckle, and she felt a rush of exhilaration. Such a small gesture, but it affected her to the core.

He released her hand, and she could have sworn she heard a giggle from beneath the bed. With a stomp of her heel, she silenced their hidden audience and snapped her senses to attention.

"I came to tell you that I spoke to your . . . patient today."

Louisa felt mildly disappointed. Her brother had come out of this mess smelling like a daisy—no offense to Daisy—while she'd been the one judged. Cradling her recently kissed hand, she asked, "How is he?"

"I've arranged for him to receive a special commendation for bravery, and he's already back on duty."

What could be better news? Readjusting her expectations, Louisa responded with practiced grace. "How wonderful."

"I thought that would please you," he said. "And in return for the good news, I have a favor to ask."

The silence was deafening. Obviously Caroline and Daisy were hanging on every word, but now Louisa was concerned they'd stopped breathing.

Daniel ran his hand through his hair, a gesture he rarely made while in uniform. "I don't mean to tie this favor to anything relating to Private Willis. It would be ungallant of me to expect something in return, because why should you care if I promote him or give him special honor? I just thought the good news might make you look more favorably toward any request at the moment."

He was rambling. If they were at the chess table, Louisa would suspect that he saw a trap ahead and didn't know how to avoid it.

"What I'd like to ask is if you'd allow me to escort you to dinner tomorrow night. Not here at the house, and not at the mess hall—that would be a disaster. Instead, I will take you to Lieutenant Hennessey's next door. With Darlington evacuated, there aren't any restaurants around in which to court a lady, and it seems lazy to stay here at home if I want to give you a special evening."

"I'm sorry," Louisa gasped, "did you just say *court*?"

He squared his shoulders. "Yes, I did. Court—exactly what a widower with a fine position in the U.S. Cavalry might do with a beautiful woman whom he regards highly. And it shouldn't be a huge inconvenience. I've already arranged it all with Jack. We'd just go next door—"

He turned his back to point in the direction of the lieutenant's house. There was a sudden whisking noise, a puff of air against Louisa's arm, and scuffling from the floor behind her.

When he and Louisa both turned, the blue gown lay on the bed.

Louisa wanted to run away.

Daniel stepped inside the room, his eyes filled with wonder. "Has that been there this whole time?" Reverently, he reached out and brushed his fingertips against the blue silk. "It's perfect for tomorrow evening," he said. "I can't wait to see you in it." He dipped his chin in a ghost of a bow and added a single word that would cause Louisa no end of trouble from the girls beneath the bed. "Again."

～❦～

Bradley Willis was Miss Bell's brother—not her friend, not her beau. Daniel would have danced a jig if he hadn't been in the middle of small arms practice with his men. His thumb found the hammer. He pulled it down and cocked it, sighted along the barrel, and then squeezed the trigger. The gun barely jumped in his trained hand. He didn't have to wait for the smoke to clear before squeezing off a few more rounds. He knew where the target was, and it didn't take but a moment for one of the troopers to check it and holler back the results.

Daniel coolly holstered his pistol—*Bradley Willis is her brother!*—before repeating the steps for the troopers who were just learning how to shoot. Here was another area in which Bradley Willis would be an asset. And it was to his credit that he had a sister as refined as Louisa, too. Hadn't Louisa mentioned being an orphan? That accounted for Bradley's lack of discipline, but with a few years' maturity, just think of all he could accomplish.

And no, Daniel didn't think it at all hypocritical that he

now esteemed someone he'd despised earlier. In fact, he was relieved to be able to find value in the private. He hated being completely negative about anyone.

He stayed at the shooting range long enough to see everyone perform once. He made corrections where needed but knew that his officers would continue to enforce whatever orders he gave even after he was gone. Getting on his horse, he decided to ride the perimeter. The whitewashing had been completed while Willis was recuperating. The stable had a healthy number of remounts, which would be needed by the reinforcements when they arrived after their long journey. At the armory, the gun powder was dry and stored correctly. The supplies were ready, should General Sheridan instigate a counteraction against the threatening tribe. The agency families had settled into their temporary quarters. It was nice to hear the voices of women and children at the fort again. He hoped the new officers being stationed with them would bring some families as well.

Before he could consult the quartermaster about their supplies, a bugle sounded. Daniel turned his horse toward the coming messenger, who rode with a plume of dust behind him. Jack appeared from the adjutant's office, having heard the signal.

The sergeant saluted. "Four companies of the Fourth Cavalry are arriving. They're making the river crossing now."

"Have they encountered any trouble?"

"No, sir. They are a fearsome sight assembled. General Sheridan and General Miles should arrive shortly after with the infantry."

"Excellent news, Sergeant. Our displaced guests will be glad to hear that they will soon be going home. Report in at the office. Tell them to prepare for the Fourth's arrival."

The trooper, anxious to spread his news, rode off, leaving Jack with Daniel.

"While I'm glad for the reprieve, it's bad timing for you," Jack said. "I hope Miss Bell will be gracious enough to reschedule after General Sheridan's visit has ended."

"Nonsense," Daniel said. "I'll greet the troops, introduce them to my best lieutenant, and he can direct them to their barracks while I enjoy my dinner. It cannot wait."

"I have to host eight hundred sweaty, dusty men while you entertain a beautiful woman in my dining room? I should file a grievance."

Daniel laughed. "Don't worry, Jack. Someday I'll repay the favor. You just wait."

Chapter Twenty-Four

"Oh, Pa will think you look so beautiful." Daisy danced in front of the door to Louisa's room. Since the girls had heard their father's request the night before, Louisa had been forced to wear her favorite dress, no matter how out of place it looked at the isolated outpost. But before she'd donned it, she'd spent hours with it and the sewing machine, adjusting the neckline and weeding out the frills and lace until it looked more suitable for her station.

"How could she not look beautiful?" Caroline said. "Just look at that gown."

Maybe she should have done more weeding. But if Louisa detected a hint of envy in Caroline's tone, she wasn't bothered. It was the healthy response of a young lady who had never been to a dressmaker in her life. Even the new gown Louisa had sewn for her didn't compare.

"Your father wouldn't allow you to wear this gown," Louisa said. "A young, pretty girl like you doesn't need finery to catch a young man's attention. Only someone older like me . . ."

She didn't need to finish her sentence. Caroline rolled her eyes, but her smile told Louisa that she believed her. Louisa twisted another lock of hair and pinned it into place. She studied herself in the mirror. If she were at the Cat-Eye, she'd reach for a pot of rouge to complete the look, but she was surprised to find that she didn't need it. Somehow the thought of Daniel asking her to spend special time with him brought color to her cheeks.

What was she doing? Someday soon she had to tell Daniel the truth. No longer would her conscience allow her to live a lie. She didn't know everything that God expected from her, but this was a sin she had to account for before she could be settled. She had to give Daniel up. But maybe not yet.

"Look at her," Daisy fake-whispered to her sister. "She's thinking of Pa."

Louisa saw her own thick lashes flutter in shock before she could turn away to answer. Unable to deny it, she instead took a pillow off her bed and, much to Daisy's delight, began to pummel her with it.

Daisy shrieked, rolled off the bed, and scurried beneath the springs.

"Be careful, Miss Bell," Caroline said. "You don't want to muss your hair."

No, she didn't. She stood and smoothed her hands over her skirt, feeling more confident in her modified performance clothes. This Louisa knew what she was about. This Louisa awed her audiences with her talent. This Louisa didn't hesitate before answering a question from a ten-year-old. And she wouldn't cower, even before a major as majorish as Major Adams.

There was a knock downstairs at the front door.

"Who's that?" Daisy asked. "Do you think it's Frisco Smith?"

Caroline flew out the door. After pinning a rose in her hair, Louisa followed.

"Major Adams?" Evidently Private Gundy had opened the door before Caroline reached it. "What are you doing, knocking on your own door?"

Louisa stopped at the top of the stairs. She shouldn't eavesdrop, but somehow she knew his answer involved her.

"I'm calling on Miss Bell. Is she receiving visitors?"

Louisa could only imagine the old private's expression. She heard his uneven tread thumping away toward the kitchen. He clearly had no answer for such a ridiculous statement.

"Pa, you're being silly," Daisy said. "You live here. You don't need to knock."

"When a gentleman calls on a lady, he doesn't just walk into her house. He shows her respect and waits to be asked inside."

Louisa felt warm and toasty. What would it have been like to have had a father like Daniel who demonstrated the correct behavior of a gentleman? How different her life would have been! Then again, as she looked forward to their evening together, she could only be thankful for the good turn it had taken since she'd reached Fort Reno.

And if he was going to demonstrate correct behavior, so must she. She couldn't do anything tonight that would embarrass him in front of his daughters.

Lifting her chin and trying to suppress her excitement, she descended the stairs like royalty. At first glance, she saw Daisy's eyes grow wide at her approach, and Caroline bit her lip as if studying her for clues. But then she saw Daniel, and after that, he was all she could think of.

With his polished boots, the golden shoulder straps denoting his rank, and the double row of gleaming buttons down his chest, he cut an impressive figure. Then he removed his hat and reached to take her hand for the last few steps. Louisa accepted his help daintily, her wrist at just the correct angle as she descended, her pinkie finger raised slightly. Daniel bowed low over her hand with his back straight. Her heart sped at the memory of his kiss, but this time he skipped that ritual.

"You look beautiful this evening, Miss Bell," he said.

Daisy giggled.

"There's nothing wrong with a gentleman expressing his appreciation for a lady's beauty," Daniel said, "if it's done tastefully and is not repugnant to her."

"I assure you, it's not repugnant," Louisa said.

"That's a start." He smiled. "Then if you are ready to depart, may I escort you to dinner?"

"I'd be delighted."

"Girls, Private Gundy should have your dinner ready. Eat up, then get yourselves to bed."

"Can't we go with you?" Daisy asked.

Caroline took her by the shoulders and steered her toward the dining room. "That would defeat the purpose, little sister. Don't worry, Father. I'll explain it to her."

"Thank you, Caroline. I'll leave it to you." His eyes shone with equal parts humor and pride.

He opened the door, and Louisa passed through, being sure to inhale the unfamiliar scent of sandalwood he was wearing. He'd gone through extra efforts in his presentation, just as she had. The thought that he'd done all of this for her amazed her.

But that was just the beginning.

"I wish we had a longer promenade before us." He took her hand and tucked it into his arm. "More time to enjoy the evening. But walking in circles around the fort isn't a viable activity."

Sure enough, the new troops that had arrived that afternoon were taking notice. Louisa felt a twinge of misgiving. What would the agency ladies think of her? But they made the short walk to the lieutenant's house quickly.

At Daniel's knock, Lieutenant Jack swung open the door. His face registered happy surprise, reminding Louisa once again how drastically different she was presenting herself tonight.

"I thought you were looking after the new troops," Daniel said.

"I just dropped in for a moment. Miss Bell, may I be the first to tell you how beautiful you look?" As ever, Jack kept one amused eye on his commander.

"No, you may not," Daniel groused. "Don't you think I took care of that? First, indeed!"

"Relieved to hear it, sir," he answered. "A good assistant always looks to make up for his superior's weaknesses. Come this way." Jack led them through his quarters, a mirror image of Daniel's but with simpler furnishings and more books stacked in odd places.

"You knew we were coming," Daniel said. "I thought you might have cleaned the place up."

"You said you were coming for dinner, not for an inspection. Besides, I have too many books to keep them all in my office. Nothing shameful in that."

If he were that smart, Jack should have been teaching the girls. At least she and Private Gundy were better housekeepers.

She didn't need Daniel to escort her to the dining room, since the house was so similar, but when she turned the corner and saw the lit candelabra on the table and the two bowls of lilies flanking it, she stopped in her tracks. Instead of the cotton tablecloth they used daily, a cream-colored damask cloth draped the table. Two china place settings anchored the picture with real silverware, more forks and spoons than she knew what to do with.

The men in the room didn't say a word, waiting for her pronouncement. She had to say something, but the realization that this had been done on her behalf was more than she could account for.

Her throat closed up. Her hand tightened on Daniel's arm.

"Thank you, Jack. I've got it from here," he said.

She was barely aware of the lieutenant fading from the room before Daniel stood before her. He bent so that even with her bowed head, she couldn't avoid his tender eyes.

"What's the matter, Louisa? Can you tell me what's wrong?"

Could she? She had so many secrets from him that anything close to the truth would likely expose something else. But as she gazed into his caring face, she wanted to give him something true. Something of herself. "I've never had anything this fancy done for me." Wait, that wasn't true. She'd had sets and stages designed for a princess, but it was all counterfeit. How to make him understand? "Nothing authentic," she added. "Nothing real. I don't know how to . . ." She gestured to the elaborate table set for a formal dinner. She'd had enough trouble making it through a family dinner with the children. What hope had she of keeping up the ruse here?

Daniel took a deep breath and stepped back. His normally granite posture relaxed as he studied all the glasses, forks, and spoons on the table. "I just figured that anyone who could play chess as well as you wouldn't have any problem figuring out how to move each of these implements."

He was back. The man who'd spent those long summer evenings—that were never long enough—challenging her across the chessboard had returned. Whatever had kept him away didn't matter now, and Louisa couldn't be happier.

"Forgive me for losing my composure," she said. "I'm ready to eat with you . . . or best you at this new contest. Whichever you prefer."

He eagerly pulled her chair out for her, then tucked it in as she sat. His jaunty steps around to his side of the table made the silver rattle. Once in place, he fixed her with a devastating smile that could have no response except for her own grin. With a flourish, he flung his napkin high and then laid it across his lap. She already knew that much. Then he reached for a brass bell. It was clanging before Louisa realized she didn't have a bell of her own. How about that? A chess game where the pieces were uneven from the beginning? But before she could protest, the door to the kitchen flew open.

Louisa startled. She gripped the sides of her chair, but her fright was only brought on by a skinny man bursting through the door with a large tureen.

"Miss Bell, this is Sergeant Nothem," Daniel said. "He is our resident culinary expert, and he's serving us tonight."

As the sergeant ladled turtle soup into her bowl, Louisa marveled at his hair. It was as white and curly as lamb's wool.

She waited until he left the room before asking, "Does the cavalry approve of you using your staff for events such as these?" The longer she sat in this fine atmosphere, the more comfortable she grew.

"They expect us to be able to entertain in style, and that takes practice. Since General Sheridan will arrive any day now . . ."

"Oh." Louisa picked up a blunted spoon as Daniel reached for his. "This is to practice for General Sheridan, is it?"

He pursed his lips and blew on a spoonful of soup. "It's for you. Only for you. Nothem's getting practice is just a nice coincidence." No trace of flattery. Just sharing information.

Sergeant Nothem scurried back into the room, bubbling with apologies. Crystal chimed as he filled their glasses. "Sorry, sir. I should've seen about this first." It was a startling reminder of Daniel's authority here and the fact that he, for whatever reason, was elevating her to sit at his table. Being equals in the privacy of his office was one thing, but to expect honorable men like Nothem to serve her was another. What good could come of it?

Determined to think of something else, she asked, "When will the Darlington people be able to return home?" She lowered her arms so Nothem could take her soup bowl away.

As hoped, Daniel launched into a litany of steps that would

likely be undertaken to restore order. With him droning on, she could sort through her turmoil. Keeping her head bent over her venison steak also kept the bright light of the candelabra between them as she tried to identify what had changed. Why had Daniel suddenly decided to put on this show?

He was going through the schedule of events planned for the general's arrival now. His head was tilted to look around the candelabra she'd been hiding behind. The flame illuminated specks of auburn in his wavy hair. It bounced over a happy crease on his cheek when he smiled, warmed to red a slight scar on his forehead. Not only had he forgiven her, but his attentions appeared to be of a personal nature. Could it be true? Everything he was doing was the recommended, prescribed method for courting a woman. And if Louisa knew anything about Major Adams, it was that he would do everything by the recommended, prescribed method.

But she was hardly the recommended, prescribed mate for the major.

Then a phrase drew her out of her morose musings. ". . . and Private Willis is embarrassed by his commendation, but grateful." Daniel was smiling, just like he did when he thought he had her game piece trapped by a subtle move. "What do you think of that?"

She lifted her glass, then deciding she couldn't get a drink past the lump in her throat, lowered it. "I'm . . . I'm glad that he is pleased."

"Louisa." He lifted the candelabra and set it to the side of the table, giving him an unobstructed view of her tapping nervously on her plate. "I know."

"You know? You know what?" She folded her hands in her lap, assuming a serene pose that couldn't be shaken, even if a drunk mule skinner started firing off a shotgun from the audience.

"I know about Bradley. He's your brother. It explains everything."

Her unshakable poise was failing. She looked past the flowers, the fine china, searched the room for some diversion.

"I don't blame you for not wanting me to know," Daniel continued with maddening calm. "It must have been difficult for a lady of your education to be associated with him."

Her fear arose again. The major thought she was so far above Bradley. If he only knew.

"I don't mean to insult your brother," he said. "I'm only repeating what Bradley told me himself. How you tried to look after him when he strayed. How you set the example of industrious work and insisted on his taking a commission in the army." Daniel smiled, unaware of the turmoil he was causing. "You were right. The army is exactly what he needed. While I sympathize with your earlier embarrassment, I believe Bradley is going to fool around and turn himself into a man you will be proud of . . . as a sister." The last words were added with an unusual amount of emphasis.

"You mean you aren't mad?"

"Just relieved. If I had caught you talking to him again, I'm afraid it would've meant trouble for both of you. But now that it's all cleared up, there are no more secrets."

She closed her eyes. Oh, but there were a few.

⁓ꙮ⁓

Daniel rarely started a campaign without being confident of its success—and this one had shown every indication of being a rousing victory.

He needed a mother for his children, and Louisa had already proved that she could take on that task. The girls loved her and responded well to her direction. She was an asset to his household.

Many women weren't suited to the isolation that came from being married to a cavalry officer on the frontier, but it didn't seem to bother Louisa. In fact, she preferred staying away from society. Unlike other officers' wives he'd known, she wasn't eager to meet every stagecoach for news from Kansas. Instead, she preferred the open air of Fort Reno and the big skies, as he did.

Then there was the matter of accepting him as a partner. If he possessed any uncertainty over his campaign, it was in this area. Testing her success as a teacher was one thing, but testing her affection for him personally was another. He had much to lose if he was mistaken, but the reward was too great to be ignored.

As Nothem served them blackberry pudding for dessert, Daniel tried to look at the situation from a tactician's view. Louisa enjoyed his company. She eagerly sat in his office for hours, just the two of them, when she could have easily excused herself for the day. Although younger than he, she wasn't naïve—not the woman who'd held him so tenderly when he fell. She had to know his intentions when he invited her to a private dinner.

The sky-blue of her silk dress shimmered in the candlelight. The rose in her hair and the shell earrings he'd bought at Darlington evidenced that she knew exactly what this was. A woman didn't array herself like that for a meeting to discuss her pupils' progress.

Dinner ended with them sharing a laugh over Caroline's paintings.

"She continues to give Daisy pointers," Louisa said, "when Daisy's already better than she is."

"That's Caroline for you," he replied. "Her confidence knows no bounds."

Their plates were empty. No excuse to linger any longer in Jack's house, although being away from the girls did have its benefits. It looked like Jack might be inconvenienced more often.

Daniel stood. Louisa started to rise, but he held out a hand to slow her down until he could assist her with her chair. She turned pink beneath his gaze, the fair skin on her neck blushing a delicate shade.

"Thank you, Major Adams."

"Why not call me Daniel?"

"This just seems like more of a formal occasion."

"I intended for it to be an intimate one." He was pleased by his boldness, and if he wasn't mistaken, so was she. A stroll through Jack's dusty parlor wasn't quite moonlight and magnolias, but at least it wasn't under the eyes of his perpetually curious daughters.

"Thank you for a wonderful evening." Her musical voice was low and dusky. "You went through so much trouble."

"It's what a man does . . ." *For the woman he loves.*

They stepped outside and took the short walk next door. He had to laugh at himself for his dread of saying good-bye, when he knew that she would be right there with him every day. He just wasn't ready to end this special evening.

He reached for his own door, but to his surprise, she stopped him.

"Daniel, I'm sorry I didn't tell you about Bradley. I was afraid of what you would think. There are things you might not approve of. Things that might shock you."

Her fingers trembled beneath his. Daniel hesitated, fully able to conjecture any number of damaging secrets, but he had one of his own.

"Louisa, there's something I need to tell you. Something I should've confessed earlier." He took a deep breath. "That letter you found, it was never meant to be seen by anyone. I wrote it. To you."

She frowned as if her hearing had failed her. "That's impossible. You wouldn't . . . you couldn't . . ." Her lashes fluttered as she lowered her eyes. "I won't presume anything. As you said, you didn't mean for anyone to see it, so it'd be wrong for me to dwell on the words."

"No, it'd be right. Perfectly right for you." He leaned a shoulder against the wall next to her, to better appreciate her profile by moonlight. "I wouldn't have expressed my feelings for you that early—or this early—but it seems that my secret has been revealed, and I'm not one to retreat from the truth."

She turned and matched his posture, leaning against the support of the wall. "I'm sorry, Daniel. I can't comprehend what you're telling me. Not right now."

"I'm not asking you to respond. My announcement is premature and only prompted by my clumsiness in leaving a rather embarrassing letter on the ground."

Her eyes widened. "Oh no. I showed it to Bradley."

Daniel had to appreciate the irony. While he was fuming over the trooper, Willis knew why his major was guarding the governess so carefully. "Someday I'm going to ask Private Willis to describe his amusement at reading it."

"Bradley's not in more trouble, is he?"

"No. This is all my doing." A shadow passed over the green as a silent owl swooped down to pluck its dinner off the empty parade grounds. "It could've been much worse. I could've written more."

Perhaps it was the late hour or the long day, but Louisa's defenses had softened. She no longer acted as if she were afraid of him.

"What more would you have said?" she asked.

His eyes traveled her heart-shaped face. The generous cut of the blue silk gown perfectly framed her porcelain shoulders.

"That I'd be willing to fall off my horse and suffer a cracked skull again if it caused you to hold me like you did on our first meeting."

Her chest filled with a long breath. Her eyes darted to his forehead, where the scar was still visible. She moistened her lips, then with a tentative reach, smoothed back his hair. He leaned into her palm. Her skin was smooth and cool. Her touch was light as she combed her fingers through his hair.

"Please don't attempt any more stunts," she said. "At least until after General Sheridan has visited."

"I make no promises." But there were a lot of promises he wanted to make to her, and soon.

Chapter Twenty-Five

Did you dance?" Caroline asked over her botany text.
Louisa looked up from the arithmetic book, which she was still working through day and night to stay ahead of Daisy.

"Did I dance where?" she asked. Breakfast had been a quiet affair, with Daniel treating her with the same courtesy and friendliness as before, leaving their romance to develop out of sight of the children.

"Caroline, Pa said we aren't to pester Miss Bell," Daisy said. "If we have any questions, we are to talk to him."

"He said that, did he?" Louisa asked. Major Adams took care of everything.

"Father is gone, and Miss Bell is my governess. I'm of age to get instruction on courting," Caroline insisted.

"Not when it's our own father." Daisy wrinkled her nose.

"We did not dance." Louisa kept her finger under the arithmetic problem she was tackling. "It was only dinner."

Forgetting her own rules, Daisy asked, "Then why did you have to go to Lieutenant Jack's? That's just peculiar."

"Did Father tell you how pretty your dress was?" Caroline

again. And this time her botany text had closed. "You have to tell us what's going on."

"Ask your father," Louisa replied. How could she explain to the girls what had happened when she couldn't make any sense of it herself? The fearsome, powerful Major Adams in love with her? The world had turned upside down.

A bugle sounded. Books dropped, cushions flew, and heels pounded across the floor as all three ladies ran to the door.

General Sheridan had arrived.

Two columns of spry horses trotted through the high golden prairie toward the fort, carrying men in blue uniforms. The flags at the fore of their procession snapped in the stiff wind. The dust stirred by the hooves trailed off behind them like a rooster's tail. Had Daniel given the girls instructions on their reception of the general? Louisa hadn't heard anything, which was fortunate, because she was already too late if she'd wanted the girls to stay inside the house.

They stood on the porch as the cavalrymen took their places to receive the general. Louisa's heart swelled with pride as she spotted Daniel astride his horse. His hat was jauntily pinned up on the side. His sword caught the sunlight and reflected it across the dark uniforms of his troops.

The fort had never looked better. Every wooden building was freshly whitewashed. Every fence repaired and painted, every trough full, and every woodpile stocked. He'd worked so hard for this moment, even enlisting their displaced guests from the agency. She couldn't believe she'd get to share this success with him.

By the time the columns reached the fort, the men were bristling in anticipation. Through his own example, Daniel had impressed on the troopers the importance of honoring the general with their best efforts. Every chest swelled with pride as Sheridan rode past their formations to meet Daniel beneath the flagpole in the center. The general was a broad man but rode like he was born to the saddle. Upon seeing him, no one would doubt that he'd earned his rank.

Both men dismounted. To her surprise, General Sheridan had to look up to return Daniel's salute. He reached out his hand for a hearty handshake. Louisa felt a weight lifted that she hadn't even known she'd been carrying. Everything seemed to be going well. She prayed that it would continue that way.

With the general's arrival, Louisa gave up all hope of finishing the day's lessons. After the initial review, she, Caroline, and Daisy went inside to put away their lessons and help Private Gundy prepare for dinner with the general. Sergeant Nothem would oversee the main courses, but Gundy was assisting him, so Louisa set Daisy to polishing silver while she and Caroline unwrapped and washed the fort's official china, which was saved for receptions of this nature.

"What are you going to wear when we have the concert?" Caroline asked.

Louisa carefully dipped a plate into the warm, sudsy water. "No one cares what I wear. I'm just glad we have your dress ready. But the general has some important business to settle before anyone will be ready for entertainment."

Caroline looked troubled. "I don't know if this concert is such a good idea. I feel prideful getting up and singing in front of people, as if I think I'm so good that I deserve an audience."

"That's not it at all." Louisa shook the rinsing water off the plate before laying it on the towel. "You're not singing because you think you're the best performer in the room. You're singing because you want to give the people in the audience something special. All of your talent and all of your practice is a gift to them. And even if the men were deaf, they would love it because you are Major Adams's daughters. You are the young ladies

287

of Fort Reno, and they take pride in your accomplishments. Trust me in that."

Caroline traced the 24-karat gold edging on the rim of a plate. "As long as it's more about them having a good time."

Louisa smiled. "If there's anything I've learned in my years of . . . being a lady, a winsome, heartfelt performance will be more appreciated by a room of troopers than a technically perfect aria."

"I can't imagine what your coming out was like if you performed to rooms of troopers often." Caroline gave her a thoughtful look that told Louisa she wouldn't be fooled forever. Louisa was lying to the very people she was supposed to guide.

Louisa lifted the next plate off the stack. What would Major Adams say if he knew the woman he loved had been a dance hall singer? While he could overlook Bradley's reckless past, a woman was a different matter. Especially a woman you wanted to court. Even worse, the more Louisa came to know Daniel, the more she worried that it might not be her past that hurt him. What if her lies were the worse offense? She had been honest while in Wichita. People had paid for her voice, and she hadn't exaggerated her skill one jot. Here at Fort Reno, she'd pretended to be something she wasn't. For all she knew, she was teaching the girls everything wrong. She was taking Daniel's money when she was unqualified.

Loving Daniel *and* wanting God meant that she had to confess. Last night she'd been astonished by his honesty. Was she willing to be that honest? Could she return his love without telling him everything? Louisa caught a glimpse of her reflection in the spotless china plate. This had to come to an end, but how?

❧❦❧

There was nothing like the presence of a superior to make you feel like a visitor on your own base. Daniel stood aside as

General Sheridan stepped forward to greet Chief Stone Calf of the Cheyenne, Chief Powder Face of the Arapaho, and Little Medicine, a Cheyenne warrior. It had been four days since the general had arrived, and the fort had been turned upside down. A thousand extra men hadn't created the chaos that five generals did. Each of them had their own assistants who took precedence in the adjutant office, crowding Daniel's men out of the building. Each wanted the prime stables for their horses, the best cooks for their private kitchens, and insisted that Daniel be available around the clock.

He'd have to remember to cut Lieutenant Hennessey some slack occasionally.

Sheridan's ruthless reputation had guaranteed that the Indians came in for a council, but even Daniel could tell they were skeptical. Unlike the fighting warriors, Stone Calf wore a navy button-up vest over a white long-sleeved shirt and fringed buckskin trousers. The other two chiefs were dressed similarly in a mishmash of white and Indian items. Behind the three leaders was a youngster no bigger than Daisy, with dark eyes that seemed to be roving quickly, taking it all in. Daniel wondered what his role was. A chief's son, perhaps?

The generals escorted the chiefs inside the council room. Daniel paused to make sure that Ben Clark, the fort scout and interpreter, was on hand before he followed.

General Sheridan didn't even wait for everyone to take a seat before he picked up the typed treaty and announced its terms: All cattle leases canceled. Texas cattle forbidden to cross the Cheyenne and Arapaho lands. Rations to be returned to their original quantities for six months, after which the U.S. government would evaluate the tribes' progress in farming and adjust.

Ben calmly repeated each point. Stone Calf stopped him. He wanted to know where the cattle trails would go, if not through their land. Would another tribe collect the toll and leave the Cheyenne and Arapaho without this income?

Instead of addressing the Cheyenne, Sheridan looked at his own men. "They're worried about a few cowboys crossing their lands every day. What they don't understand is that this land will soon be opened for settlement. The cattle trails will end when this country is divided up between farms and roped off with barbed wire." Then he nodded to Ben Clark. "Tell him that we can't predict the future, but for now all standing contracts between the tribes and the ranchers are null and void."

Ben Clark dutifully reported as he was told, but the junior member of the delegation stood and respectfully tapped Stone Calf on the shoulder. The wizened patriarch waited until Clark was finished before turning to the youngster, whose black braids swung forward as he whispered into the ear of Stone Calf. Daniel suddenly remembered where he'd seen this boy before—at the school, where he was learning English.

Stone Calf's jaw tightened. The words he spoke to the rest of his delegation were short and gruff. Ben Clark folded his hands on the table and looked away as their faces hardened. Then, speaking to the officers, the boy said, "You speak to us of treaties, but you speak to each other of dividing our land. Where is the truth?"

⊰❈⊱

Besides practicing at the commissary, Louisa and the girls were doing their best to stay out of sight. Now that the fort was filled to the gills with soldiers, they had no business lolly-gagging outside, which was fine with Louisa. The fewer people who saw her, the better.

Sitting in the parlor, Louisa paged through the grammar book, seeing things that she knew somewhat instinctively written down in rule form. She turned the book over to look at the cover. What would it be like to read a book of chess rules? Would it make some plays clear to her, like this? Seeing how she was much better versed in chess than writing, probably not.

"I heard that Chief Powder Face is coming in." Daisy twirled around the room with an open parasol. An occasional feather dropped out of her adorned braids. "Do you know why they call him Powder Face?"

Louisa wrinkled her nose. All she could think of were her neglected cosmetics.

"Because gunpowder exploded on him. They say his face is burned up from it."

"That wasn't what I was expecting," Louisa said.

Daisy looked wistfully out the window. "I want to see him. Don't you?"

"Not if it interferes with your father's work. And you have work to do, too. Get your slate."

"Yes, ma'am." Daisy paused. "I think I left it in the kitchen."

Louisa continued reading about homophones, surprised to find that popery and potpourri were different words. Sword and soared. Colonel and kernel. What in the world? Whoever decided to pronounce colonel like that? It didn't make sense.

The metallic click barely registered, but something bothered her. That sound, she'd heard it often and should check after it. And where was Daisy? She hadn't come back in with her slate.

"Caroline? Daisy?"

"I'm sitting here," Caroline called from the staircase, where she had her composition book spread on her lap. "No need to yell."

Had the noise been the latch on the back door?

Louisa tossed her book aside and hurried to the kitchen, but it was empty. She rushed out the back door and saw Daisy running down Officers' Row behind the stately homes. Louisa didn't have to wonder where she was going.

That child would be the death of her. Louisa snatched up her skirts and gave chase. No time to worry about what she looked like. She had to catch Daisy before she interrupted Daniel and the generals.

But Daisy had too much of a lead. She disappeared around the corner, no doubt headed straight for the council room.

~≈)(≈~

Sheridan was good at maintaining control in many things, but being accused of lying wasn't one of them. "It's you who aren't keeping your word," he growled. "You charge the cattlemen a toll to cross your land, and then you let your people rob them. That's what started this mess."

Ben Clark didn't even try to intervene. The young Cheyenne boy was already relaying the inflammatory statement. Quick as a flash, he had his answer and reported, "The agency has cut our rations. We're hungry."

"You wouldn't need rations if you'd learn how to farm."

"Farming isn't our way. We're hunters. We see no reason to change."

This was getting nowhere. So far, even through their discontent, the Cheyenne had tempered their response. Darlington was still standing, and the teachers had been returned to their posts. Now that the fort was fully manned, the troopers and soldiers could protect Darlington, but if they made the Cheyenne angry enough, they would attack as a matter of honor.

"I don't see how we can come to any reasonable agreement while overlooking the trouble you've caused recently." Sheridan leaned back in his chair and crossed his short arms over his round chest. "Unless you—"

The door burst open. Daniel sprang from his seat, but the sight that met his eyes was worse than an ambush. Daisy stood framed by the open door with feathers randomly protruding from her braids.

"I came for the treaty, Pa. Am I too late?" she asked.

Daniel's stomach dropped. "Excuse me, gentlemen." He took Daisy by the arm. "You know better than to come in here. Apologize, and then go to Miss Bell."

Her eyes filled with tears. He'd stunned his sensitive child with his tone, but he couldn't afford to spare her feelings. Not when so much was at stake.

Stone Calf asked the boy a question, then looked down and nodded. After another question, he smiled. They were talking about Daisy. That much was clear.

Ben Clark leaned toward Daniel. "The boy recognizes your daughter from the agency. They are commenting on her clothing."

In general, Daniel didn't like any man making comments of any kind about his daughters. He looked again at Daisy's new dress with the Indian beadwork and the feathers she'd woven into her hair. He could only hope the Cheyenne weren't offended by her choice of decorations.

"He's asking about Daisy," Ben said. "The boy is telling him that she's your daughter and you've let her play with the girls at the Arapaho school."

What did it mean? The room was quiet as the chiefs and boy talked. A tentative knock at the door announced the arrival of Miss Bell, who was flushed and breathing hard. He motioned for her to wait as Stone Calf pointed to Ben and gave a pronouncement.

Ben looked nervously at General Sheridan, then translated, "Stone Calf said he will only talk to Major Adams. He wants the generals to leave, or the council is over."

Daniel shook his head. "That's not for Stone Calf to decide. General Sheridan is the senior commander. He doesn't take orders—"

But Sheridan stood. "I've had enough of this nonsense. You

are fully capable of getting what we want, Major Adams. I don't need another feather in my cap." He flicked one of the feathers in Daisy's hair as he passed out the door.

The room emptied quickly as the generals and their aides exited. Louisa steered Daisy toward the door as well.

"Stop," the boy said. "They want your daughter to stay, too. They say it's important for the young ones to know what is decided so they will keep the treaties in the future."

Daniel squeezed Daisy's shoulder. This wasn't what he'd expected at all. He tried his best to smile at Louisa. "It's going to be okay," he said, trying to believe it himself. "I've got her from here."

Chapter Twenty-Six

Daniel's meeting had been a success. While he couldn't change the terms of the treaty, he could offer more help. If the Cheyenne would skip their slaughter of the cows for one week, Daniel would send his men to build a corral for a tribal herd. Perhaps before the Bureau cut their rations again, they would be able to supply their own meat and milk.

Independence was what everyone craved for the Cheyenne and Arapaho, but they all needed to get a realistic picture of what that would look like.

Daniel stood on his porch and watched as the chiefs rode proudly away. They'd gotten the government's attention, so they were satisfied. No bloodshed showed a developing restraint on their part. The last of the agency workers and Mennonite missionaries had been escorted back to Darlington, where Agent Dyer was waiting, overjoyed to have the freedom to light a fire in his hearth and to walk the streets unmolested. Of course, he didn't know that General Sheridan was recommending that he be removed from his appointment, but the general did what the general wanted and cared little that the agent and his wife had risked life and limb to stay at their post.

And the general was the fearsome person expected at Daniel's table for supper that night.

With the tribes simmering down, the stagecoach could resume its route, as it was at that moment. Birds fluttered up from the high grass as the coach rumbled along the ruts toward the fort. With half the U.S. Army already stationed here, who was left? Maybe one of the officer's wives.

The battered coach swayed as it made the turn, then leveled out on the straightaway to Officers' Row. Losing interest, Daniel went back inside to check on dinner. Sergeant Nothem and Private Gundy had been fighting over the kitchen's territory all day. He hoped they'd come to a truce.

He didn't get very far before there was a knock on the door. Caroline popped out of the parlor and beat him to it. Sergeant Byrd stammered a greeting. His fluster was going to get him into Daniel's black book very quickly. The troopers were supposed to ignore his daughters. Then again, maybe it wasn't Caroline who had him shaken. Maybe it was the crone with him.

"Major, this is Mrs. Woodward. She's here at your request."

Caroline's forehead wrinkled as she looked to Daniel for answers, but he had none.

The woman was thin—thin like the steel rails the trains ran on. She came inside and stood as if she was trying not to take up any room. Content to stand and appraise the situation before pronouncing her judgment.

"I'm Major Adams, ma'am," he said. "How may I help you?"

Her eyes lit on Caroline and assessed her from crown to heel. "I came to be of help to you, sir. I've come to teach your children."

Daniel's mouth went dry. "Caroline, go upstairs."

"Where's Miss Bell going?" Caroline demanded. "You can't send her away."

"Upstairs, Caroline."

"Miss Bell is my friend. I have a right—"

"Young lady!" Mrs. Woodward's voice stabbed the air like an icicle shot from a cannon. "You aren't listening to your father."

Daniel eyed her warily. "This is your last warning," he said to Caroline. Caroline raced up the stairs and flew into her room. It didn't escape his notice that she left the door open and would be listening to everything said between them.

"Come in my office, please." He had to figure this out. He remembered asking Agent Dyer to check on Louisa's references. After that, well, he had an uprising on his hands. Someone should cut him some slack.

"I'm sorry to be obtuse," he said, "but how are you here, again?"

His uncertainty did not please her. "Didn't you receive our letter?"

Oh, the letter. His eyes darted to the fireplace. "I did, but it became damaged before I read it."

"You requested a referral for a good Mennonite governess. Upon learning that Mrs. Townsend had turned back and that you had someone of unknown character serving in her place, I was dispatched. I come with all the necessary references and qualifications. And I know Agent Dyer personally, so there's no doubt as to my suitability."

Daniel swiped his hand over a dusty corner of his desk. All this time, he'd had his doubts, and yet he was shocked to hear definitively that Louisa was not who he thought she was. Hadn't he known it, though? Why else had he decided that he'd rather burn that letter than read it?

Well, he couldn't toss Mrs. Woodward into the fireplace and do away with her, too. He had to make a decision in light of this new information, and he was surprised to find that his decision hadn't changed.

With her slight frame and tight gray bun, Mrs. Woodward

was exactly what he'd imagined when describing his ideal teacher to Agent Dyer. A mature older lady who didn't look susceptible to frivolity or idleness. She wouldn't sit with her feet up on the couch. She wouldn't roam the fields looking for wildflowers. She wouldn't have let Daisy sneak away and interrupt his council.

Mrs. Woodward might be a good governess, but she wasn't the best. Not for his family.

"I'm sorry, Mrs. Woodward, but the position has been filled."

"Nonsense. By whom?"

"I will have you accompanied to Darlington tonight, where you'll find comfortable accommodations and your friends Agent Dyer and his wife."

"Major Adams, I must insist that you carefully consider your decision. How could you allow someone who has misled you to remain in your household?"

Daniel had always thought of himself as a rational man, but even he didn't understand. He didn't know how Louisa had ended up at his house, but he wanted her to stay because he trusted her. Was that crazy? He didn't believe everything she'd told him, but he trusted that she would do right by him and the girls.

But there was no way to explain that to Mrs. Woodward.

"I apologize for the inconvenience. I'll telephone Agent Dyer and tell him that you are on your way. Now, if you'll excuse me . . ."

Daniel went to the door and motioned for a trooper to assist her. Determined and persistent, she protested all the way to the wagon, but Daniel was resolute. He wouldn't trade Louisa now.

Caroline rushed down the stairs, leaned against Daniel's arm, and watched Mrs. Woodward be escorted away.

"Miss Bell isn't a governess?" Caroline said.

"She's teaching you, isn't she? That makes her a governess." He sighed. "You won't say a word to her."

Caroline tucked her hand beneath his arm. "Don't worry, Father. You made the right decision. It'll be our secret."

While knowing that Louisa wasn't a Mennonite missionary didn't trouble him overly much, Daniel had many questions. Where had she come from? How had this governess shown up on his doorstep when he'd needed her?

"Where is she?" he asked. He hadn't seen Louisa since he'd returned.

"She's upstairs fixing Daisy's hair. All those feathers made a mess."

And with Sheridan coming for dinner, they needed all the spit and polish they could muster.

~~∘)|(∘~~

That evening, Sheridan was complimentary of Daniel's command, even after the slight he'd received at the council meeting. In the end, his pragmatism won out, allowing him and the other generals to enjoy their time at Daniel's table. But how could they not? Daniel had three of the loveliest females on the planet gracing his dining room.

"It must be a trial, Major Adams, raising such beautiful daughters amid these men. That you aren't concerned about them speaks well of the discipline of your troops," General Sheridan said.

"Thank you, sir," Daniel said. "I couldn't do it without the invaluable services of Miss Bell. She has been an excellent instructor for my daughters."

Caroline's brow rose while Louisa squirmed in her chair. Why didn't Louisa just tell him the truth? She had to know he loved her, no matter what her reasons for coming to the fort were.

"And I understand we are to be entertained tomorrow night," Sheridan remarked. "But not until we return from the hunt."

"We've heard you can't pull a trigger without hitting a turkey here," General Miles said.

"You will see plenty of game," Daniel assured them. He could make plans for the hunting and entertainment, but the truth of the matter was that they were all at the mercy of Sheridan. If he decided to hunt from sunup to sundown, that was what would happen.

Daisy had been quiet all evening, not wanting to push her luck after interrupting the officers' meeting with the chiefs, but Daniel should have known it wouldn't last. "I like to hunt turkey," she said. "I'm a crack shot."

General Sheridan beamed at her. "Aren't you a little pistol? Of course you like to hunt."

"But I must be careful of hornets' nests," she added. "I stepped into one and it nearly killed me."

Daniel supposed it had only been a matter of time before Daisy worked that into the conversation. She wanted everyone to know. The officers murmured their concern.

But Daisy hadn't gotten enough attention with her hornet story, so she tried again.

"Miss Bell and Father are courting."

Louisa froze with her fork in midair. Every eye turned from his striking governess to rest on him. Daniel fixed a death glare on Daisy while Caroline elbowed her.

"Ouch, stop it," his youngest protested.

"Isn't it your bedtime?" Caroline asked.

Daniel managed to make it through the rest of the dinner without further embarrassment. Sheridan didn't say a word about Daisy's pronouncement, but that didn't mean he approved. Only that an officer didn't discuss a soldier's performance in the presence of his family. Daniel would hear about it tomorrow.

Dinner was over, and the party was breaking apart. Daniel

picked up his hat to walk the general and his staff back to their quarters for the night. Louisa herded the girls upstairs as Sergeant Nothem and Private Gundy cleared the table. The men were sharing hunting stories as they passed outside, giving Daniel a chance to catch Louisa by the wrist before she accompanied the girls to their room.

"Meet me in my office?" he whispered. "I'll be back directly."

A timid smile was her only answer.

Daniel couldn't get the general and his men to their quarters quickly enough. The lamp in his office was lit when he came back across the damp grass. What if he'd gotten what he'd asked for and Mrs. Woodward was waiting in the house for him instead of Louisa? But that wasn't happening. Yes, he had questions, but he'd wait until she was ready to tell him.

Daniel entered his office. He dropped his hat on his desk and removed his belt and saber. Louisa fidgeted in her chair by the chessboard. Maybe removing a belt was considered disrobing in some circles. Was he treating her too familiarly? It was hard to remember she wasn't already part of his family.

He took a seat opposite her, glad to see the chess pieces ready to go. "Thank you for tonight," he said. "I hope it wasn't awkward."

She ran her hand over her cascade of curls. "I was nervous that I would mess it up for you."

He leaned forward, a conspiratorial air surrounding them. "What did you think of Sheridan? What was your impression?"

"General Sheridan strikes me as a man who will succeed in his mission. He doesn't waste time worrying about the consequences." She chose a pawn for her first move. Then her eyelashes fluttered as she looked up at him. "There's another officer whom I much prefer."

Oh, Louisa. She had no idea how her words thrilled him.

"You performed wonderfully tonight at dinner," he said. "You have quite the stage presence."

And just like that, the moment was broken. She darted a glance at the door like she might bolt.

"Don't get your tail feathers tweaked," he said. "I only mean that you're comfortable being the center of attention. I've noticed how you like to demonstrate the singing, elocution, and deportment lessons for the girls. You have a natural grace and knack for performance. Don't forget that the first time I ever saw you, you were singing."

"The first time I ever saw you, you were hurling toward the ground, but I don't claim that you have a natural affinity for being a cannonball."

"Touché." He moved his pawn and breathed a little easier. "I spent the next day convinced you were a creation of my imagination. I didn't think anyone could be so beautiful."

She ducked her head as she moved a piece. "And I thought you were the stern, unbending commander who was opposed to my brother."

He laughed. "I was. I still am."

"And I'm glad. Without the two of us looking after him, he wouldn't have become the man he's grown to be now."

Daniel was drunk with accomplishment. Everything was falling into place, just as it should. "Hopefully we can partner in raising more promising young people as well."

"That's what you hired me to do—instruct Caroline and Daisy."

"That's only a beginning." He brimmed over with hope. The day had been a success, and the more time he spent with Louisa, the more convinced he was that he'd made the right choice, sending the other governess away.

Victory belonged to those courageous enough to pursue it, and Daniel never lacked for courage.

He moved a chess piece. "Louisa, would you do me the un-fathomable honor of becoming my wife?"

～⊶⧆⧫⊷～

He had asked her a question, but she had no answer. The chessboard blurred before her eyes, the black and white checks melting into gray.

Seeing Daniel at the council that day, and then at dinner, at the head of a table full of important men, had reminded Louisa how proud she was of him. He had endured much to rise to his position. He deserved the best.

And she wasn't the best. A man with his ambition couldn't afford to pluck a wife out of the gutter. Louisa would only hurt his career.

She hadn't realized that she was turning her queen over and over in her hand until Daniel took it from her and set it in the middle of the board.

Louisa's neck tightened. She hadn't meant to touch it. And the queen couldn't move there, anyway. The path was blocked. Besides, the queen was vulnerable there. She could be taken out by the weakest opponent, the row of pawns staring her down.

She hated to be vulnerable.

"I don't know if it's possible," she said.

"Most officers are married," Daniel replied. "And at my rank, you could expect accommodations no matter where we're stationed."

"It's not that." Louisa kept her eye on the stranded queen, all alone in a place she hadn't earned. "What would people think?"

"Who? Do you have anyone I should speak to? An uncle? Someone from the missionary organization?"

"No," Louisa answered too quickly.

"What about your stepfather? Bradley's dad?"

When Louisa had described herself as an orphan, she hadn't

gone into detail. The fact of the matter was that her father and Bradley's were probably both alive. That didn't mean they knew of their whereabouts.

"He's gone, too." Gone to drink, gone to work, gone to Timbuktu, for all Louisa knew.

"Well then, neither of us has family to oppose us, and as for your being in my employ, I imagine that issue will be discussed with General Sheridan tomorrow, but it isn't unusual. Almost every maid, governess, or cook hired by the army ends up married to some scruffy soldier. You wouldn't be the first."

But Louisa wasn't worried about the shame of Major Adams being yoked to a governess. No, her offense was much stronger than that.

Seeing that no answer was forthcoming, Daniel took his white knight and placed it in the center of the board, next to Louisa's queen.

"I think they belong together," he said.

"You can't move there," she replied. "Neither of them should be there. It's against the rules."

"That depends on what game you're playing."

"And my queen could destroy your knight."

"I'm not afraid."

That was only because he didn't know. She wanted to accept his proposal more than anything, but first she'd have to tell him the truth. If he turned her out and forbade her from seeing the girls—which he'd have every right to do for her dishonesty—a part of her would perish. The stakes were too high to change anything.

"Courage, Louisa." His voice had an edge, deep and commanding, no hint of patience in his demeanor. "Can you tell me what the big secret is? Can you tell me what great obstacle is keeping you from what you want?"

"From what I want?"

"I've offered you my love, my hand, my family, everything I have. You're too kind to toy with me, and you haven't refused me. And when I touch you, you don't reject my caresses."

Louisa gasped. "You can't say that."

"I've treated you as a sister, trying not to take advantage of your proximity." His eyes held her pinned, unable to hide. "But your responses are anything but sisterly."

She couldn't refute him. His words alone made her pulse race. "I'm . . . I'm sorry."

"Never, never be sorry. Just tell me the truth. Tell yourself the truth." He stood and pulled her to her feet. "Louisa, if you have some reservation about my character or about my devotion, you can tell me. If you don't desire that we be united, give me a reason, and I'll stop pursuing you, but I'm very afraid I can't stop loving you."

Louisa gripped his hands as if her very life depended on it. He was so earnest as he waited for her response. What if he never found out? What if no one dared tell him?

He was reading her struggle, waiting breathlessly. He was all she wanted. Why should she break his heart? Why should she break her own?

Because sooner or later, she would have to bend her will to her Creator's. She now knew it was inevitable. She couldn't run from God, she couldn't hide, and being found meant that she had to tell Daniel the truth. She couldn't go into a marriage knowing the disclosure would come afterward.

"Daniel, you remember my questions about God?"

His throat jogged, and his brow wrinkled. "I remember."

"I haven't been sure what to do. A part of me knows that choosing to follow Christ will be my only true hope for peace, but I'm afraid. God requires so much. He demands so much."

"Whatever is holding you back, you have to let it go." If he'd been earnestly pleading with her before, now he was even more. "I can't imagine what a struggle you've had, trying to hide these doubts, but there's no reason to keep fighting. There is nothing on Earth that can take the place of a relationship with God. No matter what else you decide tonight, this is the most important."

And that was exactly what she was afraid he would say. She could feel her eyes starting to smart. "In my heart, I've already decided. I just don't know what to do next. How do I obey?"

He smiled fondly and brushed her hair back from her face. "My guess is that you already know what to do, you're just afraid to do it."

She wanted to stop time and bask in his love and acceptance forever, but it couldn't last. Her dishonesty would hurt him— had already hurt him. He just didn't know it yet.

"You're right, as usual." She caught his hand in hers and held it against her cheek. "I can't marry you. In fact, you need to find another governess for Caroline and Daisy. This isn't what I'm supposed to be doing."

His hand grew heavy as her words sank in. "You think God is telling you to leave?" He stepped away. "You can't be sure yet."

"It's not right for me to be here. I know that. It's not who I am."

"But I love who you are."

"You don't know me."

The old, questioning look that he'd worn her first week on the fort returned. Daniel was a tactician. He liked to anticipate his opponent's next move, but he hadn't seen this coming, and it obviously bothered him.

"I'm more forgiving than you realize. If there's something you've neglected to tell me . . ."

The shame was too great. Louisa shook her head.

"Louisa, I'm telling you the truth. I know something isn't right. I've known that since you arrived, and I've waited for you

306

to learn to trust me. If you leave without ever testing me . . ." When she didn't answer, he stepped back. "I've been hasty. When I learned that Bradley was your brother, I assumed my way was clear. I rushed you into a decision, but there's no hurry. You keep doing lessons with Caroline and Daisy, and we'll give it some time. Nothing has to change."

"Everything has changed," she said. "I've been hiding from God for too long. My conscience . . . I can't keep going."

How forlorn he looked. He flicked the corner of the chess table. The pieces wobbled. "The one opponent I dare not cross," he said. "How can I compete with God?"

She had no answer. He was still standing, staring at the chessboard, when she left the room.

Chapter Twenty-Seven

I f it weren't for Ben Clark organizing the hunt, Daniel would have led the generals around in circles, because spinning around and around was all his thoughts could do.

Hadn't God brought Louisa to his family? Wasn't she the perfect answer to his prayers? How could God tell him one thing and Louisa another? Had she been hiding from her calling? He tried to think critically—tried to imagine that she didn't love him and was using this as an excuse, but he couldn't believe it. Her regret was genuine. She was sacrificing him in obedience, but why? If God was leading her somewhere else, then where?

That night, the officers around his table were flushed with good humor. Their hunting stories layered over one another, each growing in volume. Daniel did his best to participate, remembering to share his appreciation for the plate of succulent turkey, but he might as well have been eating sand.

Louisa fiddled with the ribbons on her sleeve as she smiled gaily at General Sheridan's jests. Daniel knew her well enough now to recognize the performance. She was just as miserable as he was. Her jewel-tone gown was the most daring one she'd donned at Fort Reno yet. Naturally, she'd never wear the violet

bodice and off-the-shoulder sleeves for a normal day of schooling and chores, but tonight was the recital. As Caroline and
Daisy demonstrated their skills, she'd be at the piano, breaking
his heart.

"That Frisco Smith," General Sheridan was saying. "You say
you've arrested him repeatedly. Is he any danger?"

Caroline dropped her buttered roll, and it toppled onto the
damask tablecloth. "You saw Frisco?"

Daniel glared at his daughter. "We came upon *Mr. Smith*
but were unable to arrest him as he claimed to be working with
the cowboys coming up the trail. As he had no followers with
him and the cowboys verified his story, he had a right to be in
the territory."

"The trail boss isn't coming this way, is he?" General Miles
smoothed the shiny medals that hung in a row on his chest.
"They can't cross the Cheyenne and Arapaho Reservation anymore."

"No, they're going east of here, through the Unassigned
Lands, although they aren't happy about it."

"Has Mr. Smith given up his boomer work?" Louisa asked.

"Apparently not. From listening to the cowboys talk, they're
going to spread word in Texas that the land should be opened
for settlement. He's only trying a new method." Daniel paused.
"You'll be interested to know that they will be joining us tonight.
The cowboys are bedding down the herds nearby, and a few are
coming to the musical performance."

Caroline's face went white. "Frisco Smith is coming to watch
me sing?"

Louisa laid her elegant hand on Caroline's arm. "You're
going to do fine, my dear."

"Frisco Smith is coming because he'd rather sit in a lit hall
than stare at the darkness for another evening. His decision
doesn't involve you," Daniel said.

General Sheridan chuckled. "Fathers are the last ones to see it."

"See what?" Daniel asked. Then, remembering his position, he added, "Sir?"

"To see that their daughters are growing up. Every man here will be charmed by your daughters' recital. I'm sure they'll be a credit to you."

And a credit to Miss Bell, but she didn't understand how much she'd done for his family, or how badly he needed her.

After dinner, the ladies excused themselves to prepare for the great performance. Daniel led General Sheridan to the parlor, but the general was drawn to his office instead.

"I always say that you can't know a man until you see his study. Looks like your office is quite impressive."

"Thank you, sir. I appreciate orderliness. It's an important element of efficiency."

Sheridan nodded his approval as he went to the chessboard. "I've made a career out of laying waste to our enemies, so I know the advantages of keeping order. And if an outfit has a weakness, your enemies are sure to exploit it. That's why I insist my officers be flawless, and that applies to their behavior out of uniform as well."

Daniel had expected this discussion and was anxious to have it behind him. "My reputation is of the utmost importance to me."

"Your daughter claims you're courting Miss Bell, but you introduced her as your children's governess."

"She's more than the governess. We have briefly courted, and in the interest of avoiding speculation, I proposed recently."

"And she accepted?"

"Not yet." Explaining the failure of his love life to the Commander of the U.S. Army? How had Daniel gotten into such a mess?

"The sooner, the better. A scandal would hurt your career."

That was the last thing Daniel wanted.

From his window, he saw soldiers and troopers filing into the commissary. It must be time, although the enlisted men would be kept waiting until the generals arrived.

"Do you have any other concerns?" Daniel asked.

Sheridan turned, the silver in his close-cropped hair catching the light of the setting sun. "I do not. Let's go enjoy the fruits of Miss Bell's handiwork."

The excited voices and squawks of tuning strings reached them as soon as they left the house. At some point during their walk to the commissary, word reached the performers that the general was coming, for all noise besides the whippoorwills ceased. When Daniel opened the door, a hundred benches scuffed the floor as the men jumped to attention. It didn't take long to spot the only other colors in the sea of cavalry blue as Louisa, Caroline, and Daisy rose, too. Daniel stood aside to allow Sheridan to pass down the aisle first.

A banner spanned the stage, nailed to the back of the wall and draped with red, white, and blue bunting. Daniel had seen the same *Welcome to Fort Reno, I.T.* banner every time a dignitary visited, but the stage decorations were something new.

A two-handled vase filled with red roses was set atop a pedestal designed like a Greek column. A few petals had fallen off, or perhaps they'd been pulled off and left on the pedestal for dramatic effect. Jack's round parlor rug covered the new boards of the stage, and even the piano had been polished. Instrument cases of various sizes could be seen behind a black curtain that had been tacked across the corner behind the stage. From the looks of it, Jack had recruited every musician on the base.

Daniel flashed Louisa a smile as he passed the second row and sat in front of the women with the generals and officers.

Daisy leaned forward and whispered, "Where's Frisco and the cowboys? I thought they were going to be here."

One look over his shoulder confirmed that Caroline had prompted her little sister to ask. What was with Caroline's interest in the boomer? With Sheridan's warnings against chaos in the home ringing in his ears, he vowed to nip that interest in the bud.

"It's already dark, so they probably won't make it after all."

Daisy shrugged at her sister and plopped back against her seat. Caroline seemed to relax. So did Daniel.

Jack stood and, pulling from his extensive reading, made a very commendable welcome speech in which he superbly expressed his wish that the general would be pleased with their efforts. He then introduced their first entertainers—a group of men from the Sixth Cavalry who performed hymns *a cappella* every Sunday at chapel. Daniel's confidence in their abilities was strong, but he couldn't rest easy—not until Daisy and Caroline had performed. And after that, he had plans of his own.

His officers had done a thorough job impressing upon the men the importance of observing strict decorum throughout the performances. This wasn't a Saturday night jamboree, where they could get rowdy and stomp out various dances to the fiddle and piano. The hymns at the beginning set the tone, and a ballad sung by a corporal from Vermont was as fine as Daniel's mother-in-law would hear at any musical evening in Galveston. If he didn't know better, he'd think this fort was filled with genteel society men. In fact, if he had to be honest, the music was dragging on. After another melancholy performance, Daniel was relieved to see the Fifth Cavalry's band take the stage.

These troopers were a camp favorite, always called upon to call the stag dances where the men went through the steps, half of them playing the parts of the ladies. Daniel cast a glance at the door in the back of the room. No cowboys yet. That was probably for the best. He didn't want to count on some cowboys who hadn't been in civilization for weeks to observe proper decorum.

As a whiskered corporal drew his bow across the fiddle, a red-headed sergeant began a strong beat on a small barrel with a buffalo hide stretched across the open end. There'd be no lone soloist with this ensemble. Each man on the stage, no matter what his instrument, performed like he was the main attraction.

The harmonica, the trumpet, and the washboard all fired up and sent the audience into raptures. As much as the men tried, they couldn't stop their feet from tapping. Soon that was accompanied by hand-clapping. Daniel joined in. Even General Sheridan was having a good time.

And behind him . . . Giving in to the temptation to turn around, Daniel caught Louisa's sparkling eyes as she clapped along. Her cheeks were flushed and her chin was down, as if ashamed that she was enjoying the music. Daniel smiled to encourage her. The enthusiasm of the men could be upsetting to a gently raised lady. No doubt there was never such participation in the drawing rooms Louisa was used to, but he wanted her to have a good time. He wanted her to love Indian Territory and never want to leave.

An encore was called for after the first song. Daniel looked to General Sheridan to make the decision. He gave the signal, and the band kicked into another round, no less boisterous than the first.

A tap at Daniel's arm, and he turned to see Sergeant O'Hare kneeling in the aisle.

"Major Adams, a handful of drovers are approaching the fort. They claim they were invited to the musical event."

"Are they sober?"

"Appear so, sir. Dusty from the trail, but no troublemakers that I recognize. Well, besides . . ."

"Besides Frisco Smith?" Daniel already knew the boomer was with them. He also knew that Frisco wouldn't pass up an opportunity to visit the fort. He might even ask to sleep in the guardhouse, since it was his second home.

Through the pounding music, Daniel gave his consent for their guests to join them—Frisco included. Sheridan might enjoy seeing how Daniel utilized the local resources out in the territory. Despite the trouble Frisco was stirring up for Congress, he often had valuable information for Daniel.

The Fifth Cavalry band finished their performance. What started as explosive applause quickly died down as the men remembered their honored guest.

As Jack once again took the stage, Sheridan leaned over to Daniel. "You've got more talent here than many professional troupes."

If everything went as planned, Sheridan's assessment would be proved over again.

"Gentlemen, tonight we have a special performance by the youngest residents here at Fort Reno."

Every head turned in Daniel's direction, or more specifically, to the ladies who were rising from their seats behind him.

Daisy walked stiffly on account of her new shoes, which Louisa had helped her pick out in Darlington. Caroline hid her hands in the folds of her new skirt, but if Daniel could have seen them, he knew they'd be trembling. Poor girl. Being stuck out here, she hadn't had the opportunity to gain any confidence in front of crowds, an oversight that Miss Bell with her experience was correcting.

Miss Bell glided across the room in what was probably the most awe-inspiring performance of the night. Daniel had thought that his appreciation for her beauty had reached its full potential, but he was mistaken. Before the audience, her bearing seemed to refine into something regal. It was as if her allure heightened. His parlor wasn't big enough for her magnificence. The more room she was given, the brighter she shone.

Only after she took her seat and the piano hid her mostly from view did the room's attention move back to Caroline and Daisy. They looked sweet and innocent huddled next to the vase of flowers, which were exactly the virtues every father wanted his daughters to exude. Daisy stuck her nose in the roses, unable to contain her curiosity over whether they smelled as pretty as they looked. Sheridan chuckled beside him, and then the first notes of the piano sounded.

It was a few simple chords—Miss Bell had never claimed to be an accomplished pianist—but that was enough to get the girls going. Daisy started with a low verse in what sounded like Italian. Daniel's heart swelled with pride. His girls could sing in Italian. He couldn't wait to write Edna with the boast.

After a few beats of Daisy's measured verse, Caroline joined her. Instead of singing the same melody, Caroline's voice swung up to hold sustained notes in a surprisingly clear soprano. Together their voices blended, Daisy keeping the base of the song while Caroline's line trilled, sounding much more sure than she looked.

When their voices joined for the last measure, Daniel leapt to his feet to applaud their success. Finally, her ordeal over, Caroline smiled happily as the rest of the men followed her father's lead. Daniel could tell that she would want to do this again, and every time she would improve. Daisy curtsied and braved a small wave to Bradley Willis. Well, nothing wrong with that. If it weren't for Willis, Daisy might not be alive to sing anything at all.

As the girls left the stage, Daniel waved them over to himself. Dropping to his knee, he took Daisy by the elbow.

"I am so proud of you. You did wonderful," he said. Daisy threw her arms around his neck.

Caroline tried to pass, but Daniel wasn't letting her get away with that, no matter how grown-up she thought she was. He stood and wrapped an arm around her.

"You are so talented, darling. I had no idea," he said. "I'm sorry it took me so long to get you a real teacher."

Caroline laughed. "I don't know about a real teacher, but at least you got the right one."

He narrowed his eyes at his daughter. None of that talk in front of Sheridan. Then Jack stood to continue the program. Would the rest of the performance go as he and Jack had conspired?

Daniel was taking a gamble. Ever since hearing Louisa sing back at the Red Fork Ranch, he'd known that she possessed uncommon talent. The ease with which she taught Caroline and Daisy revealed that she'd had extensive musical training herself. The way she commanded the respect of the audience by merely walking across the stage showed a woman who was confident of her abilities and had no fear in front of a crowd. Added together—her talent, her training, and her presence—there'd be no reason Miss Bell should be opposed to taking the stage. No reason besides false modesty and her humble desire not to outshine her pupils.

If she truly were leaving, he wanted to give her this one chance to sing before an audience. Her talent shouldn't be hidden away forever.

Daniel stopped Caroline and Daisy from leaving. He wanted them to hear what Jack was saying from the stage.

"Before anyone leaves, we have a surprise performance planned for tonight. I say surprise, because the planning was all done between myself and Major Adams. The performer is the one who will be surprised. So if Miss Bell will kindly remain on stage . . ."

Louisa had paused by the piano so as not to pass in front of Jack when he started talking. Or maybe she'd lingered hoping for such an invitation. Daniel hoped so. He only wanted to honor her.

Jack's arm was extended toward her, offering her the stage. She looked at Daniel, uncertainty in her eyes. How well he knew that look, and how well he loved encouraging her to take the risk. But then she looked somewhere else. Her brother. What was wrong with Private Willis? He looked as nervous as she did.

"Sing pretty, Miss Bell!" Daisy cheered.

The men all laughed as they took their seats. With a flick of his hand, General Sheridan shooed two of his aides down the row, making room for Caroline and Daisy next to their father. Daniel leaned forward, ready to absorb every note.

Positioning herself by the vase of flowers, Louisa made a striking picture. It was as if the lettered banner behind her had disappeared and she were standing in a windswept olive grove, draped in some quaint garb from centuries past. The pianist from the Fifth started to make his way to the piano, but Louisa waved him back as unnecessary.

Absolute stillness fell over the room. Everyone waited breathlessly for her to begin. She rested a perfect hand on the pedestal, as much of a decoration as the vase of flowers. Bowing her head, she stood as still as the post, but then she opened her mouth and filled the room.

From the first note, it was clear that Louisa Bell had been gifted with a talent not commonly found among mortals. Daniel felt foolish that he'd had an artist of this caliber wasting her time going over spelling words and botany texts in his home, but he didn't have time for regrets. Not when he could be transported by her heavenly voice.

She too sang in a tongue he didn't recognize, but the words hardly mattered. With a hand clasped to her chest and eyes full of tears, everyone in the room felt the heartbreak of her song. Those who'd never lost a love fancied that they now knew what it felt like, while the poor men who'd been rejected mourned afresh.

Lieutenant Jack wiped his eyes, no doubt thinking of the sorry girl who'd held his heart all these years. Sheridan fidgeted, probably planning to write home to his wife at the first opportunity. Daniel's sorrow was tempered by the fact that the one he loved was with him still. He had today with her, maybe tomorrow, maybe a week. But how could he be forlorn while listening to her voice? He let her song wring his heart, knowing that he'd remember this moment for the rest of his life.

And as though she and he were reading the same sheet music, her song gradually changed. No longer mournful, a challenge entered the melody—hope, determination. Her head lifted as her voice rose strong and sure. Whatever had happened in this woman's past, she was determined to conquer it. The rest of the audience sensed the change, too. They leaned into the music, eager to be told that they would overcome whatever sacrifices they'd made.

A ruckus sounded at the back of the room. The cowboys. Although they were trying to be quiet, Daniel resented the interruption. No one else seemed to notice as the dozen or so men filed in and stood against the back of the wall. Louisa wrung out the last of her notes, her springwater-clear voice finally coming to rest.

No one knew whether to applaud, say *Amen*, or leave in

silence. Even Caroline and Daisy, who he'd assumed had heard her sing before, sat stunned at his side.

Complete silence ruled, until a grating voice bellowed from the back, "Sing another one, Lovely Lola! Carry me back to the Cat-Eye Saloon."

Chapter Twenty-Eight

Daniel jumped to his feet so quickly that he nearly knocked Daisy to the floor. Who would dare yell such a thing? What did it even mean? The culprit was a dirt-covered drover with a mouth as wide as a barn door. He was grinning at Louisa like she should know him. He was grinning so big that he didn't see the blur of blue until it was too late.

Bradley Willis socked the drover in the jaw, twisting the giant mouth to the side. Why was Willis so much quicker than Daniel? Maybe because Daniel was still trying to figure out who Lovely Lola was and what the Cat-Eye Saloon had to do with it.

"Serves you right, Slappy! Embarrassing Lola Bell like that," an old drover hollered, but the rest of the cowboys jumped into the fray.

A fellow with a neck like a bull launched into Bradley. A bench of troopers piled on to even the odds. Bradley had the instigator by the neck and was pummeling his face, forcing him backward. The drover lost his balance. Frisco jumped out of the way, exposing the shocked face of an elderly woman. It wasn't Mrs. Woodward returned to take Louisa's job. Then who? Her horrified expression was all Daniel saw before the brawlers fell into her, landing them all on the floor.

Daniel wanted to rub his eyes. Could it be his mother-in-law? Had she finally made good on her threat? This whole thing was a nightmare, but even his tortured imagination wouldn't have thought to involve Edna. He had to get his men under control. He and his officers rushed to the back of the room.

"All soldiers return to your barracks," Daniel thundered. "Lieutenant Hennessey, look after the ladies."

Jack rushed to gather Louisa and the girls. General Sheridan would have to take care of himself.

The room began to empty. A mass of blue-coated soldiers congregated at the door by the stage, wanting to stay clear of any punishment. The troopers in the back, however, were fully engaged with their enemy and couldn't hear the bugle sound retreat.

Grabbing man after man by the shoulder, Daniel pried them off and shoved them toward the back door while Frisco did the same with the cowboys. Tomorrow Daniel would have time to identify the aggressors by their cut lips and swollen eyes, but now he had to restore order. He hadn't seen the woman again and hoped he'd been mistaken, but the kink in his gut told him he wasn't.

Finally, they came down to the last two fighters—Bradley and the big-mouthed guy. It took two officers to pull Bradley off him. Considering the affront committed right as Louisa finished her performance, Daniel would have appreciated Willis's response had General Sheridan not been present. But this was the worst possible time for Willis to act recklessly.

"Private Willis, you will make a full account of your behavior." Daniel's voice shook with rage. "Until then, you will be in the guardhouse."

"Yes, sir." Louisa's brother saluted smartly, as if he'd been given a medal instead of a reprimand.

"Take him away."

Sergeant O'Hare started to drag him, but with a shake of his arms, Willis freed himself and walked calmly through the door.

The mature woman was being helped to her feet. Daniel filled his lungs with air. Time to assess the damage and plan a recovery. All under the watchful gaze of his enraged mother-in-law.

"Who is responsible for these men?" he demanded. "Who can tell me what just happened?"

"That would be me, sir." A lanky old-timer stepped forward. "Name's Cimarron Ted. I'm a mule driver from Wichita. I told the trail boss that I had a friend here I wanted to see. I brought these boys with me."

"These boys interrupted our musical evening and insulted a lady," Daniel said. "Can you account for their behavior?"

He needed to get an apology and quickly, because General Sheridan stood at his heels, ready to take over at the first sign of weakness.

"I'll explain." The big-mouthed man wiped at his bloody nose with a dusty bandanna. "That woman is the Lovely Lola Bell. She's a stage performer at the Cat-Eye Saloon in Wichita, and she ain't no lady."

The red fury that clouded his eyes should have warned Daniel that something bad was about to happen, but he didn't realize that he'd taken a swing at the cowboy until he felt the pain in his fist. So much for gaining control.

Louisa's hands had turned to ice the minute her performance had ended and she opened her eyes to see the row of cowboys standing in the back. Cimarron Ted wouldn't embarrass her, but Slappy and Rawbone didn't know and wouldn't care if they did.

And then Slappy had.

While Louisa was paralyzed, Bradley had sprung into action. But didn't he always? She watched helplessly as he took out Slappy and erased all the good merits he'd earned for rescuing Daisy. Another career she'd ruined. And who was that woman Bradley had tackled? She definitely hadn't ridden in with a herd of cattle.

General Sheridan got lost in the melee, his small stature causing him to disappear into the flying fists and struggling bodies. Daniel forged into the mix, casting troopers out behind him as he pushed forward. By that point, Jack had corralled Daisy and Caroline up on the stage with her, lone refugees from the chaos on the floor.

Daisy slipped her hand into Louisa's, and Louisa hugged her. "I'm sorry," Louisa said. "I should never have sung."

Caroline wiped tears from her eyes. "It's my fault. I wrote her."

"What? Wrote who?" Who was Caroline talking about?

"Grandmother. I should've never written to tell her about Daisy getting stung. I was worried about Daisy, that's all. I didn't think she'd come all the way from Galveston to see us."

"I don't want to go." Daisy burst into tears and buried her face into Louisa's skirt. "I want to stay here with you."

But after this night, Louisa had to leave. There was no place for her now. Not at the fort.

≈)(≈

"Major Adams!" General Sheridan was roaring orders, but all Daniel could think of was making the drover take back his insulting words.

Many hands were pulling him back. The cowboys were dragging their friend outside and out of Daniel's reach. The red haze cleared from his vision. He was in the commissary. There'd

323

been a musical evening, and then this stranger had walked in and insulted Louisa. Everything that had happened after that was a blur.

What was crystal clear was that his mother-in-law was standing before him. Her dented bonnet balanced precariously on her big fluff of white hair. She bounced as she twisted at her layers of skirts to get them where they belonged, but the whole time her eyes were burning into his.

"Major Adams!" It was the general again. Daniel's men stepped aside to make way for the fuming ball of rage rolling at him. Sheridan's face was a thunderous shade. "What in tarnation just happened here? Did one of your recruits attack a civilian during what was to be a cultured and refined evening? And then you—you—"

"I'm sorry, sir." Daniel could hear the sound of his career galloping away. "I'll make amends."

"I am taking over command of this base immediately. You go to your quarters and await my orders there. Sergeant, Corporal"—two men jumped to attention—"escort Major Adams to his quarters and prevent him from interacting with anyone else. Do you understand?"

"Wait a minute!" Edna pushed through the troopers. "Major Adams cannot leave yet. He has yet to answer for what I just saw. Was that woman performing on stage the governess of my grandchildren? Was that the purported missionary woman giving advice and guidance to my girls?"

Sheridan glowered at her. "Ma'am, I have already discussed Miss Bell with Major Adams. Right now, my concern is moving him to a location from which he is no longer a threat to our guests—"

"That might be your concern, but it's not mine." Had Edna just interrupted the Commander of the U.S. Army? Sheridan blinked in shock while she continued. "I've told him those girls have no business being raised at a godforsaken fort among a bunch of good-for-nothing troopers."

Forgetting Daniel, Sheridan turned on Edna. "Ma'am, I've taken lives for less of a provocation than that. You will not declare U.S. Cavalrymen as good-for-nothing in my presence. Those men provide protection to thousands of settlers, hunt down outlaws, and keep peace between the Indian nations."

"And they shove elderly women to the floor," she said. "Or were you absent for that part?"

Daniel tried to help. "That was Miss Bell's brother responding to her detractors. He was showing family concern."

"So our governess of questionable character has a roustabout for a brother? How charming! But then, we've already established that he's in the cavalry, so I'm being redundant."

"You are done," Sheridan said. "Depart."

"I'm not in the army," Edna said, "and I don't take orders from anyone."

"You are on army property."

"So are my granddaughters. I'll leave when they do."

Sheridan looked at Daniel. "How do you endure this?"

"We only correspond when necessary, and always at her insistence."

"I'm beginning to have some sympathy for you, Major Adams. So, Mrs. . . ."

"Mrs. Crawford."

"Mrs. Crawford doesn't approve of Miss Bell, I take it?" Sheridan's long mustache quivered with each syllable.

Daniel swallowed the lump in his throat. He wasn't sure what to think. Why was everyone saying things about Louisa? Why couldn't he dismiss them as falsehoods?

"She does not."

General Sheridan grunted. "Then I'm beginning to understand your decision." With a toss of his head, he directed O'Hare and Chandler away from Daniel. "Leave the man alone. He's the commander here, and as post commander, it's his responsibility to deal with Mrs. Crawford. I'm retiring for the evening."

Daniel exhaled for the first time. There would be reports to write and questions to be answered, but General Sheridan had shown him mercy. What about Louisa? Where was she?

He turned to the stage, but only Daisy and Caroline were still there. Louisa had fled.

Chapter Twenty-Nine

ouisa's valise was packed. It was amazing that all the shameful memories of those beautiful gowns could be contained by one leather case. One would think it would take the whole prairie to hold her secrets. Picking up Daisy's composition book, Louisa ripped a page out of the sewn spine. Carefully she printed the address:

Louisa Bell
Cat-Eye Saloon
Wichita, Kansas

After poking a hole near the top, she attached the slip of paper to the bag handle with a bit of ribbon. While she knew she had no job waiting for her at the Cat-Eye, there was nowhere else to go. She trusted Daniel to get the bag to her. He would want all memories of her out of his house.

Louisa watched the moon rise over the east barracks. She wanted to explain herself to Daniel—reassure him that she'd never intended to mislead him, not until circumstances forced her to continue the ruse. But she couldn't ask for his forgiveness. She'd betrayed him, deceived him, humiliated him, and he would think that she'd planned it to the very end. Even now the troopers were probably in their bunks, laughing at how she'd tricked their commander. She couldn't ask for his forgiveness because she didn't deserve it, and with his conscience, he'd feel that he should grant it no matter what she'd done to offend.

Her one consolation was that God knew she was sorry. God knew how it had grieved her to reject Daniel's marriage offer. God knew how torn she'd been over her decision to leave Indian Territory. At least she knew that she'd made that decision before she'd been exposed. She'd decided on her own to stop the lies and start new.

The look of shock on Daisy's face, Caroline's horror—Louisa would never be able to erase that. And now their grandmother was here to take them away, and she could do nothing about it. That was what she got for pretending to be decent. She didn't belong, and she never had.

Voices were raised downstairs. Daniel was arguing with Mrs. Crawford. Arguing over her, and Daniel wouldn't win that debate. Louisa eased down on her bed, closed her eyes, and tried to picture her next step. She didn't want to perform anymore—the demands on her appearance; the constant stream of strangers coming through, insisting that she treat them as intimate acquaintances; the bickering of the ladies over the wardrobe closet; the unwanted advances; and the shunning of every decent person in town. She was done with that.

But what came next? At least her time at the fort had taught her a thing or two. She'd buy some textbooks, maybe the same ones she'd been using here. Then, when she was ready, she'd write to the Kansas Board of Education and look into taking a teacher's exam. Wasn't that how it was done? She would prefer another family position like she had now, but who would hire her without credentials? What would they say when they heard of her previous career? Louisa would have to try. With

Bradley's help, maybe she could leave Wichita behind and start somewhere new.

The voices downstairs quieted, and then Edna could be heard next door as she settled into the room with the girls. She was their grandmother. They didn't need Louisa anymore.

After the house had fallen silent, Louisa checked the money in her reticule to prepare for her journey. She'd head to Darlington, and from there she'd catch the stage or see if she could travel the rest of the way to Wichita with Cimarron Ted and the drovers.

Praying that no squeaking hinge gave her away, she opened her door. The hallway was dark. She mustn't let Daniel hear her. Seeing him, talking to him was the last thing she wanted to do, primarily because she didn't have any idea what she'd say. There was nothing she could say.

Holding her reticule closely beside her, she tiptoed down the staircase and into the kitchen. Louisa took one last look around the room, then slipped outside. She waited on the back porch until her eyes adjusted. She'd be heading out blind across the prairie to reach Darlington, so she looked up to get her bearings, then realized she could follow the telephone line to town.

The kitchen door slammed closed behind her. Louisa nearly jumped out of her skin. It was Edna. Her ghostly white gown snapped in the wind, but her long gray braid lay still and lifeless.

"I knew it was you," she snapped. "Sneaking out after dark, are you? A secret assignation? Which trooper is it tonight?"

"It's me."

At the sound of Daniel's voice, Louisa hiccupped. He'd been sitting on the chopping block next to the woodpile the whole time. The wind teased his white shirt as he approached them.

"Miss Bell is coming to see me. I'm her secret assignation."

Edna's eyes narrowed. Louisa wanted to hide, but with a hand at her back, Daniel made her face the dragon.

"This explains much," Edna said. "I have to protest you meeting alone out here while your innocent daughters are inside."

"Where would you rather I meet her? Away from my daughters seemed like the best choice."

Louisa hung her head in shame, but no matter what he said, Edna wouldn't think any less of her. That was impossible.

"Go inside the house, Edna." He might not be wearing his uniform, but Daniel was clearly in command. "You have no business interfering with my family. If I can convince myself that your intentions are unselfish, then we'll arrange for you to see the girls, but if you continue to insult this fine lady, there's no reason for me to allow you to disrupt the peace of our household."

Edna knew when to bide her time. With a last questioning glance, she departed.

The door closed, and nothing could be heard besides the crickets and the bullfrogs bellowing their night song from the river.

Daniel's hand dropped from Louisa's back. "You told me you were leaving. I didn't think you meant in the middle of the night."

"It'll be easier for everyone." The sliver of moon barely threw enough light for Louisa to see the toes of her walking boots.

"I thought your decision was based on divine guidance, not what was easy," he said. The bullfrogs continued their song. Daniel slid his hands into his pockets. "You aren't leaving tonight. You have to face Caroline and Daisy. They deserve an explanation. And then there's your brother. He's locked up in the guardhouse for you. Are you going to leave him without a word?"

She had no answer.

"Furthermore," he said, "the army might have sent more men to hold the fort, but that won't help you any on the prairie alone at night. If you went missing, I would instigate a campaign against every man—Indian or cowboy—in this land, until you were recovered. You'd be the cause of a lot of turmoil."

"I already am." So much responsibility rested on her shoulders—Daniel's mother-in-law being assaulted, the disrespect to General Sheridan, Slappy's black eye.

"But you've caused enough for one night." That was the major. Always looking out for the best interest of everyone involved, but not one word about what she owed him. Not one word about what he felt.

"Go to bed, Louisa. And if you harbor any kindness toward my family at all, don't leave them without saying good-bye."

She was drained. Her legs felt like barrels of lead, and her eyes, sore from weeping, begged for relief. He was right. She couldn't make it to Darlington that night, and even if she did, one quick telephone call from Agent Dyer, and Daniel would send troopers to bring her back and face the music.

She couldn't escape. There was no way to bow out gracefully.

Chapter Thirty

W hat I'm saying, Major Adams, is that I see no reason to mention last night's melee in your record." General Sheridan wasn't quite five and a half feet tall, but seated in Daniel's chair behind his desk, his stern glare gave the impression that he was passing judgment down from on high.

Daniel dipped his head. "Very generous of you, sir."

"Nonsense. It's not generous, only practical. No troopers were injured, no property destroyed. The only casualty was a sloppily dressed cowboy, and he isn't my responsibility. Essentially, what happened last night was a family affair, and after consideration, I'd rather not have anything to do with your problematic family. I already have Indian relocation to deal with. That's enough."

"I understand, sir."

Sheridan fixed him with a piercing glare. Then he grunted in satisfaction. "You're doing a good job here, Major. The Cheyenne and Arapaho respect you, and you managed to hold the fort even with inadequate troops. We won't leave you shorthanded again, but I see no reason to extend my stay. General

Miles and I will spend the day dispatching orders to prepare for our departure tomorrow morning."

"Yes, sir. I'll see to it that you have—"

"You will see to nothing, Major. Nothing for the U.S. Army, anyway. I'm commanding you to get your house in order. You have a day of leave. Make the most of it."

Daniel intended to. After talking to Private Willis last night, he had a better idea of Louisa's deception. Of all the people to hire to teach his daughters decorum, he would have never chosen a stage performer. She had misled him, and he had the right to be angry, but what would his anger profit him?

Besides, he couldn't profess complete innocence. He'd burned a letter rather than read the truth about her credentials or lack thereof, and after learning that she wasn't with the Mennonite Society, he'd sent away her replacement. Perhaps he hadn't chosen a singer, but he'd chosen her.

And he'd do it again.

Footsteps sounded on the stairway. "Daniel, where are you?" It was Edna, already hunting for him that morning.

Sheridan pushed away from the desk as if he were going to dive beneath it. "It's her," he said. "What's the safest retreat?"

"You're trapped," Daniel answered.

"I'll fight my way out if I have to." Sheridan stood and picked up his hat. "It's every man for himself. Good luck." Then he strode determinedly forward, head down and ignoring Edna's sputters as he ran for the safety of outdoors.

"The rudeness of that man," Edna announced to no one in particular. "He completely ignored my greeting."

Squaring his shoulders and wishing he could ignore her as well, Daniel rode into the fray, ready to defend his choice and the woman he loved.

Mrs. Crawford was at it again. Although Louisa couldn't hear her name through the door, the references to "that woman" were clear enough. And Mrs. Crawford wouldn't be the only one talking about her this morning.

Louisa had tried to pray last night. She felt foolish talking to the ceiling, but it did seem to set her thoughts aright. Was that God answering her, or her own sense? It was too early for her to tell, but she'd realized that this was for the best. No longer would she labor under the guilt of her deception. The ruse was at an end. She had to pay the penalty, and Edna was there to make sure she did.

Louisa was dressed and her bags were packed. All she lacked was word that it was time to depart.

There was a tentative knock on her door. "Come in," she called.

The knob turned, and Daisy darted inside. Flinging her arms around Louisa's waist, she nearly pushed her off-balance. At the sight of her worried, freckled face, Louisa's throat knotted. She sat on the bed and pulled Daisy closer.

"You can't leave," Daisy cried. "Who will take care of us?"

Louisa smoothed Daisy's unbound hair. Daniel had prepared them with her sad news. Perhaps it was easier that way.

Caroline came around the corner. "You can't leave us, Miss Bell. I don't care what that cowboy said, you know you belong here." She dropped to the bed next to Louisa and laid her head on her shoulder.

Louisa hugged her tight. She didn't want to go, but she wouldn't say anything that would let them blame Daniel. With the spectacle she'd caused at the concert, he didn't have a choice.

"Girls, come down here." At Daniel's voice, all three ladies froze. Embraces tightened, snuffles ceased. "Caroline and Daisy. You heard me. Your grandmother has requested your attendance."

Daisy was the first one up. Wiping the tears from her eyes, she gazed at Louisa as if memorizing her. *Don't go*, she mouthed. Then she walked to the hallway.

Still holding Louisa's hand, Caroline stood. "I was wrong about you," she whispered. "And wrong about Grandmother. I want to stay here. If you go—"

"Caroline," Daniel called from downstairs.

Her brow settled into determined lines that she'd inherited from her father, but she obeyed, leaving Louisa alone in her room. In fact, the whole house was soon still. They had all left.

With the girls gone, she could make a dignified departure without the spectacle of crying young ladies clinging to her. And perhaps that was what Daniel intended. All that was left was for Louisa to wait for him to arrange her transportation.

She only hoped she didn't have to wait too long. The waiting was torture.

Time passed. The troopers were at drill. Officers shouted orders. Reins jangled in unison. Louisa sat on her bed and waited for the summons that her ride was ready.

The door downstairs opened and banged closed.

"Louisa?"

Louisa jumped to her feet. What was he doing here? As she stepped out of her room, Bradley saw her and bounded up the staircase to meet her. She fell into his arms. *Say good-bye to your brother.* Yes, that was her last task before Daniel would let her leave. Bradley smelled like horses and wool, but he'd smelled a lot worse in his life.

"You come see me when you get leave," she said. "Promise."

Bradley drew back. "See you where? The Cat-Eye? Ain't you done with that place, Lola?" He shook his head. "You can't go back there. You don't have a job. Besides, the major said he might be able to help us come up with a better plan."

She shook her head. "Bradley, we can't ask him for help, not after what I've done to him."

"You took him aback, that's for certain, but he's getting over it."

That was what she feared. "He's too much of a gentleman. He doesn't want anything to do with me."

"Get on downstairs and ask him. You might be surprised."

As if she hadn't brought enough shame on herself, now her brother had to twist Daniel's arm. "You should've minded your own business," she said as Bradley followed her down the stairs.

"Look who's talking," he replied.

She paused at the office door. How could she even face him?

Bradley went past her and saluted. "She's all yours, Major" were his parting words.

She heard Daniel rise. Her heart pounded in her chest. Would this be the last time she saw him? She had to live these moments, no matter how painful they were. She had to see him one last time. She lifted her chin and entered his office. He stood by the chessboard in his full uniform. When she finally met his eyes, they held a challenge, but no regrets and no sorrow.

"Good morning, Louisa."

He motioned to the chair, but she tightened her grip on her traveling case. "I don't know what Bradley said, but it'd be best if I left now. When Mrs. Crawford gets back—"

"Horsefeathers. Have a seat."

Louisa frowned. "Chess now? I have to catch the coach. It's been decided."

"This match will decide."

"What?"

A glimmer of humor crossed his lips. "All night I thought about how to best settle this problem. I had a long talk with your brother, and I came up with a solution: If you win, you can go, but if I win, you marry me."

She turned away. He couldn't want her to stay, could he? Had he heard what was said about her? Did he still not believe it?

"It's true," she said. "What Slappy said about me is true."

"I know." His riding boots creaked as he tapped his foot. "But you have to play me and win if you want to leave."

Louisa might have been exposed as having been a dance hall singer, but that didn't mean she'd lost her skills at chess. "Are you sure about that, Major?" But then her eyes fell on the board. Her black pieces were set up and in order, but Daniel's were not. He only had his king and a handful of pawns surrounding it. "Oh, I see." Her tummy flip-flopped. He could barely beat her in a fair contest. With these odds, he was bound to lose, and she would be free to go. So why the match?

Daniel pulled the seat out for her, and she gave in and sat. As he pushed her chair in, he bent over her shoulder. "I am going to win, Louisa." A warm chill ran up her spine. Unfortunately, with this setup, there was no way that was going to happen.

"Ladies first," he said.

Mechanically, Louisa moved a pawn. "Where are Caroline and Daisy?"

"Edna took them on a walk to hear about the botany you taught them. I made Daisy promise not to walk her through any hornets' nests." He moved his pawn, completely exposing his king.

Louisa bit her lip. Did he want her to win, and thus to leave? Why else would he be so obviously giving her an advantage? Well, it would take her a few moves yet to get her bishop free. Maybe he had a plan.

"I've put some thought to your situation, and I think I've figured out your dilemma," he said. "Obeying Christ meant that you had to stop pretending to be a governess. You had to tell the truth, but you thought it would be easier to leave than admit to me what you'd done." He kept his eyes on the board and moved his king over one space. "Is that the gist of it?"

Louisa's bishop came out and cut a diagonal across the board to be in line with his king. This wasn't going to take long. "Either way, I would be telling you good-bye. I'd rather leave before you found out than after."

"Did you come here because of Bradley?"

"I heard about Bradley's antics. I knew he was in trouble, and I wanted to keep an eye on him, but I'd just lost my job at the Cat-Eye, too. I came looking for work, any kind of work. Bradley is my only family. I didn't really have anywhere else to go."

"And you thought you'd try to be a governess?" Instead of moving his pawn to protect himself, he moved his king back to its original position.

His king was there for the taking. Protocol demanded that she warn him that he'd moved into danger, but she'd spare him this once. It wasn't as if she couldn't finish him off whenever she was ready.

"What I heard last night shocked me," Daniel said. "Some might say that you came with plans to hoodwink me, like a calculating opportunist, but I know the truth."

"What's that?" She moved her bishop ahead but stopped just outside his line of pawns. No blood spilt yet.

"You were so woefully unprepared. Had you come here with the intention of misleading us, you would've opened that crate and learned some basic math before you arrived. And you would've traded your fancy clothes for plainer fare." With a swift move, he captured her bishop.

But she was more concerned with explaining her story. "I met Mrs. Townsend at the Red Fork Ranch. She asked me to deliver the books and warned me that I wasn't dressed properly for the fort. Even then, I had no thought of being a governess, not until Jack assumed I was here for the job." She hopped her knight over the line of pawns, caring little about strategy.

"Blame it on Jack." But Daniel sounded more amused than

angry. He moved his king over once again, giving her another stab at getting closer. "And that's why you felt free to roam the prairie dressed in your provocative costume until you were told not to. Because at that time you were still Lola Bell and had no reason to tell me anything different."

"You can't be happy that I was a stage performer," she said.

"You're right. It'd be ridiculous for me to pretend that it won't affect the way people see you . . . and the way they see us." Somehow, in two more moves, he'd captured two more of her pieces.

"And most will accuse me of worse." For the first time, she took one of his pawns.

"There are things you don't ask a woman's brother," he said softly. He reached for another piece, then paused. His confidence had slipped.

He didn't know, but still he was here, asking her to stay. She looked at the forlorn pawn in her palm. "I sang," she said. "I've been propositioned, threatened, and witnessed things I wish I hadn't, but I was lucky."

"Louisa, if you go back, your luck might run out."

She didn't want to think about that. She'd felt so safe here under Daniel's protection that she'd forgotten the daily fear she used to live with. Fear that one day her walk from the stage to her room would be interrupted and she would be accosted, but also fear for the future.

With only pawns and the king, Daniel was limited to moving only one square at a time. Dutifully he marched another pawn forward into her line of fire.

"I'm not going back," she said. "I'll earn my teaching certificate. My reading and writing are good. If I spend some more time with my arithmetic, I'll have a shot at another position." She hardly noticed that she had moved another piece diagonal to a pawn.

"Why not stay here?" he asked.

The board was becoming evenly matched. Soon Louisa would start fighting for her right to leave. Soon she'd make her escape. "Everyone at the fort and probably everyone at Darlington knows about me now. I can't stay here."

"Doesn't everyone in Wichita know?"

That was pure meanness.

"I won't go back to Wichita, or at least not for long. But here, everyone will laugh to think that I tried to be a proper governess. I was even going to be your wife. Just imagine."

"I am imagining." His pawns advanced. Soon she would have to promote one, and then the game could become a challenge.

Louisa stared at the board. Why was she even playing? It was ridiculous. One didn't agree to marriage based on the outcome of a match.

Daniel nudged her foot with his. "You talk like Lovely Lola was an evil, wicked person, but I don't have that opinion at all. Was Lovely Lola selfish? No, it seems she loved and sacrificed for her brother. Was Lola stealing from people or hurting people? No, she worked for her wages. She was a woman of character before she arrived at Fort Reno. The important things about her were all true."

"But my conscience . . . how can I keep pretending? God knows, and I can't disappoint Him."

"What pretending? Tell everyone you used to be a singer. I don't care, if it's the truth."

Louisa moved a knight to protect her king. Daniel took it.

"Do you love me, Louisa?"

She sacrificed another piece, but he was unrelenting.

"The game is almost over," he said. "Win or lose. Go or stay. The choice is up to you."

Did she love him? Undoubtedly. She'd treated him wrongly, had deceived him, and what was even worse, didn't trust him with the truth of her story. But he was showing her the grace that the church people always talked about. Turning her back on love like that didn't make any sense.

There were one hundred moves she could make on the board, but now that she knew the outcome she was after, it changed the game entirely. One by one, she marched her pieces to his paltry pawns. One by one, he captured all her defenses.

"Are you sure you want me to stay?" she asked.

"I'm about to beat you with six pawns and a king. What do you think?"

"I think this is the worst game of my life."

His eyes twinkled. "But the best prize." He didn't announce his win, just took her last piece off the board, then moved his chair away from the table. "Come here."

Louisa's heart rocked in her chest. Could she really begin a life with him? Was there anything she wanted more?

She stood. He took her hand and pulled her onto his lap. Not satisfied with the arrangement, he slid an arm beneath her knees and settled her more fully against him.

"It's the middle of the day," she whispered. "What if Edna comes back?"

"Jack is standing guard outside. No one is coming in."

"Jack?" Louisa sat up and cast a worried look at the window. "Does he know—?"

"Shhh. He's the soul of discretion." Daniel brushed her cheek with the back of his hand. His eyes roamed her face. "I love you, Louisa Lola Bell. Marry me today and make my life complete."

She couldn't help but laugh at him. He'd always been an impatient opponent. "Maybe we should wait until General Sheridan leaves."

"But he could be my best man," he said.

"I'd prefer Bradley, since he's newly released from the guard-house. But if you'd like, Edna could stand up for me."

He groaned. "On second thought, going straight to Darling-ton this morning and finding a preacher has its advantages."

How she loved him. Louisa snuggled her head against his shoulder. "We need a few weeks at least. A proper lady wouldn't elope first thing in the morning."

"An impatient major might, but I'll defer to your sensibil-ity." His hand skimmed over her blond ringlets in unhurried, contented strokes. "Louisa, would you please sing for me?"

Her heart overflowed at his words. How completely he had accepted her talents and her past.

"I'll sing for you, but first I have to learn a new song. Some-thing I've never sung before." The sun's rays bathed the room in pure light. "It should be about a stubborn man who pursued a woman when he should've let her go."

He sat up straighter and rearranged her. His contentment was fleeting. Major Adams was about to make his next move. "How could I let you go?" he asked. "You have my heart."

She looked into his eyes and saw everything she'd ever dreamed of. "I'll take good care of it," she said. "I promise."

Then his gaze strayed to her lips, and a new song began.

A Note from the Author

Dear Reader,

Thank you for sharing your time with Daniel and Louisa at Fort Reno. While as far as we can tell, no dance hall singer ever masqueraded as a governess at the fort, the true history of the area did provide several exciting events to include. A Cheyenne uprising did indeed prompt General Sheridan's July 1885 visit. During the crisis, Agent Dyer and his wife, Ida, stayed behind and hid in Darlington, although their marriage did not survive the publication of her memoirs. Vigilante Texas cowboys shot Running Buffalo while hunting down their stolen horses, which incited Running Buffalo's family to trap the drovers inside a stone bakery. All this was going on while David Payne's followers, the boomers, were leading illegal tours of the Unassigned Lands. Other historical figures that made appearances in *Holding the Fort* are Ben Clark, Chief Powder Face, Chief Stone Calf, Marshal Bass Reeves, General Miles, and Ralph and Hubert Collins.

Although my family visits Historic Fort Reno regularly, it was a rainy day in April when I, with two kids in tow, showed up with a notebook of specific information I needed to hunt down. Sarah Overholser and Rick Owens spent considerable time sharing their knowledge and presenting photographs and maps when words weren't enough. Their help was invaluable. Any mistakes or fabrications are on me.

Pat Reuter and Kendall Watson presented me with precious, out-of-print booklets on the history of the fort. Go visit them at the Canadian County Historical Museum if you get a chance. You might catch a ride on the trolley, if you're lucky.

Gaylene Siemens and Wendi Oberholtzer directed me in regard to the Mennonites who assisted in the Indian resettlement and the Darlington Agency work. It's wonderful to have such resourceful people available via social media.

On the editorial side, you should know about Dave Long and Jessica Barnes, who apply their wisdom and talent to each of my projects. And even before they see it, my stalwart critique partners Stephanie Landsem and Kristi Ann Hunter work with the manuscript when it's still rough and green. I owe them all. Massively.

But the most thanks go to you, reader. Yes, you. Without you, this series would not have happened. If you're ever on Route 66 (or I-40) just west of OKC, stop by and say *howdy* to the folks at the fort. You might hear one of Louisa's songs still being sung in the General's House.

And feel free to drop me a line on Facebook or Twitter. Or if you want news about sales, upcoming books, and events delivered right to your inbox, sign up for my newsletter at www.reginajennings.com. I love hearing from you.

Sincerely,
Regina

Regina Jennings is a graduate of Oklahoma Baptist University with a degree in English and a minor in history. She's a winner of the National Readers' Choice Award, a two-time Golden Quill finalist, and a finalist for the Oklahoma Book of the Year Award. Regina has worked at the *Mustang News* and at First Baptist Church of Mustang, along with time at the Oklahoma National Stockyards and various livestock shows. She lives outside of Oklahoma City with her husband and four children and can be found online at www.reginajennings.com.

Sign Up for Regina's Newsletter!

Keep up to date with Regina's news on book releases and events by signing up for her email list at reginajennings.com.

More from Regina Jennings

Betsy Huckabee dreams of being a big-city journalist, but first she has to get out of Pine Gap. To that end, she pens a romanticized serial for the ladies' pages of a distant newspaper, using the handsome new deputy and his exploits for inspiration. She'd be horrified if he read her breathless descriptions of him, but no one from home need ever know....

For the Record

More from Regina Jennings

Visit reginajennings.com for a full list of her books.

When Miranda Wimplegate mistakenly sells a prized portrait, her grandfather buys an entire auction house to get it back. But they soon learn their new business deals in livestock—not antiques! While Miranda searches for the portrait, the handsome manager tries to salvage the failing business. Will either succeed?

At Love's Bidding

To fulfill a soldier's dying wish, nurse Abigail Stuart marries him and promises to look after his sister. But when the real Jeremiah Calhoun appears alive, can she provide the healing his entire family needs?

A Most Inconvenient Marriage

When an abandoned child brings Nick Lovelace and Anne Tillerton together, is Nick prepared to risk his future plans for an unexpected chance at love?

Caught in the Middle

Young widow Rosa Garner and her mother-in-law return to Texas with nothing. But when help is offered with unwanted strings attached, how far will she go to save their futures?

Sixty Acres and a Bride

◊ BETHANYHOUSE

You May Also Like

When paid companion Gertrude Cadwalader is caught returning items pilfered by her employer, her friend Harrison's mother jumps to the wrong conclusion. But Harrison quickly comes to Gertrude's defense—and initiates an outlandish plan to turn their friendship into a romance.

Out of the Ordinary by Jen Turano
APART FROM THE CROWD, jenturano.com

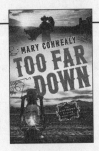

When an explosion at the mine kills workers and damages the CR Company, the Boden family is plunged deep into the heart of trouble yet again. As they try to identify the forces against them once and for all, Cole Boden finds himself caught between missing his time back in the east, and all that New Mexico offers—namely, his family and cowgirl Melanie Blake.

Too Far Down by Mary Connealy
THE CIMARRON LEGACY #3, maryconnealy.com

While fleeing the villain who killed her father, Grace Mallory is waylaid by Amos Bledsoe, who hopes to continue their telegraph courtship in person. With Grace's life on the line, can he become the hero she requires?

Heart on the Line by Karen Witemeyer
karenwitemeyer.com

Evelyn Wisely works daily to help get children out of her town's red-light district, but she longs to help the women as well. Intrigued by Evelyn, David Kingsman lends his support to her cause. Though they begin work with the best of intentions, complications arise.

A Love So True by Melissa Jagears
TEAVILLE MORAL SOCIETY, melissajagears.com

🕮 BETHANYHOUSE